MW01125606

GROUP, PHOTO, GRAVE

BOOK #8 IN THE KIKI LOWENSTEIN MYSTERY
SERIES

JOANNA CAMPBELL SLAN

spot on publishing

Group, Photo, Grave: Book #8 in the Kiki Lowenstein Mystery Series

© 2016 by Joanna Campbell Slan

Joanna Campbell Slan

Spot On Publishing

9307 SE Olympus Street

Hobe Sound FL 33455 / USA

http://www.SpotOnPublishing.org

http://www.JoannaSlan.com

Publisher's Note: This is a work of fiction. Names, characters, places, and incidents are a product of the author's imagination. Locales and public names are sometimes used for atmospheric purposes. Any re-semblance to actual people, living or dead, or to businesses, companies, events, institutions or locales is completely coincidental.

Revised 08/10/2020

Covers: http://www.WickedSmartDesigns.com

Zentangle® is a registered trademark of Zentangle, Inc. For more information, go to Zentangle.com.

Group, Photo, Grave: Book #8 in the Kiki Lowenstein Mystery Series by Joanna Campbell Slan. – 3rd ed.

ISBN-13: 978-1978137172

ISBN-10: 1978137176

CONTENTS

Who can find a virtuous woman?
For her price is far above rubies.
The heart of her husband doth safely trust in her,
So that he shall have no need of spoil.
She will do him good and not evil all the days of her life.

Proverbs 31:10
King James Version of the Bible

1

~ In Memoriam ~

A Special Edition of the
Time in a Bottle Newsletter

*A*s many of you know, this month we said our final goodbye to Dodie Goldfader, the founder and former owner of our store, Time in a Bottle. The cancer that Dodie had fought so long and valiantly finally won the fight for her body. But even her passing cannot rob us of her memory. Dodie has been and will continue to be a blessing to all of us who think of Time in a Bottle as a second home.

Dodie is survived by her husband, Horace and her daughter, Rebekkah. She was preceded in death by her son, Nathan. In keeping with her wishes, immediately after her death there was a brief graveside ceremony for family members only.

We invite you to stop by Time in a Bottle and create a page with your memories of Dodie. At some point, we'll collect all these, put them in an album and give them to her family.

Thanks for the memories, Dodie!

Kiki Lowenstein

2

Saturday/Second week of June
Webster Groves, Missouri

*M*y mother-in-law Sheila's wedding wasn't totally ruined by the discovery of a corpse in the punch bowl. Okay, I lie. The corpse wasn't exactly inside the punch bowl. The body had simply hit the punch bowl on its way down to the ground. One of the wait staff was walking through the catering tent and found the limp figure sprawled on the grass with a punch bowl over its head.

Except for the corpse, every other part of Sheila Lowenstein and St. Louis Police Chief Robbie Holmes's ceremony had been lovely. Joyful, too, and I badly needed a spot of cheer after the death of my friend and mentor, Dodie Goldfader.

Sheila had beamed with happiness as she and Robbie Holmes had said their wedding vows. The day was beastly hot, but the sun was bright in a cornflower blue sky, and a light breeze carried the scent of roses. All in all, a wonderful (pre-dead guy) omen for the new couple. Sheila's attention to detail had paid off handsomely. The dresses of the brides-maids were a lovely visual counterpoint to the vibrant pinks, deep reds, rich magentas and royal purples of the garden owned by my landlord, Leighton Haversham.

My thirteen-year-old daughter, Anya and I were Sheila's maid and matron of honor, respectively, so we wore dresses in shades of soft pink with navy trim. Mine had been altered repeatedly to fix my expanding waistline. Right now, I'm six weeks pregnant with my second child. Everything they say about second pregnancies seems to be true, especially when it comes to how much faster you show the second time around. The rest of the bridesmaids, Sheila's best friends, a group that went by the nickname of the "Jimmy Girls," wore plum-colored silk. Ester Frommer from Los Angeles, Toby Pearlman from Palm Beach, and Leah Ginsberg from Chicago had pinned narrow navy ribbons to their chests in remembrance of a fourth friend, Miriam, who had recently died. Sheila had a ribbon, too, but hers was more discretely tucked into her bouquet so as not to ruin the lines of her dress. The quintet had been best friends since their years at the Charles and Anne Lindbergh Academy, known locally as CALA, the same school my daughter attends.

On the groom's side, we had Sheila's new husband and his best man Detective Chad Detweiler, the father of the child in my belly. Detweiler and I were planning to get married, although we hadn't set a date, due to a variety of complications. To elope or not to elope, that was the question. There were pros and cons on both sides of the decision.

Over and over in my head, I repeated my mantra, "Love will find a way." The words might seem trivial in the face of our obstacles, but I believed them with all my heart. Already, Detweiler and I had been through so much! The drama surrounding us wasn't surprising when you considered the fact we'd met because my husband, George Lowenstein, Sheila's son, had been murdered.

As Dodie used to say, "Man plans and God laughs." Right now, the good Lord must be rolling on the floor and clutching his sides with hilarity. "Unplanned" could be the one-word theme for my entire life. Both of my pregnancies had been unplanned. Anya had been the result of my drinking too much Purple Passion at a frat party, and this one was what Detweiler called, "Equipment failure."

But unplanned did not mean unloved or unwanted. Anya was the light of my life, and I had no doubt that this baby would be just as precious. With a sigh, I brought myself back to the here and now, lest I allow my daydreaming to rob me of this beautiful moment.

Rounding out the groom's attendants were Detweiler's partner Detective Stan Hadcho; Lieutenant Milton Lesher; Sergeant Donald Tomatillo; and Captain Prescott Gallaway. Prescott was a *nebbish* (a Yiddish term loosely translated as an ineffectual person) who nobody liked, but as I understood it, Prescott and Robbie were somehow related. The man was also Robbie's second-in-command at the police station, so an invitation had been mandatory. Sheila didn't like Prescott, but she wasn't in a position to complain, partially because Robbie's side of the invitation list was embarrassingly short. It seemed that his kids had decided not to attend their father's second wedding. Since Robbie's first wife, Nadine, had died ten years ago, I found their behavior puzzling to say the least. I mean, come on! At fifty-nine, didn't the man deserve another chance at happiness?

With or without his adult children's blessings, Robbie

Holmes was a happy man. When Robbie and Sheila had turned to face the crowd after saying their vows, his grin split his face in half. Sheila had looked radiant as joyful applause drowned out the music of the string quartet playing "Pachelbel's Canon in D." The bride and groom made a handsome couple as they started arm-in-arm down the flagstone path. My mother-in-law's denim blue eyes and silver-white hair were offset by her periwinkle gown. The navy blue sling that kept her broken collarbone in place contrasted nicely with her dress. Robbie looked especially dashing in a newly designed navy blue uniform that signified his position as Chief of Police for the City of St. Louis.

The newlyweds' expressions were priceless. I couldn't wait to create a wonderful wedding album for my mother-in-law because that's what I do.

My name is Kiki Lowenstein, and I'm a scrapbooker. It's my hobby, my passion, and soon it'll be my business because I'm finalizing the arrangements to buy Time in a Bottle, a scrapbook store where I've been working since George died.

As per our rehearsal instructions, my honey and I had to wait until the happy couple reached a half-way point on the flagstone path before we linked arms and stepped forward together. Next, Anya and Hadcho stepped off with Gracie, our harlequin Great Dane, trotting along between them. Around my dog's neck was a wreath of silk flowers, matching our bouquets of white Shasta daisies, pink Gerber daisies, sprigs of lavender and pink roses. Given Gracie's natural black and white coloring, the effect was stunning!

Two by two, the rest of the wedding party processed away from the *chuppah,* the ceremonial canopy that's a standard feature of Jewish weddings.

As we moved past the seated guests and spilled onto

Leighton's lawn, I caught a glimpse of my friend Cara Mia Delgatto, who was catering the wedding banquet. Standing in the back in her simple black shift and pearls, she'd been waiting for this moment to set her staff into action.

Yes, although her broken collarbone had confined her to a recliner, Sheila had polished every bit of the ceremony to a high gloss of perfection. From the handmade invitations I'd created and assembled to the wisteria and roses running up the poles of the *chuppah*, she'd taken care so that the colors, sounds and fragrances would evoke a romantic ambiance.

Everything was absolute perfection—and as a result, I was exhausted by Sheila's demands. Er, requests. That and the fact I was now twelve weeks pregnant. I had worked like a fiend to accommodate Sheila. Even clothing factory workers in Bangladesh were allotted more breaks than I had been.

"Looks like she pulled it off, sweetheart," whispered Detweiler. "Now you can relax and get back to running your scrapbook store."

"Can you see the relief on my face?" I said quietly. I was holding my bouquet so that it partially covered my baby bump. I felt a tad embarrassed about my condition, but it was nothing I couldn't handle. Lately, I had started caring a lot less about other people's opinions. Instead, I concentrated on what I wanted out of life.

A brush with death can cause a rearrangement of your priorities. Sheila and I had both nearly died in an event we now wryly called "the shoot-out at the slough."

But we'd foiled the bad guy and lived to tell about it. Today was truly a milestone to celebrate.

3

$\mathcal{T}$he gun fight at the slough hadn't been pretty, and I wasn't proud of what happened. But out of necessity, I'd killed our captor, my husband's former business partner. My choice had been to shoot him in the head or let him kill all of us: Sheila, me, my unborn baby and Johnny Chambers, the brother of Mert Chambers, my former cleaning lady and best friend.

My best friend.

I still thought of Mert as my BFF (Best Friend Forever), even though she still wasn't speaking to me. She blamed me for her brother's involvement in the mess. I had high hopes that when she learned the truth, she would come around, but Mert is a Scorpio, and once they decide they've been wronged, they want nothing to do with you.

As yet another consequence of the melee, Sheila's injuries forced her to change the original date of her wedding. So this lovely event was special for many, many reasons. Not only to Sheila and Robbie, but to all of us. It was a triumph, considering what we'd endured.

Leighton used the event as an excuse to add a creek and

goldfish pond to our shared backyard. As his gift to the newlyweds, Leighton put up two white tents, one for the ceremony and one for the reception so a sudden shower couldn't possibly ruin the day.

That meant there were three tents, two large ones for the guests, and one small blue awning where Cara Mia's crew had set up coolers, bins, and containers.

At Sheila's urging, Leighton had also installed a temporary flagstone path for the bridal party to take on our way to where a priest and rabbi waited to perform the ceremony. Yes, Sheila had thought of absolutely everything. And she wanted absolutely everything. And she expected and got absolutely everything. As my friend and co-worker Clancy Whitehead said, "Nothing is impossible when you are willing to spend money hand over fist."

Although Robbie never voiced a word of complaint, the staggering sums they'd spent on the wedding were a source of concern to him. I'd overheard him asking Sheila to be more cautious about spending. In response, she'd laughed and given him a kiss. The cost of their honeymoon cruise alone was absolutely staggering. At least to me, it was.

Once the ceremony had started, Cara Mia's wait staff had migrated to the back of the tent to watch. Word had spread that our entourage included a "real, live, flower dog" the size of a small pony, so the servers wanted to see my Great Dane. Gracie charmed the socks off of everyone by walking along slowly between Anya and Hadcho, wearing her collar of flowers, and wagging her long black tail.

Now these same servers raced back to the catering tent. Appetizers, champagne, soft drinks and sparkling white grape juice would mark the start of a wonderful repast. I'd seen the menu, and I knew that Cara wouldn't disappoint. The tables were decorated with tulle, tiny hearts and doves punched out of paper, and lavish floral arrangements. Guests searched for their tables with their decorated name cards.

Not a cloud marred the celestial blue sky. Birdsong mingled with the Bach played by a string quartet. The sweet smell of petunias and roses scented the air. Sheila's bell-like laughter and Robbie's booming bass rose over the appreciative murmurs of the crowd.

All in all, this was a wedding to die for.

4

As per the bride's prior instructions, Detweiler, Anya, Gracie and I headed to the fishpond for formal portraits by Vincent, the photographer. But I didn't go there directly. I stopped by my own house to use the bathroom, drop off Gracie, and grab my purse with my camera. By the time I arrived at the fish pond, Anya was posed, sitting on the edge of the goldfish pond and dangling her fingers in the water. The koi bubbled up to the surface eagerly, hoping to be fed.

"Watch out, Anya," warned Detweiler. "You're liable to lose a finger."

In response, she flicked water at the long, lean cop. Their playful relationship brought a smile to my face. Soon we would be a real family. We would be united by our marriage, as well as by the addition of our baby and Detweiler's son Erik, a child by his first wife, Gina. What a wonderful blended family we were going to have!

"Gents? Ladies? Group photo, please." Vincent herded us together.

Sheila and Robbie joined us.

"I hope you hurry with those pictures," said Milton. "My stomach is rumbling, and that food smells delicious. If we don't get over there soon, I bet it will be all gone."

"Not likely," said Robbie, clapping a hand on his officer's shoulder, "unless we're joined by the Russian army."

That brought a big laugh. Sheila had ordered enough food to feed the hungry hoards on a thirty-day march. Cara had kindly squeezed Sheila into her catering schedule at the last minute and cheerfully put up with my mother-in-law's ever changing demands.

"If I were you, I would have shoved a plate of meatballs in her face by now," I told Cara after Sheila had made yet another change to the menu.

"It isn't personal," said Cara. "Sheila can't keep changing the menu forever. Sooner or later, we'll be right back where we started. You're a fine one to talk about dealing with her. She keeps adding to the guest list so you have to keep making more handmade invitations, envelopes, place cards and so on. Your poor hand is swollen from hitting those punches over and over!"

"Too true. I've been soaking it in ice water at night. But there's a light on the horizon. She can't keep inviting people. She's bound to run out of friends sooner or later," I said. "Knowing Sheila, it'll be sooner rather than later. In fact, I suspect she's bribing strangers with the prospect of an open bar and the promise of your food!"

"In less than two hours this will all be over," Cara had whispered to me when she and her catering crew had pulled up next to Leighton's house so they could unload. Vincent's photo van was parked nearby. "Your mother-in-law will be on a cruise, and we won't hear from her for an entire thirty days."

It would be good for Sheila and Robbie to get away for

awhile. Especially, to a place where cell phone coverage would be iffy. I watched as he slipped a proprietary arm around Sheila's waist. They'd fallen in love in high school, married other people and found each other all over again. Really romantic.

"Hey, gorgeous." Detweiler came up behind me and kissed me on the neck. My knees went a bit wobbly at his touch and the scent of his cologne.

"No PDA," sniffed Anya. "That means no public displays of affection. You two need to get a room."

"Maybe we will," said Detweiler. "You can go on home and babysit Gracie."

A scream split the dense summer air.

5

—————

*D*etweiler and Hadcho took off running.

Usually I would tag along, but the heat was really doing a number on me. Besides, the yelp probably came from someone who'd spotted a garter snake or a big bug, common uninvited guests at an out-of-doors function. Instead of chasing after the boys, I grabbed a folding chair and took a load off my feet.

Robbie took two steps in the same direction as Detweiler and Hadcho before Sheila hauled him right back with a curt, "Oh, no, you don't, buster."

Vincent glanced around nervously. I couldn't blame him. A scream like that will put anyone's nerves on edge.

"Could I have the bride and groom again?" Vincent recovered quickly and gestured to the couple.

Sheila had hired Vincent because he was the brother of a friend. But what really cinched the deal was the fact that his photos were always picked up by a local society magazine.

While I sat off to one side, the bridesmaids chatted with each other. They'd been cordial enough to me, but since they hadn't seen each other in ages, they had a lot of catching up to do, so they mainly talked to each other.

"Wait," said Toby, a statuesque brunette who favored really big false eyelashes. "Where's Ester?"

"I think she ran to the ladies room," said Leah, nodding her head toward Leighton's house. Leah was slightly plump with a ruddy complexion.

Almost on cue, Ester came walking along on my landlord's arm. Leighton's salt-and-pepper gray head bent close to her sunny blond hair as they conversed. He's a slender, classy looking man, and Ester, an aerobics instructor for seniors, looked perfectly at ease on his arm. Once the couple came closer, the other bridesmaids clustered around them.

The women all began talking at once, complimenting Leighton on his flowers. I could see my landlord pinking up with pleasure; his home was his palace. As an author who traveled the world, he tended this little patch of land with great reverence, as it was his touchstone. This acre-and-a-half lot provided him with a great deal of happiness, particularly after Anya and I moved into the garage he'd converted into a small cottage. He often said that he considered us his family. That seemed pretty sad to me because Leighton had a daughter somewhere, but they were estranged.

"Ladies? A few more pictures, please." Vincent took a few more quick shots of the bridesmaids, all women who were aging gracefully. "Mah-vel-lous ladies. That's a wrap for the formal shots. I'm going to break all this down and then wander around at the reception."

The bridesmaids and Leighton gathered around Sheila and her husband, talking happily about how well the ceremony had gone. Anya joined them. I couldn't haul myself out of my chair. Instead I glanced over my shoulder, wondering why Detweiler and Hadcho hadn't returned. Sheila noticed, too. She lifted an eyebrow at me, and I shrugged. The guys were taking their time, but I figured they'd run into well-wishers or other friends from the police department. I had struggled to my feet and was considering hunting the guys down, when a familiar voice stopped me.

"Yoo-hoo! There's that photographer! Oh, Vincent!" called my mother as she trotted toward us, her large handbag flopping at her side. In her pink polyester blouse and skirt, she looked her best, and I made a mental note to thank my sister Amanda for overseeing Mom's wardrobe. When Mom angled closer, I spotted a small flesh-colored bandage on her temple where Mom had had a pre-cancerous growth removed. Since my plate was full, Amanda did an amazing job taking care of our mother.

"I know you'll want to take my photo. Remember? At the Senior Center, you commented on how photogenic I am." Mom tossed her purse to the ground and posed with one leg cocked suggestively. Grabbing her skirt in her hand, she managed to show an awful lot of leg.

"Sorry," mouthed Amanda as she brought up the rear. I shrugged a "what can you do?" at her.

My mother doesn't understand that she can't always be the center of attention.

Vincent, bless his heart, either took the photos of Mom or pretended to do so. He offered a bit of direction, suggesting that my mother show off her "good side," the one without the bandage.

"Now I want one with my lovely daughter," said Mom. As I started toward my mother, she gestured wildly to Amanda who rolled her eyes at me. I did feel a smidgeon of satisfaction, however, when Mom clutched Amanda and crowed, "Everyone thinks we're sisters!"

Amanda looked horrified. I certainly hoped Vincent had caught that expression for posterity!

As a scrapbook professional, I should have suggested a real family portrait, but frankly, the urge to up-chuck overwhelmed my feelings of familial affection. Could be morning sickness or mom sickness, either one. I was betting the latter. As Vincent finished, Mom waved wildly again. "Yoo-hoo! Penny! Over here so we can take your picture."

I gasped as Morticia Addams walked toward us.

My Aunt Penny wore that iconic black gown, complete with gauzy trailing sleeves, and ribbons crisscrossed under the bust. Fortunately Sheila and her friends were so busy talking to well-wishers that none of them noticed the wedding had become a Halloween party.

"What on earth are you wearing?" I grabbed Aunt Penny by the arm. My goal was to get her out of Sheila's line-of-sight before the bride threw a wonky, as the Brits say.

"Sorry, Kiki," said Amanda. "I was so busy helping Mom that I didn't check on Penny until it was too late."

"Like it?" asked my aunt, spreading the gauzy black skirt. Okay, she's not a blood relative, she's my mother's best friend, and we've adopted her because she's the nearest thing to a real relative we have.

"Where? Why?" I stuttered.

"Remember? Those guards at the Mexican border confiscated my luggage."

"That happened because you were packing heat," added Amanda. "What were you thinking? You can't carry guns in and out of the country."

"It slipped my mind. That gun was just a little bitty thing I picked up in a shop, but they made a huge fuss about it.

Took everything! All my dang clothes were in that suitcase. Lucky for me, I found myself a Halloween shop going out of business."

"She dresses with her eyes closed," muttered Amanda.

"Not too picky about the fit either," I added.

"Family photo!" called Vincent.

My sister grabbed me by one arm and Morticia by the other and dragged us over by Mom.

"Is this your family, Kiki?" asked Vincent, as he fussed with a setting.

"Yes. Mom, sister, and aunt. Could you hurry that shot? I'd rather Sheila not see us."

Two seconds later, Vincent said, "All done!"

Amanda started herding cats, that is, moving my mother and aunt to the reception tent. They were ten feet away when Vincent called, "You forgot your purse!" to my mother.

Amanda race-walked back and thanked Vincent. "Mom's always misplacing this." She waved toodles with her fingers toward me and caught up with Aunt Penny and Mom.

"That's a wrap for the posed shots," said Vincent to no one in particular.

Sheila was chatting with Sharon DiPrima, a pretty woman with hazel eyes hidden behind glasses. Sharon was bubbly and warm, always ready with a hug and a big laugh that instantly made Sheila want to befriend her when they met at a silent auction fundraiser. Robbie had been standing by and listening in when he withdrew his phone from his pocket. His relaxed posture changed, and he started swearing under his breath. Sheila noticed, too. He tilted the screen of his phone so she could read it.

Her hand flew over her mouth. "No, no, no."

"Anya?" Robbie reached around two bridesmaids to tap my daughter on the shoulder. "Could you escort your grandmother over to the head table for me? I have an errand to run. I'll be right back."

Sheila didn't want to let him go. Even as Anya took her grandmother's arm, Sheila kept her grip on Robbie. "Can't someone else handle this?"

"Just let me check into it. Probably the unfortunate result of the heat and humidity, but better safe than sorry," he said, before he headed in the direction of the scream.

6

We were half-way to the reception tent when Sheila crooked her finger at me and whispered, "Kiki, would you go check on what's happening? And report back to me?"

"Sure." I grabbed my purse and started in the direction that Robbie had taken. With every step, my kitten heels punctured the turf and threatened my balance. After a few wobbly steps, I slipped off the shoes. The grass blades felt cool and delightful between my toes. I made a semi-circle from the fish pond in the back all the way around to the front quadrant of Leighton's huge Victorian house. I was almost within sight of the catering tent when sirens whoop-whoop-whooped in the distance.

"Uh-oh." I picked up my pace and caught sight of Detweiler. He hurried toward me and folded me into his arms.

"You don't need to see this." He blocked the view of the area between the blue tent and Leighton's house.

"I love it when you act all manly," I said. "It makes me

feel so cherished." Ever since I've become pregnant, he's very protective.

"You are cherished." He stared down at me with those amazing Heinken bottle green eyes.

"But I'm also curious," I said, as I leaned to one side to see what was going on. An ambulance pulled into Leighton's circular drive, and a crew of EMTs hopped out with some of their equipment. Right behind it was a police cruiser with its red lights strobing. An unmarked cop car pulled up next to the cruiser. A policewoman jumped out with a roll of yellow crime scene tape.

"Yes, you are that, too," he agreed.

Despite Detweiler's strong arms, I pulled away to stare. Hadcho was writing in a Steno pad. Where he'd found one, I couldn't guess. He appeared to be interviewing one of Cara's servers, a young woman, mopping her eyes and trembling.

"Someone trip and fall?" I asked.

"It's a bit more serious than that. One of the catering staff members found a dead guy, face-down in the grass with a punch bowl next to his head. He was between Leighton's house and all those coolers they unloaded."

"Wow," I said. "Any idea who it is?"

"Hadcho's checking the guy's pockets. Looks like he just keeled over onto the table. Might have been the heat. We figured Robbie or Sheila will know him. He's obviously a guest. Do you still have a copy of the list?"

"In my purse." Since Sheila had added names several times a day, I kept the list with me at all times. I worried that otherwise I might scribble down a name on a scrap piece of paper and forget to create the invitation, envelope and name tent.

"Hang on to it."

I turned to see Robbie talking to Hadcho. They waved over a medic and pointed to the ground.

"Looks like they've got this under control. Hadcho is calling the crime scene unit. We can't get sloppy even though I'd lay odds the man died of heat prostration. Let's go get you under the shade and off your feet. You've been working too hard lately," Detweiler said.

He was right. The news that Detweiler had a son he'd never met, a five-year-old boy named Erik, caused us to rearrange everything in our tiny house. Anya had been adamant that she didn't want to move. With a new brother and a baby on the way, Detweiler and I decided to tough it out rather than add more stress to her life.

To create a small bedroom for Erik, in advance of him joining us, I'd emptied out a small room where I'd been keeping my crafting supplies. Consequently, I was working all day at the store and coming home at night to a mess. As Detweiler and I walked back to the reception tent, I looked forward to a relaxing meal and some dancing. But that never happened.

7

---

*R*obbie arrived just as Detweiler and I took our seats. He leaned close to Sheila and whispered in her ear. She went white, then red, and finally pink with anger.

"I did not!" she said. Although she was keeping her voice low, the tone was unmistakable as she and Robbie went back and forth. Finally, she nodded sadly and squeezed his hand. Robbie kissed her forehead, hugged her, and walked over to the microphone. The leader of the dance band they'd hired stopped the music with a curt motion of his baton.

"Hello? Testing? Can you hear me? Sheila and I want to thank you all for coming and making this a special day for both of us. Unfortunately, we have a situation here. Nothing to worry about, but it's a bit of an inconvenience. Did any of you come with Dr. Morrie Hyman? Ride with him? Bring him as a plus one?"

No one raised a hand.

"Okay, thanks," said Robbie, as he stepped away from the band podium.

"Dr. Morrie Hyman? That name sounds familiar, but I'm pretty sure he's not on the guest list. Here," and I handed my list to Robbie. Luckily, I had kept a pretty complete copy on my computer.

Robbie's eyes widened as he stared at it.

Sheila leaned in close. "See? I told you. And no one is claiming him as their date. I'm telling you, Robbie, that man crashed our party."

"I think we can forgive him for being a crasher," said Robbie. "Now that he's dead. Probably had heat stroke. Or a heart attack. What is he, eighty? Nearly ninety?"

Sheila's lower lip trembled as she reached for her water glass. "I guess."

"Let's get this show on the road," said Robbie with a nod toward Detweiler. "Are you ready to start the toasts?"

The rest of the afternoon passed as a pleasant blur. Detweiler's toast was short and sweet. The food was incredible, especially the red sauce and the toasted ravioli. The band played quietly until the dessert was served, and then the band director (who was also the keyboardist) tapped the mike and said, "Now for the first time anywhere, ladies and gentlemen, please welcome Mr. and Mrs. Robbie Holmes to the dance floor!"

The new couple waltzed for a while before circulating among their guests. I noticed that Captain Prescott had disappeared right after the ceremony. Hadcho had finished up with the crime scene investigators and, after reporting to Robbie, sat down to a well-deserved Bud Light and a meal.

Except for the dead guy outside of the catering tent, Sheila's wedding had gone according to plan.

When a white Rolls Royce pulled up across from the reception tent, Captain Robbie Holmes swept his bride off her feet and carried her to the car. As tin cans clattered behind them, they took off for the Ritz Carlton where they would spend the first night of their honeymoon. Tomorrow, they would fly to New York City, and from there to the port in Europe where they'd embark on a month-long cruise, Robbie's wedding gift to Sheila. Her lifetime dream had been to take a luxury journey through parts of India, through the Maldives, and winding up in northern Africa. She was nearly as thrilled about the cruise as she was about her wedding.

While the Holmes were honeymooning, the bridesmaids would bunk up at Sheila's house. Since the three old friends hadn't been back to St. Louis for years, they'd taken Sheila up on her offer to let them stay in her place long enough for a proper visit.

As for me and my little tribe, we were happy to see Sheila and Robbie off to start their lives together. Tomorrow was Sunday, our traditional family day, and I was looking forward to spending alone time with Detweiler and Anya before our lives changed in a big way. On Sunday evening, Detweiler would fly to Los Angeles to meet his son. Soon after, he would bring the boy home. In about five months, our small family would grow yet again with the birth of our child.

"Alone at last," said Detweiler, as he kissed the back of my neck. "Sort of."

"At least, we'll get a break from Sheila," I said.

Looking back, I think I jinxed us.

8

Sunday/The day after the wedding...
Kiki's house in Webster Groves

The Detweiler-Lowenstein household likes to sleep late on Sundays. For brunch, we whip up a big batch of pancakes, bacon, and fruit salad. After filling our tummies, we take Gracie for a walk in the park or play board games if it's too hot or rainy. Our Sunday mornings are sacred. Everyone knows not to bother us until noon.

On this Sunday, the clock had barely struck eight when my phone rang. I tried to roll over and ignore it, but the noise started again. The caller was certainly persistent.

Detweiler groaned and lifted his head. "Did I miss my flight?"

Although he was trying hard not to show it, because he didn't want Anya to think that she or the new baby didn't matter, he was terribly excited about meeting Erik. Twice I'd caught him rearranging the clothes in his suitcase and fretting over what he'd packed.

"No, sweetie," I said. "You don't leave until eight this evening. Remember?"

"Oh." He snuggled back under the covers while I answered the phone.

Before I could spit out, "Hello," Sheila started swearing like a sailor. For someone as prim and proper as my mother-in-law, her salty vocabulary always comes as a bit of a shock. Without preamble, she had launched into a series of colorful descriptions of Prescott Gallaway's parentage.

When she paused for air, I said, "Good morning to you, too. Just think! In half an hour, you'll be at the airport and ready to fly to New York."

"We're not going on our cruise," she screeched. "We're not leaving town. Come pick me up here at the Ritz. Pronto."

"What?" I wondered if the marriage was over already. I wrestled free of the covers and pushed to a seated position.

"Morrison Hyman was killed. The Medical Examiner says that someone rammed something long and thin up his nose. Since his body was found at our wedding, and since the ME put the time of death at fifteen minutes into our service, Robbie and I can't leave town. In fact, my husband has gone off to work, leaving me here alone."

"Oh, Sheila. I am so sorry." Then it hit me: The cost of their cruise was non-refundable. Not only was Sheila missing out on a great adventure, this little hiccup was going to cost her and Robbie a bundle.

"Get over here! Come pick me up!" She hung up on me.

Normally, I'd have told her to stick it where the sun wasn't shining. It had taken me fourteen years, but I finally decided that I wouldn't tolerate Sheila's abuse anymore. Whenever it happened these days, I called her on it. But I decided to make an exception in this case. She had been hysterical, and I couldn't blame her.

After I threw on my clothes and let Gracie outside, I scribbled a note for Detweiler and Anya. Our cats, Martin and Seymour, petitioned me loud and long for food. I hesitated because the smell of their canned food always provoked a bout of morning sickness. But that couldn't be helped. So I fed them, vomited, rinsed my mouth, brushed my teeth, and considered my morning officially begun.

I had one foot out the back door when my sweetie wandered in to the kitchen, yawning and scratching his stubble. He's absolutely adorable first thing in the morning. "Where are you going?" he mumbled.

I explained about Sheila's call.

Detweiler shook his head. "This is not good. Not at all. The ME sure got to Hyman's body fast. Too fast."

I froze. "What does that mean?"

"Prescott has been itching for a chance to push Robbie out of the way. I wouldn't doubt if he's behind the push to get the autopsy done quickly."

I wanted to hear more, but my phone was buzzing. One glance told me that Sheila was demanding that I hurry. As I climbed into the seat of my ancient BMW convertible, thunder rolled in the distance.

We were in for a bout of stormy weather.

9

---

*I*n damp clothes, we sat around a table in a meeting room at the St. Louis police department. From left to right, there were Sheila, me, Anya, Leah, Toby, and Ester. My mother-in-law and all her bridesmaids, including me, were soggy from running through the rain. On the other side of the door, Prescott argued with Robbie. While they traded verbal blows, I picked at a sticky spot on the Formica table. It would have been impossible not to overhear their heated conversation.

"Robbie, let me handle this," said Prescott. Through the window in the door, I watched as he squared his shoulders and invaded the police chief's personal space. Robbie frowned down at Prescott's bad comb-over and chinless face.

"You've been waiting for a chance like this," said Robbie. "That's why you told the ME this was a rush job."

"My instincts told me something was wrong. You over-looked the signs of foul play because you're too involved. You need to step aside on this one. You can't turn it over to Detweiler, because you and your wife will be his future in-laws. Hadcho is Detweiler's partner, so he shouldn't be the lead on this investigation. You have no other choice but to put me in charge." Prescott stared straight into Robbie's eyes, issuing a challenge if I ever saw one.

Behind them, Hadcho and Detweiler waited patiently. Their faces betrayed no emotion, and they said nothing.

"I am the head of the investigations department," said Prescott, with more than a touch of petulance.

I couldn't believe we were sitting here.

I'd taken Sheila to her house only to learn via text message that our presence was demanded at the police department. My mother-in-law promptly changed out of her soft-knit travel clothes and into something suitable for the muggy weather. What had begun as a soft rain became a real downpour. The bridesmaids were up and about, enjoying the morning. When they heard the news about Dr. Hyman's murder, they hurried to dress. They tried to comfort Sheila, as I started a pot of vanilla-flavored coffee.

I had just poured everyone a cup when Robbie texted Sheila to ask that she and her bridesmaids appear at the station.

This didn't sound good to me.

After the women went upstairs to put on their make-up, Detweiler and I talked by phone. He'd gotten a summons as well, and he'd been told to bring Anya down to the station.

"She's not happy about getting out of bed," he said.

"Welcome to parenthood."

I drove the ladies to the police station in Sheila's big white Mercedes Benz. Hadcho met us at the door. He directed us to the meeting room where we would wait for Detweiler and Anya. Once the bride and bridesmaids were seated, I volunteered to make a coffee run with Hadcho. Over time, Hadcho had become my "big brother" in the department, explaining the politics that happened behind the scenes. I knew he wouldn't fail me today, and he didn't.

"Prescott Gallaway has risen to the height of his incompetence," said Hadcho, as he dropped quarters into the vending machine and punched up black coffee. The brew looked thick and unappealing. I grabbed an assortment of sweeteners and creamers to dose it. He continued, "I can't explain how or why, but he's managed to climb the ladder despite his lack of ability. If it was up to him, none of our cases would ever get solved."

"At least you have Robbie," I said.

"Not if Prescott has his way." Hadcho handed me a full cup. "He's been lobbying behind Robbie's back to force him to retire."

"Can he do that?" I snapped on a plastic lid.

"Think of this as a giant chess game. If Robbie moves the wrong piece and if Prescott plays his best game, who knows?"

Hadcho and I loaded our pockets with sweeteners and creamers. Between us, we had four cups each, plus a hot chocolate for Anya. I swiped an extra handful of stirring sticks because they make great glue spreaders. When Hadcho glared at me, I shrugged. "Might as well get some benefit from this early morning interrogation. I'm not doing this for my health."

As Hadcho and I walked slowly toward Robbie and Prescott, I heard Prescott say, "Of course, there's also the matter of the cruise. You can't be on a boat and run an investigation."

A vein bulged in Robbie's neck.

Prescott rocked on his toes, trying to seem bigger than he was. As if to face down Robbie.

"Take over the command," snarled the Chief of Police. "Hurry up and ask your questions. I still want to go on a honeymoon with my bride. We've already missed our plane, but if we're lucky we can catch another flight."

"Already on it," said Prescott. "I've sent officers out to interview some of your guests."

You could almost hear the glee in his voice.

10

---

*R*obbie worked his jaw as if chewing on a big piece of gristle.

Realizing his boss was ready to go ballistic, Detweiler grabbed Robbie by the arm. He led the chief down the hall and away from Prescott.

Where and how did Prescott get a copy of the guest list? I wondered. Surely Robbie hadn't turned over the one I'd given him! So how did Prescott know who to interview?

I filed those questions away for now. This wasn't the time. Robbie was at his boiling point.

A smirking Prescott stepped into the meeting room, letting the door slam behind him even though Hadcho and I stood there with hands full of hot drinks. Fortunately, Anya had been watching for us, so she hopped up and held the door for us.

As Hadcho and I dispersed coffee, Prescott strode manfully to the head of the table. "I'm in charge here. Mrs. Lowenstein? Come with me."

A collective gasp went up from the bride and bridesmaids. Sheila turned deathly pale, the color of the creamer I held in my left hand.

"Okay," I said. I didn't mind answering Prescott's questions. After all, I'd never met the man who died.

"No! Not that Mrs. Lowenstein. The other one!" shouted Prescott, as he pointed his index finger at Sheila. It was a gesture both rude and threatening.

"She is Mrs. Holmes. Mrs. Robbie Holmes," I said. "I am Mrs. Lowenstein."

If Prescott thought he could overlook Sheila's newly enhanced status, he had another think coming.

"Right. Robbie's second wife." Prescott coughed behind his hand. A jerk of his head indicated he expected her to follow him.

Poor Sheila. She'd obviously not gotten much sleep the night before, and from the way she winced, as she got to her feet, I could tell that her collarbone was aching. It had been broken during the shootout, and it was taking its sweet time about completely healing.

Prescott didn't offer to help her with her chair. Despite her erect posture, Sheila seemed defeated and sad. Hard to believe that this was the same woman who'd beamed with happiness less than twenty-four hours ago.

At the doorway, she turned toward me, her denim blue eyes filled with misery. "Robbie," she mouthed to me.

I didn't get it. Robbie wasn't in any danger. Neither was she. What was the problem? What was she so worried about?

Then it hit me—and I realized why Morrie Hyman's name was familiar. Sheila had gotten into a fight with him last week at the country club.

11

After Prescott interviewed Sheila, he came back for me. As Prescott led me to a meeting room, I said, "I'm feeling a bit under the weather. Could I trouble you for a glass of water?"

"Not until we're done," said Prescott.

"You do realize that I'm pregnant?" I pulled out my own chair.

"The whole county knows you're pregnant, Miss Lowenstein. Your exploits were all over the news."

"That's Mrs. Lowenstein," I snapped at him, "and if you keep this up, I'll just wait for my lawyer."

"You got something to hide?" He sneered at me.

"I have nothing to hide, but I know enough about the legal process to have the utmost respect for..." and I paused "...criminal defense attorneys."

"I would think you'd be happy to talk so that Robbie and your mother-in-law can get going on their cruise."

Well, there was that. Sheila had talked about nothing else in the days leading up to the ceremony.

"Let me have that drink of water, and I'll answer your questions," I said.

"Get it yourself. You know where the ladies' room is. This isn't your first visit to the station, is it?"

Boy, was I ever tempted to wipe that smile off his face. He knew darn good and well that several years ago, I'd come to this station only to learn that my husband George had been found naked and dead in a hotel room. But a reaction was exactly what Prescott wanted, so I was determined not to let him get the upper hand. Instead, I took my time walking to the bathroom where I stuck my face under the faucet. After enjoying the cool water on my skin, I sucked up several mouthfuls of it and went back into the room where Prescott was sitting.

As I made my little excursion, I tried to remember exactly what Sheila had told me about Morrie Hyman. I'd been working on her invitations at the time, and my thoughts were preoccupied with an upcoming scrapbook event. So I hadn't been paying strict attention. Instead, I'd made soothing noises while Sheila blathered on and on about that "stupid fool" she'd run into at the country club.

"Morrie Hyman did my nose. The first time. When I was sixteen. He did everyone's noses as soon as they turned sixteen. Wouldn't touch us before that. Said we weren't done growing. He made a pile of money at it, too. But that hack messed up mine. My friends' noses, too. I've been in for corrective surgery twice."

This was a surprise to me, and I said as much. I didn't know she'd had a nose job. Furthermore, forty years had passed since she was sixteen.

"What caused you to get so upset at the country club?" I asked her.

"Ever since his wife died two years ago, he's been

moping around like a lost dog. Trying to get back into people's good graces. He says he's lonely. No one here wants anything to do with him. At least, he could have the good sense to make himself scarce. But no. No, he has to have a few too many and then bump into me. He hit me so hard that I dropped a full glass of Malbec down the front of that new St. John Knit suit I bought! Can you believe it? And I special ordered that suit! I wanted to take it on our honeymoon!"

Of course, Sheila being Sheila, she wouldn't accept the man's apology or his offer to buy her a new suit. Nope. Not when she'd been waiting for years to give the doctor a piece of her mind. So she let loose on him. The fact that she'd been drinking contributed to her loss of inhibitions.

Although I had never thought of Sheila as a drinker, she really did enjoy her liquor. Over the years, she seemed to gradually be drinking more and drinking more often. Since I didn't run in her circles, I rarely saw her at places where liquor was free flowing. But I knew from comments she made that she imbibed liberally.

Fortunately, that night at the country club, Robbie was there to intervene, although it couldn't have been easy. Eventually, he steered Sheila away from the doctor and toward the front door, where he instructed her to wait while he brought up the car.

Two truisms of life: Hope springs eternal, and booze will make you stupid. Putting both ideas in one pea brain can lead to tragedy. That's what happened.

Dr. Hyman got it into his head that he might still be able to apologize to Sheila and get back in her good books. So even after Robbie separated Sheila and the doctor, Morrie Hyman came back for more.

Not a smart idea.

"I was feeling no pain," said Sheila, "and then Morrie Hyman walked up beside me."

While Robbie pulled his car to the front door, the Hyman/Lowenstein fight entered Round Two. It must have been a heavyweight title bout because a crowd gathered. By the time Robbie managed to stuff Sheila into the passenger seat, she was hollering, "Morrison Hyman, if I ever see you again, I'll fix your nose for you for free. You can count on it. You'll wish you were dead!"

Country club members who didn't see the battle heard about it later.

"Honestly, Sheila," I had said, while I stamped romantic bouquets of flowers on her envelopes. By this point, she had my full attention. "Didn't you go a bit overboard? All that fuss about a suit?"

"The St. John Knit wasn't the point," she informed me. "This had nothing to do with my outfit. It was all about the pain and suffering he caused my friends. I'll never forgive him for that. Not ever."

12

I quickly came to a decision that Prescott Gallaway was TSTL, Too Stupid To Live. He asked me not once but three times to tell him where I was during the wedding ceremony. Duh! I gritted my teeth and said, "Standing beside Sheila at the chuppah, the canopy. You know that, Prescott. You saw me!"

"That's Captain Gallaway. Can you describe what you saw? Start with the date and time, please, for the record."

I did, repeatedly. I went over every part of the ceremony.

"How well do you know Mrs. Lowenstein's bridesmaids?" asked Prescott.

"Do you mean Mrs. Holmes' bridesmaids?" I said. "I'd never met any of them until this week. Their names are Ester Frommer, Toby Pearlman, and Leah Ginsberg."

"I know that. I'm asking if any of them have grudges."

"How should I know? I only met them two days ago. Wait. Three."

He grunted. "They all had nose jobs. Dr. Hyman did them."

"That a fact?"

"I don't like your attitude, Mrs. Lowenstein."

"I don't like yours either, Captain Prescott. Er, Gallaway."

That pretty much summed up our interaction. After going around and around in circles, Prescott decided he was "done" with me. Of course, I couldn't go home. Nope. I was forced to wait in the meeting room while he talked to the other bridesmaids, one-by-one.

When he got to Anya, I put my size seven Keds down. "No. Not without an attorney. She's a minor, and you have no reason to harass her."

Grumbling, he threw up his hands. "I guess I have no choice then."

"No choice in what?" I demanded.

He gave a heavy sigh. Never was a man so put upon. "I'll just have to explain to Mayor White that all of you were uncooperative. That Mrs. Holmes and her friends and family appear to be stonewalling the investigation."

13

Sheila's house in Ladue, Missouri

"Well," said Sheila, after we arrived back at her place. "There's one good thing about this. Robbie and I are already married."

"Huh?"

"My husband can't testify against me."

"Why would that be an issue?" I asked. Sheila leaned hard on me for support. Between the waltzing and whatever gymnastics had ensued at the Ritz, she'd irritated her collarbone. Now, she walked stooped over with pain.

"Sheila, what's that about your husband testifying against you?" I prompted her again, but she turned away from me.

"Hadcho filled me in," said Robbie, as he pulled up a kitchen chair. He'd driven right behind me as I took Sheila and her bridesmaids back to her house. "The cause of death was a long thin instrument shoved up Hyman's nose and into his brain. As a weapon, it was quick and effective."

"Why didn't he fight back?" I asked.

Sheila stared down at a placemat.

"Because the perpetrator first hit him with a stun gun. Otherwise the murderer wouldn't have gotten close enough to do the deed."

Ugh.

Robbie's cell phone rang. He covered the speaker long enough to tell us, "It's the mayor," and then after putting a finger to his lips, switched the call to speaker phone. "Hello, Mayor White."

"First, let me offer hearty congratulations on your marriage. That said, I'm sorry to be the bearer of bad news. As a member of the police commissioners' board, it is my duty to take you off this case," said Mayor White. "I can't have any whispers of impropriety, and obviously, you're too close to this situation to be objective."

"I understand, sir," said Robbie. "I have already turned the investigation over to Captain Gallaway."

"Yes, I know," said Mayor White.

"Yes, well," Robbie cleared his throat. "The transfer of authority made sense. As you know, Captain Gallaway was already tapped to take over while Sheila and I were on our honeymoon cruise."

"Scratch those plans," said Mayor White. "I can't have you leaving town while your bride is under suspicion of murder."

"Excuse me?" Robbie's face puckered into an angry scowl. "My wife has been accused? By whom? Of what?"

"One of your guests told an officer that your wife attacked Dr. Hyman at the country club. Frankly, I don't see how you could have forgotten that, Robbie. You were there with her at the time."

The investigation was less than three hours old, and Prescott was already pointing a finger at Sheila? Clearly, Prescott was more concerned about blackening Robbie's name than being fair.

"With all due respect, sir, it's not possible that Sheila hurt Dr. Hyman."

"You are too close to this situation to be objective. Don't make this any harder than it is. I expect you and your bride to cooperate fully with Captain Gallaway."

"Of course, we will," said Robbie, right before Mayor White offered a crisp goodbye and hung up from the call.

Robbie turned sad eyes on Sheila. "I don't know what to say. Or do. I think I need a drink, and since I'm off duty for a while, I think I'll have one."

With that he walked over to the pantry and poured himself a half a glass of Bloody Mary mix. Next he opened the freezer, withdrew a bottle of Grey Goose and filled the glass with vodka. I'd never seen Robbie drink anything but an occasional beer, so this surprised me.

I expected Sheila to throw a tantrum and start complaining about the mayor. The old Sheila would have. Instead, she turned crimson with embarrassment. Poor Robbie was paying the price for her bad behavior. Since agreeing to marry him, she'd become acutely aware that his job had a distinctly political aspect, one that she'd never had to consider previously. From what I understood, Sheila had already gotten cross-wise with Tom White, the mayor of the city of St. Louis. No one knew exactly how or when, and she refused to tell me, so I chalked it up to Sheila being Sheila.

Now she propped her elbows on her tabletop and stared

out her kitchen window. Robbie dropped one ice cube into his drink and said, "I'll be in my office. Playing solitaire."

"Sheila, is there anything I can do?" I asked.

"Not unless you want to play amateur sleuth and solve this crime."

Patting my baby bump, I said, "I think I'll pass. But look at the bright side. This will give you a chance to spend more time with your friends."

"Right. Instead of spending a month in a luxury cabin on a cruise ship with my new husband, I can hang out with three other post-menopausal women. We can have tons of fun comparing our hot flashes, sagging boobs and varicose veins. Woop-de-do!"

14

Sunday evening/One day after the wedding
Lambert International Airport

"Promise you'll grab a burger when you get inside and don't forget to call and tell me when you land in Los Angeles," I said, as I stood on tiptoes to kiss Detweiler. He hugged me tightly. The denim of his jeans felt alternately rough and smooth against my skin where my blouse separated from my waistband. I was still wearing the clothes I'd thrown on when Sheila had called in a panic. Our usual Sunday routine had definitely gotten thrown under the tour bus.

"I'll try to get back as quickly as possible," he said.

We both knew that he couldn't afford to be gone too long, especially since this trip was totally unexpected.

Shortly after the "shoot out at the slough," Detweiler had received a call from an attorney explaining that his first wife, Gina, had died in a car crash along with her current husband, Van Lauber. Astonishingly, Gina had left behind a little boy, Erik, Detweiler's son. A child Detweiler didn't know existed. He subsequently learned that Van's sister Lorraine Lauber suffered from MS and couldn't raise the child. The attorney wanted to know if Detweiler would be willing to come to California and take custody.

Of course, we said, "Yes!"

Until that fateful phone call, Detweiler had hoped to use his vacation time to stay home with me and our new baby. However, when discussing arrangements, Lorraine Lauber had warned Detweiler that Erik was grieving. As often happens when a child is under stress, the boy was regressing. The death of his mother and the man he called his father was causing him to act much younger than five. For several nights in a row, he'd wet the bed.

"His pediatrician advises that you spend time with him here in California before taking him home," said Lorraine, when she talked to Detweiler over the phone. "You're an unknown quantity. Another disruption to the only life he's known. For Erik's sake, I hope you won't rush this transition."

We had to do what was best for Erik. Our baby was due in January. If Detweiler's trip to Los Angeles soaked up all his paid leave, we'd just have to make do. Somehow, we'd get through this.

Adding a new baby to Erik's life was likely to cause yet another set-back, but I didn't mention that to Detweiler. He was already feeling guilty because he'd never known about Erik. Gina had simply packed up and left Detweiler one day while he was at work. Poof! Eventually, she sent back word from California that she a.) hated being a cop's wife, b.) detested living in a small town in southwestern Illinois, c.) didn't want to talk about it, and d.) wanted a divorce.

Detweiler never even knew that she was pregnant. A year passed. At the end of twelve months, he gave up and signed the divorce papers. Later, Detweiler learned that Gina had married Van Lauber, a wealthy older man. That's why Detweiler's son had spent the first five years of his life thinking that Lauber was his real father.

The call about Erik couldn't have come at a worse time. Between my ob/gyn bills and the impending birth of our child, Detweiler and I are worried about making ends meet. Not only is money tight, but I've agreed to buy Time in a Bottle, the scrapbook store where I work. That means a big commitment of both money and time. Two scarce resources.

Just a few days ago, I had discovered him pacing the living room floor late at night. "Quit worrying, and come to bed."

He held out his arms to me, and I entered the security of his hug. "Don't get the wrong idea. I've always wanted kids. Always hoped to have a large family. And you know how much I love Anya."

"True," I said, "but as my nana used to say, 'Be careful what you wish for.'"

I knew he was treading water, with his dreams weighing him down as he tried to fight the current. I decided that I would be his rock. No matter what happened next, he could hang on to me as the waters of change swirled around us. That's the sort of relationship I wanted with this man. That's what I was determined to provide.

As we stood holding each other in the drop off area at the airport. I knew I had to let him go, but I felt like I was going to burst into tears. Instead, I squeezed his hands. A sort of signal that we were united. "It will all work out just fine," I said, repeating his mantra.

"Don't forget to give Erik the books I bought him," said

Anya, leaning past me to plant a kiss on Detweiler's cheek and hand him the Pelican hard-sided case with his gun inside. "And take lots of pictures."

"Spoken like the true daughter of a scrapbook store owner," I said.

The lanky cop rested his roll-aboard on its feet and expanded his embrace to hug both of us. "Erik is such a lucky boy to have a big sister like you, Anya-Banana. He's going to be thrilled. I'll be thinking about my girls the entire time I'm away. Now Anya, promise me that you'll take good care of your mother."

"I will," she said solemnly.

With great reluctance, I tore myself away from the love of my life. Although I knew he was doing the right thing, I regretted that he was leaving us, especially now when Robbie was in such a bad mood and Sheila was under a cloud. I spread my palm over my belly. Soon there would be three children to protect. Anya, my oldest. Erik, who would join us soon. And Baby Bunting, as we laughingly called the child I was carrying.

All we could do was take things one day at a time. Thank goodness, that's all God sends us!

15

An airport traffic cop tweeted his shrill whistle at Anya and me. "Move it!" he yelled, as he waved frantically.

I hesitated long enough to see Detweiler striding through the sliding glass doors, and then Anya and I hopped into my BMW. We buckled up, and I pulled out of the drop off lane.

"What do you suppose Erik will look like?" wondered Anya.

"I hope he looks like Detweiler," I said. "I wish his aunt would have sent photos."

"Me, too," she agreed. "Maybe his parents just weren't picture people. Some folks aren't, you know. But I can't wait to see him. I like the fact that we'll be a family, whether we look like it or not. Sherrie Glover has a sister who's from China, and they look nothing alike, but that's still cool. If I had my way, I'd like for people to be able to tell that we're related. Detweiler and his sisters look kinda alike. You and Amanda look a lot alike. I think that's neat. That's a problem with being an only child. Nobody looks like you. Well, not much. Parents don't count. Grandparents either."

I smiled to myself. Detweiler and I had prepared ourselves for Anya to be upset by this turn of events. With the addition of Erik, she would be losing the limelight as an only child even before I gave birth. Fortunately for us, my daughter seemed comfortable with the change. In fact, she had shown a tremendous amount of empathy for the little boy who lost both his parents in a car accident. I was very proud of her.

As I pulled onto I-70, my phone rang. "How's my favorite niece?" chirped Aunt Penny.

I laughed. "You better not let Amanda hear you say that."

"She's an old stick-in-the-mud. I told her I wanted to go to IHOP for pancakes, and she pointed out that I'm too short to pack on extra weight. I told her that my weight was none of her business. I'm looking around for reasonable people who will eat breakfast any meal of the day. You game? Anya with you? Can she come, too?"

"You don't have to ask us twice. Do you need a ride?"

"Nope."

"Then we're on our way. We missed our pancake breakfast this morning, so we'd love a chance to make up the deficit."

"Thank goodness," said Aunt Penny, "because I was planning to dial numbers at random until I found someone willing to eat with me."

16

IHOP off of Brentwood

wenty minutes later, Anya and I sat across from Dorothy, of Wizard of Oz fame. At least, that's how Aunt Penny was dressed. I ignored the stares from other patrons. We weren't that far from Kansas, so honestly, Aunt Penny didn't look that odd. At least, not in my opinion. My diminutive aunt ordered a stack of banana pecan pancakes, two eggs over easy, a double order of bacon and hash browns. If the waiter was impressed, he didn't show it.

"Make that two," said Anya.

"Three," I chimed in. "Aunt Penny, did Amanda drop you off?"

"No."

"How did you get here? Take a cab?"

"No."

"Come on. Spit it out." I leaned across the table to urge her to speak. "You aren't up to your old tricks, are you?"

"I thumbed a ride, if that's what you mean." She punctuated her sentence with a self-satisfied nod of the head.

All I could do was groan.

I filled her in on Dr. Hyman's murder.

"Where's the list of suspects?" asked Aunt Penny.

"Excuse me?" I set down my tea cup with a clatter.

"You are planning to investigate, aren't you?"

I shook my head vigorously. "No. No way. I'm leaving this to Prescott."

"Prescott? He's the short little guy with the corn cob up his backside?"

"You noticed! He's also agitating for Robbie's job. If I get in the middle of this, my actions could be used against Robbie."

"That and Detweiler isn't here to get you out of a jam." Anya giggled.

"Hey! I'm perfectly capable of taking care of myself," I said.

"By shooting your way out of a tough spot," said Anya. "Mom, I hope you don't plan on doing that again."

"Certainly not. Besides, they are still holding my gun at the police station. It takes forever to get evidence released, I guess. You'd think I'd have it back by now, but no."

Aunt Penny reached for her handbag. "I bought one yesterday. You want it?"

"No!" I nearly shouted. "Please, no!"

"I think you should take it, Mom," said Anya. "You run into trouble a lot. More than any mother I know. Carrying a gun makes sense for you."

"Are you two out of your minds? I'm pregnant!"

"We aren't asking the baby to shoot," said Aunt Penny.

"But we are suggesting you pack a firearm," said Anya. "In your purse."

I couldn't believe I was having this conversation. Not with two reasonably sane members of my family. "Look. I plan to sit tight, and let Prescott do his job, while I work on transforming my store."

"So how's Dodie doing?" asked Aunt Penny.

A thick pain clutched at my throat. My eyes blurred with tears. "She's gone. She died three weeks ago. You were in Mexico. I guess I didn't tell you. Remember? You were out of phone service and no Internet."

"Oh." Aunt Penny shook her head. "That's too bad."

"Yes, but she was suffering. At the end, she was in terrible shape." I signaled the waiter for more ice water. That lump in my throat was too big to swallow. After he poured a glass, I continued. "She'd lost all her hair and so much weight that she was literally skin and bones. It was a blessing when she passed."

"But the timing was really bad," said Anya. "Gran expected Mom to act all skippy-yippee about her wedding, and Mom's been great, but it's still really sad. Dodie's husband, Horace is a mess."

I looked at my daughter. "How do you know that? About Horace?"

"Rebekkah told me. We chat on Facebook. She's doing everything she can to get him back to normal, but he's really lost without Dodie." Anya frowned. "I really think you should check on Rebekkah, Mom. She's kind of lost herself."

"Yes, you're right, I should. Dodie asked me to keep an eye on Horace and on Rebekkah. Unfortunately, with Sheila's wedding, I've been up past my eyeballs in alligators. But now, things should settle down a bit."

Anya snorted and water came out her nose. "Right. Because you're in the middle of a murder investigation."

"No, I'm not," I said. "But I am kind of overwhelmed at

the store without Dodie, so I can imagine how hard it is for Horace and Rebekkah. Sort of."

"Do you have any plans for the store? Any changes you want to make?" asked Aunt Penny.

"Margit suggested that they add yarns," Anya said, "because she loves to knit and crochet. Mom is going to get certified to teach Zentangle®. Clancy suggested they try offering more kinds of crafts. Since the store name is ambivalent, Time in a Bottle could mean anything, really. Mom's having that dividing wall knocked down, and they're going to expand the store by taking over a portion of the stockroom. There's always been too much stuff in storage."

I smiled. My daughter was quickly learning about retail, just as I was.

"Sounds like tons of fun. I love swinging a sledge hammer." My aunt winked at me.

"Thanks, but I've already scheduled the work with a general contractor. This is the time to get it done. We're slow in the summer."

Because the changes would put a hefty dent in my budget, I'd kept staffing to a minimum. My timeframe worked well for Laurel Wilkins, one of our staffers, who was busy with a project for her master's degree in sociology. She was also seeing a new guy, someone she'd kept to herself. However, she'd be coming back to work soon.

"Mom, you really need to catch up with Rebekkah," said my daughter.

"You're right. I thought she might need some space, but I shouldn't wait to check in on her. I'll text message her tomorrow. Maybe she's ready to come back to work. At the very least, I'll invite her to drop by and see us."

Anya smiled at me. "I knew I could count on you, Mom. I told Rebekkah that she's like an older sister to me. She was worried that after her mom died, you'd, well, kick her to the curb. But, I told her you wouldn't. I'm not sure she believed it, but we will stay in touch, won't we?"

"Absolutely, Anya-Banana." My little girl was growing up fast. Best of all, she was turning into a lovely, thoughtful young woman.

*O*n the way to the car, Aunt Penny leaned close to me. "You sure I can't help out at your store? Your mother is about to drive me nuts!"

"I'm sure I can find something for you to do. But my budget is severely limited," I said. So was my patience. If I could find Aunt Penny a chore that didn't involve direct interaction with the public, all would be well.

"I'm not asking to be paid," sniffed my aunt.

"Good. I can always use help at the store if it's unpaid or cheap labor. Do you qualify on either account?"

"Yes, and I'm a recent immigrant, too. So I'll work long hours doing thankless jobs under terrible working conditions for no benefits."

"That's the American way, right?"

She winked at me. "Besides, I pack heat. You can always use a security guard at the store."

"I hope not."

I was glad to have Aunt Penny with us. She kept a smile on her face and a firearm in her pocket. You never knew what she would do next. Best of all, she was unfailingly supportive of me and my life. In almost every aspect, she was my mother's exact opposite. I have no idea what kept them friends.

"You need to come on in and say hi," my aunt suggested, as we dropped her off back at the rental house. "Tell your mother and sister what's up with that dead guy at the wedding."

I groaned and rested my forehead against the steering wheel. "How about if I drop you off, and we'll pretend that I came inside. Tell them that I had morning sickness and needed to leave. That I got sick the minute I pulled up in front of the house where my mother lives."

"Chicken."

"Bwock-bwock-bwock. I resemble that remark," I said.

"Come on," said Aunt Penny. "Your sister will probably have a few questions that I can't answer. She might even have seen something at the wedding that would be helpful. You owe it to her to stay involved with your mom. It can't all rest on Amanda's shoulders."

My aunt was right. Amanda did almost everything for our mother. Partially because Mom loved her best. But honestly, that was a lousy trade off, because my mother was a giant pimple on the backside of the world, Amanda's world in particular. In the short time since my sister had moved here, I had a better idea of all she did for our mother, and she had a better idea of the challenges I was facing in life. Without a doubt, I had the better end of the deal. My mom was a real pill, and I often felt guilty about how much she demanded from Amanda.

They lived together in a huge house my mother and sister were renting from Clancy (or more accurately from Clancy's mother) in U City, which is what the locals call University City, the area around Washington University. The house had a full (mostly empty) basement, a nice backyard, a garage, a large living room, a library, formal dining room and four bedrooms still empty upstairs. Aunt Penny bunked there when she was in town.

I parked the car at the curb and steeled myself for a visit with my mother. I suppose I could have dropped off Aunt Penny, but she was right. I owed it to Amanda to at least check in once in a while and see if I could help. I also wanted to hear what Amanda had to say about the wedding. Had she seen or heard anything that might point a finger to the killer?

"Since your stud muffin is gone for the night," said Aunt Penny with a leer, "why not stick around and play games with us? I'm itching to beat your mother at Bananagrams. I bet neither of you can beat me."

"You're on," said Anya.

I brought up the rear as my aunt and daughter trudged up the brick walkway to the house. Even though the sun was setting, the heat and humidity had wilted Amanda's pink petunias. Still, their perfume filled the night air. I paused to glance up at the sky. Detweiler's plane would be taking off about now. I wished him a safe journey and crossed my fingers that he and Erik would get along fine.

Penny rapped on the front door. If I was lucky, Mom would already be in bed.

I wasn't lucky.

Shortly after I sat down at the dining room table with a glass of decaf iced tea, Mom walked in. "You took Anya and Kiki out to eat but didn't invite me? How could you, Penny?"

"I did invite you. You didn't want to go. Remember? You weren't interested in pancakes."

My sister rolled her eyes behind the two older women's backs.

"Does this go on all the time?" I asked.

"Every minute of every day," she said.

While Aunt Penny and Mom argued in the other room, I told my sister about the murder inquiry.

"Poor Sheila. Her honeymoon is ruined," said my sister.

"Looks like it. If they find the killer quickly, she and Robbie could fly to one of the ports of call and hop on the cruise ship. They still have three days before it leaves port. They'd planned to arrive in Dubai early and spend the extra time getting acclimated."

"Speaking of the police, that Stan Hadcho is pretty cute stuff," said my sister with a gleam in her eyes. "Didn't you tell me he's part Native American?"

"He is. His last name means 'brave warrior' or something of the sort."

"Mom's insisting he's Italian."

We both rolled our eyes. If we kept this up, they'd be calling us the Googly Eyes Sisters.

Right about then, Aunt Penny got us going on the game. The competition shut Mom up for a while. We had a good time spilling the tiles, making words, and shouting, "Peel!" Of course, my mother won. That's because she cheats. She uses proper nouns and makes up new words. That's one reason I usually refuse to play with her. But this evening, Aunt Penny kept her honest. Sort of.

After three rounds, we took a break. I helped my sister pour more glasses of iced tea in the kitchen.

"Is it my imagination, or has Mom gotten meaner?" I asked.

"It's only that you're around her more often, so she's able to vent her spleen on you."

"How's she doing at day care?"

"She complains about the other seniors, but luckily for

all of us, the therapist in charge seems to know how to handle Mom."

I took my sister's hand. "Amanda, I am so sorry that you have to put up with this."

"So am I," she smiled, "So am I."

18

Very late Sunday night/ One day after the wedding
Los Angeles International Airport

*C*had Detweiler grabbed his roll-aboard from the overhead compartment of the Boeing aircraft. Opening his cell phone, he checked the time. To get the lowest fare possible, he'd been routed through Denver, which made his trip a long six and a half hours, not counting the layover. It was late evening in California, but very early Monday morning in St. Louis. Kiki wouldn't be up yet.

The rolling bag seemed ridiculously light to a man who lifted weights regularly. But its cargo was impossibly precious: a stuffed fox from his parents, a Beanie Baby from Anya's personal collection and an album that Kiki had made for Erik.

A woman wearing cheater-readers around her neck

struggled to dislodge her belongings from the tight space overhead. "May I help?" he asked.

When she nodded gratefully, he lifted out the bag and handed it to her.

His fingers ached with nervousness. He had always planned to be a father. Always seen himself in a distant future that included being surrounded by a clutch of children who called him, "Daddy." Now his dreams were coming true. In his pants pocket was a note from Kiki, telling him to take care, that she loved him. His thumb rubbed the corner of an index card from Anya. She'd filled it with Xs and Os to symbolize "gazillions of hugs and kisses for my new brother."

By force of habit, he touched the spot under his arm. His rule was if his pants were on, he wore his gun, too, but of course, his holster was empty. When he arrived at Lambert Field in St. Louis, he had locked his gun in the case with two magazines and the ammo. After filling in the declaration form, he put the paperwork in the case and relocked the case before handing it to TSA to scan. It felt weird to check his firearm as baggage.

His seat was as far back as you could get in the plane. The passengers ahead of him seemed to take forever to retrieve their luggage and toddle off the plane. Normally, he was good at waiting. He'd been on enough stake-outs that he'd learned the value of patience. But today, he jiggled from one foot to the other. No one was moving fast enough for him.

After twenty minutes, he followed the streaming crowd through the concourse and into the baggage claim area. Lorraine, Van Lauber's sister, had offered to send a car for him. The driver would meet Detweiler at baggage claim. No matter how many times he refused her offer, Lorraine pressed him to accept. Finally, he gave in. It would save him the hassle of renting a car and navigating in Los Angeles traffic. Of course, Detweiler wanted to see Erik right away, but Miss Lauber had asked if they could have lunch first. "I'd like to chat with you before you see your son."

His son.

The words brought a smile to his face, despite his disappointment that the meeting was delayed.

Pulling the roll-aboard behind him, Detweiler quickly found his gun case as the other travelers began to scatter. His height gave him the ability to see over the heads of most. A man in a black jacket, black slacks, and a black cap held up a sign with DETWEILER in large black type. Chad switched the small case to his left hand so he could offer a handshake in greeting.

"I'm Orson," said the man. His pockmarked skin at odds with the elegant uniform. "Miss Lauber sent me. May I take your luggage for you?"

"Nice to meet you and no, but thanks. The roll-aboard is ridiculously lightweight, and this is my gun case. I never let it out of my sight."

Orson's quick blink betrayed his surprise. "Sir?"

"I'm a law enforcement officer; I always carry. Especially when I'm in a strange city," said Detweiler.

"I do, too," said Orson, as he unbuttoned his jacket to display his holster.

After Detweiler retrieved his case, the two men fell in step.

"Did you have a nice flight?" asked Orson.

"Yes. Thanks. How far are we from the hotel? And from Miss Lauber's house?" Detweiler stopped himself before adding, "And my son?"

"Not far. Miss Lauber asked that I take you directly

there. She'd like for you to call her tomorrow morning when you're up and about. Then you can schedule your appointment with her."

"How long have you worked for the Laubers?" Detweiler asked.

"Twenty years. For Miss Lauber. My job is to drive her and protect her. That's why I carry. As you probably know, she's worth a lot of money. You never know what sort of creeps are out there. Jerks who might want to cash in. You can't be too careful."

The men stepped out into the cool, gray California night. Detweiler was glad he'd worn his old leather bomber jacket over his jade green polo knit shirt. Years of controlling his facial expressions came in handy as he fought to control his disappointment. "Why didn't Miss Lauber just set a time for us to meet tomorrow?"

"Miss Lauber likes to do things her own way," said Orson. "She's not well, you know. So she has to, sort of, pace herself."

"Because of her MS?" Detweiler asked, as he walked alongside the driver.

"Most days, you'd never know it. She seems right as rain. Then it hits her, and she's a mess. Unpredictable. Except that stress seems to bring it on. Of course, hard to imagine anything more stressful than losing your brother. And sister-in-law both. Especially seeing how close the three of them were."

"What exactly caused the accident?" Even though he was off-duty, Detweiler couldn't turn off his cop's brain.

"Mr. Lauber lost control of the car and crossed the centerline. Everybody knows that stretch of highway is dangerous. They call it 'Big Bend' because it's a long narrow curve that runs through high canyon walls. Folks have been after the Laguna Beach authorities to widen it or add a median, but they won't. They claim it'll spoil the scenic beauty."

Detweiler wondered what exactly "lost control" meant. Was Van Lauber driving recklessly? Were the conditions bad? Did he lose concentration and make a wrong move? Of course, the California Highway Patrol would have used forensic specialists to check the scene. They must have found nothing, so more than likely it had been exactly as it had seemed, a case of driver error.

"Mr. Lauber enjoyed traveling with the missus. They'd been visiting friends—" Orson stopped abruptly. "I'm not suggesting that alcohol was involved, of course."

"No," said Detweiler. "You didn't say that."

But still, he wondered...

19

Monday morning/Two days after the wedding
Kiki's house in Webster Groves

he minute I opened my eyes, I checked my cell phone. There was a text message from Detweiler: *In LA. Flight was fine. Talk to you later today. Love you, D*

Anya didn't complain when I asked her get up, get dressed and eat breakfast. In no time at all, she and I and Gracie were packed into my car.

Force of habit sent me toward CALA, the Charles and Anne Lindbergh Academy, Anya's school. Most summers, I'd enrolled my daughter in a series of summer camps. This year would be different. Anya had proposed that I hire her as my assistant. She opened one sleepy eye to ask, "Mom? Are you lost?"

Gracie thumped her tail in agreement as I did a U-turn on Lindbergh. Taking my daughter to the store on a daily basis had required a new habit, but I was so groggy this morning, I'd reverted to my old ways.

"You need help at the store," Anya had presented her case to me, "and I can do that. It's better than being with a bunch of babies all day long at summer camp. I hated it. Besides, I'd like to earn a little money, if I can. I want to start saving for a car. It's not that far off, you know."

"Does that mean you'll help keep Erik occupied once he arrives?"

She nodded happily.

I was happy to pay her a pittance as long as we could lay down the ground rules: "You are an employee, not my kid. When I ask you to help, I expect you to hop to it. I also expect you to be courteous to customers and the senior co-workers. Even if you get bored with Erik, I still expect you to keep an eye on him. This'll be his first summer with us. He's bound to be lonely and emotional."

"Mooo-oom," she whined. "I know all that."

"I also expect you to get out of bed in the mornings promptly, so I don't have to nag you. We need to get to the store on time, or Margit will be cross," I had said.

"Margit wouldn't be cross with me!" Anya giggled. "She thinks I'm cute."

"Don't push your luck," I warned. "Margit hasn't had any reason to be cross with you. So don't give her one. She's a stickler for being on time, for doing things according to the lists she's made and for adhering to rules."

I didn't add that Margit and I were both on edge. There was so much catching up to do, because we hadn't realized how much Dodie's mental health had been deteriorating. She'd seemed all right, most of the time, but she hadn't been. Bit by bit, Margit and I discovered things left undone, questions unanswered, and loose ends that needed to be tied up. Before she died, Dodie had been a buffer. Now Margit and I needed to redefine our own relationship. Some days were better than others. She was no-nonsense, but that could sound abrupt and brittle. I was creative, but that often translated into unfocused and ditzy. Still, for the store to work, we needed each other. Fortunately, we knew that.

Our lingering grief cast a pall over both of us. The closer I drove to the store, the more a lump of sadness began to crowd my throat. I swallowed the pain, but a tear leaked out. Using the back of my hand, I brushed it away.

Even though Anya was singing along to "Call Me Maybe" by Carly Rae Jepsen, I couldn't muster up a smile. I missed my friend terribly. All I could think was, "Where's Dodie?" It just didn't seem right that I was here, working and enjoying the business she had started without her. I'm old enough to know that life's not fair, but my heart is having trouble accepting that truism.

I pulled into the parking lot and turned off the engine. Gracie and Anya tumbled out of my Beemer . I set my shoulders and took a deep breath. Time in a Bottle would be Dodie's memorial. As long as our doors stayed open, I would be continuing her legacy, keeping her alive. And wasn't that exactly what scrapbookers did best?

With two goals in mind—to keep Anya busy and to bring in extra income during the normally slow summer months—I'd devised a plan. We had contacted the various summer school organizations and offered crafting classes for a nominal fee. My daughter and I had combed through all my old copies of scrapbooking magazines to find projects suitable for younger kids. Since Father's Day loomed larger than life on the calendar, making a card for dear old Dad struck Anya and me both as a logical class idea.

"What are card toppers?" Anya asked.

"Imagine a blank white greeting card. Now, if you created a front for the card that could be glued on, that would be a card topper."

"Why do it separately? Why make two pieces?" she wondered. "Why not just decorate the card?"

"Card makers typically stockpile only a few card bodies and matching envelopes, but they make a lot of card toppers. That way they can add the perfect topper to the blank card and be ready for any occasion. Takes up a lot less space. Imagine if I make a card topper for every holiday, for general birthdays and for milestone life events. I could keep all the toppers in a small accordion folder and whip out whatever one I needed, slap it down on the blank card, and mail it."

"I get it. I can see another benefit. If a kid goofs up the card topper, it's easier to replace than a pre-folded card. Cheaper, too."

My daughter was learning the financial realities of retail very quickly. I gave her a hug. "You are so smart."

"I have to be. I'm soon to be the oldest of a passel of kids."

"A passel?" I laughed. "How many are in a passel? You might want to look that one up. I think a 'passel' is a large group. Last time I looked, three kids did not make for a large family."

"I like this one best," said Anya. She pointed to a card topper featuring a man's torso. By cleverly folding the paper, the artist had created a three-dimensional suit coat and collared shirt.

What made the card extra-cute was the addition of a "tie" made of brightly colored scrapbook paper. As I stared at the sample in the magazine, Anya said, "How about if we just do the tie? We could use up a lot of paper that hasn't sold well."

The tone of her voice told me more than the words did.

"Anya-Banana, are you worried about the new baby? Or about Erik? Most big sisters don't get two new siblings at one time."

"It does seem like a lot. First you get pregnant, then Gran gets married, and now Detweiler is bringing home a little boy none of us have ever met. I mean, I don't want to sound selfish, but I kind of wonder..." and a tear rolled down her face. "Will you have time for me, Mom? I sound like a big baby, don't I?'

"Oh, honey," and I pulled her close. "Forever and for always, you'll be my baby. No matter how big you get. No matter how tall you are. Even if there are two more children in our family. You were my first. You made me a mother. No one could ever take your place, sweetheart. Even if I had a dozen more kids. You're special. We've been through so much together, and I count on you. Maybe too much."

"I'll miss the times when it's just you and me, Mom. Even now when Detweiler's at the house, sometimes I just wish...I wish he'd go away."

She sobbed noisily.

"I know, honey. We're jam-packed, aren't we? I bet sometimes you just need a bit more space."

"Uh-huh," she said. "But I love that house. I don't ever want to move. Ever."

This had been a common refrain. Detweiler and I had gingerly approached the idea that we needed a bigger place to live, but when we did, Anya had gotten emotional. Her dramatic response shocked both of us. However, she was adamant. She loved our house primarily for the wonderful location, plus the beautiful and spacious lot. Of course, she adored Monroe, Leighton's donkey. She also loved Petunia,

Leighton's pug. Moving would mean saying goodbye to those two friends, as well as changing our setting. Finding homes on large lots was a challenge, especially given our budget.

Consequently, we'd agreed to drop the plan to move. I figured that once we got too crowded, Anya would change her mind. Once that happened, we could start looking for a new home.

"Promise me! Promise me that we won't move!" she said.

All of a sudden, a cold wet nose pressed against my daughter's face. Gracie had scaled the walls of her doggy playpen. Her sudden appearance shocked both Anya and me. I've never known Gracie to take a leap like that.

"She was worried about me," said Anya, reaching down to stroke the Great Dane's head.

"Of course, she was," I said. "You're her little girl. Mine, too. And everything is going to be just fine, honey. I promise."

---

20

*T*he call came while Anya was taking Gracie for a stroll around the block.

After identifying himself as an attorney working on behalf of the estate of William Ballard, my late husband George's dead partner, the man explained that forensic accountants had turned up an account in the Cayman Islands. This money appeared to be funds diverted from Dimont Development, the company George and Bill Ballard had founded. The Ballard family was willing to turn the bulk of these funds over to me if I agreed not to pursue further legal remedies against Bill Ballard's estate.

I sat back in Dodie's big black leather chair and pondered what this meant. I'd learned the hard way not to trust so-called experts. Instead of agreeing, I said, "Please send me all the particulars."

"This is a limited time offer. If you agree, I can email you a form. When you fax it back to me, we'll deposit a sizable sum in your bank account. You can have the money today."

My spidey-sense started tingling. Three years ago, when George died, I would have jumped at the offer on the table. I would have trusted the man on the other end of the phone implicitly.

But that was the old Kiki. The sadder and wiser Kiki held her ground.

"As I said, please send me the particulars. I'll get back to you."

"Mrs. Lowenstein, there's no reason for you to make this difficult. Not when we have the ability to wire transfer this sum.."

"Please listen carefully: No. No. And no." With that I hung up on him.

After putting Gracie in her playpen, Anya went to work cutting out men's jackets, shirts, and ties from a variety of patterned paper.

Since the store wasn't officially open for another forty-five minutes, after I got her started, I went into the office and sat behind the big desk. I still called it "Dodie's office" and "Dodie's desk" in my head. Converting that to "my office" and "my desk" would take time. I pulled open the desk drawer to grab a pencil. Dodie had been very particular about her office supplies. The only pencil she liked was the yellow plastic Papermate Sharpwriter, a mechanical pencil. I reached for one in the desk divider, and instead my fingers brushed an oddly shaped item. On further inspection, this proved to be a silly toy turtle with a bobbing head. I smiled at the toy and stuck him back in the drawer.

My responsibility was to review upcoming events, work on schedules and try to catch up on correspondence. I had never really appreciated the myriad of details Dodie handled, even after her cancer slowed her down. Even with my best effort, I could feel myself falling behind. Answering requests from our website took me ten minutes a day. That didn't seem like much until you multiplied it by seven days a week. Margit had calculated what my time was worth an hour, and the resultant number surprised me. Doing the math, I could see that we lost significant income when I was busy with busy work.

However, for the time being, I had no other option but to personally review all the store correspondence.

I also had to act like the owner even though, technically, I wasn't.

I'd been in the process of negotiating the purchase with Horace when Dodie had slipped into a coma. Thereafter, he'd obviously been unavailable to talk—and frankly, he didn't seem to care about the store. But I did. So I continued to monitor all the requests that came in, whether for merchandise, services or classes. Those numbers continued to grow. Alarmingly. Dodie had always been very generous. But this went beyond generosity. If I honored all these requests, the drain on resources would significantly cut into our profitability.

When I shared my notes with Margit, she had shaken her head sadly and shown me a similar list that she had started. "Ach. I do not think she ever said no. There seems to be no rhyme or reason to her responses."

"Looks to me like she didn't ask for anything in return, either. No mention in programs. No comments from the dais. I understand the concept of *tzedakah*, loosely translated as charity, but even so..." I paused and added, "With all due respect to Dodie, this was ridiculous."

"She was driving this business into the ground," said Margit sadly. "Charity begins at home. I wonder if the cancer affected her brain earlier than we realized."

"What do I do now? Tell these people that I won't honor her commitments?"

Margit took off her cat-eye glasses and rubbed the bridge of her nose. "I am not sure how to handle this."

"I know I'm eavesdropping," said Clancy, "but is it possible that these people might be lying to you?"

She'd slipped in through the backdoor while we were talking. Since Margit leaves every Monday promptly at noon, and we have a crop every Monday night, Clancy was scheduled for a full eight hours.

"Huh?" I squinted at her. "What do you mean by that?"

"Ladies, you are two kind-hearted individuals. Isn't it conceivable that people are taking advantage of the store? And of you? Kiki, do these people offer any proof that Dodie made these promises?" Clancy held out her hand, a silent demand for the list I'd made.

"No." I handed the papers to Clancy and watched as her sleek, Jackie Kennedy style bob dipped over her face. She took her time and perused the paperwork.

"This is outrageous," she said slowly. "You're telling me that Dodie agreed to donate all the supplies for a vacation Bible school? Plus a year's worth of supplies for their Sunday school? I know she was ecumenically minded, but this hardly seems possible. I bet if you look into this more closely, you'd discover that a small number of people are behind many of these requests. Especially, the large ones. I bet this is a scam. One that these folks have pulled many, many times. It's incredibly organized. Notice the same phrasing used over and over? The same style of type? The same indents on the letters? You're being hoodwinked."

I was stunned. I sat down on a nearby folding chair, unable to frame thoughts coherently. "But why would people lie like this?"

"I can think of a lot of reasons," said Clancy, adjusting her gold Movado watch on her wrist. "One might be to profit from your kindness. And to take advantage of the changing of the guard, so to speak. Another might be financial gain. And yet another might be to run you out of business. Ever since they finished revamping the overpass to Brentwood Avenue, there's been a marked increase in traffic. Have you talked to a real estate agent about what this store is worth?"

I admitted that I hadn't. My dear friend Jennifer Moore had given me loose guidelines for valuing a business. We'd intended to sit down and go over the purchase agreement before I signed it. But Jennifer's sister in Seattle had to have emergency surgery, so my friend flew to her sibling's side. I knew that Dodie and Horace weren't trying to cheat me. We'd agreed on the purchase in principle, but when Dodie had taken a turn for the worse, Horace had waved off my attempts at discussion.

I hadn't wanted to press the issue, given the circumstances. Once Dodie died—although neither of us spoke so directly about that morose event—we'd get down to the nitty-gritty of the purchase.

"Look, I understand why you're moving ahead so cautiously," said Clancy. "Dodie was more than your friend. She was a mentor, a surrogate mother and a business coach. But Kiki, business is business. Margit? I know you, too, cared deeply about Dodie."

"What are you suggesting?" I asked Clancy. "Quit dancing around."

"I'm suggesting that you, Kiki, haven't done your due diligence. The requests for charitable contributions might only be the tip of the iceberg. Yes, Margit knows the day-to-day profitability of the business, but that's only part of the picture. There's more to a business than its day-to-day expenses. When was the roof last checked? What's the status of the air-conditioning and heating units? What are the taxes? Are they paid up-to-date? Current? What's the maintenance on the parking lot? You're also buying a building and a parking lot, right? You need to get professional help in evaluating what this place is worth. You have too much responsibility riding on your shoulders to botch this, Kiki."

21

*S*itting there at the desk and looking over a fresh crop of requests, Clancy's warning came back like a smack up the side of the head. She had been right: I couldn't afford to mess up this. The truth was that I didn't know what I was getting myself into. I hadn't investigated the total scope of my obligations.

My stomach churned. I reached for the package of Saltine crackers I keep in my purse.

A tiny kick in my belly reminded me that I was a big girl now. With a baby on the way, a new son joining our family and a daughter who'd be off to college in five years, I couldn't afford to stick my head in the sand, wave my butt in the air and hope no one used me for target practice.

I needed help, and I needed it fast.

I had no idea where to turn so I shot off an email to Cara Mia Delgatto, asking her if she could meet with me.

Cara responded immediately: *I'm coming early with the food. How about if we talk before the crop?*

I emailed her: *That would be grand. By the way, how is*

your server doing? The one who stumbled over Dr. Hyman's dead body?

She messaged me back: *A bit shook up, but OK, all things considered.*

Next, I text messaged Rebekkah and asked if she'd like to help out at the store. A response came immediately, as she offered to drop by in a short while.

That would make for good timing because I had an appointment with my ob/gyn for my sonogram. I swallowed a spoonful of sadness. When I scheduled this, I had high hopes that Detweiler would be in attendance. But he would be here for the main event. That was what really mattered. I could ask the tech for pictures. Hadn't I seen more than my share of sonogram images since becoming a professional scrapbooker? Yes, indeed-y-do!

Wasn't this the perfect time to start a brand new scrapbook? One including photos of Erik, as soon as they were available?

Yeppers!

"Anya?" I called to my daughter. "Let's start a new family album. What do you say?"

When the door minder rang a half an hour later, we had pulled out all the albums and narrowed our selection down to two. Looking up from the work table, I spotted our guest, a woman who did not look happy. The customer turned in a tight circle, studying the store, taking in all the racks of paper and studying the sample pages on the walls.

"Welcome. How can I help?" I walked over to greet her with a smile.

"Where is Kiki Lowenstein?" The customer looked to be in her early thirties, but that was only a guess because she was a person with a mouth that naturally turned down in a frown. The fixed expression aged her. In her arms was a cardboard shoebox labeled Christian Louboutin.

"I'm Kiki." I extended my hand to shake, but she didn't respond. After an awkward silence, I let mine drop.

She stared at my baby bump and said, "You aren't married."

"I am a widow." I put a lot of nice into my voice.

"Bonnie didn't tell me you were pregnant."

"Bonnie Gossage?" I found it hard to reconcile Bonnie, whose favorite accessory is a smile, with this crabby woman. Bonnie is not only one of my favorite people, and a long-time customer of the store, she's also the woman who got me out of the county slammer when I was unjustly accused.

"Mrs. Gossage is our attorney." The woman shifted her weight. "I'm Bernice Stottlemeyer. I have a little job for you."

Uh, a little job for you?

"Nice to meet you, Bernice." A voice inside me cried out, "Not so much!" But I ignored it. "Why don't you come on over and sit down? This is my daughter, Anya."

Just as she'd been taught to do, Anya stood up and extended her hand for a shake. Bernice ignored my daughter's good manners. In fact, she withdrew from Anya, while holding the box to her chest like a shield. Anya, fortunately, was far too polite to comment. Instead, she offered Bernice a cold can of cola.

"I don't drink carbonated, sugary beverages," the woman sniffed.

"Coffee? Tea?" Anya continued.

"No," said Bernice.

Just plain, "No," without a smidgeon of graciousness.

Anya wisely went back to her work, and I gestured to a stool where Bernice could sit. "What sort of scrapbook would you like? Are those your photos?"

80

Bernice sat stiffly on the stool. "Actually it's not a scrapbook. That's a hobby. This is different. It's important. What I need is an adoption profile book. My husband Wesley and I need it to show women who don't want their babies."

I winced at her awkward terminology.

Women who don't want their babies?

That was both judgmental and cruel.

Many of these birth mothers wanted their children but found themselves in impossible situations. As a result, they had come to a courageous decision to give up their babies, believing that another family could give their children a better start in life. It was a gut-wrenching choice, one that would haunt these mothers forever.

How dare Bernice Stottlemeyer stand in judgment of the very people who were making her dreams come true?

"With all due respect, Mrs. Stottlemeyer, I believe you are jumping to a conclusion. I have met many of these young ladies, and I can tell you that most of them really do want their babies. However, they've come to the painful decision, that another family can offer their children a better future."

Her hard little eyes stared at me as if I was a specimen of beetle, and she was hoping to pin me to a cork board. A tiny *tsk, tsk* came from her mouth. Although I hadn't changed her opinion, I had stood up for the birth mothers.

Dodie had taught me that once in a while, you simply must take a hard line. Especially, when confronted by issues of morality. Dodie never allowed her customers to get away with acts of prejudice. If she overheard a cruel comment, she called the person on it. If unkind behavior persisted, she "fired" the customer. "All it takes for evil to flourish is for good people to turn their backs on it," she often said. "All of us must serve as reminders, lest in a weak moment any one of us weaken and loosen our grip on the moral fiber that makes us righteous people."

Dodie would have had a field day with Bernice Stottlemeyer. But Dodie had gone to her reward, so it fell on my shoulders to keep this little shop as an oasis of goodwill. Watching Bernice's lip curl, I realized this might be the biggest job I would ever tackle. Even bigger than balancing the year-end inventory.

After a long pause, Bernice asked, "Do you guarantee your work?"

"Excuse me?"

She had to be kidding.

Nope. She wasn't.

"I mean to say, can you guarantee that the birth mother will like this profile?" Bernice squinted at me, assessing my abilities.

"No. People are subjective, and everyone has different tastes. Furthermore, I can only work with what you give me. This album will tell only one part of your family's story. The birth mothers will interview you, right?"

"Yes. But not unless they like our profile. And there's no reason they shouldn't, if you do your job correctly. We have so much to offer a child. Wesley and I are well-educated, well-to-do and we attend church regularly. No child could hope for a better family."

Humility not withstanding.

I thought I'd gag; instead I pinched my thigh hard.

"Bonnie says you're the best person to do this." Bernice fingered the fringe on her jacket, which I recognized as being from Chanel because Sheila owned one just like it. I also recognized her purse. The weave was unique to Bottega Veneta®.

Jennifer Moore had purchased one for herself to celebrate her thirty-fifth birthday. I'd gone with her to pick it out. Bernice's purse was bigger than Jennifer's. I guessed it cost her somewhere around two grand.

"Bonnie is wonderful. I'll certainly do my best for you, but you have to realize, I can only work with the materials you provide."

"You've done one of these before and not this for a first time?"

"Yes, I have done a half dozen or more. In fact, we have a group that meets here every Wednesday night. They are all parents who have adopted."

"Why?"

"Um, pardon?"

"Why would they meet here?" Bernice glanced around. I have to admit, the store wasn't at its best because we were ready to knock down a wall.

I chose to ignore the implied insult.

"To support each other. They want to give their children a feeling of belonging. As you probably know, there are issues unique to adopted children. One is a sense of rejection. Also a sense of loss. Problems with identity. The mothers come here to create albums that will help their families work through those core issues." I paused to give her a reassuring smile. "You are very welcome to join them. Even if you simply want to stop in and say hello. They have a wealth of information."

"No. Not interested. How much do you charge for an album like what I want?"

Making this woman look warm and fuzzy was not going to be easy. Over the years Clancy has taught me to add a "hassle fee" to my calculations. She explained it this way: "When a customer is a pain in the backside, you should be paid extra for the aggravation."

"But if I'm charging an hourly rate, how is that fair?" I had said.

"It's fair because projects with nasty customers suck up a lot of your creative energy. They take more time because those customers are difficult to please. Even when you aren't at the work table, I bet you're thinking about the project, right? In your non-work hours?"

"What non-work hours?" I couldn't imagine any time when I wasn't working or thinking about work.

"See? People who are tough to please inevitably take extra time, even if it's off the clock. You have to talk with them longer before you get started. They call you multiple times. You wind up fine tuning your work to make them happy—even if your work was perfect from the beginning. I know this is the case, because I've watched you." She brushed a strand of her auburn hair off her face. Clancy could have gotten work as a Jackie Kennedy double, and she dressed the part. Her looks, wardrobe and regal bearing made an elegant addition to our store. But I prized her for her brains. She was a no-nonsense person with all sorts of practical smarts.

Clancy was teaching me not to take guff off of anyone. She was a great role model. As was my Aunt Penny. And Margit. And of course, Dodie had been, too. What I lacked in my mother, I'd found in my women friends.

"What's my deadline?" I asked Bernice Stottlemeyer.

"We're meeting with the agency and the donor this Thursday at one p.m."

"Wow. That's a tight timeframe," and I doubled my usual fee.

"What does that rate include?" Bernice's frown deepened.

"Everything but the photos. The album, the plastic page

protectors, the paper, adhesives, embellishments, stickers, my time and labor."

"All right. I guess I need to give you this. Our family pictures are inside." She practically thrust the box at me.

"Thanks," I took it from her. "But we're not done here. You need to fill out a couple of forms for me. Or you can take them home and return them."

"When do you need them back?"

I checked my calendar. "Wednesday. If you stop by at six, you'll be there for the adoptive parent's crop, in case you change your mind."

"If I'm paying you, why do I have to fill out your forms? Isn't that part of the job?"

"No, first of all, the forms provide raw material that I can't provide and I can't fake. I've worked with the local adoption agencies to develop a list of questions that most birth mothers want answered. Obviously, I can't answer those for you. There's also a list of pictures that I need, photos you might or might not have in this box. Third, I can't identify the people in your photos. You'll need to do that. Last but not least, I have a contract for you to sign. It also serves as your receipt. Before I begin a project like this we ask for a deposit of half up front."

"You're asking me to pay in advance?"

That was her main concern. Not a word about the contents of the album or how we might work together to put her best foot forward. Assuming, of course, that she had a best foot. So far, things weren't looking optimistic. Unless Bernice had another side, a persona that she wasn't sharing, I couldn't imagine any young woman wanting to bless her with a child. In fact, I wouldn't trust Bernice to dog sit for me.

"Do you really insist on half up front?" she repeated.

"Yes."

Because you're exactly the type of customer who'll find some odd-ball reason to jerk me around when it comes to paying your bill.

"You are welcome to take this project to someone else," I continued, "but as far as I know, all the scrapbook stores in the St. Louis area charge half up front for similar jobs."

With a sigh that sounded suspiciously like a hiss, Bernice reached into her purse and said, "Will you take a check?"

22

"Are your customers always so mean?" asked Anya after Bernice left.

"Nope. Fortunately." I walked around the store misting it with a lavender spray that we bought to purify the air of nasty vibes. We didn't use the spray often, but today it came in handy.

"What was her problem?"

"I suspect she's desperate to have a child. When people are at the end of their ropes, they usually aren't at their best." I pointed to my burgeoning belly. "Here I am already a mother, pregnant again, and she thinks I hold her future in my hands."

"But you don't."

"No, I don't."

"If I were a birth mother, I wouldn't want to give my baby to her."

"Neither would I. Let's play our 'benefit of the doubt' game, shall we?"

This was a game that I invented when she was little. The

goal was to remind ourselves not to take things personally, to extend grace to others by recognizing that we don't know what's happening in their lives. What started as a way to teach empathy wound up being a wonderful tool for me. Whenever people were nasty, mean or downright rude, I returned to our "benefit of the doubt" game and imagined all the extenuating circumstances in their lives that might excuse their behavior. Over the years, Anya and I had only to say, "benefit of the doubt" to each other, and we both were more forgiving.

Bernice's bad attitude could either infect our day or be brushed aside. The choice was ours.

Anya pursed her lips and thought a second. "I'll give her the benefit of the doubt because I bet she had a bad morning. Maybe she didn't have time to buy her favorite latte from Starbucks. Or the cat coughed up a hairball in one of her shoes. Seymour did that this morning to one of mine."

"Lucky you. I'll give Bernice the benefit of the doubt because her husband sent her in to get the profile done, and she hates crafts."

"I'll give her the benefit of the doubt because maybe she's been trying to get pregnant for a long time," said Anya.

"See?" I put my arm around my daughter. "I feel better about Bernice already, don't you?"

"Sort of. Kinda." She hugged me and then went to the restroom. I was alone on the sales floor when Rebekkah entered.

When I'd last seen Dodie's daughter, she was twenty pounds heavier. She'd long been wanting to lose weight, but grief was not a healthy weight loss tool. I hugged Rebekkah and asked how her father was.

"Not good. He wanders around like he's lost. He won't

eat. Doesn't sleep." She paused and brushed the tears from her eyes.

"How can I help?"

Anya came out from the back. She took one look at Rebekkah, rounded the worktable, and gave the other girl a big hug. The affection between the two delighted me, as I'm a firm believer that every kid needs all the positive influences that he or she can muster. Rebekkah needed Anya, and Anya needed Rebekkah right now. Their lives were changing. Rebekkah's family had shrunk, and ours was growing. Both girls were forced to make adjustments.

"I'm not sure how anyone can help my dad," said Rebekkah.

"Have you talked to Rabbi Sarah?" I asked, thinking back to how our rabbi had helped me after the shooting. "She's wonderful. I bet she can help him."

"I didn't think about that."

"Look, why don't I call the rabbi for you? Maybe she can drop by and see your dad."

Rebekkah nodded. "That might work. I think he needs help. I'm trying to cheer him up. Honestly, I am, but..."

"Honey," I said, "there's only so much you can do. You'll always be his little girl. Rabbi Sarah has training in grief counseling. I'll tell her what's happening. Meanwhile, how are you?"

Her smile was weak as she said, "Okay. Sort of."

"If you'd like to be on the work schedule, I could use your help. We've missed you. And it goes without saying that if you ever need someone to talk to, I'm here for you, Rebekkah. I promised your mother I'd look after you, and I keep my promises."

Anya hugged Rebekkah again. "I'm here for you, too. You're a big sister to me, Beckkah. You know that."

"I know. It's...it's just so hard." She pulled away from my daughter. "I thought that after my mother died, we could move on, but we can't. It's like I walked through something sticky, and it's pulling at my feet. Whenever I laugh, I feel guilty. When I quit thinking about her, I feel like I'm a bad person. I worry that I'm going to forget her."

"You won't. But you will go on with your life, and that's what she wanted for you. No mother would want her child to be sad forever. That's not a memorial to anyone. That's self-indulgence. Self-pity. When you are constantly sad, you are negating the joy that person brought to your life and to this world. What sort of remembrance is that?"

"But it seems so weird. I look for her, I expect to see her, and she's nowhere to be found."

"That doesn't mean she isn't nearby," I said. "Can you see Alaska from here?"

"No."

"But you know it's there, right? And you can't see your heart, but you feel it beat, right? That's what faith is about. We believe in what we can't see. Instead, we look for signs. Like this store. It's a sign your mom was here, that she's still here and her life force brought—and keeps—all of us together as a family."

Rebekkah thought about this. "I'm glad you mentioned signs. There's something that's been happening. It's faintly creepy, but comforting. Do you remember how she liked turtles? Well, that turtle nightlight she bought me keeps turning on. By itself."

"After George died, I found a message from him on my cell phone. I have no idea how it got there."

"I found a Scooby Doo video that Dad bought me in the VCR," said Anya, "a whole month after the funeral. And I hadn't played that video for years! In fact, I thought we'd given it away, but there it was!"

"Did you know that the word 'angel' means 'messenger'?" I asked. "It's true. So there have always been messages and messengers from the other world doing their best to communicate with us."

"I guess." Slowly, Rebekkah smiled. "Yeah, I think you're right, Kiki. She's trying to tell me everything is okay. When I got in my car this morning, for some reason I opened the glove compartment. There was a flyer there about how to save sea turtles. I sure didn't put it there."

"See, honey? She wants you to continue her good works. You'll be okay. I just know it," I said. But then I bit my tongue. Dodie had been Rebekkah's rock, while Horace had been a good father, but a bit of an absent figure. How would Rebekkah cope without that firm foundation? My mother was more like gravel. The kind of gravel that flies up and chips your windshield. I would never know how it felt to lose someone who had your back, someone who had loved you your whole life. Worse luck, I couldn't even really imagine it. So how could I honestly reassure Rebekkah that she'd be fine?

I had to have faith. Just like I'd counseled her.

"I can't imagine what you are feeling," I said to Rebekkah. "But I miss her too, and I'll do everything I can for you. You will always be welcome at our house. I hope you'll think of us as extended family."

Once more, I hugged her. Rebekkah had lost a lot of weight. She was still a big girl. She would always be bigger-boned and taller than I, but she definitely must not be eating well.

When I let her go, she and Anya ran to the back to let Gracie out for a piddle. Through the display window, I watched as the two girls chattered happily while Gracie tugged them down the street.

Thank you, God, for unexpected joys. For the simple moments in life that make me smile. For the precious gift of loving friends and pets.

23

*W*hile the girls were walking Gracie, I struggled to get my emotions in check. I checked my phone, but there weren't any messages from Detweiler. A quick trip to the bathroom gave me the chance to splash cold water on my face. I longed for a Diet Dr Pepper, but I'd decided that colas with artificial sweeteners might not be good for my baby. I contented myself with an iced tea sweetened with Truvia.

I phoned Rabbi Sarah and left a message on her answering machine about Horace's state of mind.

After all that was done, I dialed Sheila to see how she was doing.

"Hadcho called us on the QT. That no good piece of garbage Prescott isn't making one bit of progress. He's told my bridesmaids they shouldn't leave town, and if they do, it'll look bad for them. He's strutting around the police station like he owns the place. He even moved into Robbie's office, claiming that he needs privacy for this investigation. How dare he use this murder to further his career at the expense of my husband!"

As is typical with Sheila, her reaction seemed over-blown. Sure, she had reason to be put out, but asking the bridesmaids to hang around didn't sound unfair to me. He hadn't ordered them to stay, after all.

I wondered if she'd been drinking. On occasion, she had a mimosa or a Bloody Mary before lunch.

"Is this a real imposition on your girlfriends? Or is it an inconvenience for you, because they're in your house?"

"I can't very well kick them out, can I? They had planned to stick around and catch up with family. The flight schedule in and out of Lambert isn't what it used to be, so they figured they'd take advantage of being here, because it's not like they can pop in and out of town."

"How's Robbie taking all this?"

"Not well. He wants to be involved in the investigation in the worst way. He's apologized twenty times for not flying out for our cruise, as if it's his fault. But mainly, Prescott has nipped at Robbie's Achilles Heel. My husband has been wondering if it's time for him to retire. Please don't go blab-bing that to anyone."

"I won't."

"I have no idea how that loathsome doctor wound up at our wedding! He's not on the copy of the guest list that you handed to Robbie. Did you add him?"

"Of course not. I don't know the man."

"But you sent him an invitation."

"No, I did not." I reminded her that I had carefully crafted each and every invitation and its matching enve-lope. As we talked, I pulled up the list in my computer and checked it again. I'd used a program that alphabet-ized names as a way to keep organized. Sure enough, Hyman wasn't on the list. "I kept my own copy of the list to mark off the names as I worked my way through the project. I've just double-checked it, and his name isn't there."

"But Hadcho told us they found an invitation in Dr. Hyman's pocket."

"Then whoever sent that is the murderer."

"But right now, the only people who could have sent it are you or me," she said.

"You know that old Sherlock Holmes saying. Something about when you've eliminated the impossible, whatever remains, however improbable, must be the truth. It was impossible for me to send the invitation. Impossible for you, too, because I made them, and you didn't have any extras. That means the invitation is a forgery."

She was quiet for a long time before adding, "Or someone re-used an invitation. My poor husband. Marrying me has already brought him grief. All right. I have to go. Robbie's calling for me."

The back door to the store flew open, and Aunt Penny marched in ceremoniously.

"Hope you don't mind me dropping by, but I couldn't take Lucia's griping one more minute. Law's a-mighty. Your mother sure has become a sour puss," said Aunt Penny. As she talked, the lace bobbed on her Little Bo Peep costume, a blue gingham dress with puffed sleeves. On her feet, she wore white socks with lace trim and black patent leather shoes. A mob cap sat crookedly on her white curls. Over one shoulder was a tote bag that screamed, "Mexican tourist."

"You're always welcome in the store, but how'd you get here?" I asked. U City was an easy ten miles from where we stood, and several highways crisscrossed the path, so you couldn't hoof it even if you tried. Aunt Penny didn't have a car here, at least none of which I was aware. Mom didn't either. Amanda had taken away Mom's driver's license after she backed over a neighbor's metal trashcan and didn't even notice. Amanda couldn't have driven Aunt Penny because she was at her job at the law office in downtown Clayton.

"I hitchhiked."

"Again? Is that even legal?"

"Probably not. But who's going to arrest an old woman for sticking her thumb in the air?"

"You could have been killed," I sputtered. "Murdered. Did you know that St. Louis is the second most violent city in the country? In terms of murders?"

"Yes," she said solemnly. "That's why I took hitchhiking in Detroit off of my bucket list."

"Oh, my gosh, Aunt Penny, do not do that again. Please, promise me! I'll come get you. I'll do whatever it takes. You can't put yourself at risk like that."

"*Pshaw*. No one is going to mess with me. Like I told you, I'm packing heat."

This was too much. I sank down on a stool and braced myself against the worktable.

"I told you that I had a gun while we were eating pancakes at IHOP. Did you forget? You are starting that placenta brain pretty early in the pregnancy, aren't you?"

I put my head down on the worktable and hoped the store would quit spinning.

She kept talking. "I don't know why you're making such a fuss about this. I never shot anybody. You're the only dead-eye Dora in this family."

I snapped to attention, ready to defend myself, but I stopped when I saw the mischievous twinkle in her eyes. "Ha, ha, ha. Very funny."

"Actually, I'm durn proud of you. You saved yourself, your baby, your mother-in-law and that hunky brother of Mert's. How is he, by the way?"

"Even though Johnny is much better, his sister still hasn't forgiven me."

"Forgiven you for what? Saving his cute little bacon? Last time I saw that young man walking away from me, I thought I'd have to roll up my tongue to stick it back in my mouth."

"Let's not go there."

"Don't never give up on a friend," said Aunt Penny, putting a hand on my forearm. "You can't choose your family, but you can pick your friends. A good 'un is worth every cent in your bank account."

"I agree, but maybe she's not such a good friend. Anyone who refuses to hear the truth, who thinks badly of me, and won't let me defend myself—"

"Sounds like a Scorpio."

"She is."

"Whewie." Aunt Penny scratched a mosquito bite and left a smear of blood on her calf. "That's one hard nut to crack. You gotta wait until she sets down that stinger-tail of hers. Then maybe she'll listen. Maybe she won't."

"She's sure taking her time," I said.

24

*A*unt Penny looked me up and down. "What's going on? You look as wilted as yesterday's lettuce."

I blurted out my concerns about buying the business, Rebekkah's news about Horace, and Sheila's report on the murder investigation. "On top of everything, Detweiler is out of town."

"You have a lot on your plate. Even if the mix didn't include a five-year-old boy who's lost his parents," said Aunt Penny, as she pulled up a stool and sat next to me.

"Yes, and I feel horrible even admitting that."

"Why? You'd have to be a total fool not to recognize that y'all have a tough row to hoe. That little tyke has lost his parents. He's being transplanted into an entirely new environment. He's going from an only child to one of three. As is Anya. This is not going to be an easy transition. You're going from single parenthood to shared responsibility. The new baby is the cherry on top of your sundae. But it might also be the straw that breaks the camel's back. You've got plenty on your plate already."

Her mixed metaphors tickled me and brought a half-smile to my face. "I'll survive," I said.

"Yes, you will. But that doesn't mean you don't have cause to worry. I'd be more than happy to move in with you and help, but you don't have enough room to swing a cat by its tail. Not that I'd ever do such a thing, but still."

"But still," and then a few tears leaked down my cheek.

"Where is Anya?"

I explained that she and Rebekkah were taking their sweet time walking Gracie.

"Better dry your eyes before they come back. Your mission is to be as strong and invincible as the Statue of Liberty."

"Don't I know it," I said.

Once again, I went into the bathroom and splashed my face with cold water. At this rate, I wasn't getting anything done but worrying. As I dried my hands on a paper towel, I heard a man's voice.

I walked out to find Aunt Penny talking to Roy Michelson, the contractor I'd hired to knock down the wall dividing the sales floor from the back room. Although he was trying not to stare, her strange get-up obviously had him scratching his head.

Aunt Penny had switched into her Southern belle, charm-the-pants-off-of-him mode, even though he was at least thirty years her junior. I felt torn between letting her continue, watching her do her thing and extricating him from her attentions. She was harmless and cute. Three decades earlier, she must have been a real hottie.

"I see you've met my aunt." I offered Roy my hand for a shake.

"The family resemblance is striking," he said.

Aunt Penny and I exchanged looks. We've heard this so often that we've long since dispensed with explanations.

Roy shuffled his feet and looked everywhere but straight at me. "I have bad news."

"It's a load-bearing wall?" I had been worrying about that. If the wall was load-bearing, we would have to add a header and a column. The costs of my renovation would sky-rocket.

"No."

"Whew."

"Another problem. Because of another job I'm doing. Those rains we've been having? That high wind? Knocked down two walls we'd framed and ruined the subfloor. I hate to do this, but I have to move all my crew to that job. As I told you originally, I could do your work at the low price I quoted you only if we didn't run into trouble at my other job."

Yes, that had been exactly what he'd said. I could see how the rain and wind would have caused a problem. But if he couldn't get to my job quickly, it wouldn't be done by the fall. I'd lose out on precious sales, money that I'd counted on having. My pregnant self was stuck between a rock and a hard place.

"What all needs to be done, Kiki?" Aunt Penny perked right up and took command of the conversation.

I wished she'd given me some privacy. This morning was not going as planned. My hormones were waging a full-out war on me. Tears threatened. I wanted to run back into the ladies' room and sob. But instead, I pulled up my big girl maternity panties. "Roy was bringing in a crew to knock down the wall dividing the sales floor from the back room. We planned to expand the sales floor all the way to the back on this, the right side of the building."

"Is that all?" She waggled her eyebrows at me.

"Um, what do you mean by is that all?"

"Great day in the morning, girl. I can knock down that wall and frame up your new one. Do the drywall, too."

Before I could challenge her carpentry skills, Anya and Rebekkah joined us with Gracie in tow.

"In fact, I see my construction crew approaching right now," said Aunt Penny.

"What?" Rebekkah turned to Anya who shrugged and said, "Huh?"

"I'm thinking you two could help Kiki with a little construction project. I'd act as your boss, and I'm a great person for whom to work. I've knocked down a lot of walls in my time. Put 'em up, too. Nothing like good old physical labor to cure what ails you," said Aunt Penny to the girls before turning back toward Roy. "All I need, young man, is for you to continue to act as the G.C."

"G.C.?" I asked.

"General contractor. Your aunt is suggesting that I oversee the work, while she oversees the crew. I can check in with her daily and make sure nothing goes wrong. Honestly, knocking out a wall like this one isn't difficult. It can be time consuming and labor intensive." He studied Aunt Penny. "You know how to frame in a wall, too?"

"Sure do," she said with a wide smile. She crossed her arms over her chest, a stance totally at odds with her costume as Little Bo Peep. "I can put up drywall, tape it, mud over it, and sand it smoother than a baby's backside."

"You'll call me if you run into any problems?" Roy frowned.

"Of course, I will. You can cut off the electricity to that wall?"

"Sure."

"Then you got yourself cheap labor, Kiki," said Aunt Penny. She narrowed her eyes. "You will, of course, reduce your price to my niece to reflect that you only acted as her G.C."

"Absolutely," and he stuck out his hand so she could shake it. "I'll go hit the fuse box and turn off the juice."

All four of us females watched him walk to the back of the store. Aunt Penny purred, "Be still my heart. I love that view of his caboose. Choo-choo."

Anya giggled.

"Can you really get this done?" I asked. "If you can, it'd be great, because I wanted it done by the end of the summer. This is our slow time of year. I don't want to be tripping over equipment and lumber. Especially, in the fall. That's when our customer count really increases."

"I wouldn't have offered to help if I didn't know for sure that I could get it done. As long as I can depend on these two helpers, we should be good to go." Aunt Penny cocked her head toward my daughter and Rebekkah.

"I've never done anything like this, have you?" Anya asked Rebekkah, who shook her head no.

Both girls wore expressions of eagerness. A certain electricity crackled around them, and I realized that even if the wall didn't get done perfectly, it would be a wonderful experience for them. Physical exertion forces you out of your head. Although I didn't make it to Jazzercise as often as I'd like, when I did, there was no room in my mind for fretting. I had to stay in the moment and pay attention. The choreography occupied me totally. The movement kept my stray thoughts marching in sync. When I did indulge in wool-gathering, I'd inevitably lose track of the beat or move in the opposite direction of the crowd.

Besides, how far wrong could Aunt Penny and her makeshift crew go? If Roy checked on them daily, he could set them right. Yes, it would probably take much longer to have these unskilled workers on the job, but that was to my benefit. I'd been wondering how I could keep Anya occupied all summer.

"All right, but what safety concerns might we have?" I asked.

"Nothing a little equipment can't solve," said Aunt Penny. "Toss me your car keys, and I'll take the girls to buy hard hats, safety goggles, and any other equipment we need. You both up to date on your tetanus shots?"

The girls nodded.

"We'll test the outlet on the wall after Roy hits the switch in the fuse box. Then we should be good to go, except for a liberal usage of common sense," said Aunt Penny.

"Are you planning to work in that outfit?" I asked. I could see her getting one of those flounces caught on a nail. "And Anya? Those are nice pants that Gran just bought for you."

"Is there a thrift store nearby? We can stop, and I can buy me some jeans and old tees. Stuff for the girls, too."

"I can drive," volunteered Rebekkah. "I know where all the good thrift shops are."

"After we get our clothes and our safety gear," said Aunt Penny, "we can come back and start moving stuff out of the way. Tomorrow, we'll put up plastic sheeting to protect all this merchandise from the dust. Believe me, there'll be tons of dust."

"My aunt seems to have a game plan. This is your last chance to back out," I said to Roy and waited.

"I wouldn't miss this for the world!" He rubbed his

hands together gleefully. "Let's go check that fuse box. I'll show you both where it is, and what I'm doing with it. After that, we'll test the socket to see if it's live. Wouldn't do to get zapped the first day on your new jobs. Not when you have such a fine career ahead of you."

25

*a*unt Penny and her construction crew returned shortly after noon. They were loaded down with bags. My stomach had been growling for the past half hour, so I was glad these bore the familiar soft green and peach tones of St. Louis Bread Co. From each sack wafted the delicious fragrance of fresh bread with a savory overtone promising that at least one held a cup of soup.

"I don't get it," said Aunt Penny as she handed the bag to me. "How come y'all call it Bread Co-oh? Why not Bread Company?"

All three of us shrugged. "Everyone calls it 'coh' to rhyme with 'dough,'" explained Anya.

"But isn't it the same company as Panera Bread?" asked Aunt Penny. "The layout and the menu look the same."

"Actually," said Rebekkah as she sipped on a plastic cup of green iced tea, "the company began in 1981 as Au Bon Pain. In 1993, they bought out a local chain called Saint Louis Bread Company. Eventually, they morphed into Panera Bread. But luckily for us, they kept the name we all know and love. At least they did here in the Lou."

"It's a bit pricey," said my aunt.

I lifted a spoonful of soup to my mouth to hide my smile. My Aunt Penny had been appropriately named, because she knew the art of making a penny holler for mercy. To my mind, Bread Co. was incredibly reasonable, especially given the high quality of the food. But Aunt Penny could find the lowest price vittles in any town where she landed. I remember watching her carefully wrap up the extra bread from our table at a cheap cafeteria. I protested, but we ate peanut butter sandwiches on those leftover slices for the next three days. In retrospect, she'd taught me that valuable lesson: Waste not, want not.

That lesson served me well, especially after my first husband died. George had provided a comfortable lifestyle for us. Unfortunately, his partner, Bill Ballard, had conspired to have George killed. I was so stupid back then. When Bill told me that George had embezzled money from the firm, I moved heaven and earth to pay back what I thought my late husband "owed." I was more worried about saving his good name than questioning Bill's claim. If I'd been a smarter, wiser woman, I would have found a good attorney and demanded a forensic investigation of Dimont Development's finances. But I knew nothing about business. I'd dropped out of college because I was pregnant with Anya. I assumed I was too ignorant to question a "respectable" businessman. To my everlasting shame, I'd acted like a helpless ninny.

Fortunately, Dodie set me on the right path. She offered me a job at Time in a Bottle. When I dithered over accepting, she put a bit of starch in my undies by reminding me that I had a child to care for, my primary concern. Dodie suggested that I grow up...fast. She became my mentor. Besides teaching me to make smart business decisions, she took the time to help me make a budget. When I had questions about money management, I took them to her.

Although I wasn't the daughter-in-law she wanted, Sheila had always been a wonderful grandmother to my child. After George died, Sheila paid the tuition bills at CALA so that Anya could continue there. The swanky private school would have been beyond my humble means, but Sheila came up with the substantial extra financial "gift" expected of all attending families, took care of Anya's books, and made sure my daughter was dressed to the nines. She also provided pocket money for Anya. In short, Sheila and Dodie had helped me grow from a child into a responsible adult.

Now, I would have the chance to pay it forward by mothering Anya, Erik and Rebekkah.

While I finished my lunch, Aunt Penny and her crew talked about the project. Anya changed into a pair of jeans I'd never seen before, and an old AC/DC tee. Aunt Penny disappeared and came back in a Led Zeppelin tee and a pair of jeans. Next, Rebekkah slipped into the back room and walked out wearing a Grateful Dead tee and a pair of jeans. By the time they were all changed, I was busy choosing papers and embellishments for the Stottlemeyer adoption album.

"What thrift shop did you visit? I've never seen cool stuff like that at the Goodwill store."

"Mooo-oom. We went to Plato's Closet. Everyone sells their old clothes there. Pretty cool, right?"

I had to admit I was impressed. "They have any maternity clothes?"

Anya is nearly as good at rolling her eyes as I am or my sister is, and she proved it. "Duh."

"I bet you could find stuff that would fit," suggested

Rebekkah. "They have a variety of different sizes. Or you could shop in the guy's area. I used to get all my tee shirts from that side of Plato's."

"An excellent suggestion. Thanks," I said. My cell phone beeped to remind me that in an hour I was due for a sonogram at my ob/gyn's office. I took the opportunity to send Detweiler a text message saying that I loved him. Given the time difference, he was probably starting his day.

As I finished eating, Rebekkah and Anya began moving more stuff away from the wall that would be coming down. Aunt Penny finished her food, picked up after herself and went to join the construction crew.

They'd been at it for twenty minutes when Clancy walked onto the sales floor to begin her shift. "Whoa. What's with the jeans and Heavy Metal tee shirts? Is there some reason that you are dressed like refugees from the 70s?"

"Rebekkah and I are going to knock down the wall and build the addition," Anya explained. "With Aunt Penny's help, of course. See? We're moving everything away from the wall."

"Right, but you need to keep it organized, otherwise we'll never be able to find anything." Clancy fisted her hands on her hips.

The two exchanged sheepish expressions.

"Sorry," said Rebekkah, staring at piles upon piles. "I guess we got carried away."

I got up off my stool and wandered over to check on them. Clancy was right to be upset. All our merchandise had been dumped onto the floor in untidy heaps while I'd been eating.

"This is my fault, Clancy. I should have been supervising. We can help you put it away. I've got an hour, before my appointment for the sonogram."

"Get back to work on that adoption album." She waved me away. "It's not as bad as it looks. It probably needed to be sorted anyway. I have to think through how we'll jam more stuff in less space."

"Is today the sonogram? Can I come? I want to see my baby sister," Anya pleaded with me.

"That will be so cool," said Rebekkah.

"Can you really see anything?" Aunt Penny asked.

"You can not only see the baby, but using the stethoscope, you can also hear his or her heartbeat. Tell you what. How about if we all pitch in to get this picked up and you can come."

"Could I?" Her eyes brightened.

"Rebekkah, do you want to come, too?" I felt weird asking her, but I also felt weird leaving her out of our plans. "We've got an hour before we need to leave."

Inclusion always beats exclusion. By offering Rebekkah the chance to come with us, I was making good on claim that she was family. I don't have long arms, but my embrace could expand to include Rebekkah as well as Erik.

"Thanks, but no thanks," she said. "I'll help Clancy get organized, and then I better go home and check on my father."

"Y'all planning to be here tomorrow? I need to get our names on our hard hats," said Aunt Penny.

"I can do that," I said. "I'll use letter stickers. Are the hats all the same size? Then that shouldn't be a problem."

After Rebekkah confirmed her interest in slinging a hammer, Aunt Penny suggested a 7 a.m. starting time. "We want to get all our banging around done as early in the day as we can. From what I've seen, most of your customers show up in the afternoon."

Once again, I was amazed at my aunt's keen perception.

I'd noticed the same. As the temperature rose outside, customers came inside to shop.

St. Louis helps Missouri live up to its nickname of the "Show me" state, because most of our homeowners like to deck out their yards with colorful flowers. Drive down any street in any one of our 91 municipalities, and you'll treat your eyes to a profusion of brilliant pinks, tangy oranges, sunny yellows and snappy shades of purple. We also suffer from miserable summer weather. From spring through early September, you can count on the days getting hot, muggy and unbearable. As a consequence, smart folks schedule their lives accordingly. Scrapbookers, as a group, are a touch above average in intelligence. (Okay, I admit to a certain prejudice!) So they finish their gardening chores in the cool of the morning and take advantage of the air-conditioned comfort of stores in the afternoons.

"You can't start any earlier than eight," said Clancy. "We have private homes behind us. We don't need complaints from the neighbors."

"Eight is plenty early for me," I said, after making a quick calculation. Starting that early would involve my getting up at 6:30 a.m. to feed the animals and do a few loads of laundry before getting myself and my daughter ready for the day. Six-thirty wasn't much earlier than my usual start.

With that settled, I went back to the Stottlemeyer album. An hour later, I left the store in Clancy's capable hands. "I'll be back before six for the crop."

While Aunt Penny and Anya piled into my car, I gave Rebekkah one last hug for the day. "Call me if you need me," I told her. "I think you'll probably hear from Rabbi Sarah very soon."

26

I felt like a circus sideshow lying there on the examining table with Anya on one side and Aunt Penny on the other, but I'd asked for the audience, hadn't I? While Anya practiced acting calm, cool and collected, Aunt Penny was busily collecting pamphlets about pregnancy.

"This gel will feel cold," said the sonogram tech as she squeezed goop from a tube onto my belly.

I shivered as she smeared it around.

"Did you know that your blood volume will increase by 40-50% before you have the baby?" my aunt asked, reading straight from one of the brochures. "And your bra cup will grow by one or two sizes?"

"You should see her pregnancy underpants," Anya said. "They are so funny looking."

"Anya? Too much information," I said. "Be nice to me. Someday if you're lucky, you can wear my hand-me-downs."

"Yuck," said the princess.

The tech grabbed a flat-tipped wand called a transducer. It looked a bit like something straight out of a Harry Potter movie.

"This emits high-frequency tones. When they bounce against the baby, we can read them as a picture. It's the same principle as Doppler radar. Now, watch the screen," the tech said as she pressed the flat edge of the wand into my jelly. We all turned our faces toward the screen, although I had trouble seeing because of the tears in my eyes.

They spilled over my face. The import of the moment hit me hard. Detweiler wasn't with me, and I keenly missed his rock-solid presence. What if I saw something amiss? What if something was wrong with our baby? I hadn't planned on getting pregnant. I'd taken none of the prenatal vitamins that might ensure our child's good health. I couldn't help myself: I started sobbing.

"Mom? Does it hurt?" Anya was holding my hand and now she peered at me anxiously.

"No," I gasped.

"You okay, Kiki?" Aunt Penny's face creased with worry.

"Emotional," was all I could manage.

The tech smiled at me and then at them. "It's not unusual. This is exciting and scary, and her hormones are cranked up to their maximum levels."

That felt like I was given permission, so I really let loose. I thought about Dodie's death, about missing Mert, about the responsibility of adding Erik to our lives. I also thought about the new financial pressures of owning the business— and how unprepared I was for all of this.

"I'll go get you a cup of water," said the tech.

"Mom? You sure you're okay?" Anya repeated desperately. "Did you see something? Is something wrong?"

"Noooo," I wailed. "I'm just being a big baby."

The tech returned with a Dixie cup of lukewarm tap water. I gulped it down and yanked a tissue from the box she offered me.

"Do you want to reschedule, Mrs. Lowenstein?" asked the tech. With her strawberry blond hair and freckles, she looked like an ad for wholesome living.

"No. I'm sorry. Go ahead," but as she reapplied the wand, I babbled on, unable to stop myself. "It's...it's...just so much happening all at once. My baby's father just learned he has a son, who's five, and that little boy is coming to live with us. And...and..."

The tech started to move the wand around. An image appeared on the screen, but you couldn't tell what it was. The edges wobbled as the tech tried to get a better angle.

"And what?" demanded Aunt Penny. "I'll help in any way that I can."

"Me, too," said Anya.

"How can you help me?" I whined. "Go into labor for me?" Mustering up my courage, I looked at the screen.

"Ah," said the tech. "See that? It's an arm. Your baby is waving at you."

The tiny limb mesmerized all of us. My jaw flopped open. In the years since I'd had Anya, the technology had improved greatly. The tech had been right. As we watched, five tiny little digits waved at us.

Temporarily, I had been distracted, but now I imagined those little fingers holding mine, looking to me for guidance. Right now, Anya held my hand, but soon I'd be juggling a babe in arms and a little fellow who might have tons of trouble adjusting to his new family.

A little fellow, a boy.

The image on the screen grew indistinct again. The tech's mouth pursed with concentration as she moved the wand, almost as if stirring a pot. I guess she was trying to get the right angle, but it seemed like she was chasing shadows. Okay, so we'd seen fingers. What I really wanted was a full-body image of the baby, enough of a sighting that I could put aside my fears.

What if something was wrong? How would we cope with a child with a disability? The wonder of it, the miracle, was that all those chromosomes and cells knew their jobs. They arranged themselves in a predestined order so that they could structure a human being. How could they be so tiny and yet so intelligent? What unearthly hand arranged them with such love?

Surely the possibility of problems outweighed the likelihood of perfection! One in every thirty-three babies was born with a birth defect. That meant that 120,000 children were born annually with problems, and of these, 3% were considered "major."

Would ours be one of the unlucky ones?

Even if everything was hunky-dory, A-Okay, would I be able to cope? I hadn't slept much last night. I woke up worrying about the murder investigation, Detweiler's trip, remodeling the store and our new addition. Scratch that: additions, plural.

How would Erik adjust to losing his mother and accepting me?

I tried to hold back a sob, but I couldn't. "I don't know anything about raising boys! I grew up in a family of girls. And now Detweiler is bringing back his son. He's five. I won't know what to do. I know girls, but what do you do with a son?"

"Tucson," said the tech.

"Tucson?" I repeated. "You're suggesting we move to Arizona?"

A gap-toothed smile appeared on that freckled face. "No, not Tucson. I said 'two sons,' as in congratulations, you're definitely having a boy."

27

Early Monday
Los Angeles, California

*D*etweiler woke up at 6:30 Central Standard Time and used the early hour as a chance to go down to work out in the hotel's fitness center. After a hearty breakfast of eggs, two strips of turkey bacon, whole wheat toast and black coffee, he showered and changed.

Time seemed to drag as he waited for Lorraine to call and say that Erik was up and ready for the day. He texted Kiki several times but didn't call. He knew she was trying to catch up on paperwork at the store. Between reading the *USA Today* slipped under his door and working Sudoku puzzles, he paced the floor. When the phone finally rang at nearly eleven, he had to calm himself before answering.

"I'm sending Orson for you," said Lorraine after she politely asked how he had slept and if the accommodations were satisfactory. "He'll meet you in the front of the hotel. Where he left you off last night."

"That's kind of you, but if he'll just drop me off over at a rental car agency—"

She interrupted. "No need. Orson is at your beck and call. Didn't he give you his card?"

"Yes, but—" Detweiler started to explain that this situation made him uncomfortable. However, once again, Lorraine derailed him.

"Good. He's actually on his way. I'd like to have a few words with you before you meet Erik. He went to summer camp this morning, which is what the counselor suggested. Keeping his life as normal as possible for as long as possible. I'm sure you'll understand. After we have lunch and a chat, Orson will take us to pick up Erik. That way, you can see his camp and meet his camp counselors. The camp is held at his regular school, so you can see the place. We'll have to make an appointment with his kindergarten teacher. As for today, I hope you like seafood!"

With that, she said goodbye before he could respond.

"Crud," he snarled to the empty room. "She's out-maneuvered me again."

Lorraine had this way of taking control and not pausing for breath so that he couldn't get a word in edgewise without being rude. Once more, she'd delayed his meeting with his son. Detweiler had a good mind to call her back and demand that he be allowed to see Erik, but in his head, he could see his father winking at him. "Son, there's a reason people say that patience is a virtue. That's because it is. See, it's easy to run headlong into foolishness, just because you want to prove yourself. A wise man bides his time. Shows his maturity. Allows other folks to set the pace so they feel comfortable."

His father had been right. Detweiler had seen his wisdom proven time and time again. In situations where other officers pressed the point, Detweiler stepped back, waited and assessed his options. Taking his cues from others, Detweiler trained himself to respond to their rhythms not his own. For this reason, his interviews were far more productive than those of his fellow officers.

But being patient at work was one thing. This was his personal life. His son—the boy he'd wanted his whole life— was out there, somewhere. A small hot spark of anger flamed up inside him. Why couldn't he see his boy?

What was Lorraine's game?

She seemed to have her reasons for dragging her feet. But what were they? She'd set this transfer in motion. Why was she putting on the brakes now?

He remembered what Kiki had said. This was exciting for him, yes, of course, but it would also be terrifying for Erik. First, he'd lost his parents (or more correctly his mother and the man she'd married), and now he was meeting a stranger who would take him away from the life he'd known. Perhaps Lorraine Lauber really did have the boy's best interests at heart. Perhaps she was only being cautious. Getting a feel for Detweiler, sizing him up before turning the boy over to this stranger.

If so, he should thank her for her diligence.

With that resolved, he calmed himself. He would meet her for lunch. He'd hear what she had to say. But no more delays. Reaching into the roll-aboard, he grabbed the back-pack that Anya had chosen for her new brother. His fingers curved over the now-familiar lumps of gifts inside, and he paused long enough to center himself. Glancing into the full-length mirror, he straightened the collar on his shirt and smoothed the front of his navy blue jacket.

Would he recognize Erik? Would the boy look like him? Or like Gina? Would it take him a while to feel comfortable with Detweiler? Or would they establish a bond quickly? What if the child didn't like him? What if he couldn't overcome the boy's loss?

His eyes grew misty, so he stepped into the bathroom, wet a washcloth with cold water and wiped his face.

Now the voice in his head was Kiki's. She said to him, "It's going to be okay. It might be rough going at first, but we'll make it work. You'll see."

"It'll be okay." He repeated and thanked his lucky stars that he'd found such a wonderful partner. With a quick nod to the mirror, he closed the door of his hotel room and started for the lobby.

28

—————

 sing his cell phone, Detweiler snapped a photo of Cafe del Rey for Kiki. The outside of the building offered no clues as to the ambiance of the interior, but he knew that Kiki would enjoy the tiny white holiday lights sprinkled in the palm trees.

The hostess clearly had been expecting him. She chattered happily, asking how he was enjoying his visit, as she led him past clusters of tables covered with crisp white damask clothes, sparkling glassware, candles and heavy china. The deeper they went into the restaurant, the more glimpses Detweiler could see of the startling green-blue water. Even before they reached a bank of wall-to-ceiling windows, Detweiler could smell the tang of saltwater and see the masts of sailboats bobbing in the distance. It was a magnificent sight, but again, one that a photo couldn't capture.

The hostess took him to a table set off by itself where a woman stared out at the water. The back of her carefully groomed hair gave no indication of her age. But her hands were freckled and gnarled and her skin on her neck sagged slightly.

"Miss Lauber?" Detweiler said.

She turned and smiled. The light glinted off the water, making it difficult for him to see her clearly. He judged her to be in her mid-sixties. Lorraine Lauber had never been a classic beauty, but she was a handsome woman with eyes of an undetermined color and beautifully highlighted blond hair. Her shake was firm and her gaze direct as she assessed him without trying to disguise her interest. In return, he looked her over, too. She was impeccably groomed and dressed in a simple, black top and matching slacks of nice material. A gray shawl draped over her shoulders. Her jewelry was heavy, which meant it was probably real. From working around the well-heeled people of Ladue, he knew she was expensively attired. There was a casual attitude about her that said she had always had money. However, Lorraine spoke kindly to the waitress and thanked the bus boy as he refilled their water glasses.

As he took a chair, Detweiler dropped the backpack he was carrying into one of the empty chairs between them.

Her lips twitched in amusement. "Do you always bring your backpack? How long have you been a Superman fan? That's the new version, right? Henry Cavell? Marvelous actor."

"It's for Erik. All the women in my life insisted that I be the bearer of gifts. My fiancée Kiki, her daughter Anya, and my mother all had their own ideas. Anya chose the backpack. I hope he likes Superman." Detweiler tried not to sound embarrassed. In truth, he was happy to be bringing gifts, but the childish packaging wasn't his style. However, Kiki and his mother had assured him that Erik would love the backpack. And he trusted their opinions.

Lorraine Lauber's laugh reminded him of the music from the carillon in Luther Tower at Concordia Seminary in Clayton. The forty-nine bells rang out on special occasions and in the summer months. He counted it a special blessing if they happened to be playing as he drove past.

"He'll be delighted with her choice. I told him he was getting a sister. Many of his classmates have siblings, so he seems to think this might be a good thing. But he's not entirely convinced. Now shall we order? Drinks first? And appetizers? I'm famished."

Letting her set the pace, he asked for a Bud Light while she sipped a Campari and orange. Deferring to her judgment, he let her choose a starter of flatbread with figs and goat cheese. The waiter rattled off the list of fresh catches. Detweiler selected the first dish offered. Honestly, he couldn't care less what he ate. He was hungry for news about his son.

"Tell me about your fiancée." Lorraine smiled at him. "How does she feel about welcoming your son into her life?"

"She's delighted. Kiki is wonderful," said Detweiler. "I think she's as excited about Erik as I am. She's very good with children. In fact, she's expecting. Due in January. I'm missing the first sonogram. "

"A baby on the way and a daughter?"

"Yes, Anya will be thirteen this month. A great kid. I've known Kiki and Anya for nearly three years, so I've had the chance to watch Anya grow. She's thrilled about having siblings. Her best friend Nicci has a brother, and Anya envies her. I think the two girls are already counting on making babysitting money."

"Gina told me you have extended family in the St. Louis area." Lorraine fiddled with the orange slice balanced on the edge of her glass.

"My mother, father and two sisters live just across the river. I have one niece, Emily, who is Anya's age. The two are great friends. Kiki's mother and sister live ten minutes away from us, as does her mother-in-law from her first marriage. We met after her husband George was murdered. But her mother-in-law, Sheila—George's mother—has stayed close to Kiki and Anya. Sheila recently married my boss, Chief of Police Robbie Holmes."

"My, my," said Lorraine. "You do indeed have family nearby. How lovely! Erik won't grow up in a vacuum, will he? How are the schools there in St. Louis?"

He explained that because Anya attended CALA Erik should be considered a sibling, and therefore, he should be able to get into the prestigious institution. "It's pricy," Detweiler admitted, "but I have money in savings that we'll use for his tuition. Having him there at CALA will make life easier for all of us. There'll only be one school schedule. One pickup and drop off time. One administration and their quirks to navigate." He continued by explaining that CALA's educational prowess was second-to-none in the area.

"How about your home? Do you have enough room for another child?"

The flatbread arrived. Detweiler was relieved to discover that "flatbread" was nothing more than thin crust pizza. The sweet taste of figs mingled pleasantly with the pungent flavor of the goat cheese, making the food surprisingly delicious even without tomato sauce. He'd have to tell Kiki about it.

"We'll be cramped. There's only one bathroom. But Anya doesn't want to move. Since we're asking so much of her, Kiki and I have decided that we'll wait a bit before bringing up moving again."

"Why doesn't Anya want to move? I should think she'd

value her privacy and want a bigger place with more bathrooms." Lorraine seemed genuinely concerned.

He laughed. "My sisters would be the first to agree with you. However, this little house is special. Particularly to Anya and Kiki. The landlord is an author named Leighton Haversham."

"Really? The man who wrote The Everland Trilogy? Those fabulous suspense novels! How fascinating! I didn't realize he was from St. Louis."

"Yes. He grew up out in the country in Southwestern Missouri, but he went to school at Washington University in St. Louis. You see, he built out his garage intending it to be his office. But once he finished it, the view was so terrific, he couldn't get any writing done. And it's way too big to be an office, so he decided to rent it out. Kiki's house is on the edge of his property, in a picturesque St. Louis suburb called Webster Groves. The place also comes with a donkey named Monroe. Frankly, I think the donkey is as much of the charm for Anya as is the scenery, a large wooded lot that Leighton has filled with flowers."

Lorraine laughed out loud. "A donkey?"

"Yes," said Detweiler. "I think Leighton rescued Monroe. He also has a pug named Petunia. When Leighton travels, Kiki and Anya watch his pets for him. We're all animal lovers."

That led to talking about Gracie, Seymour, and Martin. By the time he'd finished his meal, Detweiler felt talked out to the point of exhaustion.

"Kiki is buying a scrapbook store?" Lorraine seemed content in her role as interviewer.

"Yes, she's extraordinarily talented." Detweiler reached inside the backpack and withdrew the album Kiki had made for Erik. While handing it to her, he signaled the waiter to bring him the check, a subterfuge that Lorraine didn't notice.

As he slipped the man his credit card, Lorraine turned the pages of the book slowly. He couldn't help but feel proud of the memory album. Kiki had done a wonderful job of showing off his family, his home, her home, the animals and Anya. In short, the book was an accurate representation of the loving world that Erik would be entering.

As she closed the book, Lorraine lifted her cloth napkin and dabbed at her eyes.

"This is beautiful." Her voice was husky with emotion. "A paradise for a little boy. What a lovely family! I didn't realize there's so much to see and do in St. Louis!"

"We want to do everything possible to help him make the transition," said Detweiler, reaching once again into the backpack. He pulled out a thin three-ring binder. "Kiki sent questions to ask you, Erik's teacher, his doctor and anyone who matters in his life. I'm under strict instructions to tell her what she can buy or do to make him feel at home as quickly as possible. Whether it's singing endless rounds of 'The Wheels on the Bus' or buying SpongeBob SquarePants sheets for his bed. I'm to report to her tonight so she can be organized for his arrival."

Lorraine sat back in her chair. She crossed her arms over her chest and studied Detweiler. "You really have given this a lot of thought, haven't you?"

"Yes, ma'am. We have. We know it won't be easy for him. We can't bring back his parents. That is, we can't replace Gina and your brother. But we can make this transition as seamless as possible. He's my son. I'll move heaven and earth to make him happy. I can promise you that."

29

*L*orraine was shocked to learn that Detweiler had paid their bill. "I'm unaccustomed to having my guests pay, and you are my guest. That was totally unnecessary," she said as she text-messaged Orson to come for them.

"Ma'am, where I grew up, the gentleman always picks up the check."

"Well," she said slowly, "that's utterly charming of you and completely unexpected. Thank you very much."

She tried to push back her chair but found it troublesome. Detweiler noted her struggle and went to her aid. Using both hands, she pushed down on the table to lever herself into a standing position.

"Could you open my walker and hand it to me?" she asked, her head peering up at him from an odd angle. In the blare of the sunlight he hadn't noticed the dowager's hump that forced her neck to jut out at an awkward angle.

Her hands grabbed the walker, clenching it until her tendons stood out in stark relief. One foot shuffled forward slowly. The other followed painfully. Moving was a chore for

Lorraine. Her final configuration was a stiff right angle, a geometric shape that seemed likely to topple over at any moment.

Detweiler held his breath, worrying about her. No wonder she couldn't keep Erik. An active child would find his life severely limited by Lorraine's handicaps. For a boy, this would be devastating. She could never keep up with him. She could only hold him back.

Orson pulled up in the big black Escalade. Before the driver could hop out, Detweiler moved to open the passenger side door for Lorraine, but she pointed to the back seats. "I was hoping we could sit side-by-side so we could continue our conversation."

"Of course," he said. "Whatever you'd like. Don't forget that the running board on this car pops out. I hit my shin on it this morning."

She laughed. "That's why I've taken to wearing pants. I can't tell you how many bruises I'm sporting."

After they were seated and belted in, she turned to him. "Detective Detweiler," she started before he suggested that she call him either Chad or Detweiler, "I have a letter for you. It's from Gina. She made me promise to hand-deliver it, if need be. I hope you won't mind that I haven't offered you more privacy. However, once you read it, I think you'll understand why I haven't."

He opened the plain security envelope. The message was printed in Gina's strange scrawl, a script unmistakably hers. It read:

Dear Chad,

I had worried that something like this might happen, and it must have or you wouldn't be reading this. I wish I could answer your questions, but I can't. I'm not even sure that I have all the answers.

Remember how you always told me that sometimes things aren't what they seem? That you wanted to be a detective because you liked solving puzzles? Getting to the heart of a situation?

Keep that in mind. The minute you see Erik, you'll have to make a decision. You'll have a choice to make. You're the only person I can trust to do what's right. The only person I can trust with my child. As you can see, Lorraine's health precludes her caring for my boy.

I should have talked to you right away and taken responsibility for my actions as soon as I learned I was pregnant, but I was ashamed. I couldn't face you or your family. Not when they'd been so kind to me. And when I heard the news about Trevon Jackson, I got scared. Really scared. If someone had known I was pregnant, with Trevon's child, who knows what might have happened next.

So, I told you that I was leaving because I hated Central Illinois and being a cop's wife. That was unfair to you. I know that now. But back then, I was in a panic. It was cruel of me to let you think any part of this was your fault. That's a burden I'll carry to my grave. I hope you'll forgive me.

You can see why I didn't sign the divorce papers right away. This way no one will ask you to take a paternity test. Everyone will have forgotten about Trevon by now. Certainly, they won't connect me with him.

I can imagine how hurt and angry you might be. You have a right to be mad—but I hope you can get over it. Erik Chandler Detweiler is a wonderful little boy, and I named him after you because you always wanted a son. What I did was wrong, but I didn't see any other way.

You don't have to worry about my parents. We're still

estranged. But from what I've heard, Dad's had another stroke; Mom has been hospitalized. Her Alzheimer's is much worse.

I met Van the first week I was in LA. My car broke down. You remember that old Ford Escort I had? Always overheating? There I was on Santa Monica Boulevard with smoke billowing out, and cars honking behind me. Van stopped to help. He was so kind. He kept checking on me, and our friendship led to something more.

I told him everything. I had to having learned the hard way what one little secret can do to a relationship. Since Van couldn't have children of his own, he was delighted about Erik. He treated him like his own son.

As you probably know by now, Van has plenty of money, but he'd also been burned several times. I signed a prenuptial agreement. Not that it mattered. Van's been very generous to me and to my son. I have lived a good life. I was even able to buy a policy and put a little money away for Erik's education. That should make things easier on you.

I heard through the grapevine that you've moved to St. Louis. I also heard about what happened to Brenda. I'm sorry about that, but it's probably for the best. My friends tell me you're engaged to a wonderful woman. Good. That will make the transition easier for both Erik and you.

Lorraine has been my best friend. She was happy that I made Van happy—and she's been wonderful to Erik. I hope you'll find a way to keep her in your lives.

Please apologize to your parents for me. And to your sisters. I hope that they can forgive me.

I hope you can, too. If not for my sake, for Erik's—

I know you'll make a wonderful father, and I trust you to do what's best.

Sincerely,

Gina

P.S. I really did love you, but it just wasn't going to work.

Detweiler shook his head and read the letter a second time. Then a third. Instead of asking Lorraine all his questions, he stared out the window. Trevon Jackson? And Gina? No wonder she fled. Trevon had been running an internal affairs investigation when he was found shot to death outside a bar. Everyone knew what happened, but no one could prove anything. Trevon's death was one of the many reasons that Detweiler wanted to get out of Illinois and join the St. Louis police force.

But Gina had been having an affair with Trevon? The man who'd been his friend and mentor? An instructor at the academy?

He closed his eyes. Snippets of scenes came to him.

Yes, he could see it now.

A fresh pain began in his chest. How could she have done that to him?

And then, he realized he had to let it go. She was gone. So was Trevon.

Only their son remained.

A boy without a home. No mother. No father. No one.

Lorraine studied him quietly. Her eyes were wild with worry. She seemed smaller and more broken than before. "If you don't want him, I can try to care for him. There's always adoption."

"You've talked to her parents?" he asked. "Gina's father?"

"She asked me not to, but I made contact."

"And?" He tried to sound calm, although what he wanted was to punch a hole in a wall. Or two.

"When I told her father that his daughter had died, he interrupted to say, 'I have no daughter.'"

Detweiler shook his head. He couldn't imagine his parents ever cutting him out of their lives.

"You have every reason to be angry with her," said Lorraine. She was staring down at her hands.

"I am."

"But there's a child involved."

"Who is blameless."

Lorraine nodded slowly. Her eyes were wet. "Yes. Blameless. And adorable. Will you at least meet him? Before you decide?"

30

Same day
Metro St. Louis

*A*nya clutched the sonogram images in her hands. "Wait until I show Nicci. She's going to flip."

I smiled at that. Nicci Moore was Anya's best friend. Because Jennifer Moore's sister needed her help, Nicci and her brother Stevie were with their mother in Seattle. However, thanks to the wonders of social media, Nicci could still see the images of my baby. The sonogram tech offered to email images to us.

"Can I forward the images to Gran?" asked Anya.

"Sure," I said, knowing that Sheila would enjoy them. "Why don't you compose the email and send it to all our family members?"

"Yup. You're having a son!" said my daughter in what sounded like a cheer.

My son.

Our son.

One of my two sons.

Wow.

Aunt Penny was unusually quiet.

I was driving her back to my mother's house, taking the most scenic way possible, winding through the streets of Ladue so she could see the grand houses. Our convoluted route also took us past the St. Louis Cathedral. I found a parking space nearby and suggested we see if we could go inside.

"Since when did you become Catholic?" asked Aunt Penny.

"I'm not," I said. "But I certainly am an admirer of great art and beauty. Wait until you see this."

From the street, we craned back our necks to follow the curve of the green-tiled dome that rises 227 feet. "Remember what you see from here when you get inside," Anya told Aunt Penny.

Built in the Byzantine style, the church is impressive from the outside. However, it is the interior of the cathedral that I wanted to share with my aunt. We moved quietly through the entry hall, and I paused with my hand on the central door to the Cathedral. "Prepare to be amazed," I said.

And she was.

Aunt Penny is a world traveler, but she'd never seen mosaics that matched the splendor of those in the St. Louis Cathedral. With her mouth open and her eyes wide, she stared at the glorious images covering 3,500 square feet, some of the finest mosaics in the world.

Slowly we worked our way down the aisle until we were nearly beneath the central dome. "Half of the churches in the country could fit under this," Anya told her aunt. "I remember that from the guide book."

"Notice the windows?" I said, as I pointed out the sixteen stained glass windows that circled above us. "Remember the outside?"

Aunt Penny nodded. "There weren't any openings in the dome."

"That's right," I said. "The windows are fake."

Next, we moved to the northwest corner of the building and visited Our Lady's Chapel. There I knelt at the altar rail and prayed for my unborn baby and for little Erik. When I rose to my feet, Anya beckoned us toward the All Saints' Chapel. From the ceiling were suspended several red hats. "Those belong to the Cardinals," explained Anya. "They say that whenever one of the hats disintegrates, a Cardinal is admitted into heaven."

The interior of the southern dome of the Cathedral is devoted to local history. The mosaics show four saints who served in the United States. "That's Mother Philippine Duchesne." Anya pointed to the woman for whom one of the local private schools was named. "She became a missionary at age 70."

We ended our tour by stopping to view the statue of a young King Louis IX, the medieval ruler who tried to bring justice to all his people, including those who were poor. "He's the patron of the Cathedral," said Anya, as we paused to stare at the young man wearing a crown and holding a sword, "and the namesake of our city."

With that, our sightseeing was concluded. But back in the car, Aunt Penny seemed unusually quiet. "What's wrong?" I asked her when I stopped for gas. Anya had hopped out to buy three bottles of water so the time seemed right to query my aunt.

Her smile was wistful. "Nothing's wrong. I'm just feeling overwhelmed at seeing so much beauty, and such a miracle as that little baby floating around inside of you. Thank you for letting me share this day with you."

I hugged her tightly. "Thank you for being here with us. That means a lot to me and to Anya." And it did, especially since my own mother had never accompanied me to any of my appointments.

Anya chattered happily, coming up with a list of possible boy's names.

"Detweiler will have some say in this, you realize," I told her.

"I know. But I thought I could help," and she bent her head to add yet another name. Suddenly, she looked up at me. "Mom? I've been thinking."

"You have?" I grinned at her. "By the size of that list, I can tell."

"No, I mean thinking about you getting married."

I glanced at my rearview mirror. Aunt Penny was watching the scenery go by. I prompted Anya, "What's up? You getting cold feet? Thinking I should ditch Detweiler?"

"If you do, I get first dibs on him," said Aunt Penny. "He's my kind of man."

Anya blushed. "Of course not. I mean that I've been thinking about whether you should wait or not. You've said all along that you wouldn't marry him before the baby came. You promised me."

"That's right. I did. I intend to keep my promise."

"I've changed my mind."

I nearly stood on the brakes.

"Geez, Mom, you're going to kill all of us." Anya had one arm out to brace herself against the dash.

"Sorry. Not my fault. You surprised me. You okay, Aunt Penny?"

"Never better."

I eased off the brake pad. "Anya, did I hear you right? What are you saying? And more importantly, why are you changing your mind?"

"While you were getting dressed, I asked the tech how much it cost to have a baby. It's really expensive. I asked how much all your doctor visits would cost. That's a lot of money, too. If you were married to Detweiler, his insurance would cover you, wouldn't it?"

"Yes," I said, "but I'm not going to marry him for the insurance benefits. There's money owed me from your father's business. They actually called me to say they're ready to release some of it. That should cover my hospital and doctor costs."

"But we're going to need that money for the store," said Anya. Those beautiful denim blue eyes of hers, the same shade as Sheila's, blinked at me.

"It's not your job to worry about money, sweetie."

"I'm not a baby anymore. I understand how important money is."

I turned into downtown U City and headed toward my mother and sister's house. "I never said you are a baby. It's abundantly clear you're growing up so very quickly. However, I refuse to make an important decision like this based on money. Or more to the point, based on your worries about money. That shouldn't be a consideration. You told me that you didn't want to give up your last name. I respect that. I don't want you to forget your father. Your last name is an important link to him."

"I will never forget my father," she said, as she chugged most of her bottle of water.

"Of course you won't. Anya, I am impressed that you would be so unselfish about this. It shows a lot of maturity for you to think about the financial aspects of having a child. But again, it's not your problem."

"Well, it's a problem for our whole family—and I have been thinking about it. And about weddings in general. I think you ought to marry Detweiler, Mom, and I think you should do it before this baby comes."

he crop would start in an hour, and customers would begin arriving before that. My phone rang as soon as my daughter and I walked through the back door of Time in a Bottle. Before answering it, I asked Anya to take Gracie for a piddle-walk. "Go through the front, please, so Clancy knows we're here." I hit the button to connect with my caller.

From the other end of my cell came a strangled sound.

"Hello? Rebekkah?" I panicked. Was it possible that Horace was in worse shape than we'd suspected? Or was she in need of my help?

"No. It's me," said Sheila, in an uncharacteristic breech of good grammar. "I am so angry I could spit."

"Whoa," I headed for the bathroom where I could close the door and have a modicum of privacy. "What's happened? Are you all right? Is Robbie okay?"

"Prescott is making my husband miserable. That little weasel. So much for family loyalty. He isn't much of a brother-in-law."

"Brother-in-law?" I was shocked.

"Kiki, you can be so stupid sometimes. Of course, Prescott is Robbie's brother-in-law. You knew that."

I knew very little about Robbie's family, picking up bits and pieces here and there. His wife, Nadine had died ten years ago, but how or why I didn't know. I was aware that she and Robbie had four children, and only one of them lived here in town, Reena Marie. I also knew that Reena wasn't married, but I didn't know whether she had ever been. I had never met her in person, because she had rejected every invitation Sheila had issued, giving me the distinct impression that she wasn't happy about her father's upcoming marriage. Sheila had been strangely close-mouthed about the tiff between father and daughter.

I figured that this particular problem wasn't my business. My plate was already full. My cell phone had been curiously quiet despite the fact that Detweiler had promised to send me a photo of Erik. Where was it? What was the problem? I was definitely sensing something had gone awry.

"Kiki? Are you listening to me?" Sheila was on a rampage.

"Of course, I am. I just need time to absorb all this," I said.

Robbie always struck me as a stoic figure. He didn't gossip about his employees or his job. At least, if he did, I never heard it. My sense was that his first marriage hadn't been great, but that he was too loyal to his late wife's memory to complain about her. Now I wondered: What else had happened to Robbie and his first wife? What had gone on between them, behind closed doors, that played into the situation today?

Ten years is a long time between spouses. In my book, at least. I couldn't imagine why Reena's tail feathers were in a twist. When I had asked Sheila—and I had only indulged my curiosity once—she was evasive, which I translated to mean, "None of your business."

Now she prattled on and on about how Prescott had Robbie over a barrel. How he was simultaneously goofing up the investigation and blaming Robbie for his lack of progress. How Prescott kept running to Mayor White complaining that Robbie was blocking his efforts to solve the murder.

"How do you know all this?" I asked. With Detweiler out of town and Hadcho off the case, Robbie's connections to the department were severely diminished.

"Most of the officers are still loyal to Robbie. They've kept him informed even though they aren't supposed to be talking to him. Prescott has threatened them. If he hears they're in cahoots with Robbie, he'd take drastic measures, whatever that means."

Prescott probably knew that officers were talking behind his back. Perhaps that's what drove him to heap even more blame on Robbie. He might be whining about Robbie as his own twisted sort of damage control. Especially, if the investigation wasn't going well.

My mother-in-law had worked herself into a real tizzy. While I tried to sort fact from fiction, she babbled non-stop. Slowly a storyline emerged. Prescott and Robbie had never gotten along, but their dislike for each other got out-of-hand when Nadine was diagnosed with diabetes. She'd been a two-pack-a-day smoker and a big sweets eater. Robbie begged her to take care of her health, but she hated the idea of limiting her intake of sweets. A weight gain inevitably followed as did numerous trips to the emergency room.

She grew heavier and heavier. She started to have problems with her feet.

Robbie wanted to take her to the Mayo Clinic. She

refused that, too. She didn't want to be far from home. He kept taking her to the doctor, to the emergency room, to support groups, but Nadine seemed to be on a self-destruct mission. She refused to change her eating habits. By the time she died, she was wheelchair bound, after having to have one foot amputated.

All the while this was happening, Prescott told people Robbie should be taking better care of his wife. Robbie and Nadine's daughter Reena was the baby of the family. She was also her mother's favorite. Since she was unmarried and living at home, she was able to spend most of her time caring for her mother.

"Nadine was angry and bitter. That's how everyone has described her to me. She hated Robbie's job with a vengeance. She used to call and check on him constantly, refusing to believe that he was at work." Sheila hesitated. "I think Nadine enjoyed being sick. The worse she got, the more frantic Robbie became. So she got a lot of attention."

"But it backfired."

"It sure did. At least, that's what I surmise. Robbie won't discuss it with me."

"Is that why his kids didn't come to the wedding? I remember something being said about how they couldn't come because you changed the date, but I take it that there are hard feelings?"

"Natalie is a licensed nurse," said Sheila. "She knows her father did everything he could to help his first wife. J. R. believes whatever Natalie says, so he's never thought Robbie was negligent. James seems to go along with the older kids. But Reena Marie is like her mother. Bitter. Unhappy with her own life."

"So she blames Robbie for her mother's death?"

"It's more complicated than that."

I waited.

Finally, Sheila said, "Nadine loved stirring up trouble. I think that's one reason her older children were eager to move away from her. They'd had enough of their mother's drama."

"What kind of drama?"

"Nadine was vicious. It wasn't enough to stop other people from having a drink of water. No, she had to dump poison in the well. Nadine told her friends not to expect Robbie to grieve for her. She said that when she was dead, Robbie would finally be free to marry the woman he really loved...me."

I did a quick calculation. I knew that Sheila and Robbie had been high school sweethearts. Anya was turning thirteen later this month. Sheila's first husband, Harry, died right after Anya was born. Doing the math, that meant that Nadine was accusing Sheila of carrying on with Robbie after Harry died but while she and Robbie were still married. That didn't sound like the Sheila I knew, although love and lust in tandem can make anyone pull stupid stunts.

"Believe me, I stayed as far away from Robbie as I could after Harry died. I knew how attracted we were to each other. Given that and how lonely I was, I didn't trust myself. That's what makes her accusation so horrible. He and I would bump into each other at social events and act like we barely knew each other!"

"You are thinking that her accusations are behind Prescott's malice and Reena's distance?" I asked.

"Yes, I believe so. The older kids were fine when Robbie first told them we were getting married. But they have a different relationship with their father from Reena. She's always asking for financial help. She's never really made a successful life for herself. The older ones have made their own way in life without relying on their dad. J.R. has four kids and another on the way. Natalie and her husband have one and another on the way. James has four kids, two sets of twins. They're happy for Robbie and me."

Right. But they hadn't shown up at the wedding either. Maybe Sheila had underestimated their displeasure.

"What a mess."

Despite her many faults and her rampant narcissism, Sheila put a high value on family. Causing a division within Robbie's family must have pained her greatly.

"Marrying me has brought Robbie nothing but grief."

32

*S*heila's phone call took a chunk out of my crop preparation time. Clancy stuck her head inside the office door to tell me she'd done her part.

"The handouts are copied. The name tents are out. The kits are ready." Handing the class roster to me, she said, "Thirty-two people coming tonight. I've checked the supplies, and we're good. We have enough for the students, plus extras to sell to customers who can't make it tonight. All are paid in advance except these two."

"Thanks for your hard work," I said. "Have a good evening."

She gave me a stiff hug. Since we'd become friends, she'd grown accustomed to my affection and tried to return it, but she would never be wholly comfortable with a physical response. Still, I always appreciated that she was making an effort. "I heard about that doctor's murder at Sheila's wedding. It's all over the radio. Try not to let it bother you too much. You don't need more stress on your plate."

"Thanks," I said. "I'm trying my best to stay out of it. That's why I didn't mention it to you."

I let Clancy out the back door and looked around for Anya. She was taking her sweet time about getting back to the store, but on occasion, Gracie flat out refused to hurry along. Even so, my arms ached to hug my daughter. I was so pleased that she'd changed her mind about when I should marry Detweiler. It meant she was over her worries about being the only Lowenstein. She accepted the fact that she would be part of a family, a family with different origins and names.

But Sheila's unhappiness cast a shadow over me, one that I needed to shake before our croppers arrived. I used the toilet, washed my hands slowly and adjusted my voluminous top before stepping out of the bathroom.

As a consequence, I nearly collided with Cara Mia Delgatto, who'd come through the backdoor, arms laden with shopping bags full of food.

"Let me help you." I relieved her of one bag. "I'd totally forgotten that I asked you to come early so we could talk. I'm sorry, Cara. Things have gotten crazier than usual."

"No problem. I heard Prescott talking about the murder investigation on the radio."

I grumbled and shook my head.

"Why do I get the impression he's happy this happened?" Cara asked.

"Probably because he is. At least, that's the way it looks to me."

"Your poor mother-in-law. How about if we talk over your business questions while I get this ready? The salad and fixings are in that bag," she said. "The pasta is in here. There's also garlic bread. You do have a toaster oven, right?"

We carried the food to the crop area, aka our sales floor.

Clancy had rolled the shelving units off to one side to give us more room for tables that she had prepared. A few weeks ago, we'd had casters added to the bottom of all our shelf units. Where the units had been attached to the floor, the old linoleum was missing. But it had gotten very worn and tired looking anyway, so we replaced it with new flooring that looked like tile but wasn't. The process forced me to close the store over one weekend, but it was worth every penny. Now, we could push the shelf units to one side. Moving the shelves doubled our cropping area. I recouped the cost of the flooring and casters in two weeks because we made more money from crops than from any other single activity.

When the shelf units were clustered more closely together, customers could still wander through the displays, although not if they were pushing baby strollers. I had a hunch that this change would continue to pay dividends because when customers came for crops or classes, they always spent money on consumable supplies. Although Margit hadn't worked up the figures, I knew our sales total was higher since we could accommodate more scrappers at the crops.

As I looked over the list of attendees, I realized there was yet another benefit to the enlarged space. We'd been turning people away from our crops. Even though most people were understanding, they weren't happy about being put on a waiting list. We lost the income from their crop fee and from any sales that would have naturally happened during the crop breaks. More importantly, we also lost good-will. That was priceless.

Thanks to the new configuration, we could designate two tables for food. I set down one shopping bag and started toward the back room for the toaster oven. Since the toaster oven is awkward to carry, I perched it on top of the wheeled picnic cooler full of iced drinks and rolled both to the front of the store. Cara Mia lit several small cans of Sterno to keep the pasta warm. Everything smelled delicious.

After we set up everything, we headed back to the office. I briefly described to her my dilemma regarding purchasing Time in a Bottle. "I thought I knew what I was doing. Jennifer Moore and I discussed how a business is valued. I knew what Dodie paid for the building and the parking lot because she told me."

"But real estate values are never static," explained Cara. "Especially when the city has made improvements that change traffic patterns."

"Right, and I forgot to take that into account." I stopped. "I feel like I'm being disloyal to the Goldfaders to question the price tag they've put on the business."

"Disloyal?" Cara raised an eyebrow. "Dodie always encouraged you to think in a businesslike fashion. Besides, what if they've seriously undervalued the property? That could be the case, too."

"Wow. If that's true, what will I do?"

"Cross that bridge when you get to it. Right now, you need good information. As it stands, you're buying the proverbial pig in a poke."

"I'm still clueless, Cara. Chalk it up to pregnancy brain."

She laughed. "I remember that! Okay, let me contact a friend who's a commercial realtor. It won't cost you anything to have him come and look over the building. I bet he won't even have to come inside to put together comps."

"Comps?"

"A list of comparable properties and what they're valued at. By looking over what similar buildings sold for, you'll have a better idea whether the price you're paying is fair."

"I feel like an idiot. I should have thought of this."

"How many businesses have you bought? How many pieces of commercial real estate do you own?"

"Uh, none and none."

"Exactly," Cara said. "I wouldn't know all this except for my father. He made a lot of mistakes in his business career, so I benefited from his hard won education. Now, I'm sharing it with you. High-five, girlfriend."

The sound of our palms slapping each other sent a happy ring through the store.

33

When Cara Mia reached into her jeans pocket and withdrew her wallet, I waved her money away.

"Heavens, no. Especially after that talk we just had. This class is on us. So are all your supplies. You saved us a bundle with your quick thinking. It's a pity that people were too distracted by Dr. Hyman's death to really dig in and enjoy the food. The pasta and that salad would have gone to waste."

"I also have a full pan of tiramisu tucked in a cooler sitting outside in Black Beauty."

"Black Beauty?" Anya joined us with Gracie in tow.

"That's what she calls her black Camry," I explained. "Cara loves to name things. Her Golden Retriever is Sven because he's blond and Nordic looking. Isn't that funny?"

"He's getting so old and feeble," Cara said. "I'm taking him to the vet's office tomorrow. I don't like how he's been coughing and losing weight." Her eyes avoided mine. She'd had a really tough year, and we were only half-way through. Her mother had died of breast cancer right after the holidays. Then her father had a heart attack and followed her mother to the grave. In a month, her son Tommy would be going off to school in Miami, Florida, and Cara would be alone, rattling around in her house.

Although she'd worked in the restaurant her entire life, that particular business wasn't really her passion. She never said as much, but I could tell. After Tommy went off to school, she planned to explore her options. "Time to move into Phase Two of my life," she'd said. "We've got a great manager at the restaurant, so I'm free to move on to whatever. I know the place will run without me."

"What's your plan?" I'd asked.

"I have no idea," she said. "None. I think I'll start with a road trip. Maybe I'll hop in the car and see where I wind up."

I would hate to see her go, but I knew she needed to make a change. Lately, she'd become an unofficial member of our team while Laurel took off some time. In exchange for coordinating our food offerings, I gave Cara a monthly "allowance" of scrapbook supplies. Time in a Bottle had become "home away from home" for her, just as it had been for me.

Experts often say, "Don't mix business and your personal life," but that wouldn't work in a scrapbook store. Our business is all about our customers' personal lives.

Cara Mia Delgatto was an example of a customer who'd become a dear friend. I could think of countless others. But I didn't think I'd be adding Bernice Stottlemeyer to the list. No way.

I dispatched Anya to check in customers as they came through the front door. With her clipboard in hand, she looked very, very mature.

"Your daughter does well with responsibility," said Cara.

"Yes, she's growing up fast," I agreed. "I depend on her a lot. With two new siblings on the way, I hope I won't be asking too much of her."

$\mathcal{T}$he card toppers proved to be a huge success. My scrapbookers quickly realized that following my simple formula would provide a great way to use up odd scraps of paper while saving them the cost of buying expensive greeting cards. We finished our "make and take" portion of the night quickly, and the croppers segued into working on their own pages. At seven, we suggested that folks help themselves to the food. The wonderful fragrance of garlic, butter, tomatoes, and cheese had permeated the air since our guests arrived, so they didn't need any urging to fill their plates.

"You met with Bernice? She stopped in to see you?" Bonnie Gossage asked me as she headed toward her seat after visiting the food table.

"Yes. Thank you for the referral. She came in earlier today. I gave her the forms and asked her to return them by Wednesday at six. I understand she needs the album by Thursday at one."

Bonnie nodded. In her hands was a plate piled high with salad. She had carefully avoided the pasta, which I took to mean that she was on yet another diet. Bonnie was having trouble shedding her post-baby pounds. I understood entirely. I still hadn't lost the weight I'd gained when I was pregnant with Anya, and now I was adding to my already fulsome figure.

"I hope you'll still be thanking me after the job is over," Bonnie glanced sideways at me and picked at a piece of lettuce.

I walked with her to her seat and pulled out the chair for her. "Bonnie, I always appreciate new business. You know I'll do my best for her. I am missing a few photos. I don't have many of their home. Especially the nursery."

"Uh-oh," said Bonnie. "That's really important. I told her you'd need them."

"She doesn't seem to grasp what I'm trying to do for her."

"I know. I keep trying to stress the importance of the album, but Bernice seems to think that..." she stopped. "Look, I hate to ask, but would you do everything you can for her? I mean, I know you always do, but a senior partner at the firm asked me to take over for him on this one. I'd really like to do a bang up job."

I owed Bonnie. Big time. She had provided countless hours of free legal aid to me. This was my turn to repay the favor. "Of course, I will. I'll go the extra mile. I'll do every-thing I can—"

"But?" Bonnie's eyes narrowed speculatively as she stared at me. She is a good attorney, although your first impression is of a harried, frazzled mom. The minute she opens her mouth, however, you realize what a brilliant mind churns behind that rumpled exterior.

"I didn't say 'but.'"

"No, but you thought 'but.'"

"But I didn't say 'but.'"

"But you wanted to say 'but,' even if you didn't say 'but.'"

I frowned. "You know I don't gossip about my customers. It's a rule that Dodie set down on Day One."

"I'm not asking you to gossip. I'm asking your opinion. As an expert. Do you think you can create an adoption profile album that will make the Stottlemeyers look appealing to a birth mother?"

I squirmed. Rather than look Bonnie in the eyes, I chomped on a carrot I had in my hand. She wisely said nothing. She was waiting me out to speak.

"I have no idea what birth mothers find appealing or how they make their decisions."

Bonnie squared her shoulders and scowled at me. "You've done six of these albums. How will the Stottlemeyers' album compare with the others you have done?"

"I will do my best craftsmanship. I've found some lovely new—"

"Let's go in the back." She sounded a bit upset. We both put down our plates and headed for Dodie's office.

Once I'd closed the door, Bonnie turned to me. "Look. I may have made a mistake by sending her here. She needed the work done, and you're the best. I've seen your albums, and the birth mothers have always responded positively. You seem to bring out the warmth of each couple and flesh them out on paper."

"I always appreciate the work. You know that."

She blew out a sigh and rubbed the back of her neck. She was wearing her after-work uniform, mom-jeans, a faded polo shirt, and running shoes. "Let me go about this another way. I can see this blowing up in both our faces. I'm worried."

I let down my guard. "I am, too. I owe you so much! But

I'm not sure that I can work magic—and I don't want to lie to you! I can't and won't fabricate a warm family that doesn't exist. I told Bernice and I'll remind you: I can only work with what she gives me."

"I know," Bonnie said. "I really shouldn't have gotten you involved, but I figured that if anyone could help them, it would be you."

"Thanks for the vote of confidence, but I can only work with the photos I have." I felt stupid repeating the same excuse over and over, but what other choice did I have?

"Argh," Bonnie groaned. "I wish the senior partner would have assigned them to someone else. Anyone else! But he said that he thought I could help the Stottlemeyers because I'm a mom. Can you believe that? If we weren't a law firm, I'd consider suing for sexual discrimination."

"You know how he meant that. Right? He was hoping you have extra insight. That's all."

"Right, but he didn't consider that maybe the men in the firm wouldn't have such strong feelings about parent-hood as I do. I'm usually a lot more dispassionate when it comes to my clients, but Bernice has really gotten under my skin."

"So what can we do?" I decided to be proactive. "This is your job—and mine. They still have a right to want to adopt a child. In the end, it's the birth mother's decision, isn't it?"

"You're absolutely right. It's my job to give them their best shot—and your job, too. How about this: Would you go to the Stottlemeyers' house and take photos of it and them?"

That was the last thing I wanted to do. I'd have to bath in anti-cootie gel for a month. But I wasn't doing this for Bernice. I was doing it for Bonnie.

"Sure," I said. "Um, but I do have a question. How do you manage to overcome your gut on this? Although you haven't said as much, I get the impression that you aren't sure they'd be good parents."

"I didn't say that. In fact, I can't say that."

"No, but I can. So what's the deal here? Why do they want a kid? I don't see them walking the talk."

"Due to attorney-client privilege, I can't say more." She lifted her chin and stared straight ahead as if she were in court giving testimony. Her whole body went rigid.

"Sorry," I said.

After a minute, she said, "This is the way my job works, Kiki, and it puts food on the table. I am obligated to do my best for our clients, no matter what I feel toward them personally. It's not up to me to vet them. That's up to the adoption agency."

"Bernice might be different when she's with the birth mom, but she sure doesn't strike me as the warm and fuzzy type."

"That doesn't mean she wouldn't make a good mom," said Bonnie. "You never know about these things. How she acts toward you is not indicative of how she would act toward her own child."

Bonnie was right. I always marveled at the way people's voices changed when they answered a call from family. Especially, from their kids. Even the toughest cookie on the baking sheet would soften. There was nothing else to do, but resign myself to helping Bonnie by helping the Stottlemeyers. "Regardless, of whether she's a worthy candidate or not, rest assured that I'll do my best to portray her in the best possible light."

"Your best might not be good enough."

That stung. I sank down into Dodie's big office chair. "Not be good enough?"

"You know exactly what I mean," she rubbed that spot

on the back of her neck with more gusto. "This isn't about you, Kiki. I'm between a rock and a hard place. Your hard work can't compensate for everything. Off the record? I've never worked with less appealing mother material than Bernice Stottlemeyer. But don't you ever, ever repeat what I said."

35

*B*onnie and I decided that I should send a text message to Bernice Stottlemeyer explaining that I still needed candid photos of her and her husband in their home to complete the album. I showed the text message to Bonnie who helped me write it. Then I hit "send."

Bernice responded by sending a message to Bonnie asking if I were an idiot.

Bonnie sent Bernice a text message explaining that she'd seen the album, and she agreed with me about what it needed. She further explained that she (Bonnie) was here for a crop and had asked me (Kiki) to show her (Bonnie) how the job was going.

How's that for confusing?

After a brief pause, Bernice agreed to let me come to their house. Of course, she chose a totally inconvenient time for me. I could have thirty minutes of their time the next morning, between eight-thirty and nine.

I showed the message to Bonnie who gave me a thumbs-up.

"I don't have their address," I said. "Do you?"

Bonnie grabbed a sticky note and a pen from the dispenser on the desk.

When I saw the address, I nearly fell off my chair. The Stottlemeyers lived around the corner from the house I'd built with my late husband George.

I took care not to let Bonnie see how uncomfortable this made me. I'd told her I'd take care of the photos and, by golly, I would. But she would never ever know how hard this assignment was. Particularly right now when I was so hormonal.

With a quick glance at the office clock, I suggested we needed to rejoin the croppers lest I appear rude.

The crop ended as crops do, with some people rushing out the door and others lining up to buy merchandise. Bonnie thanked me profusely for my extra effort regarding the adoption album.

I continued at the cash register, making small talk and trying not to show my feelings. Seeing my old home would just about kill me. George and I had worked hard together on those plans. In the end, the house was more his than mine because he called in a professional decorator, whereas I'm so much more of a do-it-yourself type of girl. But still, it had been the place where we'd raised Anya for the first eleven years of her life. I had strong attachments to it. Going back and taking photos of a house around the block would be tough on me.

But there was nothing to it but to do it. I was the owner of a business. Well, almost. And I'd given my word.

After the last customer left, Cara kept a look-out from the back door as Anya took Gracie out for a piddle. I did a quick survey of the sales floor, checking for stray merchandise and noting spots that needed filling. That done, I took the change from the cash register, counted out the fifty bucks we open with, and zipped the rest of the money into a bank deposit bag. Even without looking at the detail tape, I knew that the crop had gone well. The shelf units had already been rolled back to their usual spots, so everything looked to be in order. I took a few minutes to straighten a row of pots of glitter, shiny bits of plastic that add so much fun to every layout.

After putting Gracie in her pen, Anya helped Cara clean the food service items. When they were finished, I had two containers to take home, one of pasta and one of salad. There was also a half a pan of tiramisu in the refrigerator. I turned off all the lights, except for those in our display windows and headed to the back door.

Cara walked with us to my car. Anya and Gracie followed along behind us.

"What's happening tomorrow?" asked my friend. "I noticed the hard hats."

"We're knocking down that wall," said Anya with more than a little pride in her voice.

"Wow," said Cara. "That's really cool. I love big projects like that. Kiki, what's on your agenda?"

"I want to work on Sheila's wedding album. She's pretty upset about the murder investigation."

Cara leaned against her Black Beauty and nodded at me. "I can imagine."

"And I have an adoption profile album to finish."

"What's your day like tomorrow, Cara?" I asked.

"Same-old, same-old. Tommy and I are trying to get his stuff sorted and packed so he's ready for college. Take note, Miss Anya, that'll be you someday soon."

"Nope," said my daughter. "I'm not going away to school. I'm going to stay right here. I'm never leaving my mom."

My heart fluttered in my chest. I was glad she loved me so much, but I hoped when the time came, my little girl would feel free to go away to school if that was what was best for her.

36

"Hello, babe. How are you? How's Anya?" The deep voice of Detective Chad Detweiler never failed to bring a smile to my lips. Even when he was far away, like now, he made me happy.

"She's sound asleep. It's been a long day. Better yet, how are you? And how's Erik?"

"I don't know," he said.

"What?"

Bit by bit he told me about his meeting with Lorraine Lauber. Their lunch had lasted longer than expected, so Detweiler hadn't had the chance to see Erik. By way of explanation, he read to me the letter that Gina had left behind.

"So, he's not your biological son."

"No."

"But he doesn't have a home."

"No."

"And Gina wanted you to raise him."

"Yes."

I couldn't help myself. I needed to hear the facts once

more. This whole...mess...was just inconceivable. I didn't know whether to laugh or to scream.

My first thought: It takes a lot of nerve to cheat on your husband and then ask him to raise your bastard child.

My second thought: It's not Erik's fault.

My third thought: If I died tomorrow, I'd want Detweiler to raise Anya. He'd do a great job of it.

Maybe great minds do think alike. Maybe if I'd been in Gina's shoes, I'd have made the same choices.

"What are you thinking?" I asked Detweiler.

"I was hoping to hear what you are thinking."

"No," I said. "You first."

His voice took on a raspy quality as he said, "I'm not sure what to think. One minute I find myself thinking I'd like to wring Gina's neck. The next, I feel sorry for her. I guess when Trevon died, she thought she might be in danger. After all, he was investigating an, um, situation. Just because I didn't realize they were lovers doesn't mean that other officers on the force didn't know."

Wow. I couldn't imagine what he was going through. First Gina leaves him, and now he discovers she was cheating on him but wants him to raise her son? It was outrageous.

"What did Miss Lauber say? Was she aware of the contents of Gina's note?"

"Yes. She said she's sorry that she couldn't tell me this over the phone. That she resorted to subterfuge to get me out here."

I nodded even though he couldn't see me. "Anything else?"

"She wanted me to give this some thought. With the traffic and the timing of our lunch, I missed my chance to meet him today. But I suspect that was her plan all along, because she thought I should consider things carefully. She urged me to see Erik before I make a final decision, but she hasn't told him that he might come home with me. She did tell him he might get to meet a new sister, but otherwise, nothing about moving away. Or leaving her. Obviously, she kept all her options open and left the details sketchy."

"That was decent of her," I said with a snort of derision.

"She's a nice woman, Kiki. You'd like her. Remember, she's not responsible for this mess either."

This whole "mess" sounded like torture for Detweiler. Here he was on the brink of being united with the son he'd never met, and then he got the rug pulled out from under him. Oops. That dream you had? Consider it cancelled, buddy. You've been tricked.

Except...

"Well," I said, "there is good news on the horizon. You're going to have a son."

"If I decide to bring Erik home with me."

"No, I mean the sonogram. The tech is pretty sure I'm having a boy."

A whoop of joy went up from his end of the phone.

"Hot dog! Can you believe it?"

"Now these things are never one hundred percent certain," I cautioned him.

But he was having none of it. "Kiki, what would I do without you?"

"You'll never have to find out, my love."

37

———

"The long and short of it is that Erik needs a home," I said, while talking into the phone and rubbing Gracie's silky ears. Martin, our yellow cat, padded out of Anya's room and hopped onto my lap.

"And Gina trusted me to take care of her son. Sort of like being a guardian. Except, most people get asked before they accept the job. Even when people leave you their pets, they usually give you a heads-up first."

That analogy tickled me. I knew how much he loved Gracie, so it wasn't a big stretch. "I'll support you no matter what you decide."

"I thought you'd say that. In fact, I would have bet money that you would." He went silent.

I didn't need to remind him that this was a long term commitment. Nor would I mention that the boy might have a hard time adjusting. Erik would be caught between the twin challenges of grief and new surroundings. About the time he would adjust to those, we'd be adding a new baby to the mix.

I also decided not to say a word about the cost. Kids are

expensive. That's all there is to it. As a parent, you hate having to deny your child anything! You want the best for him or her—and you want your child to fit in with his peers.

Closing my eyes, I tried to get in touch with my gut and my heart.

What should we do?

In truth, I couldn't imagine leaving the boy behind with his aunt. My heart ached for the child, and I knew I could love him.

But this had to be Detweiler's decision, not mine.

I stopped myself: *That wasn't right.*

It was our decision. I would help raise Erik. Much of the burden of childcare would fall on me. Detweiler and I would function as a couple, moving forward together in a way George and I never did.

Now that Anya had spoken up strongly in favor of an early wedding, we could wipe that problem off the charts. Detweiler and I would be man and wife. I no longer worried that he would be marrying me just because I was carrying his child. I'd moved past that.

And with our marriage would come other support for our decision to bring home Erik. When Detweiler and I were wed, his insurance would help with our financial burdens.

But the emotional ones? Those would still be there.

How would Detweiler feel about seeing the evidence of Gina's cheating on a day-in, day-out basis? Would it tear him apart?

I asked him.

"No," he said slowly. "I don't think so. I think I can separate what she did from the result. This little boy didn't cheat on me. Besides, that's all water under the bridge. It's over. Has been for years. We were never really right for each other. We were just two horny teenagers playing house. We weren't really a couple, and looking back, we weren't really even friends. Not like you and I are. When it's all said and done, I'm happy that she found a man who could love her and provide for her the way she wanted. From all I've seen and heard, Van Lauber was good to her and good for her."

"Lorraine Lauber really is incapable of raising the boy? She can't or she won't?"

"She can't. It's just not feasible. If you met her, you'd realize how frail she is. Her health isn't up to the task. And she's too old, really, to be there for the long haul. Well, she's not chronologically too old, but because of her health she is, if you catch my drift."

I snuggled down into the sofa with Martin in the nook of my legs and tried to imagine that Detweiler was right next to me. If he were here, we could have this conversation face-to-face. I could look at him and tell what he was thinking. But this would have to do.

"Distract me," he said. "I need a bit of breathing space. Tell me about your day. Anything interesting happen? We can come back to this."

I told him what I'd learned about Prescott and about my new construction crew. "Anya is so tickled to be doing manual labor. It will be good for Rebekkah, too," and I told him about Horace's tenuous mental state.

Then, I told him about Bernice Stottlemeyer. As I spoke, it became clear to me: Someone just like Bernice Stottlemeyer would try to adopt Erik or a younger version of him. Panic raced through me, and I sat bolt upright. "Detweiler, we can't let that little boy go into the system. There's no way. We can't let that happen!"

For a moment, there was silence, and then finally, "I was hoping you'd say that. I didn't want to push him on you. I needed to be sure—and I wasn't trying to play games, but I really, really needed to hear you say just that."

In a ragged voice, he added, "I love you. I know we have hard times ahead, but that's okay. As long as we're in this together, we'll make it work. As for this little boy, he needs us. I used to fantasize about adopting when I worked in the Big Brothers program. This isn't much different, except... except...Gina asked this of me. Even though I get really angry when I think about how she lied, I can't hate her. If our positions were swapped, I might have asked the same from her. And I know she would have done it for me. She and I were just in the wrong place and the wrong time when we married, and we were too young to know better."

38

*T*he decision was made. Now we could move onto the practicalities. The questions tumbled out in a hurry.

"Lorraine will take you to meet him tomorrow? And do you still have the list?" I asked. Before he'd left, I'd sat down and typed up an exhaustive list of questions he should ask, and people he should interview.

"Two copies of it," he chuckled. "I intend to go over your list with Lorraine. She promised to set up appointments for me to visit Erik's pediatrician and his camp counselor. She's trying to set up a lunch meeting with his kindergarten teacher. I guess his nanny is working on the list of his friends and favorite activities."

"Nanny?" Oh, to be wealthy enough to hire help!

Creating continuity would make Erik's adjustment easier. Of course, the scrapbooker in me was thrilled to have a new subject for memory albums. My customers often asked for ideas for the boys and men in their lives. It's comparatively easy to create a scrapbook for girls and women, but there are fewer cool products for the guys.

Having Erik around would force me to re-think all our supplies. That would be good for our customers.

"I can't believe I missed the sonogram," said Detweiler.

"I have pictures," I said. "But you can't have them until you get home."

"You are such a tease."

"It's a bribe so that you'll come back to me."

"Babe, I thought I'd made it perfectly clear. You are stuck with me. Forever and for always."

My heart did a happy dance.

We circled back to the situation at hand with Sheila. Detweiler's tone turned serious. "I don't trust Prescott. He's had his eye on Robbie's job far too long. He and Mayor White would love to drum up some sort of a crisis to make Mayor White look like a hero. What's Hadcho have to say about all this?"

"I haven't seen Hadcho since we were all interviewed at the police department. Why?"

"He and Prescott have gone 'round and 'round."

"Tell me more."

"Prescott has spread rumors that Robbie is a bigot. Remember that big splash in the newspapers last year? That source that spoke off the record? I'm pretty sure it was Prescott, which is weird, really weird because he's the real problem in the department. He made some crack about how Hadcho should be paid with wampum."

I knew that Hadcho had Native American blood in him, but other than to admire his coloring and high cheekbones, I'd never given it another thought.

"In this day and age, who makes comments like that?"

"An idiot." Detweiler sighed. "An idiot who's now in charge of an investigation that could reflect poorly on his supervisor."

39

Tuesday/Three days after the wedding...
Kiki's house in Webster Groves, Missouri

he next morning Anya woke up bright and early, ready to knock down my wall. Her enthusiasm for this project tickled me.

She wasn't alone. When I swung by the house in U City, Aunt Penny stood on the curb, hopping from one foot to the other. When we pulled into the parking lot of Time in a Bottle, Rebekkah was already there, bubbling with excitement.

At eight on the dot, we opened the front door to Roy Michelson, the general contractor, who looked approvingly on Aunt Penny, Anya and Rebekkah standing at attention with their hard hats under their arms and their safety goggles dangling from around their necks, like a troop of soldiers ready to do battle.

My crew looked cute as all get-out. Using letter stickers,

I'd spelled each person's name on her helmet. Just for fun, I added stickers of butterflies, ladybugs, and flowers. Once the ladies put on their helmets, Roy's plain orange hat beamed like a beneficent sun in the midst of a field of light-hearted insects and flowers. I posed all my workers and took a photo that would make a super cool scrapbook page.

Despite the dark circles under Rebekkah's eyes, she seemed ready and raring to go. I ached to ask her if she'd heard from Rabbi Sarah, but I figured that could wait.

"You're certainly getting your money's worth," said Aunt Penny, looking over my shoulder at the photo.

"Yes, I am," I said proudly.

"*Guten morgen,*" Margit called from the back room. She was on a one-woman mission to teach all of us rudimentary German. As a result, I'd expanded my vocabulary to include *roulade, stollen, spätzle,* and *sauerbraten.* I was eager to expand my vocabulary, especially if it involved food.

"*Ja,* we are here," I sang out in return.

She came out to admire our workers. In their worn jeans and tees, they were the picture of a proper construction crew. "Good. I like the helmets. Being safety conscious is good. Kiki, I will do the paperwork first thing. We can talk later about profitability of the crop. You have an appointment outside the store, *ja?*"

"Yes, a command performance at the Stottlemeyer house," I said.

"*Oh, das ist toll!*" Some days Margit is more German than others. I suspected that after spending half a day with her mother, she swung a bit more toward her heritage. Since her mother's mind is failing, the older woman often talks in her native language. That's normal for Alzheimer's patients. They lose their short-term memory and regress to their childhood. So rather than resent Margit's attempt at internationalizing our happy little band, I appreciated that she had found a coping mechanism.

All three of us—Margit, Clancy, and I—had aging mothers who made demands on our time. One night over a pot of hot tea, we'd made a pact to be supportive of each other, even if that meant occasional inconveniences. For example, Clancy's mother had fallen and lived in an assisted care facility. Some days, Mrs. Clancy (my friend went by her family name) had called the store six times in a row to ask what time it was. My mother often called to fuss at me for whatever sundry problems she encountered. The day before Sheila's wedding, Mom had phoned to say, "The clothes washer is off balance. Can't you come fix it?" When I explained that I was working, she got huffy. Margit's mother wasn't allowed to make phone calls, but her nursing aides often called with requests like, "Your mother is out of those hard candies she likes and wants you to bring her some. Immediately."

Everything was an emergency as far as our mothers were concerned. One day when I complained about this pseudo urgency, Dodie looked up from her paperwork and said, "If you don't have long to live, it is an emergency, isn't it? Time doesn't mean the same thing to them as it does to you."

"To you" not "to me." That hit me hard, because Dodie was acknowledging that she didn't have long on this earth either.

Thinking about my old boss put a lump in my throat. As did contemplating a change in the store. I saw Dodie's touches everywhere I turned. She'd opened this store when scrapbooking was at its apex, and despite a downturn in the hobby and in the economy in general, she'd managed to keep it going.

Her health problems had offered me an unbelievable

opportunity to own my own business. She and Horace had come to me with two possible payment plans. One would allow me to buy the business outright for a comparatively modest sum. The other was to buy the business "on contract," making payments over time, which would add up to a larger sum. After last night's crop was over, Cara and I talked about my options as we finished putting the store to rights.

"The longer pay-as-you-go contract isn't your best option. Not when interest rates are so low. Have you thought about a business loan?" she asked.

Actually, I had. After George's death, I tried to rebuild my credit, and I'd done a pretty good job, but I couldn't say it was perfect yet. I wasn't sure that any bank would loan me as much money as I needed.

"I could loan you the money," said Cara. "I have money in the bank from selling my parents' house. I planned to invest in a business or a building or both."

"No. That's very kind, but I wouldn't feel comfortable with that," I told her. The evening ended with her promise to pull together various numbers for me so I'd have a better idea what this place was worth. She would also email me a list of questions I should ask Horace.

The store wasn't mine yet, so I was taking a risk in treating it as though it were. However, I had gotten Horace's approval to take down the wall. I took a few more photos for our blog before leaving the wrecking crew to their job. A flicker of the overhead lights informed me that the contractor had located and turned off the power to the wall, just as he had practiced yesterday. Aunt Penny stopped by the office to ask where the first aid kit and fire extinguisher were. That panicked me, but she explained that she wanted to check the extinguisher's expiry date and have both items handy "just in case."

"Fiddle-dee-dee, I forgot to buy us tool belts," Aunt Penny grumbled.

"Will these work?" I walked her over to a display of tool belts we'd purchased for our crafters.

"Perfectly!" she crowed, taking them from me and admiring them. "Our hammers can go there, and the pockets will work for the nails we'll pull."

In her Rolling Stones tee shirt, she seemed as happy as a kid with a new toy. "Hey, y'all, lookee!" she called to her crew members who admired their new gizmos.

"Okay, I'm off to my appointment with the Stottlemeyers," I said, glancing at my watch. "They're graciously allowing me thirty minutes, so I should be back momentarily."

"Have fun," said Anya with a knowing grin.

"Right. Rebekkah? Don't forget to listen for early customers, okay? Margit's got her nose in the books, so she might not hear the door minder. I should be back around nine fifteen or so. Unless I stop and buy donuts. Anyone, anyone?"

A general cheer went up from the crowd.

It was nice to know I could make them so happy!

There's no trauma in life so awful that it can't be eased by large doses of sugar and fat. That's my story and I'm sticking to it.

$\mathcal{I}$ climbed into my car feeling slightly sneaky. I hadn't mentioned to Anya where the Stottle-meyers lived. I knew she would feel as emotional about our old neighborhood as I did. Not surprisingly, my car made the turn into our old lane rather than waiting to turn on the Stottlemeyers' street. I pulled up in front of our old house. Sitting there and staring, I wondered who lived there now. The family who had purchased it from me had been trans-ferred six months later, so now the house had yet another owner. Like all real estate in Ladue, my house had sold quickly. Ladue is small in acreage, but big in prestige, so even the crummy lots (those with bad slopes, no backyards, etc.) sell for high prices. George had purchased this lot from an old school chum, and he'd gotten a wonderful piece of land at the end of a lane, nearly invisible from the main street. Only three other houses were on the same side of the street. This was the end lot with a lovely maple tree that we carefully worked around as we built our house.

But our maple tree was gone. So were the neon flash

spirea bushes usually bursting with hot pink bouquets of flowers. Of course, the purple petunias I usually planted were missing, too. There was no white ageratum either. The new owners had opted for sturdy green yews. Boh-ring! But basically, maintenance free.

Whereas, I'd painted our front door a cheerful blue, they'd changed it to a stodgy gray. That color choice along with the off-white bricks made the house look like an aging elephant. A lump formed in my throat. Fortunately, I hadn't turned off my motor, so I quickly did a u-turn and drove away while fighting tears.

Two blocks over was the Stottlemeyers' house. There were no extraneous flowers, just yews. The front door was a shiny black. Nothing about the house seemed welcoming.

Bernice answered the door. She was dressed in a black jacket and pants. Underneath was a French blue blouse. It should have looked stunning, but the frown on her face trumped her clothing choice. In her ears, she wore diamond studs. Her only other accessories were her watch, wedding and engagement rings. I like minimalism, but this was absolutely Spartan.

She didn't offer me a greeting, so I began working.

"I thought I'd take a photo of you and your husband in your favorite room of the house," I said.

"He's busy."

"This will only take a minute, and Bonnie cleared it with you." I kept my voice level.

"All right then," she huffed. Moving at a fast pace, she led me down the hallway into the ground floor office. The walls had been paneled in a dark oak. The carpet was a cream Berber. The room had no personality.

Wesley Stottlemeyer looked up from his computer monitor.

I didn't know what to expect, but he jumped to his feet and offered me a firm handshake. He wasn't a handsome man, but he was attractive in his own way. He greeted me and tried to make small talk, but Bernice wasn't having any of it. Each time he'd ask me a question, she'd answer it for me. When her back was turned, he shrugged and gave me a "What can I do?" sort of look.

I directed them into a pose where she was looking at the computer monitor with him. That's when I noticed that all the books in the bookshelves were arranged by color and size. Obviously, they weren't for reading. In fact, I was pretty sure they were fakes. No one who loves to read buys his books by size and color.

I snapped several photos. Anyone with half a brain would immediately pick up on the tension between them. I reminded myself that I wasn't there as a marriage counselor, only as a scrapbook consultant.

"Where do you sit at night when you are relaxing?" I asked.

I knew perfectly well where the great room was, having visited this house once for a block party, but I waited.

"There's a great room," said Bernice.

They led me into the "family" room. A similar room in our house had been the place where George, Anya and I spent hours playing Candyland. But this room was missing the comfortable sofas and the low oak coffee table. Instead, a white leather sofa and matching chairs faced a glass and chrome coffee table. Definitely not kid friendly.

I directed Bernice to sit close to her husband on the sofa. They didn't take each other's hands. They barely touched. "I think you need a prop," I said. So, I went to the shelves that flanked the fireplace and tried to pull down a book.

"Don't!" yelled Bernice.

Not that it mattered. I couldn't move the book. It was glued in place.

"Do you have any magazines you could hold?" I asked. Eventually, they remembered a copy of Forbes that had just arrived in the mail. Wesley went to retrieve it from his briefcase.

That helped. But not much.

"Okay, I think that all I need is a photo of the kitchen and the nursery."

"Nursery?"

"Uh-huh." Seeing the confusion on their faces, I added, "Or child's room. Where your child will sleep."

"We're not remodeling until we have the official word that we'll be adopting," said Bernice.

"Oh." In my mind, I saw Bonnie banging her head against a wall. Honestly, Bernice Stottlemeyer was doing everything possible to make adoption impossible. One glance at Wesley's face told me that he was concerned. A hashtag formed between his brows. He seemed to be avoiding my direct stare. His body language screamed that he was uncomfortable. Did he realize how difficult his wife was making this? Had they talked this through? Clearly, they were not in sync with this process.

"We have a guest bedroom that we'll redecorate," said Wesley. "Why don't you show her that, Bernice?"

She led me upstairs. The space we entered reminded me of a hotel room in any major chain.

"Um, should I say you are waiting to redecorate? That when you see whether it's a boy or a girl, you'll change out the furniture and colors?" I asked. The room smelled of lemon-scented furniture polish.

Bernice crossed her arms over her chest and glared at

me. "We only want a boy. I suppose we'll add a crib. It can go there, in the corner."

"You'll need a changing table," I suggested.

But she didn't say anything. Her face was set in stone.

41

I thanked Bernice for her time, though she should have been thanking me. I really was going above and beyond on this album. As we started toward the front door, she sniffed. "As you can see, this is a very upscale neighborhood. I'm sure that most of your customers don't live like this."

"Most don't," I agreed.

Most people find a way to express their personalities in their homes. No matter how meager their income, they find a way to make their décor a reflection of their innermost selves. Most people consider their homes a welcoming sanctuary, a place of comfort. This house, although large and expensive, was cold and cheerless. I wouldn't want to live here. I didn't even like visiting.

She noticed my car. "BMW."

"Yes," I said. "An oldie but a goodie."

"Shame about the color," she said. "Black is so much classier." She slammed the door behind me.

I climbed into my car and sat there, trying to get my wits about me. I've never had such mixed feelings. Wesley seemed nice enough. But Bernice? What was her major malfunction? What was she trying to do? Why go through this process if she didn't really want a child? I remembered a woman I knew from Jazzercise, who had gotten pregnant and announced, "This baby isn't going to change my life. I'm the adult. I'm in charge."

Boy, had she ever been in for a shock! That baby had her wrapped around its tiny fingers in no time and happily so.

Maybe Bernice would come around. Maybe a child would defrost her heart.

I doubted it.

As I turned over the key in the ignition, Detweiler texted me to say he loved me. It was almost as if he knew I needed him, right then and right there. Surprisingly, when I checked the time, the message had been sent late last night. But that didn't matter, it had come when it was supposed to come. Right on the dot.

On that happy note, I swung by a Dunkin' Donuts, picked up a baker's dozen, and headed back to the store. Yes, I missed my old house in Ladue for its spaciousness and the nice lot. But I wouldn't trade one second of my life then for my life now. No way!

As I walked in the back door, a ripping sound greeted me. The store smelled like fresh plastic. Duct tape was being unrolled. Roy was helping Aunt Penny hang a heavy plastic drop cloth between the wall and our merchandise. Anya and Rebekkah held opposite ends of the sheeting as Aunt Penny fed it to Roy who had the tape in one hand.

I took a dozen photos. With each one, I grew more and more excited. Using duct tape on a scrapbook page is my idea of fun, and I couldn't wait to play with the silver tape and these shots! It would make a great "make and take" class. In fact, I got so enthralled with the idea that I almost forgot about the box of donuts, until Margit carried them from the back room into the construction zone.

"How did your visit with the Stottlemeyers go, Mom?" asked Anya, as she took a bite of a cake donut with pink icing.

"Uh, okay," I said. I was determined not to allow Bernice Stottlemeyer's negativity to spread by sharing my experience.

I allowed myself one chocolate cake donut and then went back to work on the custom album. My first task was to print out the Stottlemeyer photos.

They weren't bad, although they were stiff. Really, really stiff. The strained expressions on the couple's faces didn't help their cause.

Choosing embellishments proved an easy task, because every aspect of their home was neutral. I started with a simple brown faux leather album. For the pages themselves, I chose ivory paper, a darker khaki lettering and a scrolled corner embellishment. I took a quick photo of the elements and sent it to Bernice. She approved the colors via email. Each photo was matted in both ivory and the dark khaki. The look was elegant and expensive, although usually my albums for adoption profiles are more playful. I really regretted the lack of a nursery photo, because those are typically the most fun of all! Now that I had all the photos I needed, I finished the form I'd begun for the Stottlemeyers, scanned it, checked off the boxes for the new pictures and sent the finished paperwork to Bernice via email.

Waving a jelly-filled donut in one hand, Roy was talking to my construction crew, going over how to tear down the wall.

I didn't want to take any chances on bringing Bernice's bad vibes into this space. Especially when my daughter, aunt and friend were going to be doing dangerous work. I rummaged around in Dodie's big desk until my fingers seized upon a smudge stick. I carried it to the front of the store and lit it, letting the sweet smell of sage wander through the open area. When I thought I'd chased away the lingering Stottlemeyer cooties, I took the stick back to the bathroom and set it carefully inside an empty tin can so it couldn't start a fire.

From his accustomed spot in his glass bowl, Danforth, the red-eared slider that Rebekkah had brought to the store winked at me. He was a sweet turtle, a quiet guest who never failed to bring a smile to my face. As I watched, he dove off his rock and paddled around in the water. In honor of Dodie, I gave him an extra pinch of turtle food. Why couldn't everyone be as serene as Danforth?

After leaving the bathroom, I checked my computer for messages. "Do your job! This is what I'm paying you for!" read the note from Bernice. "Quit wasting my time sending me emails!"

"Lovely. Just lovely," I muttered.

On days like this I sorely missed the Wendy Ward Charm School, of which I am a proud graduate.

"Wendy Ward, I summon your spirit. Come and knock some sense into this boorish woman, Bernice Stottlemeyer!"

I grabbed a black candle from under the front counter and lit it. As I did, I muttered to myself. "Go away, all of you negative cootie bugs. Let me finish this project so I can get that woman out of my life."

42

$\mathcal{I}$ didn't notice when Roy left. My crew went at the job with a vengeance. After an hour and a half, the banging and clanging of hammers against drywall and concrete started to give me a headache. At noon, we all took a lunch break. Rebekkah offered to fix peanut butter and banana sandwiches on Ezekiel raisin cinnamon bread, much touted by her as being "sprouted." I wasn't sure why that was so cool, but she sure seemed gung-ho, and it tasted good to me.

After the break, the crew cleared debris while I sorted photos for Sheila's wedding album. Months earlier, I had ordered a wedding gift for them, a custom album in ivory faux leather, engraved with Sheila and Robbie's names. I was eager to fill that memory book with wonderful pages.

When it comes to putting together an album, it's all about the organization. I have a pretty good method, a sort of twist on "speed scrapbooking."

I love how all-consuming my work can be. While my construction crew worked to pull nails and sort through rubble, I explored different ways of showcasing Sheila and

Robbie's journey as a couple. The images and colors were so lovely that I could almost forget that the wedding had been marred by a murder investigation. All that was missing were Vincent's professional photos and a photo of the original five Jimmy Girls, as well as an explanation for where they'd gotten their odd nickname.

At two o'clock, Clancy came in to take my place. Usually she's scheduled from noon on, giving me half a day off, but she'd text messaged me earlier to ask if she could come in late. I knew Margit had been itching to debrief me about the Monday evening crop, but I badly needed a breath of fresh air. The weather outside was beautiful, but only for a brief while. Rain, rain and more rain were in the forecast. I really needed a chance to stick my head outside.

"Margit? Could I just take a break, please? Could we debrief when I return?" I asked. "I need to grab some fresh air and run an errand."

The lenses of her cats' eye glasses magnified her irises so that her eyes looked like twin goldfish in bowls. *"Ja,"* she said in a grumpy tone.

My crew had gone from pulling nails to cleaning up the dust and tearing off drywall by hand. Aunt Penny assured me that she would keep a watchful eye on the girls. Anya turned to smile at me. "Mom, I didn't think I could do this, but look! And it's fun. I'm stronger than I thought."

Out of the corner of my eye, I noticed the look of satisfaction on Aunt Penny's face. As a single woman who'd never married, her circumstances had forced her to be self-reliant. A firm believer in *mens sana in corpore sano* (a healthy mind in a healthy body), she often surprised me with her physical strength. Combined with her sharp mind, she would live to be one hundred.

This had been her goal: teaching the girls how strong

they were. Pretty sharp cookie, that Aunt Penny. None of us had realized this was a lesson disguised as a building project.

"I'm very, very impressed," I said. "Looks like I need to keep supplying the donuts, huh?"

Clancy joined me. "Mainly, all I see is one heck of a mess."

"You always say that about my projects. Can you keep an eye on my construction crew? I'd like to run over to Sheila's house. I've told Margit we can debrief when I get back."

"Is there a problem? With Sheila?"

"Other than an ongoing murder investigation being carried out by a man who wants Robbie's job, no. No problem at all."

"You haven't been listening to the local news, have you?" She raised an eyebrow at me as we stepped away from the dust and chaos.

"What's up? That man, Preston?"

"Prescott."

"Should be Press-con. He's held a press conference."

"Saying what?"

She glanced away from me. "Saying nothing. Implying all sorts of things."

"Such as?"

"Those unsympathetic members of the department with competing agendas are working to stonewall his progress."

"Holy guacamole," I said. "Talk about a knife in the back."

"That's how I saw it, too," she agreed. "He's suggesting that the department has become complacent. That the investigators are not as skilled as they should be. 'Cronyism' was the word he used."

"That could come back to bite him on the rear-end considering that Robbie is his brother-in-law."

"From your lips to God's ears," Clancy grinned.

43

_____

After hearing about the news conference, a trip to Sheila's house seemed imperative. I climbed into my car, a simple daily activity that was getting harder and harder given my changing shape and center of balance. I'd only just put my backside on the seat when I felt something hard under me. I stepped out of the car and stared.

Sitting on my seat was that silly toy turtle that Dodie kept in her desk.

"Listen, bub, this is my spot. I claimed it first," I said, as I scooped him up and slipped him into my purse.

I had no idea how he'd managed to make it from his home in the drawer to my driver's seat.

Was he a message from Dodie? If so, what was she telling me? Go slow? I laughed to myself. That was pretty silly stuff.

As I headed toward Sheila's house, I noticed the mature flowers in her upscale neighborhood. St. Louisans seemed to compete when it came to dressing up their yards. Witness Leighton and his freshly landscaped flowers. The old plants surrounding his house had been just fine to my way of thinking, but he hadn't been content. His weigela with its merry goblets of pink and white, his hydrangeas in bright blue and his bushes of pinkish orange honeysuckle delighted my senses and filled the air with sweet fragrance. However, he pointed out that in their maturity, they produced fewer blooms. So away they went. New varieties replaced the old.

But here in Sheila's section of town, Old Money dictated restraint. Houses were still surrounded by encampments of flowers, but the stems were sturdy with age, giving the landscaping a look of unplanned elegance.

I pulled my convertible into Sheila's driveway behind Robbie's police cruiser. With a baby coming, I'd need something else to drive, aka the dreaded Mom Car. I kept my fingers crossed we could find a car in a pretty color. Yes, it was silly of me, but despite Bernice Stottlemeyer's nasty comment, I've loved this shade of candy-apple red. On dreary days like these, it never failed to cheer me.

"Good to see you," Robbie said, as he met me at the door. "And, with a smile on your face no less. Sheila's in a foul mood. The cruise company refuses to refund our deposit or apply it to another trip. Instead of privacy with my bride, I'm living under the same roof with four postmenopausal women. This isn't how we intended to spend our first week of married life."

No, I imagined it wasn't.

"That said, they're happy enough for me to do the cooking and cleaning. I'm making steaks tonight. Sheila is hungry for raw meat. Preferably, a piece of Prescott's backside."

"At least she gets to spend quality time with her friends," I said. Just call me Little Suzy Sunshine.

"Huh. She's embarrassed about all this. They're actually

taking Prescott's demands pretty well since they'd planned to visit old haunts anyway. But Sheila, well, you know Sheila."

"Maybe this will help." I pointed to the tote bag on my arm. "I have part of your wedding album done."

He cocked his head and stared at me. "Where did you get the photos? Vincent told Prescott that his shots aren't developed yet."

"I left spots for photos from Vincent. The book starts with your early years and ends with the wedding ceremony. I'm working in reverse chronological order. Remember when I asked you for those old pictures? The black and whites? That's what I have so far, plus the candid shots I took and blank spaces. I'm just checking to make sure that Sheila likes this before I go any further. Any idea when Vincent will have your pictures done?"

"At least by the end of the week. He uses film."

"You have to be kidding me!"

"Nope. Prescott demanded that he drop off the canisters, but Vincent pointed out that it's simpler for him to process it, since he's worked with us before developing photos for the station. In the old days, we used Fox Photo. I'm not even sure they're still in business, but short of taking the film canisters to Walmart, I don't know how we'd get film developed. Not these days. Everyone uses a digital camera."

I stood there with my mouth catching flies. I couldn't believe what I was hearing. Letting anyone other than a police technician touch that film was, in my humble opinion, a big mistake. Even though I'm not well-versed in PhotoShop, I can still monkey with a picture. So, can just about anybody with a lick of sense.

"Robbie, what's to stop Vincent from altering a photo?" I asked.

"He'd have to convert it to digital to change it, wouldn't he?" The big cop rubbed his chin thoughtfully.

"No. He could use light techniques to make changes. They call it dodging and burning," I said. I knew this because those were the terms that PhotoShop used, and I had looked up where they originated.

"Yes. I see what you mean. But that would have to happen in the printing process, when he transfers the images to paper. I'll suggest that we ask him for a copy of his negatives."

I still wasn't satisfied, and my face betrayed my emotions.

"Kiki, this whole situation is out of my hands," said Robbie. "Believe me. This is not how I would have handled the investigation."

Sheila stuck her head out of the family room. "Why are the two of you still standing in the foyer?"

Robbie nodded a goodbye and took off for the small butler's pantry off of Sheila's kitchen. She'd converted it to a sort of "man cave" for him, since she'd never really used it as a place for storing extra serving pieces. This had been a big compromise for both of them. Robbie wanted her to sell her house so they could buy something together. Something much, much smaller. Sheila resisted that. She loved having one of the biggest houses in Ladue. Furthermore, the real estate market had not fully recovered in the metro St. Louis area, and she complained that they wouldn't get top dollar. I thought her priorities were all wrong. This house had been Sheila and Harry's. Of course, Robbie wanted a place free from the ghost of Sheila's first marriage.

I didn't blame him one bit.

Sheila had a lot of good qualities; however, sensitivity was not one of them.

She took her accustomed spot in a recliner, the chair that offered the most support for her still healing collar-bone. I grabbed a chair from the dining room and brought it over so I could sit next to her, because that's the easiest way to view an album. I handed her the shopping bag. The album was wrapped in tissue paper the same way we package every album that comes from Time in a Bottle. Even though the book wasn't finished, it was still a gift, so I wanted this presentation to be special.

Taking her time, she withdrew one piece of tissue after another. Finally, she opened the album. "Robbie? You should come see this."

He couldn't hear her from his spot in the pantry. I don't know why she didn't realize that, so I said, "It's okay that he isn't here. The book isn't finished. I was hoping to show you the design and get your approval. I'm missing photos of you and the Jimmy Girls from your school days. I don't have an explanation for where you came up with that nickname. Could you tell me?"

Since Robbie didn't come and join us, she flipped the book open and started looking through it. I could tell she was happy. She's not a big smiler, but the intensity of her attention told me she was pleased. That didn't surprise me. She had micro-managed every item I'd created for her wedding, and I'd recycled many of those images for this album.

Flipping through her childhood photos and a family picture of her with her parents, she paused at the blank space where I'd put a sticky note and jotted, "Jimmy Girls."

"Behind those doors in the bookcase, there's an old album. It's black." She pointed to the first bookcase in the row of built-ins. I retrieved the album for her.

"Someday soon, you need to let me scan these pages and

put them on acid-free paper. This old stuff is starting to crumble, see? That's because of the wood pulp in it. The pictures will suffer," I said.

"I'm not sure I want you to see this," she said, holding the album so that the inside was hidden from my view.

"Why?"

"I didn't like the way I looked."

"We've all changed over the years."

"No, I said I didn't like the way I looked, past tense. I'm comfortable with who I am now."

"Is this about your nose job?"

"Yes," she said, but she didn't offer to show me the photo. She kept the album on her lap, using the cover as a shield.

"Since I know about your surgery, what difference does it make?"

She glared at me. "For goodness sake, Kiki, use your head. It makes a difference, because it was embarrassing. We got our nickname—the Jimmy Girls—because of Jimmy Durante. Remember his nose? He joked about it. All five of us had huge honkers. You can't imagine the sort of teasing we endured. Day in and day out. We were young, sensitive girls, but even the teachers poked fun at us."

"Why? That doesn't make sense. CALA values kindness and civility. They make a huge deal of those virtues."

"Today they do. Back then, people thought teasing wasn't a big deal. 'Sticks and stones will break my bones, but words will never hurt me.' Remember that? If I heard that once, I heard it a million times."

"I'm sorry you had to endure that, Sheila. That must have been awful. But I still find it hard to believe. You couldn't possibly have looked that bad. Not you."

With a tiny "huh" of disgust, she thrust the album toward me. I took it from her carefully, worried about her range of motion and about the weight. I shouldn't have been.

There were only a dozen photos in that black book. Sheila had curated them, culled them down to the bare minimum. The images had faded, as I had suspected they would. The family room wasn't well lit, so I had to squint to parse my mother-in-law's features in the picture. She stood at the back of a group shot, which also made it harder to see.

When I did, I almost gasped.

Her nose had been the size of a Greyhound bus.

I've lived in apartments smaller than her nose was.

Not only was it large, it also bent to one side. The size of it totally obscured her other features. Her eyes—one of her most stunning assets—were nearly non-existent by comparison.

There are large noses that are lovely, but this wasn't one of them.

"Oh, my," I said.

"The surgery made a huge difference in my looks. My self-confidence soared." She spoke very matter-of-factly. "All of us Jimmy Girls suffered until we had our noses done."

Turning my attention to her friends, I could barely figure out who was who. Only one other woman had a nose as bad or worse than Sheila's. "Okay, I see Leah, Toby and that's Ester in the front. So, is that Miriam standing beside you in the back row?"

"Yes," said Sheila. "Poor Miriam. She was as ugly as I was."

I couldn't dispute this. The other girls sported big noses, but the shape and size of the schnozzles on Sheila and Miriam were disfiguring.

I dithered. I wasn't sure whether I should include this picture or not. While I tried to decide what to do, Sheila interrupted my thoughts. "I guess it doesn't matter now. Robbie actually met me before I had my nose done. You are welcome to take the photo, although I'd really rather have you bury it than show it off."

"What happened to Miriam?" I asked. "How did she die?"

---

44

*B*efore she could answer, Robbie stuck his head around the corner. The dark circles under his eyes reminded me of cast-off tires. "I talked with Hadcho," he said. "The situation isn't good. Prescott has named you a person of interest, Sheila, because of the invitation found in Dr. Hyman's pocket."

"But we didn't put him on the invitations list!" Sheila said.

Now Robbie stepped into the room and sank down into the chair closest to Sheila's. "Hon, we look like liars. We told Prescott that we didn't invite Dr. Hyman."

"We didn't!" Sheila puffed up like an angry barnyard hen. "I didn't. Did you, Kiki?"

"Never met the man. Like I told you earlier, I went over the list I have in my computer and his name isn't on it."

"There's only one way this could have happened. The killer or an accomplice must have put his or her invitation into an envelope and sent it to Dr. Hyman. Tell you what—ask Hadcho to check out the envelope," and with that, I opened the wedding album to the page where I had included a sample of the invitation and the matching envelope. Unhooking the page so I could pass it to Robbie, I explained, "I customized every one of those envelopes with a rubber stamp. See? That image of the two flowers intertwined? With your names under it? I had that custom-made for Sheila. Remember?" and I turned to her. "You approved it yourself. We wanted to put punch-art flowers on the envelopes. Those would have been 3-D, but the post office was going to charge extra, because the envelopes couldn't go through their machines, so we settled for the customized rubber stamp. To make each envelope, I stamped the image and then hand-colored it with markers."

"Every envelope?" Robbie sounded skeptical.

"Every envelope," I assured him. "Trust me, there's no customized envelope sent to Dr. Hyman. Can't be. No way."

He nodded slowly. "I see what you mean. How about if you explain that to Hadcho. He's not on the case, but he's still in contact with the officers who are."

"Certainly." After he handed his phone to me and clicked it onto speakerphone, I told Detective Hadcho what I'd explained to Robbie and Sheila.

Hadcho's response was a grunt, but I'm accustomed to his way of non-talk talking. "Too bad we can't go to all the guests and force a show of invitations," he said.

"Invitations and envelopes," I said. "The killer must have been sent an invitation. So, you can cross off the wait staff, the musicians, and the photographer. And the rabbi and priest. It would have to have been someone who was on the guest list. This also means the murder was premeditated. The murderer went through quite a bit of trouble to get Dr. Hyman to the event where he could be killed. That might tell you something about the weapon. It had to be portable. Easy to hide. Or something so common that no one would notice. Have you figured out what the weapon was?"

"No," said Hadcho. "The ME says it could have been a skewer, like they use for shish kabobs; a long nail, such as a ten-penny nail; a screwdriver; an icepick; an awl; a small gauge knitting needle; a small wooden dowel; and, possibly a hat pin, but not likely."

"But the ME hasn't narrowed those down?" asked Robbie. "Surely if it was a dowel or a bamboo skewer there'd be splinters. Also, there's a wide variety of circumferences in that listing. Has he decided exactly how wide the hole is that killed Dr. Hyman?"

"No. Prescott didn't think about that. The other detectives have tried to talk to him, but he's refused to listen to any suggestions. Prescott isn't exactly the sharpest fish hook in the tackle box, if you get my drift. He copied this list and told the detectives to go back to Mr. Haversham's house and look for these things. Outside. In the grass. Can you believe it?"

"That's ridiculous. He released the scene. It's not that the murderer was likely to leave a bloody awl in a flowerbed. Maybe in a trash bag. Did he search those?"

"No. Believe me, I suggested that," said Hadcho. "He's never run an investigation like this, and he's making mistakes left and right. He's so busy granting interviews about how his—your—office should be run that he's not focused on directing the efforts of the detectives. Worst of all, he doesn't listen to what anybody has to say!"

"Keep your head down, Hadcho. If he learns you've been talking with me, he'll make you pay."

"I realize that," said Hadcho. "Hey, Kiki, where can I get a copy of the right envelope? Maybe they brought in the bogus envelope and entered it into evidence. If they did, I can compare it to a copy of the bona fide item. That should make it pretty clear that you and Mrs. Holmes didn't send the doc his invite."

"Of course, I kept one. I have it at the store."

45

*A*lthough my fingers itched to text him, I didn't send any messages to Detweiler about Prescott. This was a big day for him, and he would have his hands full. After breakfast, he and Lorraine had a meeting with Erik's pediatrician. Then came lunch with the boy's kindergarten teacher. Later, they would go to the school where Erik was attending summer camp.

Not only was I eager to hear more about Erik's world, I also wanted the boy's reaction to the album I'd made. Anya had her fingers crossed that he would love the Superman insignia on the backpack and the stuffed animal she'd chosen for him—a turtle in honor of Turtle Park and Dodie.

All in due time, I told myself. But patience has never been one of my personal virtues. In fact, I think it's highly overrated. You wait too long and your ice cream will melt. Trust me on this.

I walked into Time in a Bottle, signaled to Margit that I'd be ready in ten minutes for her meeting, let Gracie out, checked on my construction crew, grabbed a bottle of cold water and sat down next to my co-worker's desk.

Shortly after she came to work at the store, Margit had carved out a makeshift space where she could keep her paperwork. She'd appropriated a blank portion of the back wall. By adding a wood-grained Formica desktop, we converted a pair of two-drawer file cabinets into a desk. Over that, we had added a cork board, with a strip of peg board along the top. Above all that we had positioned three shelves on an adjustable system. These held three-ring binders neatly labeled with such information as suppliers, outstanding orders, special orders and so on. The weekly work schedule was in a plastic sleeve, pinned to the corkboard in a spot that never varied.

At first, the corkboard was bare except for the occasional piece of paper that needed to be filed. But as Margit became more settled, she added postcards of Germany, a pattern to a knit sweater she liked, and a lovely photo of her mother in her youth. When Margit pinned anything to the cork, she did so at exacting right angles, which tickled me to no end. Since she liked labels so much, for her birthday I bought papier-mâché letters that spelled out her name. These I collaged with scraps of paper in her favorite colors of green, yellow and red. She loved my gift, and her name marched proudly across the top of the corkboard.

A three-tiered in box on the desktop proper was labeled with incoming, pending and to be mailed. Since she didn't have a supplies drawer, I'd grouped cans, collaged them with her favorite colors, and hot glued them to an old lazy Susan. In these, she kept scissors, a stapler, a ruler, a magnifying glass, pens and pencils. Along the bottom edge of her corkboard, she'd added a strip of clear pockets cut from a shoe bag. In these pockets, she'd put stamps, coupons, menus and paperclips.

In short, her workspace was a sacred spot dedicated to

the muse of organization. As I pulled up my chair, I couldn't help but smile about how precise Margit was. I liked that about her. I would never be so tidy, but after working with her, I did find myself aspiring to a higher level of neatness. Whereas Clancy had become my fashion icon, Margit was my organizational skills mentor. Both women brought much more than friendship to my life.

From her in-box, Margit withdrew a debriefing form that I'd been filling out for our Monday night crops. If we didn't have a form for a job, Margit invented one.

To my comments, she had added a collated version of the evaluation forms. We always asked customers to rate the "make-and-take" on a variety of variables. Now I handed over a sample of the project, a handout and a cost breakdown.

Reviewing the form, Margit told me that we'd had three newbie customers who had come to the class solely for card making ideas. Calculating our costs, including my time and supplies, she proudly confirmed the profitability of the event. As a follow up, she would email the newbies and offer them a coupon for their next store visit. She also showed me the sales tally for the event. We deducted the cost of supplies that I had "gifted" to Cara, a deduction we agreed was totally worthwhile. I noted any glitches, including the fact we should have made more card making kits for our customers. Margit suggested that based on sales I should create an entire line of these.

By the time we had finished our debriefing, we had decided that particular "make-and-take" was worth repeating. Some projects weren't. Although at first it seemed just nit-picky, I'd come to realize how valuable Margit's assessments were. Thanks to Margit's careful analysis, our profitability had increased. Sometimes, I grew tired of justifying absolutely everything, but the benefits outweighed the hassle. Adding Cara Mia to our team for the small net cost of supplies proved another wise move. Before she had agreed to work with us, I had wasted hours coordinating what food we'd serve. Scrapbookers can't crop without food! It's as necessary as adhesive.

Now that Cara handled that portion of our crops, I was freed up to do what I do best...being creative.

After checking on my construction crew's progress, I went back to work on Sheila's album. Understanding Sheila's concerns about her looks, I added the old Jimmy Girls photo on a separate page under a flap. That way it was there, but not there. Sheila could be honest about her nose job if she so desired, but casual viewers wouldn't see a picture that embarrassed her. I still didn't know why Miriam had died. If it turned out to be something like breast cancer, I might want to make a page with a pink ribbon on it to memorialize her. I jotted a reminder to myself and stuck it inside the appropriate hanging folder.

A glance at the clock told me it was time to shift gears. I worked on the make-and-take for our Wednesday crop, a flip-flop album. This project was cute-as-all-get-out, even if I do say so myself.

Using fun foam (sheets of flat, brightly colored foam for crafters), I had created a flip-flop, the ubiquitous footwear of summer. The sole of the sandal formed the back cover of the album. Using two brightly colored rings, I added a dozen more pages inside. The resulting project fit all my high standards, those attributes my croppers have come to know and love: fun, funky and adorable!

As Margit and Clancy waited on customers and answered never ending questions about our construction project, I "kitted" or put together the supplies so that each of our guests could make a cute flip-flop album of her own.

"How many kits have you made?" asked Margit, standing next to my shoulder.

"Fifteen."

"We only have twelve guests coming to our crop tomorrow. The adoptive parents' crop," she reminded me.

"That's true, but we always sell extras. Besides, I wanted to make one for Erik. This will be his first summer with us."

"How is he? Have you heard anything? Seen any photos?"

"No," I admitted with a sigh. "Not yet. I have to keep reminding myself about the time difference. I don't mind telling you how nervous I am. What if he doesn't like us? What if he can't make the adjustment? How do you win the heart of a five-year-old boy?"

Margit's eyes softened as she put a gentle hand on my shoulder. "By being yourself, Kiki. You should know that by now."

46

---

*W*hen my phone rang, I was sure it was Detweiler. I scooped it up and answered, "Hello, my love!"

"Your fault!" screamed my mother. "Tell them to let me go! Right now!"

"Mom? Is that you? Where are you?"

"The county jail!" and she hung up abruptly.

My hands shook as I dialed my sister. She didn't answer. I grabbed my purse and ran to the back room. "Margit? You have to take over. I have an emergency with my mother!"

I dropped my keys twice as I raced to my car. When I got inside, I stopped myself. If I didn't calm down, I would have an accident. I forced myself to breathe deeply before I turned over the engine. Meanwhile, I called Amanda one more time.

When she answered, I barreled right over her greeting. "What's up with Mom? Is she okay?"

"What do you mean? I dropped her off at the senior center."

"She's at the county jail!"

"You're kidding."

Since Amanda works for a law firm, she promised to find a co-worker who could check out the situation—and then she'd get right back to me. Meanwhile, I hung up and concentrated on driving toward the county jail.

All sorts of images flitted through my head. One in particular spooked me. I phoned Aunt Penny and asked, "Where's your gun?"

"In my purse. Why?"

"Can't talk now. Are you sure?"

"Yes. Are we in danger?"

"No." I hung up.

Then I called Robbie. He, of course, had no idea what was happening with my mother, but he'd make a few calls and get back to me. As I hung up from talking with him, Amanda's call came through. She sounded breathless as she said, "They're arresting Mom for Dr. Hyman's murder. She had the murder weapon on her."

"But that's ridiculous! She doesn't even know the man."

"Oh, yes, she does!"

"What?"

"He's the guy who took the pre-cancerous spot off her face. He's got some sort of agreement with the senior center that he'll do pre-cancer screenings and treat seniors at a reduced fee."

I pulled into heavy traffic on 40. We were moving at the speed of toothpaste straight from the tube. "So? That's hardly a motive."

"She got mad at him."

"What?" I'd culled my vocabulary down to a single word.

"She asked him to do a facelift on her. At a reduced price. She called it professional courtesy."

"But that's a price that professionals offer each other."

"She doesn't know that. As far as she's concerned, she was a professional performer, and he should extend her the price."

I groaned. "Let me guess. He said no, and she went into one of her hissy fits."

"You've got it. They called me from the senior center and asked me to come get her. She was given a stern warning to either behave or be gone."

"And now he's dead."

---

47

*R*obbie launched right into what he'd learned: "An anonymous call came in to the precinct. The caller said that your mother had the murder weapon in her purse. An officer was dispatched to the senior center, although for the life of me, I can't explain why. An anonymous call like that is pretty flimsy stuff. Before talking to your mother, the officer interviewed the staff and heard all about her screaming attack on Dr. Hyman."

I briefly considered pulling off to the side of 40 because my teeth were chattering, and I was shaking that badly. A light rain was falling, but drivers weren't making an adjustment in their speed. Cars whizzed past me.

The smell of gas and diesel was making me sick. How on earth had my mother gotten into such a pickle? My stomach roiled. I worried that I'd puke right there in my car. At the same time, a portion of my mind stepped away, became very unattached, as I realized, "She wouldn't be this concerned about you! Don't worry yourself sick over her. Calm down and deal with this. She couldn't have killed Hyman. She's a whack job, but she's not a murderer."

I told Robbie what I was thinking.

"Right. Unfortunately, they found a small screwdriver in her purse. There's blood on it."

"But are they sure it's the murder weapon? Is it Dr. Hyman's blood type?"

"They're testing it. As usual, the labs are up to their eyeballs, so there's a wait."

Which meant it might take a while to clear my mother. "But this doesn't make any sense! How would she have subdued the doctor?"

"A stun gun. Remember?"

"Did they search her for that?"

"No, but they are getting a warrant as we speak."

"Don't they think it a wee bit suspicious that there'd be a call out-of-the-blue, and wham, my mother has means and motive? Did anyone see her interacting with Dr. Hyman? Did they check her alibi? I bet she was with Amanda and Aunt Penny the whole time."

"I'll get on it," he said. "But Kiki, my options here are limited. You know that. Prescott is under pressure to produce results. Even if he can't make this stick, he'll be more than happy to throw your mother under the bus. That way he can have a triumphant press conference and be a hero. You're smart enough to see what's what here."

"Yes," I said. "Yes, I can."

Amanda beeped through. I took her call and told her what I'd learned from Robbie.

"One of my co-workers will go with me to the jail," she said. "There's no way they can hold Mom. I can provide an alibi. Aunt Penny can, too. My colleague and I will discuss whether to allow them to search the house."

"You know better than that!" I said. "If someone was sharp enough to call and setup Mom, they'll just as easily have planted a stun gun. It doesn't even have to be in the house. It could be on the grounds."

"I know all that. I said that my colleague and I would discuss it. Where are you?"

"Um, Highway 40 at Big Bend."

"Turn around and go back to your store."

"Why? She called me. She's expecting me." I didn't add, "And she blames me."

"Because we're two blocks from the jail right now. There's no need for you to be here, too. I've got this under control."

"But—"

"Kiki, if you are there, she'll only make a bigger scene and blame you. We both know how she operates. Go back to your job and leave this to me."

Although I hated to admit it, Amanda was right. I took the exit at Big Bend and drove the back way to Ted Drewes. I parked my car and ran through the rain to the front window where I placed my order for the biggest Terra Mizzou concrete they sold. Slogging through the rain, I climbed back into my car and took my time spooning up the ice cream.

I loved how the pistachio nuts crunched. I savored the caramel. Every spoonful thrilled me.

When my cup was empty, I drove back to the store.

48

$\mathcal{B}$ack at Time in a Bottle, I toweled off, wiped the chocolate smears from my mouth and called a quick meeting with everyone to let them know what had happened. I didn't really need to include Rebekkah, but it seemed silly to leave her out. In truth, I only wanted to go over the bad news once, and I needed to warn everyone that reporters might descend on the store. They should be very, very cautious about what they shared.

"I told Lucia that her temper was going to land her in hot water." Aunt Penny shook her head. "Speaking of water, you're dripping wet."

"No kidding?" I said, as I used a paper towel on my hair. "Amanda's on top of the situation. She's got an attorney with her. They'll have Mom out in no time, I bet. But now all of you know what's up—and how desperate Prescott is. Just realize that representatives of the media might be here. If they do, say nothing. Also, don't talk about this to the customers. I mean, that goes without saying."

"You're shaking," said Rebekkah. "You okay? Or just cold?"

"I'm upset."

"I think there's chamomile tea by the microwave. Let me make you a cup," Rebekkah offered.

Anya went back to chipping away at the concrete blocks. My mother is not very nice to my daughter, but Anya knows I still expect her to be respectful toward her grandmother.

That doesn't mean Anya has to like Mom.

I don't like Mom.

Besides Aunt Penny, who does?

Around half past four, my construction crew started to pack it in for a day. They'd filled two big black plastic bags with pieces of drywall, insulation and dust.

"Not much more to do but bang this down," said Aunt Penny.

"Good," I replied. They'd kept to their promise not to hammer and make noise after lunch, but I still found their presence distracting. Every customer who walked through our door asked a million questions about the work. The wall was morphing into the Black Hole of Calcutta, vacuuming up every particle of energy usually reserved for creative endeavors.

"What happens next?" I asked, as I stared at the broken bits of concrete and wood.

"Roy will be here first thing tomorrow to check out what we're doing. He's got the plans. He's ordered the lumber so we can frame in the walls of your new hallway. Then the drywall can be attached."

I picked a piece of drywall paper off her tee shirt. "How are the girls doing?"

"They're both good workers and seem to enjoy this," she said. "There's nothing like taking a hammer to a wall to vent your frustrations. You want a turn?"

"No. The chamomile tea worked wonders for me."

Once they had most of the mess cleaned up, Anya took Gracie out for a piddle. We walked to our cars. Out of force of habit, I waited to see that Rebekkah's car started. This was a safety tip Detweiler had drummed into all of us. "Don't just drive off. What if you leave, and your friend is sitting there in the lot? She'd have to go back into the store alone or sit alone in her car until help comes."

Sure enough, he'd been right. Twice now Margit has left on her headlights, draining her battery. This time, it was Rebekkah's car that didn't start. Fortunately, Margit was leaving the store as Rebekkah struggled to get the engine to take hold. I stuck my head out my window and yelled to her.

"Could you do me a favor and take Aunt Penny home? That way I can take Rebekkah home. While I'm there, I'll stop in and see Horace. Just to check on him. I'll ask if there is anything I can do."

"*Ja,* I had been meaning to show your aunt my collection of Hummels. Penny? Would you like to have dinner with me at my house before I take you home?" asked Margit.

"Sounds super!" Aunt Penny hopped out of my car and into Margit's.

"Either my battery is dead or my starter needs to be replaced," said Rebekkah. "Dad is usually right on top of the car problems, but..." She didn't have to say anymore.

"Anya, honey? Why don't I drop you and Gracie off at home? I know you're tired. You need a shower, and the cats will want to be fed again."

As I drove to Webster Groves, Rebekkah and Anya talked happily about their progress. Clearly, the girls were enjoying themselves, but both were beyond tired. Neither had believed herself up to the demands of knocking down a wall, so their prowess surprised them. The prospect of framing in a new hallway thrilled them. Not only was Aunt

Penny saving me money, but she'd found a way to keep both young women busy, involved and happy.

At our house, I opened the back door and did a walk through to assure myself that Anya and Gracie were safe. Giving my daughter a quick kiss, I headed back to my car. Of course, I locked the house up as I left.

Rebekkah had to guide me to her house because I'd only visited there twice for errands and once to sit *shiva*. The Goldfaders lived in a neighborhood that had originally been part of a vast Spanish land grant given in 1798. All the homes looked similar, row after row of brick bungalows with a sort of gingerbread appeal. The Goldfaders' home had been built in the 1930s, and Dodie loved its beautiful molding and hard wood floors. The last time I'd visited, a neat row of marigolds marched along the sidewalk while red geraniums bloomed in pots on the stoop.

Today, the house shouldered the weight of Dodie's passing. The place sagged with sadness. The awning over the front door listed to one side. The mailbox rested crookedly alongside the screen door. The welcome mat was worn down and dirty.

I was struck anew by how much the world missed my friend Dodie.

A big knot formed in my throat as Rebekkah turned the key in the front door. When it swung open, a bad smell assailed me. I nearly gagged on the scent of dirty hair, garbage and funky body odor.

49

Rebekkah led the way, calling out as she moved deeper into the house. "Dad? Dad? I'm here with Kiki. My car wouldn't start. She gave me a ride home."

The living room was dark and the shades were drawn. It was hard to see.

Horace shuffled out of a hallway to greet us. On his feet were worn house slippers lined with sheep skin. He wore a thin seersucker shirt, buttoned crookedly. He'd hiked his britches high up under his shirt, presumably with a belt. Gray stubble gave his face the appearance of smeared dirt. His eyes were crusty with sleep.

Dodie would have been appalled at the sight of him.

I sure was.

Horace had always looked dapper, especially when compared to his wife. They'd made such an interesting couple, visually dissimilar but totally synchronized when it came to their intellect and emotions. What a pair of lovebirds! But the man before me was a shadow of his former self. His face was gaunt and drawn. His hair was greasy and sticking out every which way.

What does a lovebird do when its mate dies?

I shuddered to think. But the answer stood right there in front of me. The man was lost. Totally adrift on life's rolling seas.

"Dad? When was the last time you ate?" Rebekkah tugged at his sleeve.

"Don't know." He stared past her.

"Have you showered?" Rebekkah asked.

I could have answered that.

"Rebekkah?" I said and beckoned her to my side. "I think you need to get him to a doctor. He looks just awful!"

"I think so, too," she said. "I keep thinking he'll snap out of it, but instead, he's getting worse and worse." She turned to her father.

"Dad, did Rabbi Sarah drop by? To talk with you about missing Mom?"

Horace simply shuffled over to a recliner and stared out into space. "Dodie?" he asked in a hopeful way.

Despite the fact that Rebekkah had moved home to help her dad, the room was littered with newspapers and dirty plates. Clearly, this was beyond what she could manage. Horace needed more than Rebekkah could provide. Especially when Rebekkah wasn't her energetic self either.

"Horace?" I spoke to him gently. He didn't answer. I walked over to him. He didn't even turn to look at me. Very gently I plucked at the back of his hand. As I suspected the skin tented and stayed there, a sure sign of dehydration.

I'd made three promises to Dodie: 1.) Keep the store open. 2.) Take care of Rebekkah. 3.) Check on Horace.

No, I actually made four. She had asked, "Would you pray for me? I hope I'll go quickly without a lot of pain."

Recalling my commitments, I made an executive decision. "Rebekkah, help me get your father into my car. We're taking him to the hospital."

50

I dropped Horace and Rebekkah off at the Emergency Room entrance so I could go park. We'd gotten lucky with the timing. No one was in line in front of us. While they did intake on Horace, I called my sister. I quickly explained where I was, in case my call was interrupted by news from a doctor.

"Mom's home," said Amanda. "She's fine. We can talk later. Sounds like you have your hands full."

Rebekkah and I settled in for a long wait, but the physician actually came out quickly. Horace was, indeed, severely dehydrated. As a result, his other levels were off. They wanted to keep him overnight and run tests on him. They suspected an arrhythmia of his heart and possibly malnutrition, but they were confident he'd be released the next day. I mentioned that he had recently lost his wife. "He seems severely depressed to me."

The doctor asked Rebekkah a few questions about her dad. "I'd like to have him talk to a psychiatrist before he leaves. Your father might need to be on anti-depressants. Is he sleeping well? Regular hours?"

"No. I find him wandering the house at all hours of the night," said Rebekkah.

"Then we definitely need to get him checked over," said the doctor. "Your insurance policy is pretty good. I say we should keep him, check him over thoroughly, let a psychiatrist talk to him, and get him re-hydrated before we let him go."

After the doctor left, I asked Rebekkah if she'd like to spend the night at our house.

"Could I? I don't like going home. It's a mess there. I've tried to keep up, but..."

"It's more than you can handle by yourself," I said. "Don't forget, you've lost someone, too. I doubt that you have a lot of extra energy, especially in your parents' house. You're always a child in your parents' house."

I picked up a bucket of KFC so we'd have something to eat. I couldn't remember the last time that I'd let the Colonel do the cooking. After I pulled away from the drive-up window, I realized that I'd chosen the red and white bucket for totally irrational reasons. KFC always reminded me of my long-deceased grandmother and summers at the beach. Some part of my psyche wanted to be a kid again, sitting next to Nana on a park bench with the rough boardwalk under our feet and the sunshine beating down on my head.

I was tired of responsibility, and there was more of it on the horizon.

Tired of the drizzle, too.

Mainly I was just plain old tired and hungry. Life always improves on a full tummy.

I keenly missed Detweiler.

While we idled at a stop sign, I reached for my cell phone and called Detweiler. His phone went immediately to voice mail. Doing a quick calculation in my head, I realized I'd called at dinnertime. Given that a five-year old get pretty cranky when they haven't eaten, I reasonably assumed that Erik and Detweiler were having a meal together. In sunny California. By a beach.

Sigh.

Rebekkah leaned her head against the window. A soft snoring noise came from her side of the car. Poor kid. She was mentally and physically exhausted.

Heavy-bellied clouds dragged themselves in front of the setting sun. The sky was unusually dark for this time of year. I clicked my car radio to the weather channel, where the announcer suggested a nightlong siege of thunderstorms, possibly spawning tornadoes. The electricity in the air suggested their predictions were not only right, but imminent.

As soon as I got home, I would force Gracie outside to do her business. She hates being outside when it's raining—and thunder leaves her quaking in her black boots.

The traffic was jammed on 40, so I took advantage of the lull and punched in Mert's number. I missed our friendship terribly. Seeing Dodie's house reminded me how empty my life would be without friends. Mert had been my friend longer than anyone else in St. Louis. Sure, she was mad at me, but she had to get over it, didn't she? Maybe she was waiting for me to call.

The phone rolled over into voice mail.

"Mert? This is Kiki. I thought you might like to know that Horace is in the hospital overnight for observation. He's, um, in pretty rough shape. The house could use a good cleaning. Anyway, I hope you are well—and that Johnny is getting better."

Since Rebekkah didn't stir, I knew she was still asleep.

No one could see the tears that ran down my face. I cried for Dodie and for the loss of Mert's friendship. I cried for Detweiler, who'd been tricked by Gina. I cried for Sheila and Robbie because they couldn't go on their cruise. And finally, I cried for myself because I was plumb worn out and lonely. I was tired of lurching from one crisis to another.

I missed Detweiler. I dialed him again, but he didn't answer. I dialed Amanda, so she could fill me in on the situation with Mom. She didn't answer. I called Sheila, and no one picked up the phone.

It was one of those moments when you wonder if everyone you love has left the building without telling you.

To make myself feel better, I ripped the top off the bucket of chicken and pinched the breading from the first piece my fingertips touched. Then, systematically, I picked the piece clean.

As I drove down 40, stuffing my face with eleven herbs and spices, I repeated my new mantra: "It's going to be all right."

But I sure wasn't sure it would be.

Not at all.

51

Tuesday/Three days after the wedding...
Suburban Los Angeles, California

*D*etweiler waited on the sidewalk outside the florist's shop until Orson pulled up in the Escalade. When the driver put on his flashers, Detweiler hopped back into the car. Lorraine glanced at Detweiler's purchase. She was pleased by the bundle of carnations, Gerber daisies and baby's breath.

"Lovely," she said. Her hands picked at the fringe on her wrap as she watched the scenery roll by.

Orson drove through a clog of traffic before turning at a sign marking a cemetery. A winding road took them to a large marble marker that bore the name LAUBER. Two jagged rectangles cut in the sod suggested recently dug graves.

"Would you like to get out?" Detweiler asked Lorraine.

"Yes, please," she said, in a shaky voice.

Detweiler hopped out with flowers in hand, ran around to her side and helped her get her balance on the running board. Once she was standing on the asphalt, he offered her his arm. She leaned heavily into him, picking her way over the rough terrain.

"I'm having a bit of a flare up," she said. "MS is such a spoil sport!"

"Take your time," he answered. What irony. The malady that limited her life broadened his by offering him a chance at fatherhood.

"Sorry to be so slow."

"You are doing fine. Is this too much for you?" Detweiler had a good hold on her arm. He could tell by the way she'd pitched forward that she didn't have much muscle control.

"No. I'll be all right. Fortunately, the gravesite is nearby."

Detweiler concentrated on keeping her from taking a tumble. There was no way she could keep up with an active little boy. None. She would never be able to run with Erik, to grab him and swing him in the air.

In the restaurant, she had seemed fine. At least at first. But now, he realized why she had wanted to be seated before he arrived. How cleverly she had covered up the full extent of her disability!

Well, she had her pride. He couldn't blame her for that.

Three spaces for Lauber family members, including a spot for Lorraine. She pointed to the bare spots on the stones. "The brass plates are missing because I'm having Van and Gina's vital details added. They aren't done yet. Gina will be on our far left, then Van, and finally there's a space reserved for me."

Detweiler nodded. He had suspected as much. "I'd like to put these flowers down, but I don't want to let you go."

"Don't worry. I'll grip this headstone," she said, as she reached out for a gray marble spire.

While she watched through teary eyes, Detweiler squatted and set two bouquets side-by-side on the grass.

"Two?" she asked.

"Your brother was kind to Erik and to Gina. Of course, I never met him, but it seemed like a small way to say thanks," Detweiler explained. "If you can think of something more substantial, please let me know."

"What you can do for Van," she said, stretching forward to slip her arm through Detweiler's as he came back to her, "is to raise Erik. He loved the boy. I love him, too. Just so we are clear on this, Gina never said a cross word about you. She had nothing but praise. She was careful to explain that it was the situation in Central Illinois that caused her to run away, not you personally. Van told her she should tell you about Erik, but she refused. It was the source of their greatest conflict. In a strange way, I think he'd be happy about this resolution. But you must never, ever wonder whether Van loved the boy, because he did. So do I."

She looked away before brushing tears from her eyes. "And of course, you must only take him with you if you are confident that you really want him. We all owe Erik that. I hope you'll come to love him."

Detweiler didn't trust himself to talk.

52

*N*othing prepared Detweiler for his first look at Gina's son. One glance at the face with its oval shape just like hers, and his heart twisted in pain. He tried to conceal the gasp that escaped his lips, but he knew he'd failed. Lorraine carefully avoided the cop's eyes, and for that he was grateful.

They stood outside a viewing window, peering in at the kids. Detweiler was thankful for the one-way glass. His heart felt too big for his chest, as he watched that small version of Gina, a boy totally focused on a miniature train set. The child's loose auburn curls with red highlights brushed his collar, exposing a slender and vulnerable throat. Some distraction among the kids caused Erik to turn toward the window. When he did, Detweiler noted the boy's chocolate-colored eyes. And again, he thought of Gina.

Detweiler excused himself and hurried down a hallway, past a line of child-sized coat hooks. Once assured of privacy in a men's room stall, he clenched and unclenched his fists in frustration.

Why? How could everything with Gina have gone so wrong?

Why was he feeling emotions he thought no longer existed?

How could she have done this to him? To the boy? To Trevon?

Letting the stall door slam behind him, Detweiler washed his hands repeatedly, as if the act itself could rinse away his disappointment.

"Why did you do it, Gina?" he muttered, as the hand dryer blew its noisy, hot air on his skin. But, in truth, he knew the reason.

Gina had been wildly beautiful, and he'd been the quarterback on his high school football team. Sure, they lost more games than they'd won, but still, the experience had taught him the awesome power of being the center of attention. She'd barely spoken to him until that first home game. From then on, they were an item, despite the fact that her parents did everything possible to keep them apart. Gina's parents were older. They'd adopted her late in life and tended to be overly involved. Of course, she responded to their over-involvement by rebelling. Detweiler was part of her personal war of independence.

Her family had moved from Chicago to a small town in southwest Illinois, so her father could teach at Southern Illinois University. From the start, Gina hated it. She missed big city living, the hustle and bustle of crowds and mostly the anonymity. With her flaming red hair and big brown eyes, she was a head-turner. Yes, she could milk her looks to advantage, but she hated the cat-calls and whistles. Unlike many girls who hadn't blossomed, she was uniquely mature-looking, often mistaken for much older than seventeen. But she was incredibly insecure and often acted distant rather than affectionate. Sometimes Detweiler wondered if she really did love him, even though she said she did.

Even her best friends agreed that Gina had a habit of holding people at arms' length.

Detweiler's mother had noticed that coolness beneath the surface. She never blamed Gina or warned her son away, but she'd made mention of it. "She can't give what she doesn't have to give," Thelma Detweiler had said.

He started talking about marriage with Gina, mainly because he didn't want to lose her. When she mentioned the idea to her parents, they blew up with rejection. That only encouraged her to move at a faster speed. Gina convinced Detweiler to elope with her the week after their high school graduation. His parents did what they could to help the young couple. Hers disinherited her.

The young couple had been blissfully happy the first two months of their marriage, even though they lived in a tiny apartment filled with cast-off furnishings. They had enjoyed their new-found freedom and each other.

But soon Gina began to complain about the hours he worked. Detweiler had taken a job bagging groceries, eagerly accepting any overtime he was offered. He'd won an athletic scholarship to school, where he planned to get a degree in criminology, but given their expenses, going to school full time wasn't an option. So, he'd looked into joining the police academy and been put on a waiting list. When a spot there opened, he dropped out of college and took it—Gina had a meltdown.

Nothing prepared him for how upset she was, even when he reminded her that they'd discussed his plan.

"I can go through the academy now and return to school

later," he said. "Law enforcement officials have good benefits. We can start a family."

"I don't want to live here in Southern Illinois! Now we're stuck!" she screamed as she threw dishes. Fortunately, the plastic dinnerware bounced right off the walls.

"I can get a job somewhere else after I get through the academy," he explained. "But right now, this is what we can afford."

No matter how he explained it to her, she refused to accept the reality of their situation. Time after time, she complained that he should apply to other schools, seek out other scholarships.

"But we don't have the money for a first and last deposit on another apartment," he explained. "Besides, my parents are helping us by bringing over groceries and leftovers. We'd starve without them!"

When he suggested that she, Gina, might want to get a job, she went ballistic, slamming their bedroom door so hard that the frame popped free from the drywall and clattered to the floor. Rather than respond to her rants in the other room, he listened to a baseball game.

Detweiler was bewildered. He thought they'd agreed on a course of action. He thought Gina knew they'd have to scrimp and save at first. He thought marriage was a partnership.

Gina saw things differently.

He had felt her pulling away, but he never suspected her of cheating on him. She seemed to have come to grips with his career choice. She had a few girlfriends she liked to party with, and he didn't begrudge her the money for going out for a few beers.

After a while, Gina settled down. Although she didn't cook, she did keep the small apartment clean. They fell into a routine. When he wasn't taking classes at the police academy, he was at the check-out counter, bagging groceries. At night, after she went to bed, he studied and did his homework. Sure, they didn't have a lot to discuss, but he never realized she was so unhappy.

And he never guessed that she was having an affair with Trevon.

An older officer. An instructor at the academy. A man Chad considered a mentor. A guy that he'd invited to the apartment for chili and beer while the Rams played football one Sunday afternoon.

Trevon had repaid the favor by having an affair with Chad Detweiler's wife.

Trevon was the father of the little boy in the next room. But Gina was Erik's mother. Detweiler felt the tug and pull of opposing feelings.

Detweiler walked out of the men's room, back down the hallway, and stopped to stare at the boy on the other side of the window. The child who wasn't his son.

He wasn't sure he could do this.

Until Erik looked his way and smiled.

53

Same day...
An office building in downtown Los Angeles, California

Thornton stared out the window of his corner office. Twenty-five stories below, the streets teamed with people, most of them insignificant. They were little more than ants crowding around the anthill, unaware of the futility of their meager lives. Wearing their cheap, ill-fitting clothing, and carrying plastic satchels instead of real leather briefcases. They probably didn't have two pennies to rub together.

Thornton enjoyed his own importance. Yes, it was a personal failing, and he knew it. Right now, he had his partner, Steve Quinton hanging on his every word. And he enjoyed that. So, he spoke very slowly and deliberately.

"According to Lorraine Lauber, Detective Detweiler seems to be a man of above average intelligence. Like many in his chosen field, he carefully cloaks his expressions, making him a bit of an enigma. He's tall, muscular and seemingly healthy. Miss Lauber believes that most women would find him attractive. She certainly does," Thornton stared out the window at the cerulean sky and powder puff clouds. Another perfect California day.

"But did she tell you if he asked about the money? You're sure he didn't want to know who died first?" Quinton asked, as he adjusted his silk tie, a nervous habit of longstanding.

"No, he didn't."

Below them, rush hour had begun. What a curiously inaccurate term for the late afternoon and early morning crush of people struggling to get home. If you didn't have a driver in LA, the traffic ate up far too many productive hours. Billable hours. Driving oneself was a false economy. But he wasn't about to tell Quinton that. Quinton's short-sighted behavior had allowed Thornton to masterfully gain the upper hand. On paper they were partners, but in reality, Quinton worked for Thornton. He just wasn't smart enough to realize it. Not yet.

"But you specifically confirmed that with Lorraine? He didn't ask about the sequence of death?"

"I asked, and she confirmed. Money was only mentioned in the most fleeting of terms. The cop admitted his financial limitations. She promised to press him further. To ask more questions."

"But he knows! He would have overheard!"

Thornton sighed. "No, he didn't. Miss Lauber and I spoke while the detective was visiting with the boy's camp counselors. She called me from the car. The detective was still in the building."

"So, he hasn't said a thing about money? Nothing at all?" Quinton fidgeted with his cufflinks, yet another sign he was succumbing to a bad case of nerves.

He sighed and steepled his fingers. "He knows that Mrs. Lauber had a small amount of money set aside for her son."

"Miniscule. Not even small," said Quinton.

Thornton let his long, thin fingers flutter to signify his distaste. "Miniscule to you or me, but significant to a civil servant. To return to my point, Detective Detweiler had no questions about the money. None. He hasn't asked if the boy stands to inherit anything from Van Lauber. Perhaps, he didn't expect Lauber to give an illegitimate child anything more than a roof over his head and a pat on the back. Who would?"

"But we need to know for sure," grumbled Quinton, as he shifted his large bulk. "Is someone keeping an eye on him? Watching where he goes? With whom he talks?"

"What do you take me for, a fool?" Thornton huffed.

Quinton's cheeks turned bright red.

"What have you learned about his girlfriend? The little woman back home?" Quinton fiddled with his belt buckle. It was cutting into his large gut.

"Detective Detweiler's partner is barefoot, broke and pregnant. A total loser. He's just a hick cop, and she's his hillbilly girlfriend. A Midwestern love story. Nothing to worry about. Not for us at least. Erik is leaving a life of wealth and opportunity to go to....that."

54

Very late Tuesday night/ Three days after the wedding...
Kiki's house in Webster Groves, Missouri

*C*arrying the bucket of fried chicken under one arm,
I let myself and Rebekkah into the house. She was
groggy from her nap in my car.

"Anya? Honey?"

No answer.

I panicked, only to discover that my daughter had fallen
asleep in her bed with Martin draped over her shoulder, in
that loose-limbed way only a cat can rest. Seymour curled
up in the nook behind her knees. Gracie guarded her slum-
bering friends by planting herself in the middle of the
bedroom floor. Her uncropped ears perked up when I
opened the door. She recognizes the sound of my car, so my
entrances don't make much of a splash unless I'm with
Detweiler, who is the love of her life. Then she's up and at
the back door in a flash so she can nuzzle him.

However, if I'd been an intruder, I'd have been dead. She doesn't bark before she launches herself. When a 130-lb. Great Dane flies at you, you're going down. On the way to the floor, a great dane would snap your neck. Quiet, deadly and effective.

Satisfied that my daughter was out for the night, I made up the sofa for Rebekkah while she showered. When she wandered out of the bathroom wearing an oversized tee-shirt, I found two pieces of chicken I had missed, batter still intact, and offered them to her on a plate. All she ate was a drumstick, some mashed potato and a scoop of coleslaw. Then she ambled over to the couch and fell asleep.

"Nice not to worry about Dad," she said, before she zonked with a capital Z.

I briefly considered waking Anya so she could eat, but I learned a long time ago to let sleeping children dream. Both girls were tuckered out by the hard, physical labor of breaking down my wall.

I phoned Amanda.

"Mom's home. They had nothing on her because I presented an alibi. Aunt Penny can vouch for her, too," said my sister. "Yes, there's blood on the screwdriver, and it was found in Mom's purse, but I'm not sure they have the murder weapon. Obviously, it was a setup. Anyway, we can talk about it later. I'm bushed. I bet you are, too."

"It's just you and me, Colonel Sanders," I said to the cartoon image of the Kentucky colonel. Grabbing the plastic dinnerware, I dug a chunk out of a crispy breast. Once I had that in my mouth, I mixed the coleslaw with a dollop of mashed potatoes. Super yum.

Twenty minutes later, my stomach was full. Detweiler still hadn't called. I still had no idea what Erik looked like, or how Detweiler's day had gone. After putting the leftovers away, I took a shower and changed into a pair of drawstring pants and a loose top. To relax after a long day, I turn to Zentangle to unwind and clear my head, so I brought out my supplies and worked on a new design.

Time passed quickly. I was totally absorbed in the process when my phone rang. A warm chuckle from Detweiler released the last of the tension in my shoulders. "Babe? Did I wake you?"

"No! I was tangling. You know how I get. Better yet, how're you? How's Erik? Tell me everything!"

Delivering the CliffsNotes version of his day, he hit the high points. Men are like that. Totally unsatisfying in their brevity. I was hungry for more. "What's he like?"

"He's shy. Very sweet. He loves trucks and dinosaurs and Superman."

"Let me guess," I said. "You're totally head-over-heels in love with the child."

Again, he chuckled. "Am I that transparent? Can you see my grin through the phone?"

"Did he take to you?"

"I think it was the gun. He noticed that right off the bat. You can imagine how thrilling my firearm was for a little guy. Good thing I've installed that gun safe at your house."

"Yeah. That's not surprising." I remembered Bonnie saying at a crop that even though she didn't allow her son, Felix to have toy guns, he'd bitten a piece of toast into the shape of a revolver and pretended to shoot her. This sparked a lively conversation among our croppers. The consensus was that boys will be boys, and the appeal of guns is built into their DNA.

Detweiler continued, "That album you made? What a hit! The other kids crowded around. They loved the pictures of Gracie, but Monroe? That beast is a rock star for the under six set."

I laughed.

"So, you made lots of notes?"

"No, I recorded comments on my cell phone."

"Smart guy."

"I try hard."

"So, you've decided? He's definitely coming home with you?"

"Wild horses couldn't stop me from bringing him home."

"Did you get to put him to bed?" I'd glanced at the clock and realized I'd stayed up way past my bedtime. It was nearly midnight.

"Actually, I read him both of the books you packed and tucked him in. Tyrone the Terrible was a hands-down winner."

That was one that Bonnie had recommended because her son loved it. I'd have to thank her. Better yet, I vowed not to let Bernice Stottlemeyer bug me. That'd be a fair trade.

"What was your day like?" Detweiler asked.

"Whoa. First of all, send me a photo."

"Um, I forgot to take one."

"You didn't!"

"I did. Hon, I was busy all day. The traffic here is every bit as bad as they say it is. Orson, the driver, hustled us from the pediatrician's office to Erik's summer camp before it ended for the day. Tomorrow I'm having lunch with his teacher. She wasn't available today, because an emergency came up. Believe me, I have a whole new respect for carpool parents."

Drat. I told myself not to be such a baby, but I was disappointed. I really, really wanted those photos. Right now, Erik was just a fantasy, but a photo would make him real. I hated that Detweiler was there, and I was here, and yet we were making such a huge decision. It would be so much easier if I could look Detweiler in the face, see his expression and touch his hand.

I sighed, but not so loudly that he could hear. Right now, I needed to pull up my big girl panties and keep a smile on my face.

"Good to hear that you've been observing the rituals of parenthood," I said. "As of this fall, you are entering the carpool craziness zone. Welcome to the family rat race."

"Speaking of rat races, I knew that Lauber had money, but I had no idea how much. That nanny I mentioned? She worked full-time for Gina and Van ever since Erik was born! I guess Van Lauber was seriously rich."

"And now he's gone," I said.

"Right. Money can't buy you immortality. That reminds me. What's new with the Dr. Hyman case?"

I told him about my mother being taken in for questioning.

"I wish I'd been there for you," he said.

"Maybe it's best that you weren't, considering that Prescott is involved. Fortunately, my little sister works for a law firm. One of her co-workers went with her to spring Mom."

"Somebody setup your mother."

"Yes," I said slowly. Who? And how'd they manage it? Was it someone at the senior center? It had to be. Who else would know Mom had gotten angry with Dr. Hyman? There couldn't be a large pool of people! Or could there?

55

Wednesday morning/Fourth day after the wedding...

*A*nya gently shook me, trying to wake me from a bad dream. The fog of it lingered. I couldn't make sense of all the impressions, but I knew that I had been running and trying to hide from someone in a house where the stairs had turned to slides. Every time I started scrambling up the steps, my footing would give way, and I'd slip into oblivion. It had been awful.

"Mom? You okay? You were crying." Her hand rested on my shoulder.

I blinked at her, wiped my nose with the back of my hand, and tried to figure out where I was. Had I really fallen asleep at the kitchen table? Yup, I had. Furthermore, the foil top from a tub of butter was stuck to my face. I peeled off the lid. My Zentangle pen sat uncapped with the tip touching a paper napkin. The ink had bled. A Rorschach image had formed. The markers hold a lot of ink, but that one was now ruined. My eyes felt like I'd rubbed them with sandpaper. I bet mascara was smeared all over my face.

"Are you drunk?" Anya leaned close to sniff my breath.

"Have you ever seen me drunk?"

"No, but there's always a first time. Gran drinks. She falls asleep at her table, too."

That frosted my cupcakes. After growing up in a home with an alcoholic parent, I'd vowed not to let history repeat itself. "First of all, I don't drink. Not like that. Second, I'm pregnant. I would never drink alcohol when I'm pregnant. I haven't even been drinking diet colas. You know that. So, before you start with accusations, you better know what you're talking about, young lady."

"Geez, don't go all hyphy on me, Mom."

I glared at her. "Hyphy" is teen-speak for hyper-active or overwrought. I wasn't. I was, however, annoyed.

"Anya, there's a big difference between falling asleep and passing out."

"Morning," said Rebekkah, as she ambled in, fully dressed. "Thanks again, Kiki, for going with me to take Dad to the hospital. And for picking up dinner for us. I know it made for a late night for you."

"See?" I said to Anya. "We'll continue this conversation later. Oh, my gosh, look at the time! We better hustle, or we'll be late picking up Aunt Penny. By the way. Good news. My mother is out of jail."

Anya shrugged. "Yep. I guess that's good. Except that while she was there, she couldn't pester you."

In short order, we'd piled into my car. Gracie was scrunched in back between Anya and Rebekkah. Eventually, the big dog put her rump on the floor and rested her front legs on Anya's lap. I pointed us toward my mother's house and turned on the local news. The weatherman predicted rain and storms. After a commercial for a local dry-cleaner, the reporter announced there had been a break in the Dr. Morrie Hyman murder case.

"At a press briefing early this morning, Captain Prescott Gallaway announced that a suspect has been apprehended, following what he characterized as an arduous investigation. The police captain admitted the arrest had taken longer than he wanted. He blamed the department's slow progress on a culture of complacency that must be corrected. He ended the conference with a plea for new leadership to shake up the lackadaisical elements within the department."

"What?" I shouted at the Blaupunkt radio in my dash. "How dare he!"

"Look at the bright side, Mom," said Anya. "If he's found the killer, Gran and Robbie can go on their honeymoon. Robbie can go back to work when they return. He'll get this guy Prescott straightened out. It's all good."

She was right; the drama was over. Sure, Prescott could make all the excuses he wanted, but Robbie's record would speak for itself. Robbie was a smart man. All he needed to do was return from his vacation with Sheila and announce he was making changes. Once the media heard the sound-bite, he would regain the upper hand.

Despite the dark clouds gathering overhead, Aunt Penny fairly bounced down the brick steps of the U City house. Today she wore a Jethro Tull tee shirt tucked into her baggy jeans. "McDonald's? I'm buying!" she chirped.

It's against my religion to turn down free food.

On our way to the drive-through, I learned three things: Horace would be at the hospital all day, Rebekkah's car was being towed to a local garage, and my mother blamed me for her arrest.

A wave of morning sickness hit me when I caught sight of Aunt Penny's oatmeal.

Wouldn't you know it, I had to pull over and upchuck at the side of Clayton Road, one of the classiest streets in the area.

"Way to go, Mom," said Anya. "Totally ick-city."

"Five months to labor and counting, girlfriend. You ain't seen nothing yet."

*M*y construction crew hit the ground running. I brewed myself a cup of peppermint tea and tackled my least favorite job, paperwork.

I opened the computer and found a message from Margit. She's a newbie at email correspondence but catching on fast. Her roof had sprung a leak with all the bad weather, and she asked if there was any way I could do without her so she could call roofing companies. But to make up for her absence, she had emailed me our monthly profitability report.

I sent her an email that the crowd this evening would probably be small, especially considering the storms brewing. I wished her luck with the roofers and printed the P & L statement. What I saw was disappointing. Even though we'd improved our profitability, our overall sales were down. This was true industry-wide, but that knowledge didn't comfort me.

Somehow I'd have to keep our doors open.

Clancy called. "I have a migraine. This changing weather always sets off my headaches. Do you need me?"

"No. Stay home and take some of that medicine the doctor prescribed for you. Don't be such a martyr, Clancy. If your head hurts, take a pill."

"I hate to, but I think I'll have to. That stuff makes me groggy."

"So sleep off your migraine and stay dry," I told her.

"Love you, Kiki."

I was shocked. Clancy rarely showed affection. It just wasn't her style. Her sweet goodbye meant the world to me, and I started to tell her so, but she'd already hung up.

My friends.

This store was a wheel hub, and we were all spokes. Each of us had our strengths. But as a group, we were really impressive. We could keep a tire spinning, traveling over rough terrain. And we'd been joined together by Dodie.

Where was she now?

I ran my hand over the desktop. How could an inanimate object of so little worth still be here when Dodie was gone? How could that be right? Why did God decide that people should die and things should stick around? Where was the justice? Dodie had been bigger than life, or so I'd thought. It never really seemed possible that she would die. Even when I saw her looking so frail, I didn't believe she was leaving us. It had been too hard to imagine this store without Dodie. I couldn't wrap my head around never seeing her again. Or never hearing her call me, "Sunshine."

She'd left an imprint on every part of the store. For example, she'd purchased this big honking leather seat I now occupied, because she explained, "Men have big desk chairs. Why shouldn't I? I am a CEO. Besides, it's comfy."

I stared across from the desk at a photo she'd taken of a Galapagos turtle at the St. Louis Zoo. As a photographer, she was no great shakes, but this picture was fabulous. Just really amazing.

I opened the top desk drawer and rummaged through her office supplies. She loved her Swingline stapler, and when she discovered brightly colored staples, she switched to them and stapled every paper she could get her hands on.

I heard a rattle in the back of the drawer. Reaching in, I pulled out the toy turtle. That was odd. I'd thought I'd put him in my purse. Instead of tucking him away, I paused and studied him carefully.

A customer vacationing in Florida had bought this turtle for Dodie. The toy's head, legs and tail were loosely attached so that they bobbed constantly. Dodie had found the motion totally amusing. When she was bothered by something, she'd pull the turtle from the drawer and watch him bob-bob-bobbing along. His antics made her laugh.

"This turtle reminds me that you only make progress when you are willing to stick your neck out," she'd said.

Dodie was always sharing her silly but pertinent bits of wisdom.

How I missed her!

There had been tough times for the business, but she'd always managed to find a way to be profitable. Sometimes it seemed she kept Time in a Bottle going through the sheer strength of her personality. Everywhere I turned there were touches of Dodie, small remembrances she'd been here.

Her best memorial was this store.

Was I savvy enough to keep the doors open?

57

I didn't have much time to ponder these deep thoughts because my cell phone rang. I answered without looking at the number. Robbie Holmes' voice boomed at me before I even put the phone to my ear.

"Prescott arrested Sheila. He insisted on having her cuffed and shoved her into a police car with the Jimmy Girls watching!"

I groaned. "I didn't want Anya to hear it on the news."

"Is Sheila okay?"

"She's in booking right now."

"Have you called a lawyer?"

"Jim Hagg is on his way here right now. He's already gotten a judge to agree to an emergency bond hearing."

In a million years, I would have never guessed that Robbie would hire Jim Hagg. Hagg specialized on getting people off. Even people who were guilty. Needless to say, the law enforcement community hated Hagg. They risked their lives to put bad guys behind bars while Hagg became a millionaire several times over by getting creeps off on technicalities.

But Robbie had hired Hagg.

"Why?" I said.

"Because you don't bring a Chihuahua to a dog fight with a pit bull. He's the toughest, meanest son of a gun out there. I'm sending a clear message to Prescott. He's crossed a line. Think about it, Kiki. Can you imagine how many creeps I've put behind bars? How eager they'd be to get their hands on my wife? I have to get Sheila out of there, and frankly right now, I couldn't care less about how hiring Hagg looks. He thinks she'll be out of the slammer in time for lunch. And he better be right. I couldn't stand it if anything happened to Sheila. I don't know what I'd do."

Robbie was clearly shook up, and his fear proved contagious.

"How can he justify this? First my mother and now Sheila? Does he have any real evidence against her?" Prescott was starting to really make me mad. "Not much. No weapon, of course, because that was planted on your mother. Witnesses saw Sheila's argument with Dr. Hyman. There's the invitation, and a longstanding grudge because Dr. Hyman messed up her nose." Robbie hesitated before adding, "And some unfortunate emails."

"Emails?" A sick shiver snaked up my spine. What had Sheila said about Robbie not being able to testify against her?

"That night after their confrontation at the country club, while I was in bed, she went online. Found a website that specializes in airing grudges. Boy, did she vent her spleen about Dr. Hyman."

"She's smarter than that!"

"Not when she's been drinking. I did my best to clean up the mess the next morning, but I'm no computer whiz."

What had Anya said? About her Gran passing out? I'd

always known Sheila to enjoy a glass of wine or two. And champagne. She loved her bubbly. But when had she slipped from a casual drinker to a woman with a problem? Or had she?

"What can I do? How can I help?" I asked.

"Hadcho should arrive at your store around noon with photos of the envelope that Dr. Hyman's invitation came in. The crime scene people found it in the trash at the doctor's house. I have a hunch that you were right. From the photo, it looks like an everyday piece of stationery. Of course, I don't know what to look for, but you do, so I'm counting on you to give it a thumbs-up or thumbs-down."

"Then what?"

"We'll take it from there."

I didn't like the sound of that. "What do you mean? What do you intend to do?"

"What I should have done in the first place. I'm going to solve this crime if it kills me."

That was exactly the sort of thinking that worried me.

58

My head started to throb before I could hang up the phone. Right outside the office, boards clattered and bonked. I could hear Roy talking with my construction crew about where the wood should go. The rustle of crisp paper suggested they were looking over the plans he'd drawn up.

I knew that I should tell Anya about Sheila's arrest, but she was happy right now, working alongside Aunt Penny. With any luck, I'd hear back from Robbie after Sheila was "sprung." If the bad news could wait until then, it wouldn't be nearly so traumatic. I finished looking over the P & L statement, vowed to find a way to do more business, and headed to the worktable. I needed to prep for this evening's crop.

At quarter past eleven, Hadcho walked through the front door. The sky outside had turned dark. His jacket was dotted with raindrops that he promptly brushed off. He's really too good-looking to be a cop, and he's very particular about his appearance. But Detweiler has told me that there's no better man in a fight than Stan Hadcho. I guess when it came to knocking heads, he didn't think twice about his appearance.

"Mrs. Holmes is out on bail," he said, as he reached into his jacket pocket and set a photo on the desktop between us. "Robbie texted me as I pulled into your parking lot."

"She okay?"

"Shook up. She got a black eye from another jailbird."

"What!"

"Someone attacked her. They had to pull the other woman off of Sheila." He grinned. "Although I did hear that your mother-in-law gave as good as she got. She knocked out one of the other woman's teeth. Sheila got a whale of a gash on her right knuckles for her trouble."

"But she was attacked! And her collarbone isn't even healed!"

"I know it. Robbie was taking her to the ER when he called me. Believe me, he was steaming mad. I've never heard him so angry. That creep Prescott left her with the general population. He should have locked her in an individual cell for her protection. But he didn't. Claimed he couldn't give her special protection. Said that would be cronyism."

"What a total jerk."

"You've got that right."

I glanced at the photo of the envelope found in Dr. Hyman's trash and started shaking my head. "Nope. No way."

"You sure?"

"I'm positive. Look." I reached under the worktable and found a box labeled LOWENSTEIN, SHEILA. It was actually a clean, empty pizza box. We'd found them perfect for storing projects in progress.

My fingers quickly seized the envelope that I'd kept for

Anya's memory book, an album I updated all the time for my daughter.

"Notice the flowers in the upper left corner. There aren't any on the envelope in your photo. Next, look at the postal stamp. I bought four hundred Forever Stamps with flowers on them. Yours has a picture of the American flag. And there's the lettering. Yours is typed. I hand-addressed all the envelopes."

From a back pocket, Hadcho pulled an empty evidence bag. "May I have yours?"

"I hate to give it up, but I know it's important."

"You bet it is."

59

*H*adcho glanced at his watch and ran a nervous hand over his perfectly cut hair. "After Robbie got Sheila taken care of, they were going to meet with Jim Hagg and talk strategy. At least, Robbie was, if Sheila wasn't up to it."

"What are you thinking?" I asked.

In the distance, a crack of thunder split the heavy rain. Gracie howled in the back room. Like a lot of dogs, she hates thunderstorms.

"Usually Detweiler and I go over the case details, but he's not here. I can't talk with the other detectives because I'm not supposed to be working on this. Prescott doesn't know what he's doing. He keeps the detectives off-balance, running one way and then the other. No real progress is being made."

I closed up the pizza box and waited for him to get to the point.

"I was thinking that maybe you and I could discuss the case."

Rather than break into a huge grin, I bit my bottom lip. This was so totally cool! I felt like I'd been admitted to some sort of exclusive boys' club. Then the seriousness of his request hit me...hard. For Hadcho to turn to a civilian meant he was really, truly desperate. Although Detweiler had never admitted as much, I knew that Hadcho had given him grief about sharing his work with me. Especially since we weren't married, and I could be called to testify against my fiancé.

Wow. Talk about your stormy weather.

"I'll help in any way I can, and you know I'll keep my mouth shut. What do we have?"

"Let's go over the basics: means, motive, and opportunity."

"Start with means," I said. "The blood on the screwdriver found in her purse was definitely Dr. Hyman's?"

"We don't know yet," he said.

"So you might not have the murder weapon."

"That's right. Let's continue as if it is." Hadcho tapped a manicured fingernail against the top of the worktable. "Any idea how it got into her purse?"

"A hunch. Amanda has told me that Mom's always forgetting her purse. I figure she walked off and left it somewhere, and the killer noticed."

"Where might that have happened?"

"Probably at the wedding."

"So it could have been anybody, and since there was a lag time between the murder and the discovery of the screwdriver, could have happened any time after the killing," said Hadcho with a sigh.

"You don't have any idea who made the phone call suggesting that my mother was the culprit?" I asked.

"None," he said. "Moving right along. As for opportunity,

252

I can't rule out anyone who was attending the wedding. There were too many people milling around. Sure, we took statements. I've been over those. Usually Robbie has us re-interview everyone involved. Then we draw a diagram. Who was where and who might have seen what. That's not going to happen here. Not this time."

I reached under the work table to where I'd stashed a pack of Saltines. I nibbled on one. "Let me grab some paper." Using cheap copier paper, I drew a sketch of the three tents erected on Leighton's property that day: a tent for the ceremony, a small tent for the caterers, and a tent for the reception festivities. The catering tent was right up against Leighton's house so that the servers could also make use of his kitchen. The reception tent was parallel to his house.

To the left of Leighton's house, in the eleven o'clock position, is my house, Monroe's pen and the shed. Running along the right hand side of Leighton's house is a narrow alley that separates his home and its large acreage from other houses on the same block.

The ceremonial tent was set at a forty-five degree angle to his house, facing his new gazebo. Parallel to the gazebo, but about fifty feet to the right, is the new water feature, the goldfish pond that Leighton had recently installed. The photographer had driven up the alley and parked close to the water feature, because of all the equipment he had to haul. The only cars allowed in Leighton's circular drive that day had been the catering trucks, one of which had been driven by Cara Mia.

"Great map, doesn't tell us squat," said Hadcho.

"I agree," I said with a sigh. "What's the time of Hyman's death?"

"The ME says he died shortly before his body was found. The caterers confirm that timeframe because they unloaded their stuff from the vans, and then stayed together, as per Cara Mia Delgatto, the owner of the catering business. When someone noticed your dog in the ceremony, they all had an attack of the 'looky-lous,' and moved to the edge of the guest seating. They stood there together in a group until the ceremony was over. The entire service took about twenty-five minutes, as you know."

"That means the doctor died about fifteen minutes into the vows, right?"

"Probably."

"How did Dr. Hyman get to the wedding?" I asked. "Did he ride with someone?"

"No," Hadcho reached into his jacket pocket for his Steno pad. "He drove himself. One of the valets parked his car with all the other guests' vehicles at that nearby school lot. We verified the license plate and corroborated the valet's statement."

"So he definitely did arrive late," I said, tapping a pencil against my teeth. "That's weird. Most people try to get to a wedding either early or on time. Have you checked the time on the doctor's invitation? If someone dummied up an envelope, maybe they also monkeyed with the invitation."

"By giving Dr. Hyman the wrong time, the killer would have a window of opportunity. Everyone else would have been seated and watching the ceremony."

"Right," I said. "So the killer would have been someone who wasn't in the tent watching the service. Because the murder happened during the service. Smack-dab in the middle of it. And how did the murderer connect with Dr. Hyman? The killer had to intercept the doctor on his way to the tent where the ceremony was held. Either someone reported Hyman's arrival to the killer or—"

"Maybe Dr. Hyman had been instructed to call someone

when he arrived," said Hadcho, flipping back through his notebook. "One of the investigators was checking on Dr. Hyman's cell phone. I'll track that down. If Dr. Hyman called someone—"

"That person is probably your killer."

60

By the time Hadcho got up to leave, the rain was beating a steady drumroll against our glass display window. I walked him to the front door. The bang-bang-bang and clatter from the construction of my new addition assured me that my workers had been too busy to listen in on our conversation.

"Be careful," Hadcho said, in a low voice as he put a hand on my shoulder. "That goes without saying, but..."

Hadcho has become an unofficial big brother to me, explaining the backstory of all that happens at the police station.

"You want to borrow an umbrella?" I asked.

"Sure, if you have one."

He waited while I dug up a pink umbrella from under the cashier station.

"Right," he said, giving the thing a dubious look.

At least it would offer his silk tie a little protection. Detweiler told me that he often gets teased for caring about his appearance. Personally, I find that charming. All of us are quirky, Most of us work hard at hiding our bizarre

GROUP, PHOTO, GRAVE

foibles from the world at large. The more I get to know Hadcho, the more I appreciate his steady nature and, of course, I appreciate his friendship.

"Especially with Detweiler out of town, you need to watch your back," he said to me. "Robbie's in a vulnerable position. That means that all his minions—and that includes you—are at risk."

"I'll be okay," I said, giving him a tiny fist bump on the shoulder. "You're the only person on the force I'm talking to. Besides, I'm too busy to poke around."

"Right. But you always find a way." He smirked at me.

"What can I do that you can't?"

"If you get the chance to talk with the bridesmaids that might be helpful."

"What are you thinking for a motive?"

Hadcho burst out laughing. "Resistance is futile, isn't it? You like snooping around."

"Only when people I love are at risk."

"I haven't got a motive. No one at the station seems to have one either. Hyman's wife died ten years ago of a stroke. They had one son, who died in an auto accident when he was a teenager. Got into a car with a friend who was drunk."

"What about his finances? His private life? His practice?"

"Closed his practice six years ago. Updated his will after his wife died. Left everything he owned to the temple. Endowed a chair at Washington University. Had no private life to speak of, or so it seems. Looks like he was one of those sad old guys who retires, moves into a condo, and spends the rest of his life in a La-Z-Boy recliner, watching television in his boxer shorts. Doesn't get out much except for the work he does at the senior center to keep his hand in." Hadcho fingered his car keys. "Oh, and he liked to eat dinner at the country club once a month. Seems like the only enemies he had in the world were your mother and your mother-in-law."

"Goodie-goodie. Just what I wanted to hear." I glanced out the display window. "It's letting up. You better make a run for it."

He raced out of the front door right as Aunt Penny joined me. We stood shoulder-to-shoulder and watched Hadcho make a dash for his car. "Great day in the morning. That is one fine, fine specimen of male pulchritude."

I nodded. "Good-looking, too."

*H*adcho timed his exit just right. The rain began coming down in buckets. You couldn't see two feet ahead of you. Our big display windows turned into waterfalls.

"Great weather for an indoor picnic," said Aunt Penny.

"Yup," I said. "That it is."

I changed the sign on the front door to GONE TO LUNCH. Not that I expected anyone to stop by.

I keep a red and white gingham checked vinyl tablecloth in a basket on top of the refrigerator just for days like this. With a flick of my wrist, I spread the checked cloth on the floor. Anya and Rebekkah washed up while I grabbed the jars of peanut butter, almond butter, strawberry, and blueberry jams from the refrigerator along with the loaf of Ezekiel sprouted raisin cinnamon bread. Aunt Penny poured glasses of cold water, Rebekkah toasted the bread, and my daughter set the tablecloth with paper plates.

In the back of the refrigerator, I found a bowl of fruit salad left over from the Monday night crop.

The hardest part of lunch was lowering myself to the

floor. But once I got there, it felt perfect to be sitting next to my construction crew, listening to the rain while we were snug inside. Anya and I were knee to knee, in a comfortable pose.

"I was wondering. What if we had a memorial ceremony for Dodie?" Anya had her hard hat at her side. I could tell she didn't want it out of her sight. She turned to Rebekkah and said, "I know your mother only wanted a graveside service, but so many of our customers didn't really get to say good-bye. I feel like I didn't. I'm not thinking about something sad. I'm thinking something happy, because she always called my mom, 'Sunshine.'"

I waited because I didn't want to rush Rebekkah into responding.

"You know, I've been thinking about that, too," Rebekkah said, as she put down her sandwich. "Mom kind of underestimated how much people thought of her. She loved this store. She didn't want Dad to have to go through a big service and deal with people. But I think he'd enjoy hearing their memories. I think he needs that. He's so lost! And I'd like to hear it, too. Kiki, would you be willing to plan something?"

"I'd be honored. I'll get right on it."

"I have another idea," said Anya. "Dodie loved turtles, why not have the memorial ceremony at one of her favorite spots?"

"Where's that? The zoo?" Aunt Penny asked.

"Close, but not quite. Turtle Park. Right off of 40 in Dog Town," I said.

"Wait until you see it, Aunt Penny," said Anya. "It's the coolest place ever. There are these huge concrete statues of turtles. You can climb all over them."

"Here's another idea," I said. "What if we name this new room we're building after Dodie?"

"I think Mom would have liked that," said Rebecca. A hint of a smile showed.

"Anya? How about if you make a few notes about what you think would be a good way to proceed? After you get your ideas on paper, we can talk them over with Margit and Clancy. I want them to have input, too."

Rebekkah finished her food and went into the office where she could call the hospital and have a bit of privacy as she asked about her dad. Aunt Penny was uncharacteristically quiet while we ate. I tasked Anya with getting Gracie to go outside for a piddle, a chore that would be difficult given the rain. However, the sound on the roof suggested there'd been a bit of a let up.

"If you take Gracie out right now, she might do her business before the thunder starts again. Otherwise, she's going to fight you. Last time I dragged her outside in the rain, she waited until I wasn't paying attention and then bolted for the back door."

"I remember," said Anya with a giggle. "You should have seen it, Aunt Penny. Mom lost her balance and landed in a big mud puddle. She came in looking like someone from one of those tug-of-war competitions. Someone on the losing side!"

"Go out through the front door and change the sign to OPEN, please," I told Anya.

As my daughter shepherded Gracie, I turned to my aunt and asked for help getting to my feet. "What's wrong? I can tell something is bothering you."

"I'm feeling plum sorry for myself," Aunt Penny said, as she hoisted me to a standing position. "That daughter of yours is a peach. So is Rebekkah. I rarely wish I had children. I figure if the Lord had wanted me to be a mother, he could have worked his wonders. But seeing these girls, watching them with you, I get to thinking about what might have been, and I get weepy."

Aunt Penny used the back of her sleeve to mop her eyes. "I don't know why your mother can't see what she's got. How God's blessed her. But she can't. She's got some sort of grudge against you. She doesn't treat Amanda much better. And Catherine's given up—"

"Catherine? You're in touch with my sister Catherine?" I felt my mouth drop open. Neither Amanda nor I had heard from Catherine in fifteen years.

"I've gone and done it," muttered Aunt Penny. "And here I'd promised to keep my big trap shut."

I would have pressed her for details, but the door minder rang. I knew that Anya and Gracie wouldn't be back that quickly. There was nothing for me to do but take care of business. Two customers staggered in, shaking off raindrops. They'd come wanting help with an album they were making. For the next three hours, Aunt Penny took full advantage of their entrance to steer clear of me. She and the crew went back to work.

"Mom, I need a break from the store," said Anya, wiping the dust from her face. "I'd rather not hang around for the crop. Could I go to Gran's house? I miss her."

This was my chance to fill Anya in on her grandmother's brief stint in the county slammer. Aunt Penny and Rebekkah were near enough to listen, too.

"You're kidding," said Anya. "But she's out? And she's okay?"

"Your grandmother is fine." I explained how Prescott had arrested Sheila and put her in the general jail population. "I guess another woman attacked her. But you know your grandmother. She gave as good as she got."

Aunt Penny snickered.

"What does that mean?" Anya asked.

"That means that your grandmother has a black eye but the other woman lost a tooth. Sheila must have a mean right hook."

"That's so cool," said Rebekkah.

Anya hooted with laughter. "Gran's been doing those Billy Tae Bo videos to get in shape for her wedding. Because of her broken collarbone, she couldn't do much, but I could tell that she wanted to hit something."

A sidewise glance from Aunt Penny spoke volumes. She and I were both thinking that Sheila could have fared much worse.

"Let's see if your grandmother wants company," I told my daughter. "You are always welcome at her house, but we need to remember that she has had a really bad day."

I text messaged Robbie, and he responded immediately by calling.

"Send Anya over. I'm making steaks to celebrate Sheila getting sprung. Why don't you come over, too?"

"I can't come until after our crop," I said. "But I'd love for you to save a steak for me to eat later. I'll have Anya there in a half an hour."

By the time I got off the phone, my construction crew had finished up for the day, collecting their tools and sweeping up sawdust. Right now, the wall looked like a series of empty frames. The drywall sheets were due to arrive in the morning.

"We should be able to get a lot done tomorrow," said Aunt Penny. "Roy's bringing his nail guns."

"I don't like the sounds of that."

"Your daughter will be closely supervised," said Aunt Penny. "That's a promise."

"Good," I said. "I will hold you to it. Which reminds me. We need to talk."

She nodded and said, "Later."

Rebekkah's phone buzzed, and she checked the message. "That's my mechanic. He's going to swing by and pick me up. Luckily, my car just needed a new battery."

"Rebekkah, could you give Aunt Penny a ride home? She's on your way."

"Sure. I can even drop Anya and Gracie off at Sheila's if you'd like."

Her mechanic proved as good as his word. Fifteen minutes later, I was alone in the store. The crop would start in less than an hour. Bernice Stottlemeyer would be darkening my door as well. I took advantage of the solitude to give Detweiler a call.

62

Same day...
Metro Los Angeles, California

"Good news," said Detweiler. "The headmaster at Erik's school actually knows the dean of the lower school at CALA. In fact, he was impressed that Erik would be going to a school of such high caliber. His words exactly. The curriculum is the same, so that should be helpful. They promised to copy all his records and send them to the school. I took notes on his favorite subjects and interests. He loves animals. Likes to read. Is fascinated by trains."

"Does he know yet that he's coming home with you?" I sat on a stool at my work table and stared out the front window. The rain was coming down sideways, so thick and dense that it looked like sheets of watery plastic were being tossed from the sky.

"Sort of. He doesn't really understand that it's more than just a visit. Maybe that's okay, all things considered. Thank goodness for your album. He's showed it to all his friends. I meant to snap photos of the classroom, but I got involved and forgot. Sorry."

Drat. Another day without pictures. I took the high road. "He's going to love Gracie and the cats."

Detweiler laughed. "Wait until he meets Monroe! He's told everyone at his summer camp about the donkey in the picture."

"What's on the agenda for tomorrow?"

"Disneyland. I know it's a bit excessive, but I figured, why not? We're here. It'll allow me bonding time."

"Who can resist a man who offers Disney? I think you know the way to a little boy's heart."

"I still have a few loose ends to tie up with Lorraine, but she's having a time of it. The stress of sending Erik away is causing a relapse. She could barely get out of bed this morning. Since I hadn't booked our return flight, I figured that I might as well make the most of the visit. It's important for Erik to get to know me. Honestly, I feel for the kid. And for Lorraine."

"She's in bad shape, huh?" I asked. I really did need photos. I'd come to rely on them as a way to translate the world around me, to make sense of it.

"Yes. She has a form of MS that's particularly hard for the doctors to get under control. Her relapses are followed by things getting progressively worse," he said. "Kiki, you'd really like her. She's obviously had money her whole life, but she's not the type who's let it affect her. Very down-to-earth. The photos of our pets brought tears to her eyes. I guess she had to put her pug to sleep a couple of months ago. Oh, and she thinks Anya is going to grow up to be a real beauty."

You can't help but like someone who likes your kids. Take that to the bank.

"Disneyland. Wow," I said, "As an introduction to a new parent, Disneyland ranks right up there at the top of the charts."

"Yes, but I wish you and Anya were here with us. That would be wonderful. It doesn't seem right that you are there, and I'm here. I love you, babe. Miss you terribly."

"We miss you, too. Maybe someday we'll win the lottery. Then we could go and spend a week at Disney World in Florida. Take in Epcot. Go to Universal Studios."

"To win the lottery you have to play it," he reminded me.

"Oops. I knew there was something I kept forgetting to do. I've been pretty busy while you've been gone."

"Tell me about your day."

I took a deep breath and told him about Sheila's brief stint in the county jail. He went ominously quiet. When I got to the part about her getting into a fistfight, he actually growled. That was a new one on me. I finished by explaining that I would see Sheila after the crop, and that Anya was already there with her grandmother. I thought about telling him about my discussion with Hadcho but decided against it. Detweiler didn't need more stress in his life right now. This should be a happy time for him.

"Kiki, I'm worried," he said. "Be careful. There's a code among law enforcement officials. We serve and protect all the citizenry, but our families are sacred. Off limits. It has to be that way. Prescott has crossed a line here. This is unthinkable. For him to endanger Sheila that way, well, the guy is off his nut."

"Kiki?" Cara Mia called to me from the back. She must

have fought her way through the rain. I hadn't seen her car pull up, but then Black Beauty probably blended in with the dark scene outside.

"I've got to go," I told Detweiler. "I love you. Can't wait for you to come home."

63

———

Cara Mia and I held our "business meeting" while setting out the warming trays and food. She scooped pasta and sauce into the pans before lighting the Sterno beneath them. We left the salad in the refrigerator, choosing to dress it later. For dessert we were offering wonderful freshly brewed coffee, tiny Italian cookies, and sorbet. And if I knew my croppers, at least one of them would bring a home-cooked goodie.

We probably had fifteen minutes until the croppers arrived. Cara Mia brought her leather satchel over to my work table where we could peruse the information she'd collected.

"Let me just hit the highlights in case we're interrupted," she said. "If Horace agrees to sell this building and the parking lot for the original sum or lower, you'll immediately have enough equity to qualify for a loan at a super low rate of interest. Here's my business banker's card."

For the next five minutes, Cara gave me a crash course in buying commercial real estate. I started to take notes, but she'd written everything down for me in checklist form.

"This place is worth more money than the Goldfaders are asking," I said.

"As long as the building inspection comes back without any glaring problems, that's right. When they completed that exit off of 40 onto Brentwood, your traffic count doubled. You aren't taking advantage of it yet, because you need to enlarge your signage and get it lit. I suggest you use Metro Signage. They always stay abreast of the local codes."

I studied the sheets she'd labeled with colorful sticky notes. "I need to tell Horace that he's undervalued the building and the parking lot."

Cara said nothing. She sat across from me with a placid expression on her face.

"You think I'm a fool for wanting to tell him, don't you?"

"No, I don't. I think you're a good person with a conscience. That's how I've always seen you, and that's what you're proving yourself to be. You have to live with yourself, Kiki. Business is always about finding and exploiting advantages, be they location or talent or product. But you have to find that line between exploitation and unfairness. I think you are doing the right thing by telling Horace about the comps," and she paused. "It's entirely possible that he won't charge you the full amount. You seem to forget, you've put in a lot of sweat equity. There aren't a lot of people who could buy this business and make it work. You can. Even if Horace could get all the money due him for the building, it's doubtful that he could sell this scrapbook store to anyone but you. Think about it, Kiki. How many scrapbook stores have you seen go out of business? A lot. It's a tough market, and scrapbooking isn't the hot fad it once was. People can buy supplies in the big box stores. Running this place will take a unique skill set. One that you've got."

"Maybe," I said.

She sighed. "Has it also occurred to you that as long as this store keeps running, it's a memorial to Dodie? Maybe Horace is keeping the price affordable because he wants to see you succeed."

I hadn't thought about that. "I suppose a savvy businessperson wouldn't tell him he'd undervalued the real estate."

"You have to view information and your knowledge as if they were tangible assets that you've paid to accumulate, because you have. Therefore, they are your edge in the marketplace. But you still have to live with yourself at the end of the day. I think you're doing the right thing by telling Horace what you've found out." Then she hesitated.

"And?" I prompted her.

"And, if there's any way at all for you to take out a bank loan, I'd advise it. Interest rates have never been lower. Since the building is sure to be valued at more than what you're paying, any good bank would be happy to work with you. My banker was chomping at the bit."

"Then let me ask you about this," and I told her about the strange phone call I'd gotten from the Ballards' attorney. "How would you suggest I proceed?"

"Did he send you the paperwork?"

"In an email. I assume I need an attorney. The only ones I know are criminal attorneys."

"Actually, you're wrong. You know a great civil attorney with a super brain for trusts, wills, and family law."

"I do?"

"Saul Beck. He goes to your temple, doesn't he?"

"Saul? The old guy? He's always there at temple early? Leaves late. Talks with Sheila. Always compliments Anya. Gives me a hug."

"He was at the wedding, too. I saw him sitting near the front row."

"Of course he was. I addressed the envelope myself." I pictured a disheveled man with a rowdy head of white hair and a slow, halting walk. Sure I knew Saul. Everybody at temple did. He was a fixture like the light switches. But an attorney? My face must have shown my surprise. "Saul?"

Cara laughed. "Probably one of the richest men in town. You wouldn't think it, would you? That tweed jacket he wears is moth-eaten and threadbare. Yes, he's richer than rich. Sharp as a tack. You never hear about him because he likes it that way, but my father always used Saul for all our family trust work. Here, let me jot down his phone number. I have him on speed dial. In fact, if I were you, I'd have him handle this situation with Horace. He probably knows Horace anyway."

Didn't that just bake the crust on the pizza? Here I'd ignored this doddering old man (except of course to exchange pleasantries) never realizing he was a brain trust I should get to know on a professional basis.

"Cara, I owe you," I said, giving her a hug. "You're a peach. A bright spot on a gloomy day. That reminds me, are you staying for the crop? Oh, and a woman named Bernice Stottlemeyer is going to stop by and pick up her album around six. She should be here any time."

"Bernice? She's the one you're doing the adoption album for? How'd you get so lucky?" said Cara with a wry grin. "Unless you really, really need me, I'd rather get home. Sven is having more problems. His hind legs are giving out on him."

"I'm sorry to hear that. You know her? Bernice Stot-tlemeyer?"

"Sad to say, I've had dealings with her." Cara frowned.

"You are lucky that your encounter won't be lengthy. When she comes into the restaurant, my staff flips a coin. The loser has to wait on her! Wesley's okay, but she's a piece of work. I can't imagine her as a mother."

"Me neither."

The front door burst open, and our first guests arrived. Cara and I scooped up her paperwork. I gave her a hug and sent her on her way so I could greet my croppers.

64

*C*ynthia Farley and Mary-Ellen Lisdale both brought their little girls with them. Cynthia's daughter Bebe was a particular favorite of mine. When the Farleys had adopted her, the child was seriously underweight. Most eight-month-old babies weigh sixteen to twenty-five pounds, but Bebe only pressed the scale at twelve pounds. And there was another problem. Bebe had been born with a club foot. The child would require surgery to correct it.

"The agency in Guangzhou wouldn't let us leave until she gained a little weight," Cynthia had told me when Bebe came home with them from China six months ago.

"What was the problem?" I had asked.

"Worms. Malnutrition. Depression. Her birth mother took one look at her deformed foot and refused to nurse her. Left her to die. Honestly, it's a wonder that she survived. They warned us that she might never talk or walk."

"Wow." The girl's saucer-sized brown eyes stared at me intently. "But you still wanted her? I mean, that had to be daunting. Most people are intimidated by the thought of adopting a child with special needs."

Cynthia had been rocking Bebe in her arms as she stood there talking to me, falling into that unconscious habit that mothers have, the mimicking of our internal rhythms to sooth ourselves and our offspring. It took her a long time to speak, because her voice was thick with emotion. "Believe me, I wondered whether we should walk away. My mother acted like the voice of doom. She kept saying we were making a mistake. But I just couldn't give up on Bebe, Kiki. After we chose her and completed the home study, I knew she could thrive with our care. If she can't walk normally, we'll get braces for her legs or sign her up for PT. If she has cognitive problems, we'll work with her. Whatever it takes, I'm going to give this baby the best chance at a happy, normal life."

Six months later, you wouldn't have recognized Bebe. Her little arms and legs were appropriately chubby. Yes, she wore a big shoe on one foot, but that didn't stop her from being as fast as lightning on her feet. She called me, "Keee-keeee," and held out her arms to me whenever she came to visit. Yes, Miss Bebe knew she'd won my heart. I couldn't get enough of her!

Tonight she ran to me, although the rubber rain boots she wore slowed her down considerably. "Boots!" she crowed and pointed to her feet.

"I see! Those are so cool, Bebe." The child with the gloomy future had blossomed into a lovely and loving daughter, a delight to all who encountered her. Bebe's pediatrician had told Cynthia and Jon that it wasn't the meds or the diet that made the difference.

"It was the love," Cynthia had explained. "We gave Bebe a reason to live. And you are part of that. Thanks for your support, Kiki. I don't know what we would have done if we hadn't discovered you and the adoption group. There were times when I didn't know if we would make it."

"You would have," I said, "but I sure am glad that I was along for the ride."

Now we had to work the same miracle with Mary-Ellen and Ella because that little girl was in almost as bad shape as Bebe had been. Ella had been left to die in a garbage heap in Mexico City. Probably because she was born with a cleft palate. Ella had already been fitted with a palatal obturator until the surgery can be performed when she is between six to twelve months old. Depending on the severity of the cleft, Ella will need more surgeries as she grows up.

When Cynthia first brought her to the store, Ella was as listless as a sack of potatoes. Now, one month later, she would give me a shy smile and let me take her from her mother's arms.

"How hard is it to raise a child from a different ethnicity?" I asked Mary-Ellen and Cynthia, as I bounced Ella on my hip.

They looked at each other and laughed. Mary-Ellen said, "Since I have two children who are my biological offspring, I can tell you that every child is challenging. Going to Mexican cultural events seems like a vacation compared to dealing with a hormonal teenager."

"It's a challenge," said Cynthia, "but the benefits outweigh any hassles. We're learning as much about Chinese culture as we can. We've scheduled family trips back to the mainland."

"We've been warned that it can bother the child who comes here, because she or he doesn't look like everyone else," added Mary-Ellen. "I plan to remind Ella that my husband and I don't look alike either, and we love each other."

That made perfect sense to me. I was holding Ella and crooning to her when Bernice Stottlemeyer stomped in.

"Hello, Mrs. Stottlemeyer. So glad to see you. I have your album right back here," I said, as I started toward the counter. "You're just in time. Remember I told you about the croppers who come on Wednesday? A few are already here. I'd be happy to introduce you to several of our customers who've adopted children."

"I don't have time," she said, snapping her umbrella closed so that it sprayed Ella and me with water.

"Oops! We took a shower, Ella," I said, as I handed the child back to her mother and stepped over to the check-out counter. From underneath, I pulled the shopping bag with the album wrapped in tissue paper. At the bottom of the bag was the box Bernice had brought in with photos.

As I handed over her bag, Bernice leaned close. "Did you show this to anyone? If you've shared any of my private business, I will sue you."

I hate being threatened, and I've been threatened by much scarier people than Bernice. After all, she didn't have a gun in her hand. I didn't either, although I wished I did.

"I have said nothing to these customers," I said, under my breath. "Nor have they seen your album."

"You better hope no one saw it!"

"Cash or credit?" I asked, as I handed her the bill. I wanted that woman out of my store.

For the longest time, she studied the charges, although she didn't bother to look at the album. Not once. You'd have thought she'd want to see it first.

"This is outrageous and you know it," she said, as she tossed her credit card down on the countertop. "This is a scam. You are vastly overcharging me to slap a few pictures in an album. I plan to tell Bonnie Gossage as much."

Since she still hadn't opened the memory book, I knew she was blowing smoke up my maternity pants. She'd planned all along to get me to do the work and then complain about the pricing. Boy, was I glad I'd collected a deposit, and I had a signed contract.

"Actually I've undercharged you. You can see everything is itemized clearly. I didn't plan on making a home visit or processing those photos, so I didn't charge you for my time, labor, or supplies," I said, as I rang up her purchase. "Thank you for your business."

I knew I should wish her "good luck," but the words stuck in my craw.

Grabbing the bag, she turned to glare at Cynthia and Mary-Ellen and their daughters. In a voice just loud enough for them to hear, she said, "So this is the group you were talking about? I certainly wouldn't fit in with them. I don't want a child that's strange or defective."

I could not believe my ears.

Cynthia and Mary-Ellen went rigid. I could tell they'd overheard Bernice—and I was not happy. In fact, I was livid.

"Mrs. Stottlemeyer, that was rude and uncalled for. I think you owe these women an apology," I said.

"I don't owe anyone anything, and I've already overpaid you!" she said, as she turned on her heel and walked out.

I hurried over to Mary-Ellen and Cynthia and apologized. But try as I might, I couldn't find the right words. No matter how many ways I tried to tell them I was sorry, I could see they were shocked and hurt.

I started the crop with a heavy heart. Our evening had been ruined.

65

My flip-flop album is quite possibly the cutest craft project I've ever created, hands down, far and away. Although Mary-Ellen and Cynthia were quiet at first, once we got started playing with the fun foam, they sloughed off Bernice's nasty comments.

Because of the miserable rain, we only had five moms in attendance, counting me. That suited me fine, as Bernice had robbed me of all my energy.

When we took a break for dinner, everyone relaxed a little more. Cynthia had brought along a plate of corn fritters, dusted with powdered sugar. Pamela Hargraves brought two dozen of her dad's Peanut Butter Cookies, and I nearly ate all of them. Vicki Nellis brought a dish of Hearty Lasagna and a plate of Oatmeal Carmelitas.

Good food goes a long way toward making people feel comfortable, and this shared meal did exactly that. Both little girls had fallen asleep in their mothers' arms, so we rolled out a mat for them to snooze on.

Pretty soon, the talk turned to Bernice. Cynthia and

Mary-Ellen filled in the other moms as to Bernice's bad behavior, and I apologized yet again. Usually, I make it a rule that there's to be no talking about other customers, but since Bernice had behaved so outrageously in front of us, I couldn't possibly enforce that rule. However, I didn't add fuel to the fire by talking about Bernice's other nasty moments in my store. Or her mean text messages.

"I remember when I was trying to get pregnant," said Mary-Ellen. "I miscarried three times. I hate to admit this, but I was full of anger and loathing. I hated everyone and everything. Going through the adoption process about pushed me over the edge. Kiki, I can't describe how dehumanizing it can be. You feel like you're being judged on every level. On top of that, you already feel like a failure for not being able to get pregnant."

She laughed. "The irony of it was that after we adopted our first child, Marcus, who's mixed race, I got pregnant the next week. And then we had twins! And now we have Ella."

"But that sometimes happens," said Pamela. "Once the pressure is off, your body responds by letting you conceive."

"She's right," Cynthia chimed in. "I felt like I was the world's biggest loser. While we were seeing the fertility specialist, our romantic life really hit the skids. Jon and I felt like two science experiments gone wrong."

I nodded. "I'm trying to give Bernice Stottlemeyer the benefit of the doubt. Honestly, I am. But to look at your wonderful daughters and not see anything but the miracle of love? How can she do that?"

"Because she's hurting," said Mary-Ellen. "When people hurt, they don't know how to handle that pain. So they lash out at others."

"Yes, it's sad. Yes, what she said was awful, but here's the deal," said Cynthia. "We have children. She doesn't. So I'm content to count my blessings rather than let her steal my happiness away. It's all a matter of focus. I can dwell on her negativity or focus on how lucky I am. I know who's coming out ahead here. It isn't her."

The generosity of my customers went a long way toward helping me feel better about Bernice Stottlemeyer's visit. Seeing the cute flip-flop albums did a lot for uplifting my spirits. As my croppers started to put away their supplies, a loud boom shook the building.

"I just got a weather alert on my phone," said Vicki, pulling out her iPhone. "There's a bad storm headed our way. Might even spawn tornadoes."

Every Midwesterner knows that when the sky turns greenish-gray, you'd better run for cover.

"We're finishing up right on time," said Cynthia. "Kiki? You aren't planning to hang around and tidy up after us, are you? I think we've gotten most of this picked up."

In my customers' eyes, there was nothing left for us to do. Of course, I knew there were tons of small jobs now demanding my attention, from cleaning the bathrooms to making the deposit and ordering inventory. However, if I stuck around I would be leaving the store without an escort.

After collecting sleepy smooches from Bebe and Ella, I walked to my car with my customers. We watched to see that all of us were safely inside our vehicles, with engines started and doors locked tightly, before going our separate ways.

I had hoped to hear from Detweiler one more time. I desperately wanted a photo of Erik. After getting a little cuddle time with Bebe and Ella, I yearned to hold our little boy. It had been years since Anya was small enough to pick up and carry.

Yes, that's what he was: our little boy.

One of two, or so it seemed. I giggled.

That happy thought took me through the rain and the thunder to Sheila's house.

66

riving to Sheila's house proved to be a challenge. After George had been murdered, I sold everything except the Beemer, because it had no Blue Book value. With the top down, it was a fun summer car, but when the ragtop was up, the shape obscured my visibility. Tonight especially, I couldn't see anything. The side windows fogged up repeatedly. The rain pelted my BMW as if I were driving through a car wash.

Normally, I could have driven to Sheila's house blindfolded. But my usual route would probably take me through standing water. If my car stalled out, I'd be stranded. I decided to take the back way instead. I pointed my car down the middle of most streets, hoping to avoid the water creeping up on the sloping shoulders.

Ladue is one of the older areas of St. Louis, a neighborhood much prized for its huge trees. The power lines aren't buried here. Falling tree limbs cause frequent power outages.

A huge branch blocked one of the streets, a Bradford pear split down the middle. Of course, I could only guess that it was a Bradford pear, but I remembered seeing these in bloom just a month ago. Bradford pear trees are prone to splitting because the v-shaped junction of the branches is too slight to support the new limbs. As lovely as they are, they are often the first casualties of our bad storms. The thick tangle of branches on the asphalt didn't leave me much room to get by. As I inched closer, the skeletal shape with twig-like fingers grabbed at my car. I didn't want to ride up on the curb for fear I'd blow out a tire. The branches caught in my undercarriage and dragged along, block after block, making a terrible scraping noise.

"Made it," I said.

A loud boom of thunder shook my car, followed by the splintering of wood. Before my eyes, another tree came down, this one severed at the trunk. Branches bounced as they hit my hood. A branch scratched the paint off my door with a loud screech. The tree shook and finally came to rest. Now I could see nothing but water and leaves.

This was bad. My heart leapt to my throat. The ragtop on my convertible offered scant protection from falling objects. A multi-pronged branch could poke right through my ancient and brittle roof. What if I were to get stabbed?

I needed to get out of this weather. And I had to do something fast.

I gulped, made a three-point turn, and started back the way I had come. I went all the way back to Brentwood and decided to take 40 to Lindbergh. The traffic sent blinding sprays of water hurling against my windshield, but at least I didn't get skewered by a tree branch. Once or twice, the force of the wake churned up by other cars sent me sliding. My knuckles went white as I gripped the steering wheel.

My teeth started chattering.

I shouldn't be out here, alone, on the roads in a soft top

car. I was endangering myself and my baby. I sent up a prayer for protection.

That's when I heard a rattle in my map pocket. I reached down and pulled out that silly toy turtle. Maybe Dodie was sending me a message. Telling me she was watching over me.

I sure hoped so. I could use the help.

67

*R*obbie had been watching for me. As soon as I pulled into the driveway, he flicked the outdoors lights twice as a signal and opened Sheila's back door. I went running through the rain, skidding on the tile floor of her mudroom.

I was soaking wet. My shoes overfloweth with rain.

Robbie handed me a towel. "Is it as bad out there as it looks? I figured you'd be drenched. I just let Gracie out."

"She went outside? In this?"

"I encouraged her. Gently. She braced herself against the door and I shoved her into the rain. She was not happy with me, but once she was outside, she did her business."

"Thanks."

"You aren't planning to go back out in this, are you?" Robbie's brows puckered with concern.

"I hadn't thought that far. You have a full house, don't you?"

"The sofa in the great room is very comfortable. I've fallen asleep on it numerous times. I suggest you bunk up here rather than get on the roads. With that ragtop, you're running a risk of having a branch poke through your roof."

His worries echoed mine. I hesitated. "Are you sure? You've got a houseful of females already."

"What's one more?" he shrugged. "I always wanted a harem!"

Since I keep a set of clothes at Sheila's house, I ran upstairs to my designated guest room where I could dry off and change into a pair of drawstring knit pants and a sweatshirt. Leah had been assigned the room, but she wasn't there, so I knocked on the door and let myself in.

As I was coming out of the bathroom, I noticed a pair of knitting needles beside the bed. Without touching them, I looked them over carefully. They stuck out of a ball of very, very fine yarn. Finger-weight, I believe it's called. On the needles were several rows of tiny, tiny stitches. What Leah was making, I couldn't tell, but my stomach twisted with the realization that these needles were extremely long and thin.

Could she be the murderer? Could she have used a knitting needle? As far as I knew, the lab still hadn't confirmed that the screwdriver in my mother's purse was the actual murder weapon.

If Leah was the killer, what had been her motive?

I heard voices echoing up from the foyer. I figured I better vacate the room before my interest was discovered.

Robbie had Gracie by the collar, and they were waiting for me as I descended the stairs. I could have kissed him when he called out to his bride, "Sheila? Can we break a rule today? If I put a sheet on the sofa can Gracie sit next to Kiki? This dog is terrified. The thunder is really bugging her!"

From her spot in the kitchen, my mother-in-law hesitated, considering the problem. But one glance at the quaking Great Dane suggested this was a good idea. "All right. Just for tonight."

"How are you?" I said, giving Sheila a careful hug. Her black eye had swollen alarmingly. Since she's very fair-skinned, bruises look especially vivid on her.

"I think I got the better end of the fight, if that's what you mean. Other than that, I'm furious with Prescott. He did this for one reason and one reason only: to humiliate and antagonize Robbie. I'll never forgive him for it," she said.

When Sheila says she won't forgive someone, you could carve that in granite and add it to a national shrine, because she won't. She's like Mert that way. I have to admit in this case, I couldn't blame her. Given the animosity between the prisoners in the jail and the folks who put them there, Sheila's life had been at risk.

"For your birthday, I'm buying you a punching bag," I said, trying to make light of the situation.

"I already installed one in the basement," said Robbie. "But she could use a nice pair of gloves."

Voices echoed up from Sheila's finished basement.

"The Jimmy Girls went downstairs with Anya to try and find our stash of board games. I have a hunch we're going to lose power any minute now."

Anya led the pack coming up the stairs, as she carried a dusty Scrabble box. I greeted the women, but I felt awkward around them. I hadn't had much chance to get to know them. Their comfort with each other left me feeling like an interloper.

Anya set down the box and threw her arms around me. "Any word from Detweiler?"

"Not yet."

"I'm getting a new brother," she announced. "Actually two of them."

"So we heard. Via email. A novel way to make a birth announcement," said Sheila. The look she gave me was neither warm nor fuzzy.

Oops. I'd neglected to call Sheila after the sonogram. Frankly, I wasn't all that sure she would care since she's not my mother, and she's not Detweiler's either. But behind her pout was a glimmer of hurt.

"Um, sorry," I said, as I gave her a gentle hug that she accepted stiffly. "I should have told you in person, but I haven't had the chance. You've had more important things on your plate."

"For goodness sake, Kiki. Didn't you realize I could use a bit of good news?"

Wow. She really did care!

"I'm sorry. Really sorry."

"A house full of boys," said Sheila, with a touch of petulance as she pulled away from me. She headed toward her sofa, where Robbie was tucking in a sheet. "With a wonderful big sister to keep them in line. Thank you for keeping me informed, Anya. Come on, Gracie. Take full advantage of the storm, because this is a one night privilege."

Fortunately, Ester Frommer had been watching this exchange. She stepped between Sheila and me while pulling on one of Robbie's old sweatshirts. "I'd forgotten how bad the storms could get here."

Leah Ginsberg was right on Ester's heels. Tucking a strand of hair behind her ears, she asked, "Were any of the roads impassable? Flooding used to be bad over by White Road."

"I tried to come the back way, but a downed tree blocked my route. A lot of limbs have been snapped off. The water level is high in the streets."

"I hope Prescott has enough sense to send officers to usual trouble spots. There are a few traffic lights that always go out during bad storms. Maybe I should call him," said Robbie.

"No, you don't." Sheila pulled him down beside her on the sofa. "Not when he's so eager to have your job. Let him make a public fool of himself. He deserves it."

"But citizens could get hurt," Robbie said, as he rubbed the flat of his palms hard against his legs.

"If he gets your job, Robbie, you can count on citizens getting hurt," I said.

My comment put me back in Sheila's good graces. She thawed like a spring day.

"Besides, Prescott probably won't listen to you anyway. In fact, if you suggest something, he'll probably do just the opposite," Sheila said.

"Kiki, we heard you are working on a wedding album for Sheila," said Toby Pearlman. Toby wore reading glasses with round black rims, a striking accent to her silver hair. "May we see it?"

"Sure," I said. "That reminds me. Sheila? What have you heard from Vincent about your photos?"

She hadn't heard anything, so she asked Robbie to text message the photographer. Vincent messaged right back that he would drop them off at my store maybe tomorrow and no later than Friday. Seems he'd been booked for a fashion shoot in Costa Rica, and he wanted the wedding photos off his "to do" list before he flew out.

Sheila's coffee table was the best spot for viewing the album. First I grabbed a pen and notebook so I could take notes. Then we got everyone seated. Anya took a spot on the carpet near Sheila's feet. The Jimmy Girls gathered around the album with the sort of casual, polite interest that suggested they knew nothing about scrapbooking. But when I opened the book to the title page, there was a collective gasp.

I'd created blossoms in pink, purple and white, with a few tiny touches of navy thrown in. The album title was raised slightly above this 3-D layer of paper blossoms, an effect both stunning and elegant at the same time.

"What are those flowers?" asked Toby.

"Paper?" asked Leah.

"You cut every one of those? By hand?" asked Ester. "It's so beautiful!"

Indeed it was.

"How many flowers are there, Mom?" Anya knew the answer, but she was prompting me so I could share the extent of my diligence.

"Four hundred and fifty," I said. "The blossoms are layers stacked on layers. It took a lot of punching to get them just right."

"And the pistils and stamens?" asked Toby. "What are those?"

"Paper wrapped around wire. Some are very, very thin paper beads I made."

"Was it hard work?" asked Ester. She'd brought along a small bag with wooden handles. From the depths, she pulled a needlepoint belt. These belts seemed to be a sartorial necessity for CALA alumnae. Every woman of a certain age either owned one or had crafted one for her husband and son. I could see Ester had stabbed the canvas with a long thick needle.

What other needles might be in her bag? She saw me staring at her work and smiled.

I turned my attention back to Anya, who was saying, "It wasn't easy. Mom had to stop and soak her fist in ice water once every hour. All that punching caused her hand to swell."

Sheila slowly turned the page. On the left was a baby picture of Sheila and on the right was a baby picture of Robbie. Both were mounted on a background paper with a slight ivory sheen. On Robbie's side, I used the navy flowers to make it more masculine, while on Sheila's I used shades of pink.

All the women made oohed and aahed as they looked at the pictures. The rest of the album elicited the same sort of interest, until they arrived upon the pages I'd done of Sheila in high school. These pages evoked a narrative, as I'd hoped they would. Soon, my pen was flying across my notepad as the group of friends shared one anecdote after another. The stories kept coming, with one recollection leading to another. When the sharing died down, I turned the page in the album. Under a flap, my concession to Sheila's vanity, was a photo of the Jimmy Girls.

"Oh! There's Miriam," said Toby, with a hitch in her voice. "In the back. You can barely see her. Will you look at her? She was so shy back then."

"I need a glass of water," said Ester, in a ragged voice.

"Remember how the boys would tease her about her nose?" Toby turned to her friends. "She would hide her face as she walked down the halls. Her hair was always in her eyes."

"I remember how she hid behind a book in all our classes. Hoping that no one could see her, I guess," said Sheila.

"She got her nose bobbed in the summer of her junior year. Just like the rest of us. What a change that made in her life," said Leah, fingering her necklace nervously. "Boys discovered her. She went out every Friday and Saturday night. She never stayed home after that."

"I left space for a memorial page," I said. "Do you have any pictures of her? After her surgery?"

"I do," said Toby. "They're in an album I have on Snapfish."

Anya was dispatched to open Sheila's computer and search for Toby's Snapfish account. In a few minutes, my daughter came back with two prints from Sheila's color printer. The paper quality wasn't great, so she'd wisely forwarded the emails to me. When I got back to the store, I would print the pictures on high quality photo paper. But for now, we could at least take a look at the photos. I was curious about the missing Jimmy Girl.

"Wow. What a difference a nose job made!" I examined the picture closely. I set the photo of Miriam after her surgery next to the photo taken before the cosmetic procedure. Of course, you couldn't see much of her in the older pic because she stood in the shadows, but you could see enough to tell how much she'd changed.

"The rest of us benefited from the rhinoplasty," said Sheila, "but she was totally transformed."

"Who would have guessed," said Toby, "that her nose would start collapsing and couldn't be repaired?"

68

"But you had corrective surgery," I said to Sheila. "Why didn't Miriam do the same?"

Almost on cue, Gracie whimpered as the storm continued to bluster. A crackle of lightning brightened the whole house for a split second, before the boom of thunder came in reply.

"She tried," said Toby gently. "You have to understand that Miriam's transformation was astonishing. Her original nose was incredibly large and ugly. She went from major wallflower to belle of the ball overnight. She had actually started modeling, and she made a good living at it. That's why she moved to California, and there she was in great demand. So when her nose began to change, she was in denial. It was too much for her. It was like her world collapsed rather than her nose."

"Most of us needed corrective rhinoplasty," said Sheila. "But for her, it was more than a correction. It was imperative."

"Are you saying that Dr. Hyman was a quack?" I raised my voice over the pounding of rain outside.

"No," said Ester. She'd returned from the kitchen and now stood next to the sofa with a glass of water in her hands. "My father is a surgeon. He knew Dr. Hyman very, very well. You have to understand that plastic surgery has been around since the Egyptians practiced it around 1200 BC on the faces of mummies. Of course, procedures have changed over the years with the advent of modern medicine. But nose jobs have been around for centuries. Dr. Hyman worked within the protocols of the time."

"Did all of you have problems?" I asked.

"No," said Toby. "I didn't."

"That's because you had the least amount of work done to yours," said Leah.

"Dr. Hyman did what he was taught to do, in accordance with the standards of the time," said Ester. She shifted her weight and set her jaw. Her knuckles whitened as she gripped her glass.

"He was a quack," said Toby, as a loud boom of thunder shook the house.

"That's not fair," said Ester. "I know you have strong feelings about the man, but you have to be fair! Twenty-five years ago, they didn't consider how well your nose would match your facial structure. Nor did they realize that removing cartilage from the nose tip would later be a problem. Back then, all nose surgery was reductive."

"So what happened?" I asked. "You seem to be saying her nose was fine at first."

"It was," said Ester. "Her new nose looked lovely. So much so that she was approached by a modeling agency and the rest, as they say, is history. But slowly her nose collapsed because the internal architecture was compromised. Her nostrils were pinched, making breathing difficult. She started snoring."

"We all had that to some degree," said Toby, waving her hand in a dismissive gesture. "The changes, the collapsing, and snoring."

"Yes," said Ester, "but for Miriam it was different. She was overly invested in her looks. She'd gone from being the ugly duckling to the proverbial swan. Once she started modeling, she had other work done. But they couldn't do much for her nose. There wasn't enough to work with. The bridge was collapsing from the inside."

Sheila shook her head. "I've never understood this. I was able to find a good surgeon. Sure, I had to fly to Chicago, but I got mine fixed. Why couldn't Miriam do the same?"

"Come on, Sheila," said Ester. She sat back down and picked up her needlework. "You're smart enough to realize that each of us is different. She just didn't respond to surgery as well as she would have hoped."

"Anya, honey, could you bring me a refill of my tea?" asked Leah. "Thank you, dear."

When my daughter left, Leah leaned in closely. "Miriam had taken a much younger lover. He slept over one night and told her the next morning that she snored like a freight train. She was devastated."

"That's right," said Ester, in a near whisper. "She called me the next day and sobbed her heart out. Then she made the rounds of doctors one more time. They all said the same thing: They might be able to help, but they couldn't guarantee the results. Here's another difference, Sheila. You've kept out of the sun and you don't smoke. Miriam did both and her skin lacked elasticity."

"That's why she did it," said Leah

"Did what?" I asked, hurriedly. Not wanting Anya to overhear.

"She killed herself," said Toby.

69

Same day...
A suburb of Los Angeles, California

"Thank you for coming to the house," said Lorraine, as she sat in a wingback chair with her feet on a footstool. Barton, her butler, and Louisa, her maid, had helped her down the stairs and into the chair. She was far too unstable to walk on her own. "I'm afraid I'm not up to traveling downtown these days. The traffic is just horrendous."

They both knew she was having an exacerbation. But she still had her pride, and she hated admitting how weak she was.

"It's always a pleasure to get out of that rat race," Thornton said, as he eased into a chair across from her. A window was open just a crack, and on the air was the scent of young roses. It made his nose itch. Thornton hated leaving downtown LA, but what could he do? This situation was delicate, and he didn't trust anyone else to handle it properly.

Lorraine's brother, Van, had been very careful in naming Thornton and his sister as executors of his estate. Both the attorney and Lorraine had been given letters from beyond the grave, personal missives written by Van. In these he had made his wishes clear: In regards to releasing the trust fund, they were to do what was best for Gina, and in the event of her demise, they were to take care of her son. But neither Thornton nor Lorraine could act without consent of the other party. Van's goal had been to yoke Lorraine's soft touch with Thornton's fiscal conservatism.

Of course, Gina had no way of knowing that money had been put aside for her and Erik. Before she married Van, she'd signed a pre-nuptial agreement giving away her rights to his assets. Since Lauber had always been incredibly generous with her, she had no reason to question the arrangement. In fact, by saving her "allowance," she'd even put aside money for her son's education, which pleased her greatly. When anyone questioned her about the financial aspects of her marriage, Gina would point out that Erik didn't want for anything.

Although he didn't have grandparents in the picture or siblings, Erik had a wonderful life. Van made sure of it. As part of his sense of obligation, it was Van who had pushed Gina into getting her will done.

When it came time for Gina to put hard decisions on paper, she had quickly come to realize that Lorraine couldn't care for the boy. The two women had talked frankly for many weeks, reviewing Gina's options. Eventually, Gina had decided that in the event of her death, her son should live with his father. The father he'd never met. The man who didn't know he was a dad.

"Why haven't you told Mr. Detweiler about his son?" Thornton had asked Gina. "You could be collecting child support."

To Thornton, it was all about the money. Gina's secrecy made no practical sense.

But Gina had demurred. A niggling feeling told the attorney there was more to this story. He kept pressing Gina, but she wouldn't change her mind. Finally, she had thrown up her hands and said, "Mr. Thornton, if you aren't willing to leave this alone, I'll find another lawyer."

That had brought him to heel.

Although he didn't stop wondering. Information was power. What was Gina hiding? He'd sent a private investigator to look into Detective Chad Detweiler, but the man dug up nothing of interest.

But Thornton had his suspicions.

Each year during their annual review of her wishes and desires, Thornton asked Gina to reconsider. But she had stuck to her decision. If anything, she'd become more recalcitrant. "I expect to live a long life, but if I don't, Erik will be in good hands."

When Thornton tried to weasel more information out of Lorraine, she'd simply stared at him for a very long time, before saying, "If Gina wishes to tell you more, she will. I won't betray her confidences. I'm surprised you'd ask."

That warned him away from the topic. After all, Thornton had his own secrets to protect. Van Lauber didn't know that Thornton had misappropriated most of Erik's trust fund, using it as his own personal piggybank. So the lawyer's concern wasn't about Erik's welfare. No, Thornton was protecting his own hide.

This meeting with Lorraine had one purpose and one

purpose only: Thornton needed to stall. He could not afford to let Lorraine Lauber release the trust fund money.

But here she was, wanting to play the role of Lady Bountiful. She'd known the cop all of three days, but Lorraine was ready to write him a big, fat check.

A check that would bounce higher than the Arch in St. Louis.

"Come now, Thornton. Be reasonable. Detweiler's finances are meager. There's another child on the way. They're living in cramped spaces. Why not at least release some of the money? It certainly would make life easier for Erik," said Lorraine, in a peevish tone.

Well, thought Thornton, of course releasing the funds looked logical to Lorraine. Letting go of that money wouldn't make any difference to her.

When he began his business, Van had borrowed half his start-up funds from his sister. She'd been incredibly patient, never asking to be reimbursed, and never adding pressure to him. When his company went public, he'd repaid his sister's trust by giving her thirty percent of the stock. She was now a millionaire many times over.

"Isn't the point of the trust to help Erik? And doesn't that mean helping his new parents?" asked Lorraine.

Of course she was right.

But helping Detweiler and Mrs. Lowenstein would put Thornton behind bars.

If Thornton could wait her out, no one need ever know how much money was missing. Although Quinton handled Lorraine's will, Thornton had been privy to it, so he knew that Lorraine had put aside money for Erik. Thornton's plan was genius. When she died, he'd simply swap out funds from Lorraine's trust and move them into her brother's. It would take a bit of fancy footwork with the books, but

Thornton was up to the task. It was a Ponzi scheme of the first order. Unless someone hired a forensic expert, no one would be the wiser. At least not right away. By the time the swap was discovered, Thornton would be on a plane to the Bahamas, where he had a house on the beach.

Actually, the switch should happen fairly soon. Lorraine grew weaker and weaker with each exacerbation of the disease. Thornton picked up on small nuances that announced her decline. Usually she offered him tea, but not today. Usually she shook his hand, but this time when he came into the room, she carefully tucked both hands into her lap. He knew why: She didn't want them to betray her lack of muscle control.

"Of course, the money is there to help Erik and his new family," said Thornton reasonably. "But look at it this way, Lorraine. If we've misjudged the man's character, we jeopardize Erik by releasing the money. Think about it: If Detweiler has both the money and the child, he can hire attorneys to fight us. It would be much, much harder to extract Erik from a bad situation. If we wait, we'll know whether the boy is well-treated. If so, I'll gladly write the check. But once we've opened the floodgates to the money, that's like water over the dam. We can't get it back."

She nodded thoughtfully. "I see your point."

"Where is Mr. Detweiler?" asked Thornton.

"With Erik at Disneyland."

"Just the two of them?"

"Heavens, no. Not yet at least," she said. As usual, she wore weariness like a shroud. Out of respect for her brother, she'd taken to wearing black, a curiously old-fashioned gesture, but one that seemed perfect for Lorraine's sensibilities. However, the color was not good on her, sapping her face of its usual color. It made her look worse than usual. Of course, she had been stooped over for years, with her head jutting out at almost a right angle from her body. That couldn't be healthy, having that crick in her neck. But beyond the MS and the obvious osteoporosis, she was even less animated than usual. Her demeanor had changed dramatically after her brother's death. Thornton knew that the loss of her sibling had dealt Lorraine a body blow. Now, the upcoming loss of Erik was taking away Lorraine's will to live.

She continued, "Erik is intrigued by Detweiler, and likes him, but he's not entirely won over. When he gets tired, he whines for Brawny, so she is with them. Orson watches from afar."

"Of course," Thornton struggled to get comfortable, but the chair seemed too small. "So what do you think of him? Detective Detweiler, I mean."

"I like him immensely."

"The boy doesn't look much like his father."

Lorraine smiled. "Every family has its secrets. Chad Detweiler assures me that Erik is the very image of his late grandfather."

"And you believe that?" asked Thornton.

"Oh, Thornton. You are ever the skeptic. I suggest you go to Wikipedia and refresh your knowledge of pre-Civil War history. Germans came to Missouri in droves to work the land. The Detweiler farm has been in the family for more than 100 years. But the Germans weren't the only ones who wanted to put down roots in Missouri. Remember? The Missouri Compromise?"

"You don't need to lecture me, Lorraine. I majored in history as an undergraduate." His rebuke sounded more stinging than he had intended.

"Let's get back to the subject at hand," she said with a

touch of weariness. "I understand what you're saying about waiting, but really, does it make that much of a difference? If you need to fight him later, there's more than enough to cover your fees."

Thornton picked at an imaginary piece of lint on his pant leg. "Lorraine, I admire your sense of justice and your desire to help Detective Detweiler, but I respectfully disagree. This simply isn't the right time. Not yet. We have no idea whether he's taking the boy because he cares or because he suspects a windfall is attached. How can you be so sure of his motives?"

"I have always believed myself to be a good judge of character. That was proven when Van married Gina. Remember? You were convinced that she was a gold-digger. Nothing could have been further from the truth. Yes, she enjoyed the benefits of his money, but she never pressured him for more. Ever. And I would have known about it if she had. No, I think—I believe—that Chad Detweiler is a good man who will take wonderful care of his son. Furthermore, he has no idea that there's an inheritance at stake here. Why would he?"

"You've pressed him on this?" Thornton was not about to give in, but he was curious. How much had Lorraine told the cop?

More importantly, what did she suspect?

Would she have to be dealt with?

"Yes," said Lorraine with a lift of her chin. "I pressed him on the topic in a round-about way. I asked him point-blank how they would get by. How they'd make ends meet. Do you know what he said? He told me that he'd worked with a number of wealthy people in St. Louis, and then he said, 'With all due respect, ma'am, I've seen no evidence that money fixes all their problems. In fact, I'd have to say that it seems to create as many as it solves. So, while it's true that Erik might not have every new toy on the market, and we might dress him in second-hand clothes, he'll never lack for love or guidance. That's what a kid really needs, isn't it?'"

She narrowed her eyes and stared hard at Thornton. "And it is, isn't it? You have children of your own, don't you?"

Thornton squirmed in his chair. She knew he had children, and that he'd botched the job of raising them. His failures as a father were embarrassingly public.

"He made a pretty speech. Does he really mean it? Come on, Lorraine, I thought you were smarter than that."

He'd hit her Achilles heel. She hated to be thought stupid. A red stain started at her throat and crept toward her cheeks. Her nostrils flared and her mouth went flat.

It occurred to Thornton that he might have overplayed his hand.

"My brother always respected my intellect," she said.

"And he never questioned my loyalty," Thornton shot back.

That wiped the smug look off her face.

Between them sat their shared history, their memories of the past. Lorraine swallowed hard and looked away. It had been her fault that her brother had fallen through the ice in that frozen pond in Maine. She'd been charged with watching him, but instead had turned her attention to a handsome young man who flirted with her. While she'd been pre-occupied, Van had ventured out, too far from the solid edges of the pond, enjoying the fast blades on his new skates. Thornton, a newcomer to the community, and two years Van's senior, had heard the sound of the ice cracking. As he watched, a boy went down, down, down, and the water splashed up on the ice. Thornton had yelled for help, thrown himself on his belly, inched toward the hole, and pulled Van out.

Lorraine's mother never forgave her.

Van did.

He and Thornton became lifelong friends.

"Have it your way," she said at last. "Now, if you don't mind, I'll say goodbye to you. I'm feeling weary."

70

Wednesday, late afternoon/Four days after the wedding...
Anaheim, California

$\mathcal{D}$etweiler hoisted a sleeping Erik over his shoulder and started toward Pluto, not the debunked planet, but a row of parking in the vast Disneyland lot. Orson sprinted on ahead to bring the Escalade closer to the theme park exit. Meanwhile, Detweiler's long legs made short work of the distance. As he walked, Detweiler's head swiveled left and right, a habit formed by his years as a policeman. At some point, he noticed that Brawny, too, was on the alert. Without conferring, they'd both chosen to stay in the middle of the driving lanes where an intruder's approach would be immediately visible.

The overhead lights were bright, although swarms of bugs filtered the illumination. The parking lot smelled of gasoline, dropped candy, and asphalt. Erik had insisted on staying for "just one more ride." Now they joined herds of other parents, taking sleepy children to the cars. There was nothing to suggest there was any danger, except a sixth sense that told Detweiler they were being watched. He shifted Erik's bulk, to move the boy's legs to one side. This allowed the cop to lightly touch his holstered gun. Yes, his friend was there if he needed it.

"*Aye*, he's tuckered out, isn't he?" said Brawny, as she walked along next to him. "Poor mite. He had a full day of fun even though we didn't start until after his lunch."

"He had a blast," said Detweiler with a chuckle. "Too bad Emily and Anya weren't here, too. And Kiki, of course. Maybe someday we can bring all the kids. Here or to Florida. They'd love this. Kiki would go nuts taking photos. I hope we can do it sooner rather than later, because the girls will be too big before we know it."

Brawny's wingtips slapped the surface as she kept pace with the cop. The nanny seemed to measure how close other patrons came, watching them with discerning eyes. Although Brawny was only five-six or so, she carried herself as someone much bigger. Indeed, her shoulders were broader than Detweiler's.

"You want me to take him?" she asked.

"Heavens no. I love carrying him. I'm delighted he's accepting of me."

"Have it your way," said Brawny.

He'd come to realize that she didn't mean that as a jibe. It was just a figure of speech she often used. Her way of conceding his authority. Even though she was always ready to take over the child care responsibilities.

At first, Erik had run around like a crazy man, darting from ride to ride, and tugging on their hands. As the day wore on, he grew tired and fussy. Eventually, he turned pleading eyes to Brawny, and she picked him up, before

Detweiler could offer. For at least an hour off and on, she walked with the boy on one hip. If the weight bothered her, she never complained.

After a while, Erik agreed to let Detweiler do some of the heavy lifting. When they stopped for dinner, the hostess at one of the restaurants led them to a table in the back, but it was surrounded by too many chairs. Without a word, Brawny picked up one chair after another and stacked them on top of each other.

Clearly, she was "strong like bull," as Emily might say.

As they navigated the park, several Disney patrons had asked Brawny for an autograph, mistaking her Black Watch Plaid kilt, black jacket, sporran, crisp white blouse and white socks held up with garter flashes for some sort of a costume. Rather than correct them, she simply smiled and signed her name. "'Tis naught but a thrill for them. Does no harm, I expect."

The children at the park were impressed with all of her gear, but they particularly liked petting her sporran, the pouch made of rabbit hide that hung from her belt. Detweiler was curious about every portion of her apparel, because he sensed it all held meaning. Her shoes, she had explained to him, were "ghillie brogues," whatever that meant. They sure looked capable of inflicting damage on an aggressor. When he mentioned that, she nodded. "Aye. Steel toes. Can break a shin easy-peasy."

"You're from Scotland?" he asked her once they sat down at the table.

"Edinburgh."

"What is your given name?"

"Bronwyn Macavity," she said. "But I'd be pleased for you to call me Brawny."

"And you've been with Erik since...?"

"Since he was born. Mr. Lauber hired me to be his nanny."

"What do your duties entail?"

"I get this lad up in the morning, feed him his porridge, drive him to school, spend the rest of the day doing paper-work and such for Miss Lorraine, pick Erik up from school, feed him his snacks, and take him for walks in the park or to the zoo. Something educational but out-of-doors, always. Get him bathed and ready for bed."

"When did he see his mother?" Detweiler's face creased in concern.

"Brawny," murmured Erik as he roused. Half asleep he reached for his nanny. She took him from Detweiler.

"Ah," she said. "Don't be worrying about that! He spent time every day with his mum. She'd join us for breakfast. Read to him before bed. Often as not have dinner with him. Such like. I did as much or as little as she wished. She was a good mum to him, if that's what you're thinking. The best. But because I was there constant like, if Mr. Lauber wanted to travel, they could come and go as they pleased."

"This is all new to me," he said. "I've never really met a nanny. Not in real life, and definitely not one as professional as you are. I hope you won't find my questions intrusive."

"Not one bit. I've got my marching orders. You ask and I'll answer. Miss Lorraine said there were to be no secrets. It's all about what's best for the boy. My lad." With that, she reached over to stroke Erik's hair. Although no one would call Brawny pretty, her face had a nice symmetry made more pronounced by the way she wore her gray hair pulled back into a tight bun. She couldn't be much more than forty, he guessed, but the hair color made it difficult to tell. When she looked at Erik, she seemed much younger. A softness infused her moss green eyes.

As for Erik, he curved his body against Brawny's and reached for a loose lock of her hair with a familiarity that made Detweiler's heart ache.

She's just one more person for Erik to leave behind, thought Detweiler.

Poor Erik. His life had already changed irrevocably, and now it would change once more. Detweiler recommitted himself to being the best dad possible for the boy. Erik deserved no less than that.

71

Evening of the same day
Ladue, Missouri
~ Kiki~

he Jimmy Girls stayed up until midnight. They didn't realize it, but their merriment was keeping me from bed as well. Since I'd opted to sleep on the sofa in the great room, I had to wait for them to turn in. The wind outside was still blowing, and a branch clawed at the great room windows, but I was too tired to care. I knew I was safe here at Sheila's. On the streets, I would be at risk of stalling out my car or getting bonked by a falling branch.

I made up the sofa and gratefully crawled between the sheets. Before I fell asleep, I started thinking about families, and how magical they were. Soon Erik would join us, even though he wasn't a blood relative. Neither were Detweiler or Aunt Penny or Sheila. At least they weren't biological kin to me. And yet, we were family.

That got me thinking about Catherine. This was the first chance I'd had all day to ponder what little I'd learned from Aunt Penny. All I knew was that my sister and my father had a fight, fifteen years ago. Amanda and I had been quarantined in the upstairs bedroom with a bad case of the measles. We'd heard the argument, but that wasn't unusual. Not in our house. The front door slammed. Amanda and I shrugged at each other. We figured Catherine would be back after things cooled down. That was how life went in our household.

But she didn't come back. Not that evening or the next day or the day after. When we pressed our mother for details, she clammed up. Our dad refused to discuss the matter.

In our house, pushing your luck was not a good idea. Dad was violent, and Mom was vicious. When I was well enough to return to school, I talked to the guidance counselor, a man with more hair in his nose than on his head. "We're well aware of the situation," he said primly. "It's none of your concern."

I told Amanda what he'd said. She was still confined to our bedroom. I remember how she turned a bleak face to the window and stared at the sidewalk. When she turned back, she'd been crying. "I think he's telling you that Mom and Dad know what happened—and the school does too, and it's okay with all of them."

"Except for us," I said.

"Except for us." She paused. "And maybe for Catherine."

Where had my sister been all those years?

Would I even recognize her?

Why didn't she try to contact Amanda and me?

And how dare Aunt Penny keep my sister's whereabouts a secret?

I'd only closed my eyes for a minute when my cell phone started to vibrate. I nearly squealed with joy when I saw Detweiler's number.

"Erik is great," he said with a low chuckle. "We went to Disneyland this afternoon, and now he's totally pooped out. Orson, Lorraine's driver, drove us home. Erik's nanny took him up to bed. Her name is Bronwyn, but he calls her Brawny like the paper towels."

A driver as well as a nanny? Wow. What a life Gina had!

Several families in Ladue employed nannies. Two or three families had maids. I knew this because I'd seen the maids in the carpool line, picking up kids. One was an African-American woman who wore the traditional servants' attire, a black dress, white apron, and white cap. It looked totally weird. Like some sort of throw-back to The Help.

"I bet Erik had a fabulous time," I said, thinking of all the Disneyland pages I'd love to do. "Will you send me photos?"

Detweiler yawned into the phone. "I will. I meant to. They're on my phone. But can I talk to you about something? Even though Erik had a terrific time, he keeps asking me where Gina is, and why she isn't coming home. He asks about Van, too, but not as much. I guess that's normal, isn't it?"

"That's typical. She was a stay-at-home mom, so she's the one he's most accustomed to. He's too young to understand what dead really means. The permanence of it. What are you telling him?"

"Lorraine explained that Van and Gina had gone to heaven, so I'm sticking as closely as I can to what she says. I figure she knows him best, and I don't want to confuse him. We've been explaining how his parents won't be coming back, but they are watching over him and they still love him."

"That's a lot for a little guy to take in," I said. "Especially since it's both parents."

"I know," he said quietly. "I see how attached he is to Lorraine and to Brawny, and it worries me. I hope he'll be able to adjust."

"He will," I said. "Kids are amazingly resilient. Besides, he can still keep in contact with Lorraine and Brawny via Skype. Gosh, I have to admit I really envy Gina for having had a nanny. That sure would be a big help."

"Brawny is wonderful. She's a trained child care professional, so she's very calm and sure of herself. Knits like a champ, too. I've seen samples of her work. I guess she did as much or as little as Gina needed, but primarily she stepped in when the Laubers wanted to travel. She did carpool duty, too. Can you imagine how helpful that would be with three kids? Honestly, I wonder how we'll manage. I can't believe that I'm taking so much time off of work. This is time I planned to spend helping you and our baby get acclimated. I know I'm doing the right thing by Erik, but it worries me that I won't be available to help you."

"We'll manage. Erik needed to feel safe around you. How's that going?"

"As you might imagine, he's awfully clingy with Brawny. She's been with him since he was born."

"That's a normal attachment," I said. "I bet he'll miss her almost as much as he's missing his mother."

"That's what I'm afraid of."

Usually he was the one telling me not to fret. This time our roles were reversed. "Try not to worry about it," I said. "Remember, we have each other. And Erik will have us. It'll all work out."

"I love you, sweetheart," said Detweiler.

"I love you, too."

72

Thursday a.m. / Six days after the wedding
Sheila's house in Ladue, Missouri

The next morning dawned clear and fresh. You'd never guess that storms had pounded us. Outside the window, leaf litter and a carpet of twigs and branches spoke to the treachery of the night before. But birds were singing and by all accounts, it looked as though we were in for a typical summer's day.

I found Robbie in full egg scrambling mode. The sight and smell of the eggs made me queasy, so I popped two slices of bread in the toaster and waited for them. Since it was just the two of us, I pointed out to him that Ester and Leah had long thin implements that could easily have killed Dr. Hyman.

"All the Jimmy Girls suffered from botched rhinoplasty," I said, as I poured hot water over my tea bag. "Not just Sheila. So all of them could be considered suspects. Especially seeing as how Dr. Hyman died. Someone was definitely trying to make a statement. The Jimmy Girls were wandering around before the service started. Remember? They kept walking in and out of Leighton's house to use the restroom. What if we have the timeframe wrong? That could happen."

"Sure, it could."

"So?" I said. The toast was ready to be buttered and I slathered it on. "Can you check out the needles? See if there's any blood on them? At least see if they'd work as murder weapons?"

"No, I can't."

I paused in the middle of chewing. "Why not?"

"Normally, I'd be happy to look into that possibility," said Robbie. "But Jim Hagg specifically warned me about interfering with Prescott's investigation."

"But you have friends!" I waved my butter knife in the air.

"Friends who have already stuck their necks out for me."

"What about Sheila? Don't you think Prescott will continue to come after her?"

"No, I don't. He's too scared of Hagg. So is Tom White. Hagg knows where all the bodies are buried."

A piece of turkey bacon spit grease at him. To my surprise, he swore at the frying pan. Usually Robbie is calm, cool, and collected.

"Wow, this is really getting to you," I said, as I bit into the second piece of toast.

"Kiki, the day I watched them handcuff Sheila and shove her into the back of a squad car was the worst day of my life. Bar none. I've seen all sorts of creeps take a ride to the jail, but this was different. It was personal. Watching her, knowing she was innocent, and realizing that she was only being persecuted to get back at me, well, I felt about this high." He raised his index finger and thumb to measure a hair's width of space. "I always thought I could protect the people I love. Instead, I had to stand by and watch her being treated like a common criminal. And why? Because of me."

"I'm sure she forgives you."

"Yes, so she's said. But can I forgive myself?"

73

Our conversation ended abruptly because Anya wandered in. To my surprise, although she'd been up late the night before, she was eager to go back to work on the construction project. "Feel my muscle, Robbie," she told him, as she presented her bicep.

As Robbie dished out her eggs, Anya told him about how much fun she was having.

Since I'd finished my toast and tea, I went into the other room and packed up Sheila's album. I figured that after Vincent dropped off the photos, I'd finish the book and scan it. If the Jimmy Girls wanted their own copies, it would be easy enough to send them the scans. Even one room away, I could hear Anya as she chattered happily, telling Robbie about how much fun she was having doing "hard labor."

"Today we're going to use nail guns!"

"Be careful with that," warned Robbie. "You wouldn't believe all the people who get injured using nail guns. Those are lethal weapons."

Anya promised that she would. I made a mental note to get a similar promise from Aunt Penny.

In short order, my daughter, Gracie, and I were in the Beemer, headed for U City. Most of the downed branches had been pulled to the side of the road, but a few required that I steer far to one side so I didn't hit the debris. Anya stared at the broken branches, many as thick as my thigh. Her head swiveled to look at one in particular.

"What if a branch had come down on you, Mom?"

I smiled at her. "That didn't happen. Angels were watching over me."

As we drove toward U City, my phone rang.

"Hey, it's me," said Rebekkah. "Look, I need to pick up Dad from the hospital. They've finished all his tests, and they want to talk with us. I don't know when I'll be free."

I told her not to worry and to phone me if I could help.

Once Aunt Penny was in my car, I rehashed my conversation with Robbie about the dangers of nail guns.

"Shoot, Kiki. Don't be such an old lady. Anya's almost a grown woman, and she's smart as a whip. Of course, I'll watch her. Roy is going to go through all the safety points with us when he drops the guns off. Does that make you feel better?"

"Marginally," I said. To be honest, I was ticked off at Aunt Penny, and she knew it. The more I thought about her keeping her knowledge of Catherine a secret, the angrier I became.

"Shoot fire," said my aunt. The look she cast my way was one of pure disgust.

I didn't flinch. Instead, I shot my own angry glance toward her—and I must have done a great job of expressing my chagrin because Aunt Penny actually flinched.

What I really wanted to do was to get Aunt Penny in private, but it seemed that would have to wait. I sure didn't want to confront her with Anya in the car. I had a sick feeling that whatever I learned was going to be ugly. My daughter didn't need to hear the sordid details of life with my dad. Her interaction with my mother was bad enough.

"Must have been one powerful storm tore through here," said Aunt Penny.

"Yup." With gritted teeth, I turned my attention to the task at hand, getting us to the store where we would all start work on our separate projects. Normally, we would have had an easy drive, but the litter from the storm was worse as we headed south of 40.

By the time we arrived, my neck was sore with tension. It wasn't just the drive that had annoyed me. It was pent-up anger at Aunt Penny.

True to his word, Roy gave both women a safety demo. He even showed me all the safety features. I still wasn't convinced that this was a great idea, but I knew I couldn't protect Anya from every danger in life. If I held the reins too tightly, she would be more likely to rebel. I busied myself restocking shelves and filling out paperwork related to the adoptive parents' crop. The more I thought about Bernice Stottlemeyer's rude behavior, the more upset it made me. After an hour of the pft-pft-pft of the nail guns, my head started to throb.

I badly needed a distraction. I wanted to finish Sheila's album, but I'd have to wait until Vincent arrived with the photos.

Clancy walked up to my table. I hadn't heard her with all the noise.

"How're you feeling?" I asked.

"Better," she said. "Hey, have you started work on a project for our Friday night crop? We only have our regulars signed up. I think people are waiting to see what I post as the project."

"I'll get cracking on it," I said. "After I take Gracie for a walk. You still don't feel well, do you?"

"I've been better." Before heading back toward the office, she said, "I'm sending in the orders today."

Gracie and I headed out the back door, walked through the parking lot, and around the block. She took her sweet time about emptying her tanks, but gosh, since she spends the rest of the day snoozing in her playpen, I can hardly complain. Besides, her walks are my walks, and the fresh air does both of us good. By the time we'd made our circuit, I had a few ideas brewing for the crop.

Under my work table I keep a box full of "idea starters." Most are old craft magazines and super-old crafting books I've found at used bookstores. After flipping through one of them, my germ of an idea sprouted into a full-sized plant.

Lately, I'd taken to "tangling" or drawing Zentangle designs on brown wrapping paper, the stuff typically used to cover a box that's being mailed. Zentangle is an art form that's easy to teach and simple to do, but it yields wildly sophisticated results. At first glance, it looks like doodling, but whereas doodling is aimless, Zentangle relies on a vocabulary of purposeful designs made one stroke at a time. In my supplies bin, I had a collection of priority mail boxes that had already been used. Instead of pitching them into the recycling bin, I'd hung onto them. Now I painted Mod Podge on one of the small priority mail boxes and covered it with the brown paper on which I'd tangled various designs. After I adjusted the paper so it fit perfectly, I coated the brown paper itself with Mod Podge. This, I figured, would strengthen the paper, add a rich patina, and make the final product water-proof.

I set the box aside to dry and picked up Sheila's album. I had promised to scan all the pages so I could send copies of the album to the Jimmy Girls. Even though some of the pages weren't finished, I could start scanning them while my Zentangle project was drying. The minute I opened the album and detached the cover page, the door minder rang.

In stomped Bernice Stottlemeyer, wearing a face as stormy as the weather had been. In her right hand was her adoption profile album. Before I could even say, "Hi," the album went flying past my head.

I ducked.

The album smacked into a display of storage containers. Two jars hit the floor and exploded into tiny pieces of glass.

"What on earth do you think you're doing?" I jumped up off my stool.

"You sabotaged me!" she screamed.

"I did nothing of the kind!"

"Yes, you did! It's all your fault that we didn't get a kid! I want my money back!" Flecks of white spittle formed on her lips. I've never seen someone so mad. Correction: Not since my dad would go crazy have I seen someone so mad. But then I was little, and now I'm a grown woman. I don't have to take this sort of abuse.

"You need to leave," I said calmly, crossing my arms over my chest. "You are no longer welcome in my store. Either you turn around and walk out the way you came, or I'll call an officer of the law and have you escorted out."

"Huh!" She laughed. "I'm not going anywhere until you reverse the charges on my credit card. You ripped me off! That girl barely glanced at our album. She told the adoption counselor that she wasn't interested in us. It's all your fault!"

"What's going on here?" Aunt Penny approached us. Her hard hat was on her head, her tool belt was around her waist, and she held something in her right hand. I couldn't see what it was.

Clancy was right behind her.

"Give me my money back right now!" Bernice screamed, as she knocked over a display rack. Hundreds of dollars of inks tumbled onto the floor. Luckily, they were shrink-wrapped. But still, they'd been sorted by color. I was looking at an hour's work getting them back where they belonged.

"Stop that! Stop it right now!" shouted Clancy. Then she saw the broken glass. "You are destroying our merchandise!"

"She destroyed my chance at being a mother," Bernice said, as she pointed a finger at me.

"That's it," I said. "I'm calling the cops."

"It'll take them thirty minutes to get here," Bernice sneered.

"Stan Hadcho lives a mile away," I said to Clancy, as I pointed to my cell phone on the work table. "His number is in my favorites listings."

I relaxed a little when I heard her greet him.

"Mrs. Stottlemeyer," I said, as I drew myself up as tall as I could stand. "I am truly sorry that things didn't turn out as you had hoped, but you can't honestly be suggesting that the birth mother's lack of interest in you is my fault."

"Of course it's your fault! We can offer a child every advantage. Good schools, a nice home, stable family life— and there was no reason—none!—for this woman to reject us. The problem wasn't with us. The problem was this crummy excuse for an album."

"Look, why don't you just calm down?" I said, in a soothing tone while Aunt Penny edged closer to Bernice.

"Why don't you just give me a refund?"

"Hadcho is on his way." Clancy put my phone back on the work table.

"I told you my work wasn't guaranteed Mrs. Stottle-meyer. The form you signed specifically said there aren't any refunds on custom albums. Besides all that, you've now ruined a lot of our merchandise. So, while I regret that you're unhappy—"

"Unhappy? I am furious! I came for a refund and you better give me one! Every second I stay is going to cost you money!" With that, she dropped her car keys into her purse. After zipping it closed, she used her Bottega Veneta handbag as a slingshot and knocked all the punches off of a display unit.

"You shouldn't do that," I said. "That's a very expensive purse."

"You're right about that! More than you make a month, I bet. But it was also made to last, so I think I'll test it one more time," and she hoisted it over her shoulder and aimed at a display of glitter. Fortunately, our glitter is packaged in plastic bottles. Unfortunately, one container broke open as the bottles went flying and rolling all over the floor. Bernice paused long enough to turn to me and smirk. "See? I'm going to make you pay. When I finish with the store, you're next."

"Mrs. Stottlemeyer, destroying my store or hurting me isn't going to help you," I said. "If you have a police record, you'll never get a child. Ever."

Of course, I had no idea whether that was true or not, but it certainly sounded reasonable.

Bernice lowered her purse to her side. She moved closer to me, so close that I could feel her hot exhalations on my face.

Aunt Penny took a step closer to Bernice.

"You think you're better than I am, don't you? Just because you have kids? Just like that girl yesterday. Sitting there so smug. Deciding to turn us down. What a crock! People like you shouldn't be allowed to breed. Look at you!

You're poor! Unmarried. Ignorant. I can't wait to wipe that self-satisfied look off your face." With that Bernice poked me hard in the chest.

As she talked, she let her purse dangle so that it rested on my floor.

"Yes, you're on to me. I'm poor. I'm unmarried. I don't have a college degree, so I suppose you could call me ignorant." Once upon a time, an assessment like hers would have devastated me. But today, I found it somewhat amusing. Sure, I was unmarried, poor, and uneducated, but I was also happier than I'd ever been. None of those markers of success were as important as I once thought.

"Yup," I said, struggling not to smile. "That's me. Definitely the World's Biggest Loser. But what does that make you, huh? You've got all that, but so what? Frankly, Mrs. Stottlemeyer, I think that young woman showed excellent taste. I wouldn't trust you to babysit my dog!"

"Y-y-y-you, you, you—" Bernice was so mad she couldn't spit the words out.

Fortunately, she didn't have to. Aunt Penny pointed her nail gun.

Pft-pft-pft.

The Bottega Veneta was nailed to my floor.

———

74

*T*hat was not the resolution I had in mind.

Nope.

I wanted Bernice out of my store, and now she couldn't leave. Her keys were in her purse, and her purse wasn't going anywhere.

"Why you!" Bernice turned on my aunt. Her fists were balled up, ready for action.

"If I were you, I'd settle down, right quick," said Aunt Penny, as she lifted the nail gun and pointed it at Bernice. "Because I'm packing this here nail gun and I won't hesitate to use it on you! Step away from Kiki! Do it! Anya?"

"Coming." Anya walked out of the back room. In her hands was a thick roll of duct tape.

"For pity's sake," said Clancy. "Let's keep the child out of it, shall we?"

"I'm not a child, and I already heard everything," said Anya, raising her chin defiantly.

"You. Sit. Down. There." Aunt Penny pointed to the empty stool right behind Bernice.

When the woman didn't move, Aunt Penny shot the

purse again with the nail gun. "Trust me," said my aunt, "I've had enough of your baloney. Sit down and shut up, or I'll shoot you next. Like you said, it'll be a while before the cops get here. You could easily bleed to death."

That put the fear of God into Bernice, and she backed onto the stool.

Under Aunt Penny's watchful eyes, and with Clancy's help, Anya taped Bernice's legs to the stool legs. Next they taped Bernice's wrists together, behind the woman's back. The whole time Anya and Clancy worked, Bernice cursed and threatened us.

"Keep it up," said Aunt Penny, "and I'll put a piece of tape over your mouth. I promise you, when they rip it off, it hurts like holy what-for."

That only encouraged Bernice to scream and curse more loudly.

"Hand over the tape. I'm tired of listening." Clancy ripped off a piece and plastered it over Bernice's lips.

The silence that followed was strangely satisfying.

"Has anyone ever done that to you? Taped your mouth shut?" Anya asked her great-aunt.

"Of course they have," said Aunt Penny, as she scratched a mosquito bite. "Down in Bogota, ten years ago. I was kidnapped as part of a raid on our church group. I was there working with street kids."

"Wow," said Anya, as Aunt Penny's revelation totally distracted us from Bernice's thrashing about.

"Where's our camera?" asked Clancy. "This'll make a great scrapbook page."

I dug it out from under the worktable and watched as Clancy took photos from all angles. She also took shots of the mess that Bernice had made.

"Great shots," I said. "Especially since I love using duct

tape on pages. In fact, I bet we could do a whole duct tape project at our next crop."

We were printing up the photos and discussing layout options when Hadcho arrived.

Okay, I'll admit—we went a little overboard with the duct tape. Since Bernice was being such a PIA (pain in the backside), we decided to wrap her up like a mummy. In fact, we used up two rolls of duct tape in the process.

Clancy got bored with our efforts and went into the back room to fetch a clipboard. She planned to itemize the damage Bernice had done.

"Let me guess," said Hadcho, "the tin woodsman decided to terrorize your store? A mummy escaped from the St. Louis Art Museum, and you decided to paint it silver? Or maybe you had an accident with the tape runner?"

"Well, look at you. You're learning to speak scrapbook. Two years ago, you wouldn't have known what a tape runner was!" I said, as I gave him a little arm punch. "Meet Bernice Stottlemeyer. Observe the damage she was doing to my store. And of course, we've got pictures. Clancy's writing up an invoice of the damages. When I asked her to leave, Mrs. Stottlemeyer responded by threatening me."

"I used the nail gun to pin her purse to the floor," said Aunt Penny proudly. "Otherwise I'm unarmed. You can frisk me though. You might want to. You really can't trust someone like me. I could be hiding a weapon anywhere on my body."

"So there you have it, Detective Hadcho," I said.

"What set her off?"

I explained about the adoption profile album. Bernice made funny grunting noises that I took as exceptions to my narrative. "Um, Mrs. Stottlemeyer thinks the young mother made her decision based on the album. So she thinks she's due a refund. I believe she also wanted to give me a little payback for her pain and suffering."

"I see," said Hadcho, dialing in a phone number on his cell. "Since I'm officially not on duty, let me get a squad car to come pick this woman up."

"Come on, Anya, we've got work to do," said Aunt Penny, as she guided my daughter to the back room. Soon I heard the *pft-pft-pft* of the nail gun being used as nature intended.

When Hadcho got off the phone, I had another thought. "I better call Bonnie Gossage. She's Mrs. Stottlemeyer's attorney." I wound up leaving a message with Bonnie's secretary, but at least I'd given my friend a heads-up.

Clancy confirmed that Bernice had threatened me and caused the chaos. She handed Hadcho an invoice for the damaged goods. "I also included the time it'll take us to restock and reorganize this mess."

"Good job," said Hadcho. "I'll see that the booking officer gets this."

While we waited for the patrol car to arrive, I brought him up to speed about Detweiler's visit to California. I did not tell him that Erik wasn't Detweiler's natural son. This had been bothering me. I had no idea how we should handle that aspect of our new family. Obviously, Detweiler and I would have to decide what to do and how to do it, but that would have to wait until he came home, and we could discuss the matter.

"So Gina and her husband died in a car accident?" Hadcho pursed his lips. "Where'd it take place?"

"Laguna Canyon Road," I said. I'd remembered the name because I read books by Sparkle Abbey, and they're set in Laguna Nigel. Detweiler had mentioned the name to me when we'd first heard that Gina had died.

Hadcho nodded. "Interesting."

"Why?" I asked.

"No particular reason," and he started to say more, but Bonnie Gossage came walking through the front door. I shouldn't have been surprised that she arrived so quickly, seeing as how her office was in nearby Clayton. She knew Hadcho, so I explained to her what had happened while Bernice Stottlemeyer grunted loudly and fought against her bondage.

"Two uniformed officers are on the way," said Hadcho. "You can see the damage she's caused. Three people witnessed her threatening Mrs. Lowenstein."

I nodded. "She poked me in the chest. It's certainly not life-threatening, but I bet I'll have a nice little bruise."

"Kiki, I am so sorry," said Bonnie. As per usual, she wore a spit-up stain on her dark blue jacket. With two little ones at home, Bonnie struggled each morning to get dressed and out the door to her office. She'd come to accept that "a little spit up never hurt anyone." I think that was a wise decision. I only hoped I'd handle the mounting pressure at home with the same sort of good humor.

"Not your fault," I said. "You aren't responsible for her misbehavior."

The uniformed officers arrived. They cut away enough duct tape to unhitch Bernice from the stool and get her to her feet. I noticed that they didn't take the tape off her mouth. That was pretty smart on their part.

Before they could escort her out of my building, I had something to say, so I planted myself between Bernice and the door. "I told you before to stay out of my store, and I meant it. I'm telling you again that you aren't welcome here."

Then I took a deep breath and added, "That birth mother didn't turn you down because of my album, and we both know it. If you truly want to pursue adoption, I have a suggestion: Get your priorities straight. The most important things you can give a kid are love and acceptance. After that, everything is gravy."

"I'll meet you at the station, Mrs. Stottlemeyer," said Bonnie.

We watched as the uniformed patrol officers helped Bernice out of my store and into the waiting squad car.

"I can't say anything without it being a breach of attorney-client privilege," Bonnie said, "but let's talk in hypotheticals. Let's say there's a family with two sisters, and the older one is always top dog. Then the younger one has an adorable baby, and suddenly the older sister starts feeling like she's been passed over. You with me? All of a sudden, that older sister gets desperate to have a child. Even to adopt one. See how that could happen?"

"Then it never really was about wanting a child. It was about not wanting to come in second."

"You didn't hear that from me," said Bonnie. "And by the way, the birth mother loved your album. She wanted to know who did it. What's more, Bernice and I both were there when the birth mother asked who created the album."

"Let me guess. The birth mother was immediately turned off by Bernice Stottlemeyer's attitude."

"I never said that," and Bonnie winked at me.

"You didn't need to."

75
———

*A*fter Hadcho left, Clancy and I started cleaning up the mess that Bernice had made. I was sweeping glitter into a dustpan when a customer came over and asked, "Do you know whose red car that is in your parking lot?"

"Yes, it's mine." I straightened so I could rub the small of my back.

"Did you know your tires had been slashed? And that your windows are all bashed in?"

"You have to be kidding." I set the pan full of glitter on my work table. What was I going to do without a car? I marched out the front door and took a look. As I did, I noticed that more rain clouds had gathered. Yes, we definitely were in for more bad weather.

"Wow, what a mess," I said as I stared at my car. I knew exactly what happened—and whodunnit. Standing there, glancing at the damage, I phoned Hadcho and told him about the vandalism. "My car was fine ten minutes before Bernice Stottlemeyer visited my store."

"Got it. I'm headed back your way."

Soon enough, he was right at my side. "She did a number on your tires. I'll call an officer to take your statement. Meanwhile, you might want to call your insurance agency and a tow truck. Tell the tow truck to give us a couple of hours here. At the least. Do you remember what kind of tires you have? Because all of these will need replacing."

Bits of glass were scattered all over the seats. Fortunately, I keep my tire purchase paperwork in the glove compartment. I grabbed the forms and headed for the store, brushing tears from my eyes.

I tried not to react emotionally to the damage. After all, a car is a car. But that old Beemer was one of the few things left from my marriage to George. The front bumper was still dented from where I'd jumped out and let the car ram into a tree rather than allow Bill Ballard to kidnap me. The roof was tired and dull. The back bumper was scratched from where another car had bumped me on purpose.

But all in all, this car had served me well—and seeing it with flattened tires saddened me. They looked like four frownie faces, drooping there on the pavement.

I went back inside Time in a Bottle and made the call to Triple A. Because a number of drivers had stalled out in the rain, the dispatcher explained that the tow truck might not be able to get to me for hours. Maybe even until the next day. I understood. My car wasn't going anywhere, and it wasn't obstructing traffic or blocking a lane. My need wasn't a priority.

But Anya, Aunt Penny, and I needed rides home. Dropping us off was out of the way for Clancy, even though I knew she'd give us a ride if push came to shove. But that would leave me with no way to open the store the next morning.

I had no choice but to call Sheila. "Hey, I have a favor to ask. A big one. May I borrow your car?"

She listened while I explained what had happened to the Beemer. I added, "I hate to ask you, but frankly, I'm out of options."

"Since I've trusted you with my life, I think I can see my way clear to trusting you with my Mercedes," she said. "Robbie was on his way out the door to pick up more eggs. How about if I have him swing by and pick you up? Can you drop him back at the house?"

"Glad to. I really, really appreciate it. How's it going otherwise?"

She sighed. "Not well."

I conveyed my sympathies and got off the phone. Driving Robbie back to her house would mean re-arranging my work schedule. That wasn't a huge problem, but it certainly would be an inconvenience.

"We're done with your car," said one of the crime scene investigators, as he handed me his card. "But you might want to get it towed or covered because we're in for more rain."

I thanked him just as Anya ran up beside me. "Mom! Come see how much we've gotten done!" She jiggled from one leg to the other with excitement.

I walked toward the back of the store and gazed at their work in wonder. When I'd last checked on them, Anya and Penny were busy marking drywall. Since then, my daughter and my aunt had managed to hoist and nail all the sheets of drywall. As a result of their combined efforts, we now had a new yarn room. Best of all, I'd saved a bundle of money by using free labor.

"This is amazing," I said.

"Yes, indeedy-do," said Aunt Penny. "Next step is taping

and mudding. See where the panels of drywall meet? We'll spread joint compound over the cracks and then put tape on top of it. We'll smooth that out. We'll also fill all our nail holes. Got to let all of it dry, repeat the process of adding compound two more times, and then sand it all down."

"Very impressive," I said, and I meant it. "Could the two of you take a small break and do something for me?"

I explained about the damage to my car.

"That woman was such a witch!" said Anya. "I am so glad she's in jail now. That should teach her a lesson."

"I wish I'd used that nail gun on her tender bits," said Aunt Penny.

"Okay, moving right along. It's looking like it might rain again. If it does, the rain will ruin the leather seats. Could you take one of these drop cloths and spread it over the BMW?" I asked. "You might need to tape it down."

"What will we use for a car?" asked Anya.

"Sheila has agreed to let me borrow her car. Robbie will be by with it."

"Covering up your car won't take but a minute. How about if we do that and walk across the street to that convenience store before it rains?" said Aunt Penny, sending a quizzical look toward Anya. "We can pick up sandwiches for lunch. I've been hankering for pimento cheese or egg salad."

"I can drop you off," said Clancy. "I need to run by the pharmacy to get a refill on my prescription. I'll wait until you cover Kiki's car and then give you a ride."

All three of them left at once. With the store finally empty, I went back to picking up Bernice Stottlemeyer's mess. I started by retrieving the scattered bottles of glitter. Since stooping down was becoming harder and harder for me, I finally gave up on bending and started crawling around on my hands and knees, chasing after the missing containers, and sweeping up the sparkling dust.

Glitter, as any crafter will tell you, is a real pain to round up. It sticks to everything, via static cling. I managed to brush up as much loose stuff as I could. I had gotten a good start, but the longer I was down there, the more glitter I found hiding. I was down on all fours when the door minder rang and in walked Vincent. He watched as I struggled to my feet.

"May I see the album?" he asked.

"Sure."

I stood to one side as he flipped through the album I'd made for Sheila.

His eyes lingered on the photo of the Jimmy Girls.

"Interesting," he said, reaching up to adjust his black beret. He wore his hair in a low ponytail wrapped with a leather tie. To my mind, it was a bit too much. Why not wear a sign that said, "Artsy guy alert!"

"Are those Sheila's pictures?" I asked, pointing at the box he had set on the worktable.

"Yes. I do digital slide shows for each customer to use for selection purposes. Makes life so much easier than the old days when you had to print up a contact sheet and have people squint at the tiny pictures," he said.

"I can't wait to see these." I set down the dustpan and opened the box. An ivory sheet of stationery resting on the top of the stack thanked Sheila for her business and reminded her that if she wanted more copies, she would need to contact him. As with most professional photographers, he maintained the exclusive right to make copies. The letter was a classy way of underscoring that fact.

I started to put the cover sheet aside, but something caught my eye.

He'd signed the letter with his full name: Vincent Wasserman.

That rang a bell, but why?

76

"*L*ooks like my timing was perfect." Robbie walked in to join us.

Vincent Wasserman turned as white as a cleric's collar. He cleared his throat and adjusted his beret one more time.

"How are you?" Robbie extended his huge hand to the photographer for a friendly shake.

I felt, rather than saw, Vincent hesitate before he extended his right hand to meet Robbie's. Simultaneously, the photographer slipped his free hand into his black jeans. The movement wasn't casual. It was purposeful. I saw the fabric move and realized Vincent was gripping something in his pocket.

But what?

My heart did a tiny flutter step in my chest.

Oh, my gosh.

All the pieces came together.

Miriam Wasserman, the dead Jimmy Girl.

Dr. Hyman's murderer was standing right beside me.

Vincent shifted his weight. I knew exactly why. This was

a move I'd been taught in ballet class. By centering his balance, Vincent had given himself more options. Now he could move left or right. He withdrew his hand slightly from his pocket and angled his body to block my view. I responded by stepping where I could *almost see what he was doing, if the table top wasn't in my way.*

Click.

The noise was so faint that Robbie didn't hear it, but I knew what I'd heard. Vincent had a knife. A switchblade, I would guess. I rested my palms on the top of my worktable and leaned against it. By levering my body over my hands, I widened my viewing angle. A long silver blade winked at me. The quillon, the crossbeam that separates the blade from the handle, gleamed. I could make out the double edge of the blade.

Robbie couldn't see what Vincent held in his hand. Not with the way that Vincent was standing.

My heart pounded so loudly, I was sure both men could hear it. For a second, I thought I might black out. The sales floor started to spin. But I told myself I couldn't. No way. I had to warn Robbie. I had to save us!

The problem was how?

Detweiler had told me about knife fights. All cops dreaded them. He had explained the 21-feet rule to me. Even a trained marksman can't defend himself in the time it takes an assailant to travel 21 feet with a knife. Robbie was only three feet from Vincent, on the same side of the table as the photographer. I was six feet away, with a table between us. To my left was the dust pan, in front of me was Sheila's album, and to my right was the box of photos. I couldn't even remember what I'd done with my phone.

Robbie kept talking. He didn't realize what Vincent held in his hand.

Or did he?

I couldn't tell.

"Are these the photos?" asked Robbie in his booming voice. "Great! Sheila has been wanting to see them. Kiki, why don't you go call her? The reception would be better outside, don't you think?"

So he did know what was happening. He was trying to get me out of danger.

"I have a set for you, too," Vincent said to Robbie. "They're in my van."

"Great." Robbie rubbed his hands together. "Why don't you go get them? Kiki can call Sheila from the phone in her office."

No, no, no! I wanted to scream. I can't leave you alone with him! He'll stab you!

Robbie's gun wouldn't help either of us. This would be over before he aimed and fired.

My mouth went dry. I could hear my heart pounding. But I couldn't focus on what they were saying. Something about paying for the pictures. Some nonsense as they jockeyed for position.

The hairs on the back of my neck stood up. Goosebumps rose on my arms. If I could distract Vincent, Robbie could grab him.

Vincent's automatic reaction would be to lash out. To prevent that, I had to override his instincts. My distraction would have to cripple Vincent long enough for Robbie to get the upper hand.

My baby kicked. A response to my blood pressure rising. I slipped a hand protectively to my belly.

The photographer's eyes never strayed from Robbie's face. I could tell by the way Vincent moved his arm that he was ready to strike. Luckily, he didn't consider me to be a factor. Why should he?

I needed to divert his attention, so I yelled, "You killed Dr. Hyman!"

Without thinking, Vincent turned toward me. I grabbed the dustpan full of glitter. With a shoveling motion, I tossed the contents into his face. The grit, the small plastic chunks, and dirt from the floor flew into his eyes.

"Argh!" He cried out and pawed at his eyes.

Robbie grabbed at him, but Vincent twisted away.

Blinking, struggling to see clearly, Vincent raised the knife again—aiming the blade at Robbie's heart.

I let the dust pan fall with a clatter as I grabbed wildly for anything in my reach. What I found was solid, square, and heavy—Sheila's wedding album.

Vincent was struggling against the urge to wipe his eyes, while Robbie was stepping back away from the outstretched knife.

"Kiki, run!" shouted Robbie.

But I could never face Sheila if I left her husband in the lurch. Gripping the album firmly with both hands, I turned it sideways. Twisting I put all my weight behind the book. I rotated with my arms fully extended and braced myself for the impact. The book hit Vincent on the back of the head with a resounding thwack!

He froze but he didn't let go of the knife. He wasn't sure where the blow had come from. But he didn't go down.

I'd stunned him. But I hadn't really hurt him. I'd just knocked him off his stride. Robbie took a step backwards, away from the raised knife. His arms windmilled as he searched for a weapon. He grabbed a Fiskars paper trimmer and would have used it as a bat, but he stumbled over a jar of glitter, one of the few I'd missed in my clean-up efforts. With a loud crash, Robbie came down, hard. The orange trimmer skittered out of his hands and slid across the floor.

Vincent turned toward me and snarled, "Hyman deserved it! It was his fault my sister killed herself. She was beautiful. Lovely and thin. Nothing like you. You're a stupid, fat cow!"

Before I had been scared.

But now I was enraged. Okay, so I had put on a few more pounds than normal. I was pregnant, for goodness sake! It wasn't fair to call me fat! I tightened my grip on the wedding album.

After being called "poor" and "ignorant" by Bernice, my tolerance for insults had hit rock bottom. This was my store, my little slice of heaven, and Vincent was the second person this morning who'd come in and disturbed the good vibes I'd worked so hard to create.

Fat? Really? That burned my biscuits.

Robbie rolled up onto his knees, moving slowly. He winced as he shifted his weight. His face drained of all color as he tried to get to his feet.

Time for me to put up or shut up.

Vincent stepped toward me. His eyes streamed tears. He held the knife blade in a ham-fisted grip. His beret had been knocked to the floor. With his free hand, he gestured to me, wiggling his fingers. "Come on, come on—"

I shifted my weight as I considered my options.

Then he crossed a line. "Piggy, piggy, piggy," he called to me.

That big nose of his, the one he shared with his dead sister, proved his undoing. I used it as my target.

Putting my entire body weight behind me, I swung the

344

album at Vincent's face. I smacked him hard. This time my blow caught him dead center.

Crunch!

Blood spattered everywhere as Sheila's wedding album busted Vincent's nose.

*V*incent's knife hit the floor. He moaned in pain. The smell of copper filled the air. Both hands flew to his face. The blood spurted out of his nose. He stepped backwards clutching his snozzle.

I kicked the blade out of his reach.

"Grab him!" I yelled to Robbie.

Despite the pain, Robbie was on top of Vincent in the blink of an eye. After knocking the photographer to the floor, Robbie pinned both of the man's arms behind his back and handcuffed them together.

"You always carry those?" I asked, pointing to the silver bracelets. I was panting with fear and exertion. That wallop took a lot of energy.

"Never know when they'll come in handy," said Robbie. "Geez Louise, how did he get mixed up in this?"

Grabbing a tissue out of my pocket, I picked up the long, lethal switchblade and set it on my worktable, comfortably out of Vincent's reach. "His sister is Miriam Wasserman, the missing Jimmy Girl. She committed suicide because of her collapsing nose."

"You've got nothing on me!" yelled Vincent.

"Right, that's why you pulled a knife on us for no reason. I bet we can get one of the valet parking attendants to testify that you paid him to warn you as soon as the doctor arrived. I bet there's an empty spot in your tool chest and a screwdriver is missing. They'll find a stun gun at your house. Blood on your black pants. Your fingerprints will be all over the invitation you sent Dr. Hyman. Listen, buster. Don't you ever mess with a pregnant woman, hear me? I don't have the patience for creeps like you!"

"How did he get an invitation?" asked Robbie.

"Sheila insisted that I send him one," I said. "A lot of brides like the photographer to take pictures of their invitations. Sometimes they have propped one up in front of the flowers."

"So how'd you forget that?"

"He wasn't on the guest list. That's what I focused on."

"You and Sheila both," said Robbie.

Vincent kept squirming and yelling obscenities. Robbie planted a foot in the middle of the photographer's back and used his cell phone to call for assistance. When he finished, he turned to me and said, "Thank goodness you didn't hesitate. We could have both been hurt badly. That's one dandy of a switchblade. He could have poked us both, and we'd be bleeding out on the floor by now."

I felt a bit woozy and sank down onto my stool. "Thanks for backing me up."

"I've learned to trust you and your instincts."

"That's good," I said, as I put my head between my knees to keep from fainting. "Otherwise, you and I would have been goners for sure."

*A*unt Penny's eyebrows flew up to her hairline when she and Anya walked in through the front door. "Dag-nabbit. I missed all the fun. Looks like you had your-self a kerfuffle. Rats!"

"Everything is fine now," I said. My aunt and my daughter both carried bulging plastic bags and large plastic drink cups. There went our grocery budget for the week!

Anya set the food on my worktable. She gave a low whistle of appreciation when she saw the switchblade.

That knife had to go. Looking at it gave me the creeps. I grabbed a piece of cardstock from my supply bin, folded it to make a casing, and slipped the blade inside. After I taped the makeshift package shut, I emptied a plastic bag from the convenience store and used it as a carrier. The knife was unlikely to hurt anyone, and the fingerprints on it were protected.

"Gee," said Anya as she watched me handle the lethal dagger. "I thought papercuts were bad news. That could have done some serious damage. What was he planning to use it for?"

I said nothing.

It dawned on her.

"On you?" Anya squeaked. "I can't believe he'd do that! You creep!"

"She's a fat cow!" screamed Vincent. "I've been blinded! And my nose is bleeding!"

"Maybe something cold will help," said Anya, as she dumped her iced tea over his head.

Vincent screamed and cursed.

Robbie started laughing.

"You tell him, girlfriend!" said my aunt, as she raised her hand for a high-five from Anya.

This was not behavior I wanted to encourage. I grabbed my daughter and yanked her away. "Not cool. Go get towels so we can mop up. But you need to stay clear of him."

"I will. Now that he's had a bath." She practically skipped away.

"Aunt Penny, don't encourage her!" I said, but she only snickered.

"Better that she feel tough and in charge than scared of that jerk," said Aunt Penny.

"Well, maybe," I admitted.

Robbie kept his foot firmly planted on Vincent's back while he spoke to someone on the phone.

"It can't hurt that you'll get credit for this collar," I said, smiling up at the big cop when he finished his call. Anya brought out the towels we keep in the back. I dropped them to the floor and mopped up the puddle with my foot. Vincent was still bleeding, but I had no sympathy for the man.

"Sheila says you can borrow her car as long as you like!"

Although Robbie seemed pleased, I knew the evidence linking Vincent to Dr. Hyman's murder was skimpy. Of course, the man's attack on us proved something was amiss. After being knocked to the floor, he'd kept his mouth shut. That was smart on his part, but it sure wouldn't help Robbie. Especially if Prescott had botched the investigation.

I shook my head as I threw away the wet towels. If only there was a way to get Vincent to confess.

80

I was tossing a white trash bag into our dumpster when a car door slammed. It was Stan Hadcho in his Crown Victoria. Why had Robbie called him first? Did Hadcho know how little evidence we had?

"Hey!" I called to the detective. I picked my way around puddles to greet him. I told Hadcho about my suspicions.

"Vincent told us he was avenging his sister's suicide." I explained about Miriam Wasserman. "He had the means. Probably a tool from his camera equipment."

"Opportunity?" asked Hadcho.

"I think so. I don't remember him taking photos during the ceremony, do you? I was focused on Sheila and Robbie, so I didn't notice. I bet if we looked through his pictures we could tell."

"What about the invitation?"

I explained why Sheila and I had overlooked the fact that Vincent had received an invitation.

Hadcho leaned against his Crown Vic. "But how did he happen to frame your mother?

"Vincent took photos at the Senior Center. He must have

351

heard about my mother shouting at Dr. Hyman. Mom left her purse behind when Vincent took photos of her at the wedding. He probably slipped the screwdriver in her handbag before he returned it."

"Right," agreed Hadcho. "But this is still pretty lame stuff."

"I know. Can you get a search warrant and find the stun gun?"

"That won't be enough."

Side-by-side, we walked into my store. Robbie still had his foot planted in Vincent's back. Hadcho took his handcuffs out of his back pocket and linked the photographer to the support beam next to my work table.

"Don't you dare try to get up off of that floor," said Hadcho. "Or it'll be the last move you make."

Aunt Penny trotted out from the back room with her nail gun. "I'm primed and ready to use my nail gun on this here creep. Just to keep him from moving around. All you have to do is say the word, Chief Holmes. I've got pretty good aim."

Pft-pft-pft. She fired off a crooked line of nails into my floor.

"Oops," she said. "Dang it. I thought I had the safety on."

"Stop her!" whined Vincent. "Please!"

"Is that what I think it is?" asked Hadcho.

Pft-pft-psf! Aunt Penny put a line of nails in the leg of my worktable.

"Well, drat," she said. "My finger slipped."

I have to admit that the sight of a woman in bifocals waving around a lethal weapon was enough to leave me quaking in my Keds. Vincent's eyes were wide with fright. I couldn't blame him.

"Aunt Penny, why don't you put that down?" Robbie

motioned to Hadcho to come stand closer to him. That put some distance between them and Vincent.

"I will put this aside when I'm good and ready." Aunt Penny gave Robbie a big wink.

Pft-pft-pft. She let fly with another volley. One right after another. In a second crooked line. Two inches from Vincent's head.

"Stop her!" screamed Vincent. "She's going to put out my eye!"

"Okay," Robbie said. "I'm not officially working, and Hadcho isn't either, but I suppose we could take you in, Mr. Wasserman. First I will need to read you your rights. You have the right—"

"I want a lawyer!" screamed Vincent.

"Have it your way," said Robbie. "We've got a while before the patrol car gets here."

Pft!

A nail flew by narrowly missing my blue denim Keds.

"Eeek! Aunt Penny, you need to be careful!" I said.

She smirked at me. Robbie shrugged. He and Hadcho conferred in low voices.

Pft!

This nail went wide. Too wide. Aunt Penny hit one of my shelving units. Vincent squealed like a toddler on a swing set.

I squatted down so that Vincent and I were nearly eye-level and then I waved at him.

"Fat cow here. Remember me? I could call her off. If I wanted to. Where'd you put the stun gun?"

"It's still in my van!"

Pft. Another nail flew into the floor.

"Hmm," I said. "Her aim is getting worse by the minute. How did your screwdriver get into my mother's purse?"

"I put it there! Before I handed it back to your sister!"

Robbie nodded to me and gave me a thumbs up. That meant he had enough information. With a search warrant, they'd be able to gather the evidence they needed.

Anya pulled up a stool at my workbench and sat down. Once seated, my darling daughter calmly bit into her tuna fish salad sandwich. You would have never guessed we had a murderer on the floor behind her.

"Get me out of here!" yelled Vincent.

"Anya, honey, don't you want to take your lunch into the back?" I asked.

"Nope. I want to hang around and watch them arrest that creep. Should be fun."

What had I done to raise a child so unruffled by danger? I made a note to put a call into a family therapist. But until then, I couldn't bring myself to leave things alone. I whispered in her ear, "Fun? Anya, this isn't upsetting you?"

"Nope," she said. "This is good experience for me. I've decided I want to be a cop when I grow up. Just like Robbie and Detweiler. After all, being a cop runs in our family."

Oh, boy.

My baby, a cop?

No way!

I seized on that phrase, "Being a cop runs in our family," and I nearly replied, "Oh, no, it doesn't. Robbie and Detweiler aren't really your family." Fortunately a tickle in my throat caused a spasm, and I coughed. As I covered my mouth, I caught a glimpse of Robbie's face. He was practically lit up like a jack-o-lantern. I've never seen him so happy. His eyes glowed with affection for Anya.

I couldn't have it both ways.

I was caught between a rock and a hard place. If I truly believed that we were a family, how could I disagree with

Anya? How could I say, "Robbie isn't your real grandfather and Detweiler isn't your real dad, so you should become a businessman like your real father, George"? The truth was: I couldn't. Because if I did, then it followed that, "Aunt Penny isn't your real aunt and Erik isn't your real brother."

This was my chance to "walk the talk."

While my mind did these mental gymnastics, Vincent started squirming on the floor.

"If you plan to go into law enforcement, then maybe you should be aiming this here nail gun at our bad guy," said Aunt Penny, as she passed the gun over to my daughter.

"All right!" said Anya.

"No way!" I yelled and grabbed the nail gun out of my daughter's hands.

81

Late Thursday Night/Five days after the wedding...
Los Angeles, California

A surge of tenderness swept through Detweiler as he tucked the covers tightly around Erik. The child smelled of baby shampoo, the fragrance of innocence.

"You have a big day tomorrow. We're going to have an adventure. Do you remember who you're going to meet?"

"Anya," said the child carefully. "My new sister."

"And?" prompted Detweiler.

"A big dog named Gracie!"

"And?"

"A donkey. Monroe!"

Detweiler frowned. "I think you are forgetting someone. Who is Anya's mother?"

"Kiki," said Erik.

"Very good!" said Detweiler, as he ruffled Erik's hair.

Explaining who Kiki was, and that she'd be Erik's new

mother, seemed unnecessarily cruel. Especially when the boy still asked about Gina several times a day. Detweiler had decided not to press the issue. When he mentioned this quandary to his mother, Thelma Detweiler had suggested that he let Kiki and Erik sort out their relationship over time.

"I wouldn't start by labeling her 'his new mother.' Of course, Kiki will mother him, but if you tell Erik that Kiki is his new mom, that's going to raise more issues than it will solve. He might even feel guilty if he likes Kiki," Thelma had said. "So I'd let it rest. There are some problems, son, that only time can sort out."

Lorraine and Brawny had agreed with Thelma's conclusion.

"We're talking about a label," Brawny had said. "That's an abstract idea. To Erik, 'mother' and 'Gina' are inter-changeable. He's already feeling the pain of his loss. Why make it worse? Why put that burden on Mrs. Lowenstein?"

With a kiss on the boy's cheek, Detweiler stepped out of the well-appointed nursery. Erik's new room wouldn't come with a white oak bed and matching dresser, or a wall mural featuring Spiderman swinging down from the Golden Gate Bridge. Hard to believe that this was just a guest bedroom that Lorraine had tricked out for the boy. Detweiler couldn't imagine what Erik's bedroom in Van and Gina's house must have been like!

For a second, he felt the weight of what he was doing, and it pressed heavily on his shoulders. An outsider might think that Erik was being cheated. Detweiler was pretending to be the boy's biological father and taking the child away from a life of luxury. But in reality, Detweiler was following Gina's wishes. He was offering Erik a family and a loving home in exchange for the trappings of another life. If one was weighed against the other, Detweiler knew that his offering would win.

Kiki would find a way to make Erik's new room—tiny as it was—uniquely reflective of the boy and his interests. Yes, Kiki would make everything right. He could depend on her.

He couldn't wait to get back home and add Erik to their family.

Outside of Erik's room, Brawny sat rigidly on a chair, waiting for Detweiler. She did this every night, swapping places with the cop when he left Erik's side. Once he said goodnight. Brawny checked on Erik, checked all the window locks, and then presumably retired to the room across the hall. She had a portable monitor, a screen that sent images from a camera inside Erik's room. He'd seen police officers on stake-outs who were less diligent than she.

"All yours," he told Brawny. He went downstairs and found Lorraine sitting on a chintz-covered sofa, staring at baby photos of the little boy.

"About our airline tickets," he said. "I had intended to put them on my credit card. It was kind of you to take care of the travel arrangements."

"Not to worry. None of the flights to St. Louis were convenient," said Lorraine with a dismissive wave of her hand. "I booked you on a private jet. Van owned shares in it. The Gulfstream was available. No reason to let it sit there in the hanger. This makes perfect sense."

A private plane? A Gulfstream?

"That's very kind of you." Detweiler couldn't wait to get back to the hotel and tell Kiki. A glance at the clock on Lorraine's mantel reminded him that it might be too late to call St. Louis. However, a text message would be almost as good. Kiki would wake up to read about the Gulfstream and share his excitement vicariously.

"I hope you won't mind taking a cab to the airfield tomorrow," Lorraine continued. "We'll meet you there. Having Orson drive will make it easier on us. And on Erik. A familiar face and all that." Her voice frayed at the end, like a rope was coming unraveled.

"I realize this must be hard for you," said Detweiler. "You've lost your brother and Gina both. Now I'm heading out with Erik. That's a lot of leave-taking in a short period of time."

"Yes." Her voice was little more than a whisper. Silver crescents of tears sparkled in her eyes. She dug her hands deep into the pockets of the black jacket she wore. Although the style was casual, the material draped in such a way to suggest that it was expensive. As usual, Lorraine carried with her the scent of lavender and vanilla. "It's been a joy to have a child in the family. He tires me out, but I've always enjoyed spending time with Erik. I didn't realize how hard it would be to say good-bye to him."

"You don't have to say good-bye. This isn't permanent. You'll still be a part of his life. You are welcome to come and visit any time. Our door is always open to you. My parents have a big house that's been in our family for more than one hundred years. There's a lot of room. My mother loves taking care of guests."

"I do believe you are sincere." She brushed a tear off her cheek.

"I'm a man of my word, Lorraine. Gina knew that. I hope you'll take me up on my invitation. I think you'd enjoy being around Kiki. My parents would have fun showing you our farm, and you'll be enchanted by Anya. She's a doll. So is my niece Emily." He paused. "After all, we're family now. You'll always be Erik's Aunt Lori. So we'll be expecting you to visit. At least plan to come and stay with us for the holidays. We celebrate both Hanukkah and Christmas, so you'll have a blast."

Her expression was one of disbelief, quickly turning to surprise, and finally to happiness. "I might take you up on that," she said. "It certainly would be different. And I'd hate to spend the holidays alone."

82

Same day, a little later
Downtown Los Angeles, California

"Our detective friend is leaving tomorrow with the boy?" Thornton spoke into his cell phone. With his other hand, he fingered his money clip and stared out the window. Dark had fallen, but the streets were bright with headlights. Cars sat waiting at a red light. When it turned green, they still couldn't move. A perfect gridlock of traffic set horns to honking. The air grew thickened with exhaust fumes.

"Yes," said Lorraine in a tired voice. "Early tomorrow. Orson will drive us to the Bob Hope Airport. Chad Detweiler is taking a cab. He'll meet us there. Thornton, I'm going to tell him about the funds. My brother wanted that money to be used for Erik."

All right. Time to bring out the heavy artillery, thought Thornton. He had expected this.

"Lorraine, I didn't want to tell you this, because I didn't want to worry you, but I've had a private investigator look into Detective Detweiler and his girlfriend. I spent my own money to check this man out," said Thornton. This, of course, was a boldface lie because Thornton never used his own money for anything. Not if he could help it.

He cleared his throat. "Did you know that Detective Detweiler was jailed on suspicion of murdering his second wife? And that his fiancée was taken into custody on suspicion of murder? That she had to appear before a family court to win back custody of her daughter? That her own mother-in-law thought her an unfit parent?"

"Oh, Thornton, no! That can't be true!" Lorraine laughed nervously. "You know how rampant identity theft is these days. There must be some confusion with their names."

"I wish you were right. I am so sorry to tell you this, Lorraine, but it is true. Every bit of it. I have the documentation right here on my desk. I can send it over—"

"No!" she said quickly. "I wouldn't believe it if I saw it. There must have been a misunderstanding. I can't believe this of Chad Detweiler. I refuse to! I've spent the past four days getting to know this man. He's everything that Gina said he was. As for his fiancée, of course I haven't met her, but she sounds positively charming."

"I am so sorry to lay this burden on you," he said. "Honestly, Lorraine. I hoped I wouldn't have to tell you. I can imagine how distressing this is. But, here's my point: Detective Detweiler puts on a good show. I'm sure his girlfriend does, too. But we need to wait and see how these people treat Erik. Believe me, I only want what's best for the boy."

"So do I," she said.

Thornton smiled. He'd sprung this on her at the end of

the day because he knew that she grew more tired as the day went on. Lorraine simply wouldn't have the energy to fight back when he launched his attack against Detweiler.

"I'll do whatever you tell me to do," he said. Of course, he didn't mean it.

"I don't think I have a choice!" she said.

He sighed happily.

"You are very wise, Thornton," she said. "I would never have thought to have Chad and Kiki investigated. No, I'm afraid I bought into his story, hook, line and sinker. I guess that shows what a fool I am!"

After ending the call, Lorraine turned to Brawny and smiled. "Well, well, well. Thornton thinks I'm an idiot."

"Does he now?" Brawny sat with her knees pressed together. The monitor on the side table rested next to her. Her hands moved quickly to the clicking of her knitting needles. She kept one eye on the screen as she worked the thread into a pattern.

Brawny smiled at the older woman. "Aye, then, he's in for a rare treat or two, isn't he, ma'am?"

83

Friday/Six days after the wedding
Burbank, California

Orson loaded several large suitcases into the Gulfstream while Detweiler watched him from inside the passenger lounge. A hostess picked up his coffee cup and offered to make him another caramel macchiato latte. "No, thanks," he said, as he reached for his wallet.

"Are you sure? It's complimentary," she said, as she fluttered long lashes at him.

Erik was sipping a lukewarm hot chocolate and playing Angry Birds on an iPad mini. Lorraine had stepped into the ladies' room to repair the damage a few tears had done to her mascara. Brawny sat on the other side of Erik, her posture rigid and watchful, despite the plush seating and numerous pillows. In her Black Watch kilt and tasseled brogues, she looked strangely incongruous, almost like an actor playing a part. That was probably why the staff didn't bat an eye at her. Detweiler's cab driver had been quite the local tour guide, explaining that the Bob Hope Airport had been the filming location for many projects including Indiana Jones and the Last Crusade.

Today Brawny dressed like she was to be in mourning, because she'd added a black ribbon to her gray ponytail. Her ever-present knitting was nowhere to be found. As usual, she scanned their environs carefully, and she had chosen their seats so that the wall would be behind them. If she hadn't been a nanny, she would have made a fine police officer. As relaxing as the setting was, Brawny bristled with tension.

What a totally different experience this was from the cattle call atmosphere of a commercial flight waiting area! This lounge couldn't be more luxurious or relaxing. Piped in music played softly. The scent of baked goods filled the air and mingled with the pungent aroma of coffee. Detweiler did his best to savor this experience so he could recount every detail for Kiki and his mother.

As Detweiler watched through the window, Orson made yet another delivery of baggage. He handed two more bags over to a steward who stowed them in a cargo area.

"Brawny? Do all those bags belong to Erik?" Detweiler couldn't believe one little boy had so much gear.

"There's the car seat in with the lot," said Brawny. Her cheeks had pinked up and she avoided Detweiler's eyes. "Miss Lauber insisted that I buy you a new one so you'd have it."

"Yet another reason to thank her," he said.

"Aye," and Brawny hesitated as if she planned to say more.

"But I think she's gone overboard. Especially since she'll be sending boxes later." He scratched his chin. What would they do with all that stuff? Where would they put it? Poor Kiki. She'd have a huge job on her hands, sorting, separating, and storing the contents of what he now reckoned was six large pieces of luggage.

"The brown ones are mine," said Brawny.

Detweiler turned toward her, trying to read her expression. "You're going...?"

"Coming," said Lorraine, walking toward them. She planted her walker carefully and took her seat. "She's my gift to you and Kiki."

Detweiler chewed the air. He wasn't sure that he'd heard right. "Your gift?"

"My pleasure," said Lorraine. "I figured the two of you could use help, with a baby coming and all, so my gift to you is Bronwyn's services for as long as you need her."

"B-b-but—" He couldn't spit the words out fast enough.

"This will be so much better for Erik, too," said Lorraine hurriedly. "He's accustomed to Brawny. She can do carpool duty, dropping off Erik and Anya. When the baby arrives, she'll be especially useful. Best of all, she knits like a champ! Think of all the classes she can teach at Kiki's store!"

"Please, sir. Don't make me leave my wee fellow. I've been with him since the day he came home from the hospital. He's like me own flesh and blood. You can't separate us!" The nanny clenched her hands to her chest, as if she were offering up prayers.

Erik glanced up from the game he was playing. His small face wrinkled with concern. "Brawny?"

"I don't see how this will work," said Detweiler, running a nervous hand through his hair. "We live in a very, very small house. You wouldn't be comfortable."

"I grew up in a one room cottage, sir. Believe me, I could live in the shed with the donkey and be right as rain."

"I'm sure that Kiki will be thrilled! What a homecoming gift!" said Lorraine. "Erik, you want Brawny to stay with you, right?"

When Erik chimed in, "Brawny? My Brawny! You come too, right?" Detweiler knew he'd been outflanked.

"The plane's ready to go," Orson said. He stood with his cap under his arm like something out of Driving Miss Daisy.

"Brawny! We're going up in the plane!" Erik threw his arms around the nanny.

And that was that.

84

Later that same day
St. Louis, Missouri

*W*hen the windows are up in Sheila's Mercedes, the car is so quiet that you feel as if you are in a space capsule, rocketing your way to Mars. I love the silence. When I've driven her car—and I haven't had the privilege of driving it often—I keep the radio turned off. There's joy in the quiet, being alone with my thoughts. Especially when so many changes are on the horizon.

This, I told myself, is my last hour as the mother of one child, a daughter. In minutes, I'll be "mom" to two kids, a girl and a boy. In less than six months, I'll be the mother of three.

Anya had elected to stay home and decorate the house. Rebekkah had come over with a bouquet of balloons, so I left the two of them having a terrific and colorful time.

I was on 40, headed to the suburb of Chesterfield. As the

car hummed along, I sent up prayers of gratitude. I was busy thanking God for all my blessings, when my sister Amanda phoned. "Kiki, I need you to pick up Mom for me."

"I can't. I'm on the way to the airport in Chesterfield. I'm picking up Detweiler and his son. Our son."

He and I had decided that I would come alone. We figured that we would introduce Erik to his new world slowly. First he'd meet me. Then we'd go home, and he'd meet Anya, Gracie, and the cats. Next we'd walk out and take a carrot to Monroe.

On Saturday, we'd drive to Illinois and have a big lunch with the Detweiler clan. Anya and Emily could take Erik around the farm. On Sunday, we'd have brunch with Sheila, Robbie, and my side of the family. Yep, we had it all planned out.

Mom's name appeared dead last on the list of greeters.

"I have an emergency. I need to pick up someone at the Amtrak Station downtown. You have to pick up Mom. There's no other option." My sister's voice turned shrill.

Uh-oh. This was Amanda in panic mode. I knew the tone of voice too well. But I still didn't want my mother on board. Not this morning. I was not interested in putting up with her shenanigans.

"I would but..." I hesitated, caught between wanting to help and not wanting to deal with my mother.

"This is not a request," said Amanda. "This is a demand."

"Really? Okay, hang on." I got off at the Mason Road exit. There was a school parking lot on the south side of the Mason. I could stop there long enough to talk without endangering myself or the car.

"I'll pick Mom up," I said, "but couldn't I do it later? After I go to the airport? I'm heading west on 40."

"I wouldn't ask you if I thought this could wait. Please! You have to help me with Mom once in a while—and this is one of those times."

Amanda sounded weird. Totally stressed.

Well, so was I.

But she was right. She rarely asked for help. I swallowed and asked, "Could you at least tell me what the problem is?"

"I can't discuss it right this moment. You'll have to trust me. I need to pick someone up from the station. It's very important. Very, very important."

Probably had to do with her job. I inched the car around in the parking lot. Now the grill was pointed to the on-ramp that would take me east, back the way I'd come.

"Where's Aunt Penny?"

"With me."

That made no sense at all.

"Tell her I still need to talk to her!" I couldn't believe how evasive my aunt had been. Yesterday after the uniformed officers arrived to take Vincent Wasserman to the county jail, she'd managed to finagle a ride home with Hadcho. Once again, she'd managed to give me the slip, so that I couldn't ask her about Catherine. Honestly, how long could she keep up this game of cat and mouse?

"This isn't the time. Mom's at the Senior Center. Go get her." Amanda hung up on me.

"Drat, drat, and double drat," I said to my silent phone.

I gritted my teeth and conjured up fifty ways to kill my mother. None of them were quick or clean. The clock on the dash told me that I could make it to the Senior Center and get to the airport on time, just barely.

85

*a*s I expected, Mom took her sweet time leaving the Senior Center. She had to say goodbye to everyone, and of course, she couldn't find her purse. After five minutes of searching, a helper discovered it under a table.

"Nice wheels," she said, as I led her to Sheila's Mercedes. "About time you traded in that piece of junk you drive. Where are you taking me for dinner? I want someplace where I can sit down."

"Sorry. We're in a bit of a time crunch today. I promise to take you out to eat next week, but we don't have time to stop today. Detweiler is flying in, and I have to pick him up from the airport."

"He can wait," she pouted.

"No, he can't," I said. "He's bringing his son, Erik, back from California. Erik's only five. I'm not leaving them standing around at the airport. You remember about Erik's mother, don't you? I told you about it. She died in a car crash. I need to be there when he arrives, okay?"

"Tsk," she made a disgusted noise.

The Spirit of St. Louis is an airfield, west of the city

proper. The airport exit is Long Road, which must be some-one's idea of a joke because it's not long. It's short. I poked along looking for TacAir, one of four fixed base operators, or FBOs. (Airway speak for "airlines," sort of.) According to Detweiler each FBO had its own lounge facilities, with vending machines. Eventually, I found the place and parked the Mercedes. Ignoring the dust kicked up in the open spaces, I helped Mom out of the car and promised her something to eat.

As I handed Mom a can of Coke Classic and a bag of Doritos, I heard the roar of an airplane engine. It sounded like it was coming right up to the outside door. I tried to see out the window. The engine roared and the smell of fuel filled the tiny lounge. Finally, I spotted the top of Detweiler's head coming at me.

"Detweiler!" My heart turned a somersault as he threw open the door.

I ran into his arms and felt the solid strength of his embrace. As always, he smelled of Safeguard soap.

"But where's Erik?"

With a half-turn he pointed his chin at a woman wearing a tartan skirt, a stiff white blouse, and knee socks. In her arms was a little boy, who had snuggled his face into her chest, so that all I could see was the back of his head and his red curly hair.

"Um, Kiki, this is Erik and Bronwyn Macavity. She's our new nanny."

Our *what?* I tried to smile at her. Then I turned back to Detweiler with a question in my eyes.

"Not now," he said quietly.

Okay. Off to our right, I noticed that my mother was still busy with her snack. Good.

"Mrs. Lowenstein, I am very pleased to meet you,"

Bronwyn said, in a thick Scottish accent. When I offered her my hand, she shook it heartily. Erik snuggled deeper into her embrace.

"Erik? Laddie? Where are your manners?" She prodded the child, using her thick Scottish brogue. "This is Miss Kiki. You need to thank her for your presents."

He didn't move.

I sensed my mother standing behind me and smelled the Doritos on her breath. She was nearly treading on my toes.

"Kiki is the lady with the donkey," prompted Bronwyn. "You remember him?"

"His name is Monroe, and he wants to meet you," I said.

The little boy turned his head to stare at me. I gazed into a pair of chocolate eyes in a face the color of my morning coffee—and I fell instantly in love.

"Good lord!" said my mother, shoving me to one side so she could look at Erik. "That boy is black!"

EPILOGUE

Four days later...
Kiki's house in Webster Groves, Missouri

"*A*nnie! Annie!" Erik squealed as he ran through our house. I watched from my old wingback chair as he closed in on Anya.

"Ready to go feed Monroe?" My daughter snatched her new brother up and twirled him around.

"Apples? Carrots?" Erik asked. With another squeal, he locked his arms around Anya's neck and hugged her.

"Yep. Let's get them out of the refrigerator, okay?" She swung him down onto his feet.

The two of them went racing into the kitchen where I heard the refrigerator door open and shut. Gracie looked longingly after the kids, but she didn't follow them because Detweiler was rubbing her ears.

"We might have a few moments alone. Bronwyn is at the

store today until three. At least I think that's what she told me," said Detweiler.

I reached up and pulled him down for a kiss as the back door slammed shut behind the two kids.

Gracie pawed at Detweiler, eager for his attention.

"Yes, we might have all of five minutes," I said with a giggle. "Monroe will make short work of those treats. Actually I misspoke. Brawny won't be back until five. She's working up a class description with Margit. Something about knitting two socks at once. On one knitting needle curved into a loop. They're both excited about it."

"That must be what I saw Brawny working on in Los Angeles. Pretty amazing stuff. Kiki, how are we going to manage this? Our house is bursting at the seams."

"I have no idea, but we'll figure it out. Thank goodness Anya and Erik get along like the proverbial two peas in a pod. I found him snuggled next to her this morning. He must be waking up and crawling in beside her at the crack of dawn. How he manages to scoot the two cats out of the way, I'll never know."

"Brawny doesn't seem to mind sleeping on the sofa." Detweiler picked up my hand and kissed it. "I am so sorry I sprung that on you."

"I'm sorry I brought my mother along with." I kept apologizing for her rude remark. Detweiler brushed it off and Erik didn't seem to know what she meant. Brawny's face had remained stoic, but I could feel her tense up. What a miserable introduction to my family!

"Any idea what's been keeping her and Amanda so busy?" he asked.

"No, and Aunt Penny seems to have disappeared off the face of the earth, too." I sighed. "I've called several times and although they answer, they get off the phone quickly. Really fast."

"Whatever it is, I'm sure they'll come around," he said, kissing the top of my head.

"Wait until they come over for dinner. That lamb stew Brawny made last night for dinner was fabulous." I felt a tickle and stared down at my belly. "Oops. Our other son is awake and kicking. At this rate, Brawny will have her own soccer team."

"Two boys," said Detweiler. "I'm going to be the daddy to two boys and a beautiful girl."

The crunch of footsteps on gravel told us we had visitors. Gracie jumped to her feet and ambled over to the front door.

"You expecting anyone?" Detweiler asked, but he took his time leaving my side.

"No. Sheila and Robbie are boarding their cruise ship. They managed to catch up at a port along the way. Mom is at senior care. Amanda is at work. Rebekkah and Margit are at the store with Brawny."

"Aunt Penny," we said in chorus.

"But she doesn't have a car," I added.

"Maybe she rented or borrowed one," said Detweiler as he glanced out the peephole on my door. "Nope. It's Amanda. She has someone with her."

My sister gave Detweiler a quick hug and stepped into our living room. She crossed the floor to pull me out of my chair.

"I told you I needed to meet someone at the train station," she said. "You'll never guess who."

I struggled to my feet.

Detweiler stepped to one side—and I stood face-to-face with my sister Catherine.

~ THE END ~

Kiki's story continues in *Killer, Paper, Cut,* available here
https://amzn.to/2OP9V96. For a complete list of Kiki
Lowenstein books, short stories, and box sets with purchase
links, go
to https://www.booklaunch.io/joannaslan/meet-kiki

EXCERPT FROM KILLER, PAPER, CUT

A Friday evening, ten days before Halloween...
The Old Social Hall, St. Louis, Missouri

*B*lood spurted all over my hands and plopped onto my Keds.

I've seen some pretty clumsy crafters in my day, but Mary Martha Delaney took the cake and iced it, too. She had managed to cut through the paper, her mat, the table, and her palm—and we were only five minutes into our project.

Worse yet, the silly thing watched the blood run down her arm before smearing it on her blouse. At first glance, Mary Martha looked like a kindergartener covered in poster paint. There was red stuff on her sleeve, wiped across her bosoms, and dripping on her white stretch pants.

Did I mention the sight of blood makes me woozy?

It does. Especially now that I'm seven months pregnant.

But I was the C.I.C.C. or Crafter In Charge of the Crop, "crop" being the accepted term for a scrapbooking party.

My name's Kiki Lowenstein, and I'm a scrapbooker. I was also hostess of this little soiree because I own Time in a Bottle, the scrapbook and craft store that sponsored this event, a fundraiser that we'd named the "Halloween Crafting Spook-tacular."

In my private life, I'm the mother of Anya, who is thirteen going on thirty, and five-year-old Erik. Rounding out our household is my sweetheart and the father of my baby, Detective Chad Detweiler, and Bronwyn Macavity, otherwise known as "Brawny," our live-in nanny.

Yep, a lot of people depend on me. I'd promised my family that I could handle this crop, even though I was so tired that passing out sounded, sort of, heavenly. Like a brief unscheduled nap. But I couldn't relinquish my responsibilities that easily. Nope, I'm too much of a trooper.

While I struggled to keep from fainting, Mary Martha's friend Dolores Peabody reached over and pressed a tissue into Mary Martha's cut. That proved largely ineffective. In fact, it increased the flow. Now Dolores sported a bright red smear of blood across the front of her tee-shirt. Mary Martha turned and managed to wipe blood on me, explaining, "Your belly was in the way."

The sour look she cast at my tummy told me that she knew I wasn't married. I'd run into that response before, so I wasn't unprepared. Irked yes, but not totally taken off guard.

"Maybe this will help." Patricia Wojozynski was another friend of Mary Martha's. Patricia pressed her cotton hanky into Mary Martha's hand. But Patricia underestimated the amount of blood we were dealing with. Soon she too was wiping blood all over her own clothes.

Time to pull up my big girl maternity panties and take

control.

"Mary Martha, we need to get you to the emergency room." I reached down to put steady pressure on the wound. My free hand cupped her elbow and urged her to stand. This produced no result because Mary Martha was big enough to be both a Mary and a Martha.

"Heavens no. Thank the good Lord, it's just a scratch. I'll offer it up to Jesus."

Something told me he'd rather have flowers on the altar, but who am I to judge?

"Gee, I don't know. This is bleeding pretty good." The smell of copper in the air encouraged me to heave.

"Pretty well," said Clancy, from her spot ten feet away. Nothing made her madder than misuse of English grammar. Clancy was conducting this portion of our event. Although she's new to crafting, she's learning fast.

"Uh, pretty well," I repeated after my friend. "Clancy, we've got a problem here."

"Good luck," she said, without turning a hair of her perfectly shaped auburn bob. "Let's continue with our project. The next step is to rub your chalk applicator across the brown chalk and use it to edge your pumpkin."

Edge their pumpkins, my left foot. Clancy was purposely ignoring my crisis. Given a taste of teaching cardmaking, Clancy had become quite the expert. She loved seeing novice stampers turn out brilliant results. I have to admit that I'm impressed by her newfound ability. Funny how when a person finds her crafting niche, she can really shine —and that's exactly what Clancy has done.

"Laurel? Can you help Kiki?" Clancy called out to our other co-worker.

"I'm on it." Laurel Wilkins trotted over. In one hand was the first aid kit we brought to every crop. But she was stopped in her progress because of all the junk Mary Martha and friend had spread all over the floor.

"I think Kiki is making this worse!" said Mary Martha.

Nice. Really nice. I fought the urge to give Mary Martha a kick in the shins. Suffice it to say, I haven't been in a good mood lately.

"Oh, my," said Laurel. "Does it hurt much, Mary Martha? Are you okay? You poor baby. How about if we go to the ladies room and see how much of this we can get wiped off? Then I'll dress the wound."

"It's God's plan that you'd be here to help, Laurel," said Mary Martha.

"Kiki, could you help her get over to me? I'll take it from there," said Laurel, tossing that fabulous mane of blond hair out of her face. As usual, she looked as if she'd just stepped from the pages of a Boston Proper catalog. I, on the other hand, looked as if I'd swallowed a beach ball and forgotten to burp.

I could do this. I've done harder things. Taking Mary Martha's elbow, I walked her around the end of the table and pointed her toward Laurel.

My stomach heaved as I stood in the middle of a room full of crafters, soaked in Mary Martha's blood, surrounded by bloody pieces of facial tissue.

Why, oh, why had I agreed to hold an offsite crop?

Was it because the idea of helping people with diabetes had proved irresistible?

Or because I was a fool?

Kɪᴋɪ's sᴛᴏʀʏ continues in *Killer, Paper, Cut*, available here: https://amzn.to/2OP9V96

A SPECIAL GIFT FOR YOU

I am deeply appreciative of all my readers, and so I have a special gift for you. It's a full-length digital book called *Bad, Memory, Album.* Just go here and tell me where to send your digital book https://dl.bookfunnel.com/jwu6iipe1g.
All best always,
Joanna

For any book to succeed, reviews are essential. If you enjoyed this book please leave a review on Amazon. A sentence or two can make all the difference! Please leave a review of *Group, Photo, Grave* here – http://www.Amazon.com/review/create-review?&asin=B00FQ5D27C

THE KIKI LOWENSTEIN MYSTERY SERIES

BY JOANNA CAMPBELL SLAN

Every scrapbook tells a story. Memories of friends, family and ... murder? You'll want to read the Kiki Lowenstein books in order: For a limited time, you can enjoy the Kiki Lowenstein Mystery books at a discount by purchasing the box sets. All the Kiki Lowenstein books are available through Amazon. For a complete list and purchase links, go to
https://www.booklaunch.io/joannaslan/meet-kiki

Kiki Lowenstein Box Set, Books 1-3
https://amzn.to/33MFBHq
Kiki Lowenstein Box Set, Books 1-6 *BETTER VALUE!*
https://amzn.to/3gG134i
Kiki Lowenstein Box Set 7-13 *BETTER VALUE!*
https://amzn.to/3kuMClW

Love, Die, Neighbor (The Prequel)
Bad, Memory, Album
(A Full-Length Book that's an Exclusive Gift—
go to https://dl.bookfunnel.com/jwu6iipe1g)

THE FURTHER ADVENTURES OF KIKI LOWENSTEIN—SHORT STORIES

BY JOANNA CAMPBELL SLAN

Readers couldn't get enough of Kiki, so Joanna has written 42 short stories to satisfy demand! The complete box set has as many pages as four full-length books —

The Further Adventures of Kiki Lowenstein Box Set
(Adventures 1-42)

Also available as three smaller box sets:
The Further Adventures of Kiki Lowenstein Box Set #1
(Adventures 1-15)
The Further Adventures of Kiki Lowenstein Box Set #2
(Adventures 16-24)
The Further Adventures of Kiki Lowenstein Box Set #3
(Adventures 25-42)

About the author...
Joanna Campbell Slan

Joanna is a *New York Times* and a *USA Today* bestselling author who has written more than 40 books, including both fiction and non-fiction works. She was one of the early Chicken Soup for the Soul authors, and her stories appear in five of those *New York Times* bestselling books. Her first non-fiction book, *Using Stories and Humor: Grab Your Audience* (Simon & Schuster/Pearson), was endorsed by Toastmasters International, and lauded by Benjamin Netanyahu's speechwriter. She's the author of four mystery series. Her first novel—*Paper, Scissors, Death: Book #1 in the Kiki Lowenstein Mystery Series*—was shortlisted for the Agatha Award. Her first historical mystery—*Death of a Schoolgirl: Book #1 in the Jane Eyre Chronicles*—won the Daphne du Maurier Award of Excellence. Her contemporary series set in Florida continues this year with *Cast Away: Book #4 in the Cara Mia Delgatto Mystery Series.* Her fantasy thriller series starts with *Sherlock Holmes and the Giant Sumatran Rat.*

In addition to writing fiction, Joanna edits the Happy Homicides Anthologies and has begun the Dollhouse Décor & More series of "how to" books for dollhouse miniaturists.

Joanna independently published *I'm Too Blessed to be Depressed* back in 2004 when she was working as a motivational speaker. She sold more than 34,000 copies of that title. Since then she's gone on to independently publish a full-color book, *The Best of British Scrapbooking,* numerous digital books, and coloring books. Her book *Scrapbook Storytelling* sold 120,000 copies.

She's been an Amazon Bestselling Author too many

times to count and has been included in the ranks of Amazon's Top 100 Mystery Authors.

A former talk show host and sought-after motivational speaker, Joanna has spoken to small and large (1000+) groups on four continents. *Sharing Ideas Magazines* named her "one of the top 25 speakers in the world."

When she isn't banging away at the keyboard, Joanna keeps busy walking her Havanese puppy Jax. An award-winning miniaturist, Joanna builds dollhouses, dolls, and furniture from scratch. She's also an accredited teacher of Zentangle®. Her husband, David, owns Steinway Piano Gallery-DC and five other Steinway piano showrooms.

Contact Joanna at JCSlan@JoannaSlan.com.

∽

Follow her on social media by going here
https://www.linktr.ee/JCSlan

Made in the USA
Las Vegas, NV
25 October 2024